PRAISE FOR JACI BURTON

"Jaci Burton's stories are full of heat and h[...]
—Maya Banks, #1 *New Yo[...]*

"A wild ride."   —Lora Leigh, #1 *New York Times* bestselling author

"Passionate, inventive, sexually explicit."   —USAToday.com

"One of the strongest sports romance series available."
—Dear Author

"Endearing characters, a strong romance and an engaging plot all wrapped up in one sexy package."   —Romance Novel News

"Both sensual and raw . . . Plenty of romance, sexy men, hot steamy loving and humor."   —Smexy Books

"Holy smokes! I am pretty sure I saw steam rising from every page."
—Fresh Fiction

"Hot, hot, hot! . . . Romance at its best! Highly recommended! Very steamy."   —Coffee Table Reviews

"Burton knocks it out of the park . . . With snappy back-and-forth dialogue as well as hot, sweaty and utterly engaging bedroom play, readers will not be able to race through this book fast enough!"
—*RT Book Reviews*

RULES OF CONTACT

JACI BURTON

BERKLEY
New York

BERKLEY
An imprint of Penguin Random House LLC
375 Hudson Street, New York, New York 10014

ISBN: 9780425276822

An application to register this book for cataloging has been submitted to the
Library of Congress.

First Edition: December 2016

Printed in the United States of America
3   5   7   9   10   8   6   4   2

Cover photo by Claudio Marinesco
Cover design by Rita Frangie
Book design by Kristin del Rosario

RULES OF CONTACT

ONE

OF ALL THE THINGS ON FLYNN CASSIDY'S BUCKET list, opening a restaurant hadn't been anywhere even close to his top ten. Yet here he was, sitting at one of the corner tables of Ninety-Two, his new restaurant in San Francisco. He marveled that at some point in his life, cooking had joined playing football on the list of things he loved the most.

If someone had told him five years ago he was going to open his own restaurant, he'd have told them they were full of shit. But look at him now, owner of his own place.

Ninety-Two was shiny and new—sort of. He'd had the old building renovated after he'd bought the property, so it still felt like it belonged in this neighborhood. He made sure it didn't look too trendy, keeping a lot of the original details intact both inside and out. He was more in favor of restaurants that felt comfortable—like home. He wanted his customers to feel as if they could come in, sit down, and feel at ease.

They'd been filled to capacity since they opened two weeks ago and so far things were going well. He took that as a sign that his inclination to keep it simple appealed to others as well. Besides, it was damn good food, he'd made sure of that. But still, opening a restaurant was a risky proposition and he didn't want to get too cocky. He knew Ninety-Two needed all the good press and attention it could get. Which was why he was sitting here. Right now one of the major entertainment media outlets was doing a feature on the restaurant. Great for publicity, but it meant camera crews, bright lights and a lot of damn people in the way of regular business. He had already wandered around and apologized to his patrons, who seemed to take it all in stride. He hoped the crews would grab all the film and sound bites they wanted and get the hell out shortly.

"This is so thrilling, Flynn."

He dragged his gaze away from the camera crews and onto Natalie, the woman he'd been dating the past few weeks. She was a looker, for sure, with beautiful auburn brown hair that teased her shoulders and the most incredible green eyes he'd ever seen.

"Yeah, thrilling isn't the first thing that popped into my head when the crews showed up today."

Natalie grabbed his hand. "Oh, come on. Who doesn't want to be on TV?"

Him, for one. As a defensive end for the San Francisco Sabers football team, he'd had plenty of cameras and microphones shoved in his face over the years. It was the last thing he wanted now, when his fledgling restaurant was just getting off the ground. But since the restaurant was new, he wouldn't turn down some publicity for it. So he'd done the interview and now he just wanted to stay out of the way while the film crew got their overview shots.

"Do you think they'll want to get some film of the two of us together?" Natalie asked. "You know, kind of get some background on your personal life, like what you do on your off time away from football and the restaurant, who you're seeing, stuff like that?"

Warning bells clanged loud and hard in Flynn's head. He'd gone down this road with more than one woman, and had ended relationships because of women who were way more interested in the limelight than in him.

Lately he'd been careful to steer clear of any woman who had an entertainment background. No models, no actresses, no one he could suspect of chasing face time in front of a camera. He figured since Natalie was a financial analyst, he was safe.

But seeing her gaze track those cameras like a vampire craving blood, he wasn't sure career choice had much to do with someone hungering to get their fifteen minutes of fame.

He didn't understand it. Not at all.

"Maybe we should move to one of the more prominent tables, Flynn," Natalie said. "You know, that way we might be in one of the camera shots."

He forced back a sigh. "I don't think so."

She pushed back her chair and stood, ignoring him. "I'm going to go to the bar and get a drink. You know, all casual like, and see if maybe they notice me."

He leaned back in his chair. "Sure. You do that."

This relationship was doomed. Just one of the many Flynn had seen go down in flames in the past couple of years. He bit back the rising anger over having yet another woman use him to get her time in the spotlight.

What the hell was wrong with him that women craved camera time instead of just being with him? Yeah, he was a football player, and maybe that held some appeal, but he was also a nice guy who had something to offer besides photo ops. He was getting damn tired of playing this game with every woman he dated.

Maybe there wasn't a woman out there who was interested in him. Just him. Not Flynn the football player. Just Flynn the guy.

He shook his head, mentally notched up another failure and took a long swallow of his beer.

SINCE ORDERS HAD SLOWED DOWN AND SHE HAD THE kitchen under control, Amelia Lawrence washed her hands in the sink and tried to hide, avoiding the cameras. The last thing she wanted was to be on television. She was head chef at Ninety-Two. This whole publicity thing was on Flynn, and she didn't need to be interviewed, filmed or in any way noticed.

But as she did her best game of hide and not be sought, she also spotted Flynn's new girlfriend doing *her* best job to try to be seen by any of the camera crew.

Oh, no. Not another one of *those* kind of women.

She'd worked with Flynn the past couple of months, even before Ninety-Two had opened. And in that time period she'd seen him go through no less than three women, all of whom seemed to be way more interested in his prowess as camera fodder than anything else.

She felt bad for him, and nothing but disdain for the women who couldn't appreciate what a fine man Flynn Cassidy was.

He was supremely tall and ridiculously well built, with a thick mane of black hair and amazing blue eyes. She could spend at least a full day doing nothing but ogling his tattoos. And who didn't love football? Plus, the man had fine culinary taste. When he'd hired her, they'd spent several weeks designing the menu for the restaurant. She had to admit, he had good ideas.

So did she, and she appreciated that he listened to hers, and had been willing to blend their ideas for the final menu. She loved the way it had turned out and her estimation of Flynn had risen. In the past she'd worked for her share of egomaniacs who insisted it was their way or the highway, but Flynn wasn't like that. He was willing to collaborate. He also liked to crack jokes, was kind to the employees and seemed like a nice guy.

So why couldn't the man find a decent girlfriend? He kind of sucked at it, actually. If she had been a native of San Francisco maybe she could have help him out, but she'd only moved here recently from Portland. Her only ties in the city were her best friend from college and her friend's husband. Otherwise, she was pretty much alone. She'd rented a house not too far from the restaurant, and she was getting out in the neighborhood and meeting people there.

She knew it would take time to form a circle of close friends, but even with her limited contacts she guessed she could find better women for Flynn to date than the ones he'd been parading in and out of the restaurant lately. She could spot posers a mile away. Maybe she could offer her services to Flynn.

"Orders up."

Pulling her focus away from Flynn, she put her attention on the incoming orders, on directing her staff, on minding her own business, and not on Flynn's girlfriend who was currently preening for the cameras as if she was auditioning for the next blockbuster movie.

With an eye roll, she dismissed the woman and set about making scallops.

Because Flynn Cassidy was decidedly not her problem. And no matter how sorry she felt for him, she wasn't going to get involved in his personal life.

TWO

FLYNN SHOWED UP FOR PRACTICE EARLY, JUST LIKE he always did. He liked to get a run in to warm up before hitting the weight room.

After logging his three miles, he made his way to the weight room. As usual, he wasn't the first one in there. His defensive teammates—the guys he counted on—were up and at it early today, too.

He spotted Junior Malone, Alfonso Labelle, Hank "Hey Man" Henderson and Chris Smith. These guys were his rocks, the ones he depended on to be at the line of scrimmage with him and prevent the offense from moving forward. He'd worked with most of these guys ever since the San Francisco Sabers had drafted him. The only one to join the team after him had been Junior Malone, but he'd been a perfect fit to the line. They were fierce, ass-kicking defenders, and the reason the Sabers had one of their best years defensively last year. They were clicking on all cylinders and even though they were only five games into the season so far, their numbers were solid.

"You're late," Hey Man said.

Flynn laid his towel on the bench. "I'm the only one out there running three miles before workouts. You're all welcome to join me if you want to burn some of that fat off."

Hey Man looked down at his stomach. "This is all muscle, man."

Flynn let out a snort. "It looks a lot more like too much fried chicken."

Hey Man glared at him. "Don't mess with my fried chicken. You know it's my weakness."

"We all know what your weakness is, Hey Man," Chris said. "Food. All of it."

Flynn grinned, then lay on his back and started light with the bench press. Soon enough, he added more weight and the trainers had showed up to spot him. There was nothing like a pounding, sweat-pouring workout to get the blood pumping and prepare him for practice.

He finished off with an energy drink, jawing with the rest of the guys, then they headed out to the field where Mick Riley, the Sabers quarterback, was leading the offense in practice drills.

Since they weren't ready for the defense to come in yet, Flynn took a minute to watch the offense play. Defense could keep the opposing team from putting points up on the board, which was key. But if your offense failed to score, your team was sunk. Mick had been leading the Sabers offense for ten years now. He'd won two championships and didn't appear to be slowing down any time soon. At thirty-five, the man looked to be in the prime of his life, which was unusual for a quarterback.

Still, when it was time for the defense to take the field, Flynn had to take a shot at him.

"How's it going, old man?" Flynn asked.

"Hey, fuck off, Cassidy."

Flynn took his position with a grin at Mick.

"You know if you give shit to my quarterback, I'll lay you flat." Oscar Taylor, the left offensive guard, joined the fray.

Flynn crouched down in front of him. "You could try, Oscar, but you know I'm just going to run right past you."

Oscar growled. "We'll see about that, Flynn."

Flynn grinned. Shit talking was a normal part of practice. It got them fired up and ready to play. So when the ball was snapped, he and Oscar went at it, though not as fiercely as they would in a game situation. The last thing you wanted to do was hurt someone on your own team.

Practice lasted two hours. After general drills, they worked with their position coaches and went over plays for this Sunday's game against Detroit. When they were finished he and Mick headed back to the locker room together.

"How's the new restaurant?" Mick asked.

As was typical, all the trash talk ended once practice was over. "It's good, thanks. You and Tara should come for dinner."

"Yeah, she asked me about it the other day. She's eager to try it out. But it'll be a couple of weeks before she can fly out here."

As they walked down the long hallway toward the locker room, Flynn turned to him. "Well, actually, Irvin's assistant has booked the team party at the restaurant two weeks from now. Is Tara coming for that?"

Mick nodded. "Yeah, she is. So, your first big gig at the restaurant and the whole team will be there. Make you nervous?"

Flynn laughed. "Not really. I think the restaurant can handle it. And I'm grateful Irvin is giving the restaurant some business."

"I'll definitely let Tara know about the party being at your place. She'll be excited, since she's wanted to eat at Ninety-Two ever since she heard you were opening it."

"Good. I can't wait to see her."

Flynn knew that Mick and Tara made their off-season home in St. Louis, where the entire Riley clan lived. Mick also had a place here in San Francisco and Tara often came and stayed during the season, since she owned an event planning business here, along with another office in St. Louis.

Lots of juggling there, as well as their four-year-old son, Sam, and another son in college.

He didn't know how they managed. Family support, he supposed. The Rileys were a big clan, so he knew they all pitched in and helped rally around Tara and Mick and their kids.

He stripped down and headed to the shower, letting the hot steam rain down over him. Damn, that felt good. As he lost himself under the water, he thought about family.

Yeah, he knew all about family support. The Cassidys were a big family, too. And with Flynn, Barrett and Grant all playing pro football, plus Tucker playing pro baseball, it was one crazy sports-minded family. He had their dad, Easton, to thank for the guys' love of sports. Their younger sister, Mia, was the only one to escape the sports bug. She was the brains of the family.

He smiled thinking about his sister. He hadn't talked to her in a while. He needed to give her a call and check up on her. As the oldest sibling, he often felt like it was his responsibility to look after the others. Rowdy bunch, all of them.

Including Mia, though she masked it well with her ambition. But deep down inside her studious nature there lurked a wild Cassidy and he damn well knew it. Which was why he needed to check up on her.

After he got dressed and went to his car, he voice dialed his sister while he was driving home.

"Hey, stranger," Mia said.

"Hey yourself. I haven't talked to you in a while, so I thought I'd see what was up with you."

"Oh, the usual. Studying for a test right now. How did practice go today?"

Leave it to his sister to know where all her brothers were on any given day. "Good. We're ready for Detroit on Sunday."

"Of course you are."

"How's the workload for your master's program?"

"Manageable. A lot of reading and ridiculous paperwork, but that's to be expected. I'm working on my thesis now."

"I'm proud of you." He wasn't sure he'd ever told her that, and for some reason it was important to him to let her know.

She paused for a few seconds, then said, "Thanks. That means a lot to me coming from my oldest brother. And speaking of, I'm probably going to be out there sometime within the next few weeks. I'm trying to schedule an interview with Stanford."

"About their PhD program?"

"Yeah. Can I crash at your place when I come out there?"

"You know you're welcome anytime. Just let me know."

"Awesome. I'll be watching you on Sunday. Get some sacks, okay?"

He laughed. "I'll do my best. Love you, Mia."

"Love you, too, Flynn. See ya."

He clicked off, then changed lanes. Not that it did him much good since the freeway was currently a parking lot.

He tuned the radio to the sports channel and resigned himself to sitting in traffic for a while longer.

THREE

A WEEK AND A HALF LATER, FLYNN ARRIVED AT THE restaurant before it opened. He wanted to go over all the aspects for the team party Thursday night. They were going to close to regular customers, change around the seating and make sure they had adequate staff on hand for serving.

He met with Amelia, along with Ken, the restaurant's manager, the three of them sitting down at one of the corner tables.

Amelia looked over her notes. "For hors d'oeuvres, I have bacon-wrapped figs, ahi tuna, avocado and cucumber. I'm also planning crab, chili and mint crostini and goat cheese and herb mini puffs."

Flynn looked from Amelia to Ken. "Now I'm hungry. I think you should make some of those right now."

Amelia cracked a smile. "Sorry, no can do. But I do have some buffalo and black bean chili simmering in the back."

"No wonder we're hungry," Ken said. "I knew something smelled delicious."

Amelia pushed her chair back. "Give me just a minute and I'll ladle some up for you."

She disappeared into the kitchen and Flynn turned to Ken. "What else?"

"I made a chart showing how we'll arrange the tables. I thought we'd set them up along the windows here and here, to allow for viewing, with a few spread out in the middle. We're using the bar tables to give people a place to set down their drinks, but still leave room for people to mingle."

Flynn nodded while Ken went over the seating. "Great plan. You have all the liquor stocked?"

"Yes. And extra bartenders and servers will be on hand. We're in good shape."

He always had confidence in Ken. The guy was a master at managing Ninety-Two. "I knew you would be."

Amelia returned carrying a tray. She set bowls in front of Flynn and Ken, along with a basket of crackers and bread.

"None for you?" Flynn asked.

Amelia took a seat. "I taste while I cook. Trust me, I've had plenty."

Flynn took the spoon and dug in, letting the spicy chili spark his taste buds as he swallowed. "This is really good."

"He's right about that," Ken said. "It's going to be a customer favorite, Amelia."

"Thank you."

"You should definitely serve it the night of the party," Flynn said. "The guys will love it."

She shook her head. "Chili is so messy, and a lot of your guests will be wandering about. It's too hard to manage a bowl and slurp up chili while trying to carry on a conversation and walk around. Plus, it goes great with crackers. It's not a good party food."

"She has a point," Ken said.

"Yeah, you might be right about that."

"Though one of the things I wanted to talk to you about was doing a special chili night, especially during happy hour. We could set up a chili station at the bar. I know you have the games on the TV in the bar. I could make up several chilis with the appropriate accouterments and guests could sample the different ones. We could also do it in the restaurant as well. Kind of a chili sampler."

Flynn thought about it for a minute. "We could offer it on the appetizer menu in the bar and in the restaurant."

"I like that idea, too," Ken said. "In fact, it would be great to have it on the menu on Sundays during the football games."

Flynn loved that the people who worked with him had such great ideas. "Perfect. Let's do it."

Ken nodded. "I'll add it to the menu."

"And I'll start creating some different chilis," Amelia said. "When do you want to put this into effect?"

"I'll leave it to you and Ken to work out the details. Whenever you feel it's ready, do it."

"Great."

Amelia smiled as she made notes. He liked when she smiled. She was so damn pretty, but always so serious, which he supposed was good for his restaurant. Her focus produced great results, but there was nothing wrong with smiling and being happy about the work you did, either. He wasn't sure he'd ever heard her outright laugh.

"You should do that more often."

It took her a second to lift her head. "Me? Do what more often?"

"Smile."

Now she frowned. "I smile."

"No, you don't. You always look like you're in the middle of some horrible midterm exam."

"I do not."

Ken stifled a laugh. "Yeah, you kind of do. You're always serious, Amelia."

"This is my job. I'm very serious about it."

Flynn pointed to her notebook. "But you smiled when you made notes about the chili."

"See? I can smile. Therefore your point about me not smiling is moot."

He rolled his eyes. Sometimes everything with Amelia was an argument. "Okay, so what else should we review before the party Thursday night?"

"We need an estimated head count," Ken said.

"I have the RSVP list right here. We just finalized it. I'll e-mail it to you both right now." He forwarded the message from his phone.

Amelia checked her phone, scanning the list, then looked up at him. "You're bringing a date?"

He nodded. "Yeah. Why? Is that a problem?"

Amelia looked over at Ken, then back at him. "No. No problem at all. So who's the new woman in your life?"

"She's a flight attendant I met on the way back from the game in Detroit."

"Flight attendant, huh? That's great. Is the press coming to the team party?"

"They usually attend these kinds of events. Just to get some sound bites and cover the team and the season so far. Plus, Irvin likes anything involving the team to get press."

"Sure. Of course. Totally understandable." Amelia quickly focused on the list, but her lips curved.

For someone who never smiled, she sure was smiling a lot now. So was Ken.

"What?"

"Nothing," Amelia said. "I hope you have a great time at the dinner. We'll make sure it's perfect. You should finish your chili before it gets cold. I have to see to dinner."

But that smile of hers lingered as she got up and left the table. Ken's did, too, as he excused himself. And he'd sure as hell like to know what the two of them found so damned amusing.

FOUR

AFTER A LONG NIGHT AT THE RESTAURANT, AMELIA went home, kicked off her shoes, tossed her jacket on the chair next to the front door, piled her purse on top of it and went straight to the kitchen. She pulled a wineglass out of the cabinet and poured herself a nice glass of cabernet, then walked through the kitchen and into the sunroom. It was a little chilly in here, but fortunately there was a heater. She clicked it on, then sat on the sofa. She pulled a blanket over her and reached for her tablet.

After a few sips of wine she felt the kinks in her muscles start to relax.

It had been a good night. Working at Ninety-Two was a good fit for her. She liked the people she worked with, and she had creative freedom to express herself through the food she made. All in all, not a bad start to a new beginning in a new city.

Her phone rang so she pulled it out of her pocket. It was her friend Laura.

"Hey, what's up?"

"I was wondering if you were home yet."

"Just got here. It's late for you. I would have called you but I thought you'd be asleep."

"No, I switched shifts at the hospital so I'm on until eleven thirty. I just got home. Jon's asleep and I'm wired. Are you crashing or are you up for some company?"

"I won't go to sleep for a while yet. Come on over."

"I'll be right there."

Amelia hung up and smiled, then shrugged the blanket off and went into the cabinet to pull another wineglass down. She loved her rental house. It was older with tons of quirky charm like uneven wooden floors and yet the sunny, large kitchen had been updated with all new, high-end appliances, perfect for her. The house's best feature, though, was its prime location, right down the street from Laura and Jon's house. Since she didn't know anyone else in San Francisco, finding this place had seemed like kismet.

She went to the door just as Laura rang the bell. She opened it and Laura swooped in, still wearing her scrubs and tennis shoes. Despite having worked a full shift as a nurse, her best friend was still gorgeous. It simply wasn't fair.

"And how was your day?" she asked.

"My day was I hope you've opened a bottle of wine," Laura said in response.

"As a matter of fact, I was sipping on a fabulous cabernet when you called."

"See, this is why we're friends." Laura made her way down the hall, her dark brown ponytail swinging as she walked.

Amelia laughed and followed her, glad her friend was comfortable enough to pour herself a glass of wine.

"Are we on the porch?" Laura asked.

"Yes. The heater's on. Grab yourself a spot and a blanket. I'm going to go change into something more comfortable, and I'll be right there."

Amelia dashed upstairs and changed out of her work clothes and into yoga pants and a long-sleeved cotton shirt, then slid into her favorite pair of slippers. She found Laura on the wicker chair, a fleece blanket covering her legs.

October in San Francisco could be cool, but the porch was closed in and with the heater on it was very comfortable.

"Tell me about your day," Amelia said.

"Two car accidents, one drug overdose, a ruptured appendix, a broken finger and one surly drunk who threw up all over one of the other nurses."

Amelia grimaced as she tossed one of the blankets over herself. "Well, at least the drunk didn't throw up on you."

Laura raised her glass of wine. "Small favors."

"Look at it this way. At least you're not bored. Isn't that why you went into nursing?"

"True. I can't believe I started my freshman year of college thinking I wanted to become a CPA."

Amelia smiled as she remembered their first year together. "You did always score high in the math classes."

"Math always came easy to me. But I was following in my mother's footsteps. She was the finance whiz. Midway through the first semester I knew I'd die a slow, agonizing death in finance."

"Plus you were so good with people. And you knew you loved medicine."

Laura leaned back and propped her tennis-shoed feet on the old, scarred coffee table Amelia had picked up at the flea market the first weekend she'd come to town. "True. I'd have made a kick-ass doctor. It was just all those years of medical school—"

"And all that debt."

Laura laughed. "Yes, all that debt—that kept me from realizing that dream."

"You could still go to medical school if you wanted to."

"I don't want to. I'm happy being a nurse. It fulfills me."

"Then you're right where you need to be."

"As are you. I've never known anyone who loves what they do more than you. And God knows you kept the entire dorm fed the first year. I was the only one smart enough to become your best friend, thereby ensuring I'd eat well through college."

Amelia laughed. "See? You're good at math, an angel of mercy and insightful as well."

"I'm practically perfect. And so are you."

"Is that what we're doing tonight? Talking about our perfection?"

Laura swirled her wine around in the glass. "Not a bad way to spend the evening. But you could tell me about your night. Was it busy?"

"Not too bad. Ninety-Two has been bringing in a lot of patrons since we opened. I'm happy about that."

"I'm sure you are."

"And I met with Ken and Flynn before opening today. Flynn is having a team party there later this week."

Laura set her glass down. "The Sabers are all going to be there? Oooh. All those hot football players."

Amelia shrugged and took a sip of her wine. "Which means a lot more to you than it does to me."

"Bullshit. You love football."

"I do love football. I'm just not a football player groupie."

"Granted. Still, all those hot men assembled in one room. So many of them single. You could have your choice."

Amelia picked up her glass of wine and took a sip. She'd already had what she thought was a great guy. And she'd been wrong. The last thing she wanted was to go down that road again. "No, thanks."

"Oh, come on, Amelia. It's time to get back in the game."

Amelia frowned. "The football game?"

"No, doofus. The dating game."

Amelia shook her head. "I'm not ready yet."

"It's been over a year since your divorce. Have you dated even once since then?"

"Actually, I have. I went out on a date before I moved from Portland."

Laura's eyes widened. "You did? How come this is the first I've heard about it?"

"Because it was uneventful. Someone at the restaurant set me up with some friend of her husband's."

"And?"

"And he was kind of awful. We went to dinner and he complained about the food as if he was some kind of culinary expert, when the guy couldn't tell the difference between cuts of steak if they slapped him between the eyes. Then we went to a movie and he talked through the whole thing. Then he drove me home and tried to go in for a kiss when it was obvious there was zero chemistry between us."

Laura wrinkled her nose. "Yuck."

"Exactly. As soon as the date was over I promptly forgot about him."

"Can't say I blame you for that. But one date failure doesn't mean there aren't amazing men out there. It's time to dip your toes in the water again."

Amelia waved her hand in dismissal. "Honestly, I'm not interested. I have the new job, which is keeping me busy enough at work, and other things to occupy my time when I'm not at work."

"What other things?"

"The cookbook."

"Oh, right. That's an awesome thing, that cookbook you're writing, and you know I hope you're super successful. But, honey, you can't have sex with a cookbook."

Amelia nearly choked on her sip of wine. "What?"

"You heard me. It's time for you to get out there and get laid. Time to quit mourning the death of your marriage. Life shouldn't stop just because one man broke your heart."

She lifted her chin. "I'm not in mourning."

Laura shot her a look. "Aren't you?"

Leave it to Laura to tell her things she didn't want to hear. "Okay, maybe I have been. Aren't I entitled?"

Laura shifted, grabbing the bottle of wine to refill her glass before leaning back against the sofa. "Hell yes you were entitled. That asshole hurt you. He made promises he didn't keep. You were entitled to wallow for a long time. But now it's been long enough, don't you think?"

"You might be right."

Laura's lips lifted. "Of course I am. Remember that guy you dated in college? What was his name? Carey? He played violin and you were so sucked in by his musicality."

She finally relaxed against the sofa, glass in her hand. "Oh, my God, yes. Carey. I haven't thought about him in years. I fell madly in love with his magical fingers."

Laura rolled her eyes. "Right. You waxed poetic about his hands and his talents and he cast this musical spell over you. He'd put you off and tell you he had hours of practice and you waited ever so patiently for him. And then you found out he was sleeping with the dean of music."

"The bastard." She took a sip of wine.

"Let's not forget the Alpha Tau Omega guy."

She wrinkled her nose. "Oh. Frat Guy. You had to admit, though, the beer parties were amusing."

"Honey, that one spelled disaster from the first date. I warned you about him."

"I was on the rebound from Carey."

"Please. I'm amazed you didn't end up with an STD. He was such a horndog."

"True. But you can't deny the parties were a blast while they lasted."

"I'll give you that. But I'm always right about men. At least I was during college."

"You were." She smiled at Laura, remembering all the time the two of them spent together in college. Laura, full of life and adventure, always willing to pick herself up after heartbreak and go after her dreams. Laura was never one to give up, and Amelia had learned a lot of her own willingness to go after her dreams from her best friend. When she'd arrived at college as a freshman she'd been shy and withdrawn. She had Laura to thank for pulling her out of her shell, making her attend social events. Maybe that's why she'd gone out on so many dates. At first she'd been reticent, determined to do nothing but study.

That hadn't lasted long.

God, they'd had a good time together. And they'd stayed friends all these years. She couldn't imagine life without Laura. And now they were neighbors.

Sometimes life worked out perfectly.

And sometimes it didn't. Too bad Laura hadn't been around to warn her away from Frank. What might her life have been like if Laura had met Frank at the beginning? Would her best friend's "wrong guy" radar have pinged, thereby saving her years of heartbreak?

Who knew? Either way, she couldn't go back and change the past now. She could only learn from it and move on.

"So you'll at least think about ogling the hot football players at the party?"

Amelia lifted her gaze, shaking off thoughts of her ex-husband, putting her mind firmly in the present, where it belonged. "Yes. I'll ogle the football players."

Laura grinned and tilted her glass toward Amelia's. "That's my girl."

FIVE

AFTER PRACTICE THURSDAY, FLYNN HUSTLED OUT OF the stadium and headed straight for the restaurant.

He wasn't surprised at all that Ken and Amelia had everything in order. Staff was already there, tables had been moved, linens were spread out and the settings were in place.

He wasn't a fancy kind of guy. If you came to his house to hang out or watch sports, he'd cook. He wouldn't set out paper plates, but he sure as hell wouldn't fuss, either.

But this was Ninety-Two. This was his dream come true, and it was important to him. Irvin Stokes, the team owner, would be here tonight, as would most of the members of the Sabers. These were his peers. His friends. Having tonight be a success meant something to him.

"Oh, you're here, good," Ken said, grasping the sleeve of his shirt and pulling him into the kitchen. "You have got to taste the stuff Amelia and her crew have cooked up. Though she'll probably kick my butt for entering her territory."

"Then why are we going into the kitchen?"

"Because the smells are delicious, I'm hungry and you're the boss. She couldn't possibly say no to you."

Flynn cocked a brow. "Wanna bet?"

He'd been on the other side of Amelia's temper before. She was an amazing cook, but she'd made it very clear before he hired her that in the kitchen, she was the boss.

So when he and Ken walked in, she pointed to the doorway as soon as she spotted them.

"Both of you—out—right now."

"Oh, come on, Amelia," Ken said. "Just a sample. You know how I feel about bacon."

She gave Ken a firm shake of her head. "When they're ready, you can have some. Until then, get out of my way."

"I told you." Flynn held open the door for Ken. After Ken turned to leave, Flynn looked at Amelia, who glared at them with her arms folded. She looked like a Viking warrior defending her castle. Tall, blond and imposing.

And a little bit hot. There was nothing like a woman taking total charge of her turf. And this kitchen was Amelia's turf.

"You are so mean," he said to her, but his lips quirked.

"Get out, Flynn," she said, but her lips curved in a hint of a smile.

A sign that things were going well in the kitchen, which relieved some of his tension about the evening.

He went over the checklist with Ken, who had everything well in hand. Which was why he'd hired Ken in the first place.

"Your organizational skills are on point, as usual, Ken." He handed the notebook back to the manager, who bustled off to attend to the staff, leaving Flynn with nothing to do.

If Amelia let him in her kitchen he could help her. But he knew better than to go in there again, so he did what he could to assist the staff with their final prep. Once they were finished, though, there was nothing to do but wait. Ken told the staff to take a break before the party started. And Flynn headed home to change clothes and pick up his date. By the time he got back, the team should be arriving.

He hoped like hell tonight went well.

THE PARTY HAD STARTED AND AMELIA WAS PLEASED so far. The food was made and her staff had everything under control. The one thing she prided herself on was a well-run kitchen, and this one was.

She removed her apron and dashed into the restroom off the kitchen to check her appearance. She undid her ponytail and brushed her hair, applied some lip gloss and straightened her blouse, deciding it wouldn't be a bad idea to take a walk around the room to be sure the guests were enjoying the food. She knew how to do it surreptitiously, hanging back to be sure she wasn't noticed.

When she stepped out, the first thing she noticed was how big all the guys were. Not surprising considering this was a football team. Not your average men. Plenty of women in attendance as well, which was a good thing.

She grabbed a glass of wine from the bar and wandered the room. Many people were holding a full plate, which was a good sign. As a chef, there was nothing worse than people ignoring your food. Her team was refilling the serving stations and people were still eating. She was satisfied that the food was good. She'd tasted everything and approved it. Still, it was satisfying to see people appreciating it.

She found a nice spot in a dark corner and sipped her wine.

"Are you hiding?"

A beautiful, blond-haired woman found her. She smiled at her. "No, just surveying."

"Are you here with someone and avoiding them, or just avoiding the crowds in general? Because if it's the latter, I can totally understand it. These things can be overwhelming. Football players are nothing if not loud and gregarious."

Amelia laughed and held out her hand. "I'm Amelia Lawrence, head chef of Ninety-Two."

The woman's eyes sparked recognition. "Oh. I'm Tara Riley. It's so nice to meet you, Amelia."

"Thank you, Tara. Likewise. Are you here with someone?"

"Yes. I'm married to Mick Riley."

Amelia nodded. "Quarterback of the Sabers. I know him well. I mean, I don't know him at all. I've never met him, but I'm a huge fan of your husband—the entire team, actually. And now my tongue is falling all over itself. How embarrassing."

Tara laughed. "Don't be embarrassed. Let's sit down." Tara motioned to the table in front of them.

Amelia gazed around the room. "I should get back to the kitchen."

"From the looks of things, your kitchen is a well-oiled machine, Amelia. Take a minute and get off your feet."

"All right."

She took a seat, doing her best to hide her sigh of relief. It felt good to relax her tight back muscles. She was used to being on her feet all day. She'd been doing it for years. But on occasion, the tension in her lower back took its toll.

"I own an event planning company," Tara said. "And I have to tell you, over the years I've tried out many catering companies, and even hired private restaurants to cater events for me. So, I'd like to think I have a fairly sophisticated palate. I have to tell you that your cooking is beyond excellent."

Amelia beamed a smile. "Thank you. What company?"

"It's called The Right Touch. We have an office here in San

Francisco, and another in St. Louis. We're also going to branch out to the East Coast by the end of the year."

"Event planning. How exciting. And you're expanding, too. You'll be nationwide."

Tara laughed. "Well, sort of. I've wanted to do an East Coast expansion for a while, but I had another baby four years ago and he's kept me pretty busy."

"Oh, you have a son. That's wonderful."

"Two sons, actually. Though my oldest is in college. I kind of took a long break in between the two of them."

Amelia blinked. "I can't even imagine how difficult that must have been for you to start over again."

"It's been an experience, for sure. I had forgotten so much about what it was like to have a baby—and then a toddler. It's a lot harder once you're older, too." Tara laughed. "But Sam's four and in preschool now and at such a fun age. Plus, he loves his daddy and all things football."

"That must be fun for all of you."

"It is. Nathan's a senior this year at the University of Texas. He's the quarterback there, so following in his dad's footsteps as well."

Amelia leaned back in her chair, swirling the wine around in her glass. "Wow. Building a mini football dynasty, aren't you?"

"Mick would like to think so. He's proud of both the boys. And what about you, Amelia? Do you have any small cooks in your family?"

She shook her head. "Recently divorced. No kids. I moved here from Portland to take this job."

"I'm sorry about the divorce. I know how difficult it is when a relationship doesn't work out. But I'm sure Flynn is happy to have you working here."

Amelia appreciated that Tara didn't ask her any probing questions about her divorce. "I love working here. It's a wonderful environment and Flynn has given me a lot of freedom to do what I want as far as the menu. Within reason."

Tara's lips curved. "I know Flynn loves to cook, so I'm sure he has some ideas of his own."

"He does. Fortunately, they're all good ideas."

"Aha. I have it on record now that you think my ideas are good."

Amelia looked up to see Flynn and a spectacularly good-looking Mick Riley standing at their table. She'd only seen Mick on TV—both playing football and in the endorsements he did. The man was a work of art. But in person? He was so much better looking with his black hair and searing blue eyes. He was supremely tall and wow, what a chiseled body.

Tara was one lucky woman.

"Amelia, this is my husband, Mick. Mick, this is Amelia Lawrence. She's the head chef here at Ninety-Two."

Mick held out his hand. "Very nice to meet you, Amelia. The food here is great. I've already eaten way more of it than I should have."

She blushed under his compliment. "It's a pleasure to meet you, Mick. I'm a big fan. And I'm glad you're enjoying the food." She pushed back her chair. "I should go back and check on the kitchen."

Flynn laid his hand lightly on her shoulder. "Stay. The kitchen's under control. While you were out here I took a peek."

She arched a brow. "You did, did you?"

"Yes. No one was in there to throw anything at me."

Tara stifled a chuckle.

Flynn and Mick took a seat.

"Where's your date, Flynn?" Amelia asked.

"She's in the ladies' room. She should be out in a second."

Amelia hadn't noticed her. Or Flynn, for that matter. Then

again, there were a lot of people in the restaurant, and she'd mainly been focusing on who had plates filled with food, so it wasn't like she'd been searching him out.

"There you are."

The guys stood when an amazing-looking woman came over. She was slender, with chin-length dark brown hair and an incredible body. Amelia could see why Flynn would be attracted to her. She had a gorgeous smile, perfect teeth and beautiful brown eyes.

The woman reached across the table and held out her hand. "Hi, I'm Jameson."

Intriguing name. Amelia shook her hand and introduced herself, as did Tara and Mick.

"I'm with him," Tara said with a grin.

"Oh, I know you both. Doesn't everyone?"

Mick laughed. "Well, I don't know about everyone, but thanks."

"And which one of these guys are you with, Amelia?" Jameson asked.

"I'm actually the head chef here."

"Oh, I love the food. It's all fantastic."

"Thank you." So far, so good. She was nice and friendly and seemed to be content to stick right next to Flynn. Of course the camera crews hadn't arrived yet, but she was inclined to give Jameson the benefit of the doubt.

After a few minutes of chitchat, Amelia excused herself to go check on the kitchen.

"You need to come back out here when you're done," Flynn said, walking with her toward the kitchen.

She paused. "It's not my job to be the face of the restaurant. It's yours and Ken's."

He looked at her. "But I'm asking you to. I'd like everyone to meet you. They're all raving about the food."

"You can take credit for it."

He laughed. "I didn't design or prepare the dishes. You did."

"All right."

"Great. And thanks."

It was a mystery to her why he wanted her out here when this was his party with his teammates, but he was the boss. She went into the kitchen to make sure everything was running smoothly. Inventory was fine, and she reviewed each station. Her staff was top-notch. They really didn't need her assistance, but she wanted them to know she was involved and paying attention and there to help troubleshoot if necessary. Luckily, there were no fires to put out, literally or metaphorically. And once she knew everything was in order, she returned to the party.

The foursome table had broken up, and she didn't see Flynn, so she was free to wander the room. She went to the bar and retrieved another glass of wine, then headed over to Ken.

"How's everyone doing?" she asked.

"Good. The guests all seem to be having a great time and the serving stations are busy. Everyone loves the food. Which, of course, they should. It's excellent."

"Thank you. Big crowd."

"It's about to be even bigger." Ken inclined his head toward the front door. "Media just arrived. I'm going to go grab Flynn."

"Okay."

She retreated to one of the corners to watch as Ken and Flynn met the media. She also noticed that Jameson had moved to the side, out of range of the cameras, and was talking to some of the players' wives.

She had high hopes for this woman. Maybe she'd be a good fit for Flynn.

The lights went on and the cameras started rolling. Flynn

began to talk and gesture about the restaurant. Amelia was happy to see him get this amount of press for Ninety-Two. It promised to bring in more customers. The cameras panned around the room and a few of the players stepped up for interviews.

Flynn stepped out and made his way to Jameson, who put her arm around him. When the cameras made their way back to them, it was like she'd undergone a personality transplant. Her head snapped up, she plastered on a wide smile, and she was suddenly "on," flashing her pearly whites and totally ignoring Flynn.

Oh, no. Not again.

It was as if she was the only one on camera, and as the journalist interviewed her, Flynn stepped away.

But Jameson didn't stop. She kept talking, completely oblivious to Flynn, who had gone to join some of his friends.

"What's that all about?" Tara asked, coming up alongside Amelia.

"I had such high hopes for Jameson. I thought she'd be different."

Tara frowned. "Different?"

"Flynn has a tendency to choose all the wrong women. You know the types—the ones who are after a football player only to get their time in front of a camera."

Tara pursed her lips. "Oh. I know exactly what you're talking about. And unfortunately they're all too frequent in the sport. You'd think women like that would come with a warning label."

"You'd think. But Flynn's like a magnet for them. I've seen him with no less than three camera whores over the past few months."

"That's unfortunate. And he's such a nice guy, too."

"I know. I really wish he could find the right woman."

Tara glared at Jameson, then looked over at Amelia. "I know a lot of nice women."

"Do you? Maybe you could set him up with one."

"I could maybe do that. Or how about you, Amelia?"

Amelia searched the room for Flynn, found him talking with Ken. "No, I don't really know a lot of people here."

"No, honey. I meant you."

She stared at Tara. "Me? And Flynn? I don't think so."

"Why not? You're beautiful. He's gorgeous. You share a mutual love of food. You're obviously hiding in the corner because you don't want to be on camera. You'd be perfect for him."

There was no doubt she was attracted to Flynn. But the last thing she needed in her life right now was a man. Especially not a man she worked for. "No, I don't think so."

"You don't find him attractive?"

She could barely pull her gaze away from him. Despite being surrounded by a group of incredibly good-looking men, he stood out. "Oh, I find him attractive. But he's my boss."

Tara shrugged. "So what?"

She pulled her attention from Flynn and directed it on Tara. "That's a big deal. I moved here specifically for this job. I don't need to lose it because a relationship, or love affair, goes bad."

"Okay, I see your point. Still, I think the idea of the two of you together has merit. I know you and I just met, but I can see you and Flynn together. You could fit."

She hadn't thought of it. Sure, she had a physical attraction to Flynn. What heterosexual woman wouldn't? He was hot stuff. But she wasn't looking for a relationship. Or a lover. But now both Tara and her best friend had mentioned something about her getting out there and dating.

Maybe it was time. She'd have to think about it. But she wouldn't think about it with Flynn. He was off-limits.

She made her way back into the kitchen and worked, content to stay away from the cameras. Hours later, the party started to die down, so she helped with cleanup and then sent her staff home. When she came out front, most everyone had left with the exception of Flynn and Ken, who were sitting with Mick and Tara at one of the larger tables.

"Hey, Amelia," Flynn said. "Come have a drink with us."

She headed over and Flynn got up to pull a glass from behind the bar. "What would you like?" he asked.

"A glass of pinot gris would be great."

He grabbed the bottle, uncorked it, then poured her a very large glass before handing it to her. "Thanks for tonight. If I haven't mentioned it before, the food was outstanding. Everyone raved about it."

"Thank you. I thought it all turned out well. You had a great showing."

"My boss was impressed with the restaurant. And the food. Irvin loves good food and he couldn't speak highly enough about yours. And trust me, he's well traveled, has eaten in some of the best restaurants in the world. He's not often awestruck."

She took that as the compliment it was intended to be. "Thank you for that."

They made their way over to the table and she took a seat.

"I hope you all had a good time tonight."

Tara looked as fresh this late as she had when Amelia saw her earlier. "I had such a great night. We're kid-free for this trip, so I get to stay out late. Our son Sam is back in St. Louis with his grandparents."

"That must be fun for you."

"Very fun. Not that I don't miss our little guy, because I do. But this gives me an opportunity to go to the game and not have to contend with sticky little mustard fingers swiping down my pants, or worry about him running amok. I can also conduct some business while I'm here, which is ideal for me."

"I'm sure that's important for you. And relaxing at the same time."

Mick put his arm around Tara. "She needs to meet with the manager of her place here in San Francisco. And we get a couple of date nights out of it, too. Have to keep that romance alive."

Tara grinned. "Romance is vital."

Amelia could feel the love between the two of them. "Yes, it definitely is."

"They're really sickening, those two," Flynn said, though he smiled as he said it.

Amelia realized Flynn was alone. "Where's Jameson?"

"I ordered a car for her and sent her back to her hotel."

"Oh. Did she have an early flight to catch?"

"No."

She supposed from his disgruntled expression that she shouldn't ask any more questions about Jameson.

"She was a little fond of the cameras, wasn't she, Flynn?" Tara asked.

"Yeah. I have a knack for finding women who are camera magnets."

"You should let me fix you up with someone," Tara said. "I know a lot of nice women."

"No, thanks. After tonight's disaster I think I'll just take a break from women right now."

Mick snorted.

Flynn glared at him. "What?"

"Take a break from women. Like you could do that."

"I could."

"No, you couldn't." Mick gestured with his hands. "It's like the buffet here. You can't resist taking a taste of everything."

Flynn lifted his chin and Amelia noticed the firm line of his lips. "I'm not like that with women."

"Aren't you? You always seem to have one around."

Flynn narrowed his gaze. "Yeah, and you were such a saint before you met Tara."

"Hey, I never claimed to be. But I didn't lie to myself about taking a break."

Amelia wondered if the two of them were going to shove the chairs back and start throwing punches. She glanced over at Tara, who didn't seem at all concerned about the argument.

Then, suddenly, Flynn laughed. "Okay, fine. Maybe I won't take a break. But, Christ, I'd sure as hell like to find a woman who prefers me over the cameras."

Mick slapped him on the back. "I know exactly what that's like, buddy."

Tension diffused. If there actually had ever been any tension. Maybe it had all been in her mind.

"Are you two always like this?" Amelia asked.

Flynn looked over at her. "Like what?"

"Arguing with each other one second, then laughing the next."

Mick grinned. "We give each other shit all the time. Flynn knows I was just joking with him."

Flynn laid his hand on her arm. "Were you worried about me?"

"No. Not at all. I was just wondering if I should move out of the way before one of you went flying over the table. But then I noticed Tara didn't seem worried."

Tara shrugged and took a sip of her wine. "I'm used to them. They're like small boys in large bodies."

Mick leaned over and kissed her cheek. "I'm going to take that as a compliment."

"You do that. In the meantime, we should find a decent woman for Flynn to go out with before he chooses another disaster like Jameson."

"Thanks, but I can find my own woman."

"Oh, right," Amelia said. "Because you're doing such a winning job on that front so far."

Flynn's focus landed on Amelia. "Hey. Now you're joining the fray?"

"Now that I know you're not going to punch anyone at the table, I thought I might."

"Yes, Amelia told me about some of your non-success stories earlier," Tara said.

Flynn pinned Amelia with a look. "Traitor."

Amelia's lips lifted. "Sorry. I was using them in reference to Jameson, who I hoped at the time would be different."

"Now that we know you can't possibly select your own woman, Amelia and I should act as matchmakers for you."

Mick looked at them in horror. "That's got train wreck written all over it."

"How so?" Amelia asked.

"I don't know, but I've never been fond of the fix-up."

"Let me give it a try," Tara said. "I'm having a dinner party next Tuesday at our place for friends as well as a few of the guys on the team."

"Offense," Mick said to Flynn.

Flynn grimaced and Mick laughed.

"Why don't you come, Flynn, and I'll fix you up with someone?" Tara asked. "Amelia, you come, too."

"Thank you, but I'll be working," Amelia said.

"If I have to go, so do you," Flynn said. "So you get the night off."

She was about to object, but it might be fun to see how Flynn managed being fixed up with one of Tara's friends. So she nodded. "Thank you, Tara. I'd love to."

"And this way it'll give you a chance to meet some new people, too, Amelia."

"Why don't you fix her up with someone, too, Tara?" Flynn asked. "She doesn't know that many people here."

Amelia glared at Flynn before turning a gentle smile on Tara. "Oh, that's not necessary."

But Tara cast a bright smile in Amelia's direction. "That's actually a great idea. Dates for both of you at the party on Tuesday."

She couldn't very well say no since she'd just shoved Flynn into this. "Great. Thank you."

But she did send a withering look at Flynn, who only smiled knowingly at her.

Bastard.

SIX

AMELIA WAS IN THE MIDST OF PREPPING BOEUF BOUR-guignon when the doorbell rang. She grabbed the towel to wipe her hands and went to the door. It was Laura.

"Hey, come on in. I thought you were working today."

"I switched shifts with one of my coworkers who didn't want to miss her daughter's dance recital. So I'm on later, instead."

"That means no wine for you. Too bad." She took a sip from her glass and laid it on the island.

"What in the world are you making? Is that boeuf bour-guignon?"

"It is. With a little twist here and there to make it my own."

"Oh, my God. I'm so intrigued. And now I'm hungry."

Amelia slid a cheese and cracker plate over toward Laura. "Have a snack. And there's iced tea in the refrigerator."

Laura grabbed a glass and poured herself some tea, then retrieved a small plate and piled it with cheese, crackers and the olives Amelia had prepared.

"So when you cook, you get hungry?"

Amelia grinned at her. "Absolutely. Which is why I have to have snacks nearby."

She slid the casserole into the oven and set the timer, then pulled up a chair to the island and put some cheese and crackers onto her plate.

"How did the event go last night?"

"It went very well." She filled Laura in on everything, including Flynn's disastrous date, meeting Tara and Mick Riley and what happened after the party.

"So another woman decided camera time was more important than hanging out with that gorgeous hunk of man? What is wrong with women, anyway?"

"I have no idea. I'm truly flummoxed why so many women would risk a relationship with such a nice guy like Flynn to get some face time on camera. Do television cameras have some kind of bewitching quality we're unaware of?"

"You've got me, honey. If someone stuck a camera in front of Jon, I'd run like hell to get away."

"That's because you're special. And you love your husband."

Laura popped an olive in her mouth. "I do love that man. So now you've got a date next week, too? Awesome."

"Ugh. Not awesome. But there didn't seem to be a polite way to get out of it."

"Why would you even want to? This is your opportunity to meet new people. And a guy who might be perfect for you."

"No guy is perfect."

"Of course not. But some guy might be the right one for you." She sliced a piece of Gouda and laid it on a cracker. "That's what

I thought the first time. I was wrong. Clearly I have no intuition when it comes to men, and I'm not interested in trying again."

"You're burned, honey. I get it. But go anyway, have some fun. No one's asking you to marry the guy on the first date. Even if you just find someone to have a hot fling with, it's worth it. Don't you miss sex?"

She nearly choked on her wine. "Of course I do."

"All that body-to-body action, a sexy mouth kissing on you, some tongue action taking a slow, delicious ride on the Hot Body Train down to Lady Town."

She shot a glare at her best friend. "Laura. Stop."

Laura seemed unfazed. "What? You know you want some. Just because some asshole broke your heart doesn't mean your vagina has gone out of business. The two organs don't have to be connected to each other, ya know. You can have sweaty hot sex without falling in love."

Laura was right. It had been a very long time. Even before she and Frank had divorced, the sex had stopped. Which didn't mean she was ready to . . . board that train again just yet.

Still . . . just the thought of having some wild uncontrollable sex with someone sounded really good about now.

Then again, that might be the wine talking.

"I can see your mind working over there," Laura said. "You're thinking about sex."

She hid her thoughts by leaning over to jot down some notes about the recipe. "No. I'm thinking about food."

"No one knows you better than I do. And you never blush about boeuf bourguignon. You're not only thinking about sex, you're thinking about hot, dirty, up-against-the-wall sex."

Amelia shot a direct look at Laura. "I've never even had hot, dirty, up-against-the-wall sex."

Laura tilted her glass of tea toward her. "Then you've been doing it wrong. We need to find the hottest guy in the world for you. I hope he's at the party Tuesday night."

Amelia thought about denying Laura's statement, but truthfully, so did she.

SEVEN

AFTER A GRUELING LOSS TO CLEVELAND ON SUNDAY, Flynn and his team regrouped and tried to figure out where they'd gone wrong.

Special teams had made some errors, and the opposing team's eighty-yard runback for a touchdown hadn't helped. Defense had seemed off-key the entire game. The Sabers offense had put up two touchdowns and a field goal, so they should have been able to defend Cleveland and hold them.

They hadn't been, which had made them even more determined to go into their home game this weekend with a mind-set to win.

They'd watched game films today, and Flynn had paid particular attention to the defensive line. It wasn't as if Cleveland's offensive line was better. But Cleveland's offense had gotten off the mark faster, and had protected the quarterback, which meant Flynn hadn't been able to touch him. Nor had the other lineman.

Cleveland had looked solid and the Sabers defense had been scattered.

Time to shake off that loss and do what they knew they could.

It was a grueling workout, but the day was cool and they dug deep exorcising the demons from the previous game. Whatever had gone wrong last week was over. He and his line were solid now, and after the rest of the week's practices he knew they'd be ready for Green Bay come Sunday.

"See you tonight?" Mick asked as he walked by him in the locker room.

"For sure. I'll be there." Though he wasn't all that jazzed about the idea of being fixed up. He much preferred to choose his own woman.

Then again, that hadn't been working out all that well for him lately. He was still pissed about what had happened with Jameson. And if he was honest, he was pissed about the long stream of women who had been using him for camera time.

He should just give up on dating and concentrate on football. He didn't like failure. Losing wasn't acceptable to him, whether it was a game or a relationship.

At least he'd won more games than he'd lost. The whole relationship thing had been one giant loss lately, and that just fucking sucked. Something needed to change in the romance department.

Maybe having someone fix him up would work out better than him finding his own dates, so he might as well give this a try.

After he got home he checked his phone messages. One from his mother, so he clicked on her number. She answered right away.

"Hey, Mom, what's up?"

"Not much here. Wedding planning."

Two of his brothers—Grant and Tucker—were getting married next year. Which made his mom very happy.

"And how's that going?"

"It's going well, but of course there's a lot to do as you can imagine."

"Yeah, I can imagine."

"And how are you? How's the new restaurant coming along?"

"It's good. I'm glad you and Dad were able to make it out for opening night."

"We had a wonderful time. It's a lovely restaurant, Flynn. We're so proud of you."

He smiled. His parents had always been supportive of his career and everything he'd accomplished. Raising five kids hadn't been easy, and a lot of that burden had fallen on his mother when they were all younger, because at the time his father had still been playing football. He had a lot of admiration for his mom. She'd been a full-time lawyer until she'd retired, and had managed to wrangle four unruly boys and one daughter.

"Thanks, Mom."

"Anything new on the dating front?"

He expected the question. "Not at the moment. I'm . . . freelancing."

"Which means you haven't met anyone special yet. Don't worry. It'll happen for you."

"I'm in no hurry."

"Well, when it does, you let me know, okay?"

It would suit his mother to have all her kids coupled up. "You know I will."

"Oh, and Mia will be out there soon. Did she tell you about visiting Stanford?"

"Yeah, she told me. She's going to bunk in the guesthouse."

"All right. You keep an eye on her while she's there. I know she talks an independent game, but she's still my little girl."

He smiled. His sister was an adult now, but to their mother,

Mia would always be the baby of the family. "I'll keep her imprisoned in the house and take away all communication devices."

His mother laughed. "I don't think we have to go that far. Just make sure she stays safe while she's there, Flynn."

"That I can do."

"Thank you. I'll talk to you soon. I love you."

"I love you, too, Mom. Bye."

He'd avoided telling his mom about the fix-up date tonight. Mainly because he figured nothing would come of it. He rarely discussed his romantic life with his mother—or any other member of his family. They all had a tendency to butt in and offer unsolicited advice, which he neither needed nor wanted. Everyone except his mom, who never offered advice. She just got her hopes up, and he didn't want her to be disappointed.

He went to his desk and did some work on his computer for an hour or so, then kicked back and watched sports on TV until it was time to get ready. He chose a pair of dark jeans and a long-sleeved button-down shirt. Mick had told him it was casual, but since he was going to have a date, he made sure to choose a new pair of jeans and a nice shirt. After putting on his shoes, he slid his watch on, then climbed into his SUV and headed over to Mick and Tara's house.

They had a nice place over in Half Moon Bay, on the golf course because Mick liked to play golf. And since Tara wasn't often with him, it gave Mick something to do in his downtime. Flynn would sometimes go over there and play a round with him.

It was a great golf course, and Mick's house sat on the fifteenth fairway. Pretty sweet.

Flynn parked in the oversized driveway, then went to the front door and rang the bell.

Mick opened the door. He had a bottle of beer in his hand and offered up a wide smile.

"Hey, Flynn. Come on in."

"Thanks." Flynn walked inside and followed Mick to the expansive living area, where a crowd had already formed. He made a beeline for the Sabers players, since those were guys he knew and liked.

Even if they were offensive players.

"Hey, Flynn."

"Hey, Randy." Randy LaSalle was the star wide receiver for the Sabers. He'd come to the team right out of college and had done great with them.

"Where's your wife?"

"One of the kids has the flu so she couldn't make it. She's not too damn happy about it, either. Almost made me stay home so she could come. You know how she feels about Tara."

Flynn laughed. "Yeah, I know." Everyone on the team loved Tara. She was sweet and generous and truly supportive of Mick and his career. Hell, she supported all of the players.

Flynn would be lucky to find a woman like that.

Tara came over. "Hello, Flynn. I'm so glad you're here. I want to introduce you to Skylar. If you'll excuse us, Randy."

"Sure," Randy said. "Later, Flynn."

She took him by the arm and led him over to the fireplace. There was a beautiful, auburn-haired woman sitting there sipping a glass of wine and talking to, of all people, Amelia, who looked stunning in a long skirt and long-sleeved sweater.

For some reason his eyes gravitated toward Amelia, who met his gaze with interest.

"Hey, Amelia."

"Hi, Flynn."

"Flynn, this is Skylar Wilson. Skylar, I'd like you to meet Flynn Cassidy."

He held out his hand to shake hers. "Nice to meet you, Skylar."

"Nice to meet you, too, Flynn."

"If you'll excuse me, I'm going to go refill my glass," Amelia said.

"Me, too." Tara and Amelia left the two of them alone, so Flynn motioned to the fireplace.

"You found the warm spot."

She laughed. "Yes, I tend to be cold, and I forgot my sweater."

"I have a jacket in my car. Would you like me to get it for you?"

"That's very nice of you to offer, but I'm fine right now. Tara tells me you play football, like Mick."

"Yes, I do. Do you like football?"

"I do. I'm a fan of the Sabers, though I guess I don't know all the individual players. Sorry."

He gave her a smile. "It's not necessary. I'm glad you enjoy the game. What do you do, Skylar?"

"I'm an artist. I both paint and sculpt. I have a little gallery here in Half Moon Bay. That's where I met Tara."

"Sounds great. It must be amazing to have artistic ability. Mine doesn't go much beyond the stick figure variety."

She laughed. "That's okay, because I can't throw or catch a football. We all have our talents."

"I guess we do."

They chatted for a while about their respective careers. He liked Skylar. She was interesting, certainly gorgeous, and she could carry on a conversation. Plus, she listened while he talked, so it wasn't all one-sided.

So far, so good.

AMELIA ENJOYED MEETING NEW PEOPLE. SHE WASN'T an introvert, so it was easy for her to feel comfortable even among strangers.

But meeting a new guy? Now, that was intimidating. Part of her was hoping he wouldn't show up tonight, and she could engage with Mick and Tara's friends without any expectations.

She was talking to the team attorney and his wife when Tara tapped her on the shoulder.

"I'm sorry to interrupt, but do you mind if I borrow Amelia? There's someone I need to introduce her to."

"Of course," John said.

"It was nice to meet you, Amelia," John's wife, Adele, said.

"Wonderful meeting both of you. I hope you'll stop by Ninety-Two for a meal."

"We definitely will," Adele said.

"Aaron's here. He's the guy I'm setting you up with," Tara said.

"Oh. Okay. Great." So much for him not showing up.

Tara led her to the kitchen, where a very attractive guy was talking to a bunch of other attractive guys. If Aaron was in this group, at least she'd be spending the evening having dinner with one hot-looking man.

Tara touched one of the tall, well-built men on the shoulder. "Aaron."

He turned, and Amelia noted that he wore a navy blue sweater over a white button-down shirt. He had on dark slacks, had sandy brown hair and very nice brown eyes. And the guy had a killer smile.

"Aaron Brooks, this is Amelia Lawrence."

"Hi, Amelia. Tara's told me so much about you."

"Has she?" Amelia slanted a questioning look at Tara, since Tara hadn't told her a thing about Aaron.

"Yeah. I heard you're the new chef at Flynn Cassidy's restaurant. I'm kind of a foodie myself."

"So you cook?"

"No. But I do love to eat. It's one of my favorite pastimes."

She laughed. "I see."

"Excuse me," Tara said. "I think I heard someone at the door."

"Would you like to go somewhere more quiet where we can talk?" He motioned with his head to the chairs over in the corner of the living area.

"That would be great."

Aaron led her over to two comfortable chairs in the corner near the fireplace. On her way, they passed Flynn and Skylar, who were deep in conversation.

Flynn looked up at her as she walked by and smiled. She waved her fingers at him, not wanting to call attention to herself since he was with a date.

This whole thing was so odd.

Aaron had held her glass of wine as they walked, so he set it down on the small table between them.

"Tell me what you do, Aaron."

"I'm actually Mick's accountant. Not a very glamorous job like yours."

"I don't know about that. Math can be very sexy."

He laughed. "I think that might be the first time I've ever heard that, so thanks."

"You're welcome. And I assume you're a football fan?"

"Very much so. Though I have other interests besides sports. And math."

"Good to know. What would those be?"

"I love to sail. I have a boat."

Her brows rose. "Really. That must be incredible. San Francisco is amazing for sailing."

"Yeah, it is. Have you ever been sailing?"

She nodded. "I have. I used to live in Seattle. And then Portland after that. I'm a big fan of living near the water, obviously. And my ex-husband had friends who loved to sail so we were often invited out on their boat."

"Awesome. So you cook and you can sail. What else do you like to do, Amelia?"

She liked that he asked her questions about herself. She'd gone out with plenty of guys who only liked to talk about themselves. They spent a half hour doing a good back and forth getting to know each other. She liked Aaron. There wasn't a buzzy chemistry between them, but he was nice, personable and certainly good-looking.

She was good with that for a first date. Especially for a fix-up.

When Tara announced it was time for dinner, they moved into the dining room, which was beautiful and spacious.

Amelia loved everything about Tara's house here. Tara had given her a tour of the main floor when she'd first arrived. It was warm and open, with a main living area that was incredibly expansive, and floor-to-ceiling windows that looked out over an amazing terrace and golf course.

And, of course, Amelia was in love with the kitchen. Marble countertops with tons of space, a huge island, a chef's stove and a Sub-Zero freezer. Tara had told her they entertained several members of the Sabers whenever she was in town, so she liked to have a lot of room for all of those big guys. And often the entire Riley family would come out and visit, and it was a big family, so Tara enjoyed having room for everyone. Amelia understood the need for that.

As they made their way into the dining room, she made mental notes about the oversized table, the beautiful chandelier and the elegant table settings.

Someday, she'd have a big house like this with an amazing kitchen and dining room.

She and Aaron ended up sitting next to Flynn and Skylar, though with the way the seating was arranged, Aaron sat next to Skylar and Flynn was on the far end.

Which suited her just fine, because she had a nice time talking to Aaron. And Aaron apparently also had a nice time talking to Skylar. It turned out the two of them were acquainted with each other through Tara, and they really hit it off as well. Aaron and Skylar discovered they had gone to the same high school, so while they got reacquainted and talked about common friends, Amelia ended up talking to Maggie, who she discovered managed Tara's event planning business in San Francisco.

Maggie was fun and smart and had a great sense of humor. She'd recently gotten engaged to an amazingly hot guy who sat on her left and seemed totally devoted to her.

"We met at a concert in the park," Maggie said. "I thought he was kind of a stalker at first."

"Hey, I liked you," Jack, her fiancé, said. "I mean look at you. You're gorgeous. Can you blame me?"

Maggie blushed. "I warmed up to him pretty quickly once I realized he wasn't a serial killer."

Amelia laughed. "When's the wedding?"

"In April. Jack's family lives in North Dakota, but they're coming out here for the wedding. So there'll be a lot of travel coordinating in addition to the wedding planning."

Jack put his arm around the back of Maggie's chair. "Fortunately, she's an event planner, so she has all this under control. And I just nod and tell her I love everything she chooses."

"He's joking. One of the things I love most about him is that he has opinions."

She really liked these two.

After salads the caterers brought in dinner, which was an amazing seared salmon with capers and asparagus. She spent time talking to both Maggie and Jack as well as Aaron and Skylar.

It was quickly becoming apparent that Aaron and Skylar shared much more chemistry than she did with Aaron. Though Aaron was totally attentive to her and she gave him points for that. A lot of guys would just dump a fix-up and go with the girl who hit his hot buttons. He was being a total gentleman about it and she was going to have to give him an out after dinner.

After a decadent dessert of tiramisu, she finished her coffee, then let Aaron pull out her chair.

"Did you enjoy dinner?" he asked.

"It was wonderful."

"I was wondering how critical you are of food cooked by other people," he asked.

"Oh, not very critical. I mean, I sometimes think about how I might have fixed it differently, but I let the chef in me take a night off every now and then."

He laughed. "Of course."

His gaze strayed over to Skylar, who was chatting with Flynn.

"Aaron?"

He pulled his attention back to Amelia. "Yes."

She took his hand. "I've had a lovely time talking to you tonight, but it's obvious you have a much stronger connection with Skylar."

He wrinkled his nose. "Was it that obvious? I'm really sorry."

"Don't be. It's hard to find someone you connect with. And when you do, I think you should go for it."

"I don't know. What about Flynn?"

She looked over to see Skylar reaching up to give Flynn a hug, then turn to glance Aaron's way with a smile. Obviously it wasn't bothering Flynn too much, since he walked away from Skylar without a backward glance.

"I think Flynn is just fine with it."

Aaron picked up her hand and kissed the back of it. "You're a class act, Amelia. I hope you find someone worthy of you."

"Thank you."

She watched as Aaron went over to where Skylar stood by the fireplace. Skylar graced Aaron with a genuine smile.

She had a good feeling about the two of them. She had spent some time with Skylar before Flynn had showed up tonight and she really liked the beautiful, smart woman.

She headed into the kitchen and laid her coffee cup in the sink, deciding maybe more wine was in order. There was a bar set up on the counter, so she grabbed a glass and looked at the selection, trying to decide what she wanted.

"It looks like our dinner companions have found more in common with each other than with us."

She turned and looked up at Flynn. "It would seem that way."

"I hope that doesn't hurt your feelings."

She shrugged. "Aaron's a nice guy and I definitely enjoyed talking to him, but honestly, there was no chemistry between us. I can tell he's got something with Skylar, though."

Flynn nodded. "Yeah. Skylar's really sweet, super smart and funny. I liked her, but it was the same for me. No zing."

Amelia cocked a brow. "Is that zing important?"

"Hell yeah. Isn't it for you?"

"I don't know that I've ever felt a zing before."

He stepped forward. "You haven't? But you were married."

"This is true." She didn't elaborate and he didn't ask, which she was grateful about.

"Time to change that."

She definitely felt something as he grasped her shoulders and pulled her toward him. Whether it could be classified as a zing or every hormone in her body sitting up and taking notice of a hot, delectable man touching her, she didn't know. What she felt was hot fingers on her flesh, his fresh, woodsy scent and the sudden need to reach out and touch him back.

She tilted her head back and lost herself in the blue depths of his eyes.

"Excuse me, you two," Tara said. "I need to do a wine inventory check."

And just like that, the incendiary heat that had enveloped her as soon as Flynn had touched her evaporated. She took a step back and so did Flynn.

"Can I help you with that, Tara?"

"No, I've got this covered. You're here to enjoy the party." Tara looked around. "Where's Aaron?"

"Starting what Flynn and I hope is a very nice relationship with Skylar."

Tara looked at both of them. "Oh. Oops. I'm sorry, guys."

Amelia laughed. "It's not a problem. Sometimes it works out that way."

"But we appreciate the fix-up," Flynn said. "Skylar's sweet."

"She is, isn't she? Hey, at least I did fix up one couple tonight. Just not the way I originally intended."

"Better than everyone going their separate ways," Flynn said. "And let us help you with that."

They ended up pitching in and assisting Tara with her wine inventory. They headed downstairs into the wine cellar, which was pretty incredible. Flynn carted up a case of chardonnay, while Tara and Amelia each carried two bottles of red.

"Thanks for the assist," Tara said. "Now I insist the two of you go join the party."

"All right," Flynn said. "But first, Amelia, how about some wine?"

She'd gotten so caught up in being close to Flynn that she'd completely forgotten about her wine.

"Oh, right, wine."

"What would you like?"

"I'll take that merlot."

While Tara busied herself reorganizing and helping out one of the couples who'd wandered into the kitchen, Flynn expertly opened the bottle and filled her glass. Then he went into the refrigerator and grabbed a beer.

"Let's go sit down somewhere."

"Sure."

They made their way to the private corner where she'd sat with Aaron earlier. She noticed Aaron and Skylar deep in conversation at the fireplace. So much so, they hadn't even acknowledged Amelia and Flynn when they'd walked by.

Yes, those two were going to do just fine.

"It's like no one else in this entire house exists."

Flynn looked over his shoulder at Aaron and Skylar. "Yeah, I'd say they hit it off pretty well."

He returned his attention on her. "And isn't that how it should be with someone you're interested in?"

"Yes."

He picked up her hand, and she experienced that same tremble she'd felt earlier when he'd gotten closer to her.

"That zing I was describing before."

She lifted her gaze to his. "That zing."

His gaze was direct and she couldn't help but focus on his mouth.

"Yeah. It's an attraction. A chemical thing. When you feel a tightening in your body, an awareness of the other person."

His thumb rubbed over her hand. It made her breath catch as tiny sparks—she hated to use the word, but she had no other description for it—*zinged* through her. It felt like mini electrical shocks quivering within her.

"Do you feel it right now, Amelia? When I touch you?"

She jerked her hand away, forcefully rubbing her skin where, just seconds ago, she'd felt that erotic charge from Flynn. "No."

His lips curved. "You sure about that?"

"Absolutely. I didn't feel a thing."

He leaned back and took a long swallow of his beer, studying her.

There was something so intense about Flynn. She'd felt it months ago when he'd interviewed her. Back then, she'd liked that about him. So many restaurant owners had barely looked at her when they interviewed her, as if she didn't exist. Flynn was all about eye contact, which at the time of the interview she'd really appreciated. He had made her feel like a person, as if her opinions mattered.

Now, though, they weren't talking about the restaurant or food. In fact, they weren't talking at all. She wanted to look away, but there was something incredibly magnetic about his eyes. About all of him, really, from the square cut of his jaw to the thickness of his black hair to the way he smiled.

And then there was his body. She almost wished it wasn't fall and he wasn't wearing a long-sleeved shirt. She'd seen him in short-sleeved shirts before, had gotten a glimpse of his tattoos, though she wanted a closer look not only at his body art, but at his muscles.

She wasn't much for a man with muscles. Her ex had been on the lean side, and that had never bothered her. But now that she was up close with Flynn, she had to admit the idea of running her hands over his biceps or sliding her fingers under his shirt to wander his abs held a certain appeal.

Flynn cleared his throat and her gaze snapped back to his face. Only then did she realize she'd been visually mapping his body as she'd thought about him.

And the telltale smile on his face told her he knew exactly what she'd been doing.

Her face flamed hot. She stood. "Well, I should go refill my wine."

He looked at her glass. "You haven't finished what's in there yet."

"I haven't, have I?"

She abused the poor merlot by downing it in two swallows. "Now I have."

Flynn's lips curved. "Thirsty, Amelia?"

"Apparently. I'll be right back."

She made a quick exit into the kitchen, hoping there'd be someone in there she could talk to so she wouldn't have to go back and talk to Flynn.

Unfortunately, the only people in there were the catering staff, though she did take a few minutes to tell them how wonderful dinner had been. Then she refilled her wine and reluctantly made her way back into the living room.

Fortunately, there were several people sitting with Flynn now, including with Tara and Mick.

She breathed a sigh of relief.

There was entirely too much going on between her and Flynn at the moment.

Okay, actually, there had been nothing going on. But whatever the nothing was, it had been incendiary and confusing. So she was glad the two of them weren't going to be alone.

Which made no sense and she was going to chalk that train of thought up to the wine she'd consumed. And the nearness of the hot man.

She headed over to them. Tara motioned to her.

"Come sit by Maggie and me. The guys are talking football."

"Jack loves football," Maggie said, making room for Amelia on the sofa where she sat with Tara. "He played in college, so when we all get together it's like he's on the team."

"Fortunately, we can always talk our business while they talk their business," Tara said, "so it's easy to ignore them."

"Understandable," Amelia said. "And how nice that you can come out here, visit with Maggie and check on things at your shop. Plus, see your husband and watch some football at the same time."

Tara nodded. "It really is the best of both worlds. Usually I bring our youngest, Sam, with me. He does miss his daddy during football season. But he's just getting over a flu bug so this time he didn't get to make the trip."

Amelia made a sympathetic face. "Aww. I'm sure he's very disappointed."

"Very much so. But Mick's been doing video chats with him every day, and I promised him I'd make a return trip for Mick's next home game. And fortunately, the Sabers are playing in Kansas City in a few weeks. He won't play against St. Louis until later in the season, but since Kansas City is so close, we'll drive over for the game. Sam will love it."

"That's great news."

"Yes. Good for Flynn, too," Tara said. "He'll get to see his brother Tucker, who will also come over."

Flynn looked over at the mention of his name. "What's good for me?"

"That the Sabers are playing against Kansas City in a few weeks. And you'll get to see Tucker."

"Oh, yeah. It's always nice to see family. We play St. Louis here at home this season, too, which means Grant will be here."

"That's right," Tara said. "Even more family."

Flynn grinned. "Even better to play against one of my brothers."

"That competitive, are you?" Amelia asked.

"Just a little."

Tara shook her head. "I'm not sure who's more competitive—the Rileys or the Cassidys."

Both Mick and Flynn answered at the same time.

"We are."

Amelia laughed. And finally relaxed, even though Flynn kept skirting glances her way. He could watch her all he wanted to. As long as the two of them didn't have another one of those intimate conversations where he touched her and her body didn't go up in flames, she'd be fine.

The party broke up around midnight. Amelia took out her phone to call for a ride.

"What are you doing?" Flynn asked.

"Ordering a ride home."

"We live close. I'll drive you home."

"That's not necessary. I'm used to getting my own ride."

"It may be what you're used to, but it's not happening tonight. Put your phone away. I'm driving you home."

She frowned at him. "Are you always so bossy?"

"You work for me so you know the answer to that. But in this case, no. I'm a gentleman, because my mother raised me to be one. And I'd very much like to give you a ride home, Amelia, if you'd let me."

If he'd been overly assertive and an asshole, she could have easily told him no. But he had to be sweet about it, and even brought up his mother. What was she supposed to do with that? "Okay. Sure. Thanks."

They said their good-byes. Amelia made sure to hug Tara.

"Thank you so much for inviting me. I had a wonderful time."

Tara gave her a squeeze. "I'm so glad. I'm really sorry about Aaron. I had high hopes for the two of you."

Amelia laughed. "It's really fine. And I'm glad he and Skylar found a connection."

"It would seem so, since they took off a couple of hours ago. I think they wanted some alone time to get better acquainted."

Or something that had nothing to do with talking. "I'm happy to hear that."

"We'll talk soon," Tara said.

Flynn hugged Tara, then they walked out to his SUV. He opened her side of the vehicle and waited for her to get in before closing the door and moving over to the driver's side.

The night was cool, so she was glad she had her sweater to wrap around her.

"Cold?" Flynn asked after he started the engine.

"A little."

He leaned over and pressed a button on the dash. "Butt warmer. That should help."

"Butt warmer, huh?"

"Yup. And I'll turn the heat up."

"No, don't do that on my account."

He looked over at her. "Did someone tell you once that you were a pain in the ass or something, so now you never complain about anything?"

"I . . ." Actually, that's exactly what had happened with Frank. Whenever she'd asked for something more than once, he'd called her a complainer. Or, even worse, a whiner. So she'd stopped asking.

After a while, they'd stopped communicating altogether.

That had been the beginning of the end for her marriage.

He put the car in reverse and backed down the driveway. "Yeah, that's what I thought. If you want something, Amelia, just ask for it. I'll never jump down your throat about it."

"Duly noted."

They drove for a while in silence, then she looked over at him and said, "I need a couple more stainless steel sauté pans for the restaurant."

When they reached a red light, he glanced her way and arched a brow. "Taking that opening to hit me up for some inventory, huh?"

She gave him her sweetest smile. "Well, you told me to ask."

He laughed. "Anything you want, you can have."

"Anything?"

"Within reason."

"Oh, now you're putting conditions on it."

"Hey, I can't have you out buying a new stove or anything."

She frowned. "You put a brand-new stove in when you remodeled the restaurant before you opened. Why would I want a new stove?"

"I was joking."

"Oh. Sorry."

"You need to lighten up, Amelia. Not everything between you and me has to be so damn serious all the time."

"I'll make a note of that."

She was still so wrapped up in what had happened between them earlier that she'd totally missed that bit of humor.

He was right. She did need to relax. The problem was, she'd been tense ever since that moment in Tara and Mick's kitchen.

Sexual tension.

A good orgasm would cure that. She made a mental note to take care of that as soon as she got home.

Great. Now she was stuck in the car with Flynn and thinking about sex and orgasms.

She swallowed, her throat suddenly dry as she thought about how it had felt when he'd touched her, the way he'd looked at her with such . . . intensity.

She bet he fucked that way, too. He seemed like the kind of man who was all-in on everything he did. She could already imagine him giving his full attention to a woman, both with his hands and his mouth, and then later, with his cock.

Suddenly overwhelmed with heat and a quivering sensation, she blew out a breath.

"Everything okay over there?" he asked.

"Fine. I'm fine."

"You sure? I can pull over if you need a drink or you need to pee or something."

It was definitely more of the "or something" variety, and she didn't think having an orgasm at a nearby convenience store sounded all that . . . convenient.

"I'm sure." This ride home was interminable. She needed to get behind closed doors and take care of this problem. Once she had a tension release, she'd be her normal self again.

Or, at least, she needed to get far away from Flynn.

When they finally drove up her street, she almost exhaled in relief. He pulled up to the curb and it was all she could do not to leap out. But then he parked and shut off the engine. She shot him a glare.

"What are you doing?"

"I'm going to walk you to your door."

"That is not necessary, Flynn."

But he was already out the door and on his way over to her side. Dammit.

He opened her car door, so she had no choice but to step out and allow him to accompany her to her front door.

She turned around to face him. "Okay, well, thanks."

He stood there, waiting.

She rolled her eyes and fumbled in her purse for her keys. When she found them, she unlocked her door and opened it.

"I'm fine now. Thanks for driving me home."

"You should invite me in for coffee. Or something."

She knew exactly what that something was, and if she let him put one foot inside that door she'd climb him like a sex-starved monkey. And despite all the reasons that idea sounded really good at the moment, there were a lot more really bad reasons.

Wasn't going to happen.

"That's not a good idea."

He arched a brow. "Why not?"

"You know why not."

"I think you're tempted by me."

She laughed. "I am not. Nothing about you tempts me."

He picked up her hand and that shock of awareness zipped through her again.

"You sure about that?" He covered her hand with his other one.

Warmth enveloped her, and everything within her wanted to combust. She wasn't sure about anything right now. "Absolutely."

He leaned over and she braced herself for the onslaught, for the explosion of sensations.

But he kissed her cheek. "Good night, Amelia."

As he walked away and got back in the SUV, she waited, breath held, until he drove off. She exhaled and went inside, closed the door and locked it. As she leaned against the door with her eyes closed, she realized she'd never been more disappointed in her life about a man leaving her at the front door.

Which was exactly what she'd wanted. She'd wanted him to leave her alone.

So now she was alone. And damned disappointed about it.

She pushed off the door and went into the kitchen, laying her purse on the island and shrugging out of her sweater.

"You're a confused mass of contradictions, Amelia," she muttered as she made her way into the bedroom. "And you have no idea what you really want."

She turned on the light in the bathroom and laid her palms against the counter, glaring at herself in the mirror.

"No, the problem is you do know what you want. And you're too afraid to have it."

With a disgusted sigh, she wound her hair up in a clip and turned on the water so she could get ready for bed.

EIGHT

THEY WERE DEEP INTO THE THIRD QUARTER, AND THE
Sabers were up by one touchdown against Green Bay.

Flynn lived for games like this. When it was a blowout, that
was great, too, because it meant his offense was kicking ass on all
cylinders. But close games like this really put his defense to work.
It was their job to keep the opposing team from scoring. A score
by Green Bay would tie the game, and the Sabers had to make sure
that didn't happen.

Flynn wouldn't have it any other way.

They lined up as Green Bay's quarterback took the snap. Flynn
was quick off the line, shoving the offensive lineman out of the
way. Since it was third down and long, it was a pass, and Flynn had
gotten a mark on the quarterback.

He flattened him before he got the ball off, then walked away,
eyeing the quarterback to be sure he got up.

He did, brushing off his jersey.

Flynn was happy about the sack. So was the crowd, who roared their approval. He bumped fists with Hey Man, then they huddled up to do it all over again.

Offensive line for Green Bay was tough, so he had to dig in and push his way forward with every snap. They were sweating through this series with every down, but they kept Green Bay from advancing more than a few yards.

By the end of the third quarter, the Sabers were still up by one touchdown.

Mick and the offense took care of that by scoring another seven in the fourth, giving the defense a cushion to work with.

They battered Green Bay's offense, keeping them on their own side of the field for most of the fourth quarter. They gave up a few first downs, but other than that, Green Bay remained scoreless.

The Sabers got the ball with three minutes left in the game, managed to get a first down and ended the game with the ball in hand.

All in all, a solid win, especially for the defense. They'd battled hard against a really good team and won. After last week's loss, this felt damned satisfying.

"Nice sack," Junior said as they walked off the field after the game.

"Thanks. It was a solid team effort. We all did good today."

"We sure as hell did, didn't we?"

He nudged shoulders in celebration with Junior, then they headed to the locker room.

He was stopped by media so he did a couple of short interviews first, the whole time thinking of a shower and an ice bath for his sore muscles. But they mentioned his restaurant, and he wasn't about to turn down free advertising for Ninety-Two, so he gladly took the extra five minutes to talk about the game.

After, he hit the locker room, basked in the afterglow of the pumped-up team and coaches, then soaked in an ice bath for a good long time. He finally took a hot shower to scrub off the sweat and grime.

By then he was starving. He knew exactly what he wanted for dinner. He drove to Ninety-Two and parked down the street, leaving the prime parking for his customers.

He went in and greeted some of the regulars, who congratulated him on the game, so he stopped to talk to them before heading into the kitchen.

Amelia looked up at him in surprise.

"What are you doing here?" she asked. "I thought you'd be out celebrating your win with your teammates."

"Did you catch the game?"

She smiled at him. "I might have watched parts of it before I came in to work."

She had totally watched the game. Why she wouldn't admit it was a mystery to him. Maybe it was because she liked him and she didn't want to admit that, either.

"So what brings you here?" she asked.

"Hunger."

"Now, that I can help you with. What would you like?"

"I've been thinking about the black bean burger all day."

"Take a seat and I'll fix one for you. Do you want an egg on that and some sweet potato fries?"

"Yes to both."

She laughed. "I'll have it out to you shortly."

"Thanks, Amelia."

He could have sat and had one of the waitresses take the order back, but he wanted to see Amelia. After the other night at Tara's party, he realized there was something between them—something he wanted to explore further.

He stopped at the bar to grab a beer, then found a seat at a small table in the corner to sip his beer and observe. He was happy to see the restaurant busy. His staff was good at what they did so he didn't need to hover. Ken knew what he was doing, as did the managers who worked under him.

Grace, one of the waitresses, brought his burger out and set it in front of him.

"Amelia wanted me to tell you that she's trying something new tonight with the sweet potato fries. She hopes you like them."

"Thanks, Grace."

He dug into his burger, which was delicious. Then he tried the sweet potato fries, which came with a side of dipping sauce. It surprised the hell out of him because the fries were sprinkled with something hot, and the sauce was sweet. The combination was excellent.

He savored the meal, which went well with his beer. He could have eaten the entire meal twice. In fact, he just might since he'd burned a lot of calories during the game.

Amelia came out after he'd eaten the last fry.

"What did you think?" she asked.

"My mouth is on fire from these fries. What's in them?"

She gave him a half smile. "That's a secret."

He laughed. "No, seriously. They were really good."

"Some jalapeño and red peppers, along with maple syrup and caramel in the sauce. A little mix of sweet with spicy."

"Holy crap, that was such a good idea. You're adding it to the menu, right?"

"I'm trying it out on a few select customers over the next week to see how it plays out, but if you think it works, then yes, I'll add it to the menu."

"Good. Oh, and speaking of caramel—but not really—there's a caramelized bluefin tuna recipe I've been meaning to try. I thought maybe we could incorporate it here."

"Really. I'd like to hear more about it." She looked over her shoulder toward the kitchen.

"You go back to work. We can talk about it later."

"Okay. But you've piqued my interest."

His lips curved. "Have I? Good."

She wandered off and he got up and decided to do a walk around the tables. He liked to keep a low profile, but it was his job as the owner to make sure his clientele were all satisfied. And a little PR every now and then wasn't a bad thing. Some people had no idea who he was, which suited him just fine. Others knew and wanted to chat football, and that was okay, too. The important thing was the food and the ambiance of the restaurant, and that's what interested him.

All in all, everyone seemed happy, and if his customers were happy, then so was he.

He returned to his table in the corner and made some calls to his brothers. It was a little late on the East Coast for Barrett, but that never stopped him before. Barrett told him he was up late watching sports anyway.

Barrett had won his game today as well, so they talked football. Grant's game was tomorrow night, and they talked about how Grant had to win so they'd have the trifecta of Cassidy football wins.

"It's too bad Tucker's baseball team is out of the postseason," Barrett said. "Otherwise it'd be perfect."

"They made it to the division championships, though."

"Yeah, but Tucker was pissed when they got knocked out."

Flynn remembered that conversation. He'd called Tucker after the game. They all knew what it was like to get close but fall just short. His brother wasn't in the mood to be told what a good pitcher he was and how his team would come back even stronger next season. Not then, anyway. "Tucker's pissed unless he wins the whole thing. You know how he is."

Barrett laughed. "We're all that way."

"It's in the Cassidy DNA. We don't like to lose."

"He'll come back next season. But for now, it's all football, all the time."

Flynn cracked a smile. "Hell yeah. And besides football, how are things with you and Harmony?"

"They're good. She's all settled into my house now and pondering other things to renovate here."

He laughed. "That's not a surprise."

"Right? She already gutted my entire place and it's practically brand-new, but she can still come up with new ideas. Then when I told her she's obviously not busy enough at work, she gave me that look. You know that look."

"Yeah, I've seen that look from her before."

"But then I kissed her and she forgot all about expanding the guest bathroom."

"More info than I needed, Barrett."

Barrett laughed. "Anyway, things are good here. How about you? Any new girlfriends I need to know about?"

"That's not going well."

"Sorry, man. The right one is out there for you."

Flynn glanced into the kitchen and caught a glimpse of Amelia. There was something about her that made his stomach tighten. "Yeah, maybe."

"Don't give up. And quit choosing the wrong ones."

"Right. Like that part's easy."

"It's never easy, Bro. But when the right one comes along, you'll know it."

"Hope so."

After he got off the phone with Barrett, he checked his messages and saw he'd missed one from Mia, so he called her.

"Shouldn't you be studying or asleep or something?"

He heard Mia sigh on the other side of the line. "I'm a night owl and I do my best work late. Congrats on your win. You looked tough out there today."

"Thanks. How's school?"

"Tough as always, but I'm nearing the end of the road, so I can see the light at the end of the tunnel and all those other metaphors signaling graduation isn't far off."

Sometimes he couldn't believe his baby sister was close to getting her master's degree. She was all grown up and time had seemingly flown by. It didn't seem all that long ago that he had carried her in his arms while she sucked her thumb and laid her head on his shoulder.

"Good. So when are you coming out here?"

"I'll e-mail you my flight information tomorrow once I finalize my plans. I'm going to rent a car, because I'm going to be traveling around the area, plus heading down to Stanford for interviews and to look around."

"I can drive you."

She laughed. "I think you have enough going on with football and your new restaurant, which I'm dying to eat at."

"I'm sitting here right now, as a matter of fact."

"I'm jealous. And hungry."

"You can cancel the car, Mia. I really do have time to drive you wherever you need to go."

"And I'm fine with having some independence, Flynn, so I'll keep my car reservation. But thanks, anyway."

Mia always had that independent streak, even as a kid. It shouldn't surprise him that she wouldn't want to be at his mercy while she was visiting.

"Fine. I'll look for your e-mail tomorrow."

"Okay. Can't wait to see you. Love you."

"Love you, too."

After Mia, he talked to his parents. They were both doing well. Dad was busy buying some new equipment for the ranch, so they spent a lot of time talking tractors, which Flynn always found interesting. It was his goal to someday own a parcel of land that wasn't in the city.

He loved Texas. His parents' ranch was there, and while Texas might not be where Flynn ended up, he knew he wanted land and space. He loved San Francisco and everything about the city, but he couldn't deny that when he settled down and found a woman willing to put up with him, he hoped that woman would also crave time outside the city—even if it was on a part-time basis.

By the time he finished up with his phone conversations, he realized the restaurant had closed and everyone was cleaning up. He pitched in and helped the staff put up the tables so the floors could be cleaned, then made his way into the kitchen to see if he could help out there.

Amelia looked up and frowned.

"You're still here?"

He always enjoyed that shocked look on her face whenever she spotted him at Ninety-Two, as if him being in his own restaurant was unusual. "I do own the place."

"Of course I know that. I just assumed you'd be gone by now. Aren't you tired after the game today?"

"No. And I wanted to hang out and talk to you." The kitchen was spotless and she was the only one left.

"Oh." She swiped her hair behind her ears. "Sure. About what?"

She seemed flustered. Or frustrated. Maybe even pissed.

"Is there something wrong?"

"Not really. Nothing I can't handle."

He leaned against one of the stainless steel counters. "Tell me what's going on."

"I've got a handle on it, Flynn. And right now I'd like nothing more than to have a really large glass of wine."

"Let's do that. But not here. You ready to leave?"

"Yes. But let me change out of my uniform first."

"Sure."

He checked sports scores while he waited. His team was in second place in the division. Not good enough, but they were only one game behind Seattle. They could do this. They'd have to play Seattle again later in the season, and since it was a home game he was certain they'd win. He was confident in his team and their abilities. They were on the cusp of greatness. Now they just had to make it happen.

"Okay, I'm ready."

He looked up to see Amelia wearing dark jeans, boots and a white sweater. Simple, but damn if she didn't take his breath away. She had pulled her hair up into a high ponytail, and there was something about it that made him want to pull her ponytail holder out and run his fingers through her silky blond hair.

Maybe it was because she always looked so . . . perfect. So put together. He wanted to muss her up a little.

His cock tightened.

Yeah, time to rein it in a little.

They were the last two there, so they turned off all the lights and locked up, then walked outside.

"Where's your car?"

"It was a nice day so I walked. I figured I'd either walk home or grab a ride."

"Yeah, I'll drive you." He led her to his SUV and they got in. "How about my place?" he asked.

"I thought you wanted to go to a bar?"

He looked over at her. "I said a drink. Besides, you can kick off your shoes and put your feet up there."

"I'm not going to complain about that."

"I didn't think you would."

He drove to his house and pulled into the driveway. He led Amelia to the front door and unlocked it.

"I don't think I've been here since you interviewed me," she said as he opened the door and flipped on the light.

"That was a really good meal you fixed that night. My brother still raves about it."

She smiled as she laid her purse down on the sofa, then shrugged out of her sweater. "That's good to hear."

"Take a seat. I'll pour us a glass of wine. I've got a bottle of Shiraz I've wanted to open for a while now."

"But all the women you go out with keep preening for the cameras, so you haven't gotten far enough with one of them to get them back here to crack open that bottle?"

He paused, then shot her a disparaging look. "Funny."

"I thought so."

He went into the kitchen, grabbed the bottle and uncorked it. He pulled out two wineglasses, then carried it all into the living room.

Amelia sat on the sofa, her spine straight, her feet planted firmly on the floor.

"This isn't an interview, you know," he said as he set the bottle and glasses on the coffee table. "You can sit back and relax."

"I am relaxed."

He cocked a brow. "If that's you relaxed, I'd hate to see you tense."

"I'm rarely tense."

And yet she still hadn't leaned back against the sofa cushions. He had his work cut out for him tonight. He poured wine into both glasses and handed her one.

"Thanks." She took a sip.

"Now lean back against the sofa."

She shot him a glare. "Is that an order?"

"Nope."

But he waited until she finally did.

What was it going to take to make this woman relax?

He figured they had all night, and no matter how long it took, he was going to put her at ease.

AMELIA WAS DEFINITELY NOT RELAXED. BEING HERE IN Flynn's house—with Flynn, sitting in the same room with Flynn, was not relaxing.

He looked delicious in his dark jeans and his gray Henley, the sleeves pushed up his forearms revealing teasing bits of his tattoos. It was all she could do not to run her fingers over those puzzling pieces and ask him to remove his shirt so she could map his body.

With her tongue.

Dear God. Where had *that* come from?

She gave a suspicious look at the glass of wine, wondering if it had some magical, fantasy-inducing qualities, then accepted the fact that it had been a long, dry spell for her in the sex department and she couldn't blame the wine. It was just the man and her attraction to him.

The wrong man. Her boss.

So totally inappropriate.

This was a disaster and she was going to get fired for even thinking of Flynn as some kind of sex toy that she could climb on and have an orgasm with. What the hell was wrong with her? She should flee now before something awful happened. Like all her fantasies coming true.

She took a long swallow of wine.

"Good?" he asked.

She assumed he was referring to the wine and not her fantasy. "Yes. Very good."

He grabbed his glass and moved to the sofa, sitting next to her, which raised her discomfort level. He grabbed his netbook and inched closer.

"I looked over a few recipes for the bluefin tuna. Do you want to go over those?"

"Oh. Sure."

He leaned in, his shoulder and thigh brushing hers. Really, it wasn't like this was a first for her. She had male employees and worked shoulder to shoulder with them all the time.

The problem was, she wasn't attracted to any of them. But she was attracted to Flynn and that was wrong on so many levels.

When he'd first hired her, she'd noticed how incredibly good-looking he was, but she knew her boundaries, so she figured it wouldn't be a problem. Plus, she was so done with men. After her divorce, the last thing she wanted was to get involved.

But recently, something had changed. Watching Flynn choose one wrong woman after another had made her feel sympathetic toward his plight. And when Tara had matched him up with sweet, quirky and intelligent Skylar, she'd been hopeful. But she had to admit it had caused a tiny quake of jealousy, and she hadn't expected that.

She had felt bad when Skylar had turned out to be more attracted to Aaron. And then she'd felt relieved. One, because that meant Flynn would be free, and two, because Aaron wasn't a match for her.

Not that she wanted or needed a guy in her life, because she didn't. Actually, she had no idea what she wanted right now. Not a man, for sure.

Or did she? Because she was sitting next to Flynn going over recipes and she wasn't thinking about fish. She was thinking how rock hard his thigh was as it pressed against hers, how good he smelled, and how very much she wanted to climb onto him and straddle his lap.

So maybe she did want a man. At least for sex. But Flynn wasn't the man she should be having sex with.

She sighed. What a mess of contradictions she was.

"So, you don't like this idea?"

She lifted her gaze to his, realizing she hadn't been paying attention to a word he said. "What idea?"

"You weren't listening, were you?"

"Sorry. My head was somewhere else."

He laid the netbook on the coffee table and picked up his glass of wine. "Tell me where your head was, then."

Absolutely not. "Oh, it was nothing. Just a problem at work."

Liar, liar. And her pants were definitely on fire right now.

"I'm your guy, then. What's going on?"

She gave him a dismissive wave. "Nothing I can't handle."

"Talk to me, Amelia. What's wrong?"

"One of the prep cooks. I'm having problems with him."

"With his work product?"

"No, and that's the problem. He's very good at his job. When he's there. But he doesn't show up on time, and he's left mid-shift twice in the past week, claiming his wife is sick and he's had to take care of her and the kids. I'm trying to be supportive. Stuff happens. I get that."

"I take it that it's not just this past week with him, is it?"

She appreciated that he realized she wasn't falling for Jeff's excuses. "This isn't an isolated incident. Two weeks ago he came in late, claiming his wife's job had changed and they were working out scheduling issues so he had to deal with the kids and the baby-sitter and some kind of nonsense."

Flynn ran his fingertip around the rim of the wineglass. "And you're sensing a pattern."

"Yes. Other people have lives and families, too, and they manage to make it to work on time and stay for their shifts. I don't mind an occasional crisis. We all have them and everyone pitches in and deals with it. But when someone is always late or misses work on a consistent basis, it puts a strain on the rest of the kitchen staff. It's not fair to them."

"Have you spoken to him about this problem?"

"More than once. He seems very sincere and says it won't happen again. But . . ."

"You think this is a personality flaw."

"Yes. Which means I'm probably going to have to let him go. He's very talented, has a great personality and everyone likes him. But he's placing a burden on my kitchen and my staff, and I can't let that happen."

Flynn nodded. "I'll handle it."

She shot him a look. "No, you will not. I'll handle it."

"It sounds like you have more than enough to deal with. I don't mind."

"I'll handle it, Flynn."

"Okay." He took her now empty glass and refilled it, then picked up her foot and pulled her boot off, then did the same with the other foot.

She frowned. "What the hell are you doing?"

"Taking off your boots."

"I can see that. Why?"

"You're tense. And I'll bet your feet hurt standing all those hours."

"I'm used to it."

He draped her feet over his lap. "But your feet hurt, right?"

"I'm fine."

"Not much of a complainer, are you, Amelia?"

"No."

He smiled, then started rubbing her feet. Oh, God, it felt so good. She wanted to curl her feet into his hands. And maybe moan a little. Which would be very, very bad.

"After a game, it's like every part of my body hurts. I take a lot of hits, and during the game I don't feel them. It's only after, when I allow my body to relax that I feel every hit I've taken. My bones ache, my muscles are tight. Hell, even my hair hurts."

She looked up at his thick mane of dark hair. "Poor hair."

He laughed. "I know you know what that feels like."

"Being pummeled on every part of my body? No. I can't say that I do."

"But your feet know. And I'm sure your back hurts, too."

"I might get a little sore being on my feet a lot."

"There you go. Complain a little, Amelia. Whining is good for the soul."

She tilted her head to the side. "Is that cross-stitched on a pillow somewhere?"

"Hell if I know. I just know it's okay to say your feet hurt after a long night at work."

He dug his fist into the ball of her foot, and she sucked in a deep breath, then let it out slowly.

"That feels really good."

His lips curved. "It feels really good here, too."

He was not helping her saying things like that. It made her imagine being naked and him using those strong hands on every part of her body.

"But you don't have to rub my feet."

"I know I don't have to. I want to."

"Flynn. What are we doing here?"

"I'm rubbing your feet. You're drinking wine. We were talking about caramelized bluefin tuna, but you weren't paying attention."

"You know what I mean."

"I'm trying to get you to relax, Amelia. Do you have to analyze it?"

"Maybe."

"Try not to. We're just talking."

"You're touching me."

He looked down at her feet. "Technically I'm giving you a foot massage. That's not really touching."

She slid a dubious glance at him. "It's actually more than touching."

"No. More than touching would be if I slid my hand up your leg, like this."

She wasn't sure if she was happy or sad that she was wearing denim when he cupped her calf, then swirled his hand over her knee. And then farther up, his fingers teasing her thighs.

Every feminine part of her wanted to explode. She was pent up, anxious and so turned on that if he got anywhere near her sex she'd probably have an orgasm.

Wasn't that what she wanted?

No. She definitely did not want that.

Yes, you do, Amelia. Give in.

She needed to tell her inner sex voice to go to hell, because logic was going to win here.

His voice had gone deeper when he leaned in and said, "That would be touching."

Her sex quivered and she went damp, logic evaporating with his every touch. "Yes, it would be."

He stood, placing her feet on the floor, then leaned over her. "And this—this would be touching, too."

She hadn't expected it, but she didn't object when he brushed his lips across hers. It was brief, but the contact was like being struck by lightning. She wanted to reach out, to slide her fingers in his hair. Instead, she gripped the edge of the sofa cushion like a lifeline.

"Do you agree?" he asked.

She'd lost the ability to think. "Agree about what?"

"That kissing you is definitely touching."

"Oh. Yes."

"Would you like more?"

She wasn't certain if she'd nodded or not, so she wanted to make sure to give him an affirmative. "Yes."

He turned her to the side and lifted her legs onto the sofa, then hovered over her.

Right now she was barely breathing as he pressed down on top of her. She felt suspended in time, her gaze riveted on the amazing sea blue of Flynn's gorgeous eyes. He had impossibly long lashes, and the kind of mouth that was made to give pleasure to a woman.

She wanted that more than anything right now, and whatever remnants of logic were left completely shut down when his hard body nestled against hers.

"I'm so glad you said yes, Amelia, because I really want to kiss you."

NINE

AMELIA COULDN'T REMEMBER THE LAST TIME SHE'D been kissed. And she sure wasn't going to think about her ex right now. Not when Flynn's mouth was on hers, his body on top of her and his lips doing dangerous things to her senses.

She felt like every nerve ending had gone haywire. It had been so long since she'd felt anything so profoundly chemical, like a heat explosion inside of her. She was hot all over and her body tingled. She couldn't recall the last time she'd felt all these delicious sensations. It was like tasting her favorite dessert and as his lips rubbed over hers, she couldn't resist letting her tongue dart out to tease against his.

He groaned against her, and she felt the hard evidence of his erection against her sex, which only made her want more than a taste of what she was experiencing.

The logical part of her that she'd shoved way down deep in the recesses of her brain objected, but the libidinous part of her had obliterated all logic. She let her hands slide into his hair, and, just as she'd suspected, it was thick and soft.

She moaned against him and he surged against her, and all she could think about was his cock penetrating her, and how it would feel when he was inside of her. That tingling heat spread, and she arched upward, needing more of that hot contact.

He pulled his mouth from hers and stared down at her, his body continuing to move against her. "Tell me what you need."

"An orgasm would be really nice."

She couldn't believe the words that had spilled from her mouth, but now that they had, she wouldn't take them back.

His lips curved. "I think we can make that happen."

Since she was in full-out "I want sex now" mode, she traced his bottom lip with her fingertip.

She intended to touch him all over now that she had given herself permission.

He hopped off the sofa, then took her hand and pulled her up, drawing her against him. His hands roamed her body.

"That feels good."

"It's going to feel better once I get you naked. And, Amelia?"

"Yes?"

"I'm going to be honest and tell you I've imagined you naked a lot."

Her brows shot up. "Have you?"

"Yeah. Mostly when I'm in the dark at night with my cock in my hand."

Her body swelled with desire. Flynn was definitely going to make her come tonight. Just his hot words made her quiver.

She wrapped her hand around his neck to pull his lips to hers. "Now you don't have to fantasize anymore."

His kiss this time was harder, filled with passion and unrestrained need. She leaned into it, drank from his lips as he slid his tongue inside her mouth to flick against hers.

She felt weak in the knees, but also heady and powerful with desire. And now it was her opportunity to use her hands to clutch his shoulders, to feel the awesome strength in his muscles as he held tight to her.

And then she was shocked when he scooped her up in his arms. She wasn't a small woman. She was five ten, so when he started up the stairs, she gave him a look.

"Are you crazy, Flynn? I can walk and you might hurt yourself."

He laughed at her. "I think I can handle you."

He was certainly doing that. Her ex had never been able to pick her up. They had been the same height, and, granted, Flynn was a lot taller and more muscular than her ex.

And okay, she wasn't going to think about her ex-husband any more tonight. Not when a gorgeous man held her against him. This might be the first time a man had ever held her in his arms, much less carried her up a flight of stairs. It was a little disconcerting. But it also made her feel very female and, for the first time in her life . . . small.

It wasn't necessarily a bad thing to feel cared for in this way, even if the independent side of her balked. It was also extremely romantic, and when he laid her on the bed, she sat on the edge, still a bit overwhelmed by this unexpected turn of events.

"Change your mind?" he asked.

"No. Just a little surprised."

He cocked his head to the side. "Why? I think I made it clear I wanted you. And by the way you responded downstairs, it seemed reciprocal."

"Oh, I definitely want you. I'm just waiting for my head to get in line with my body."

He leaned over her, giving her shoulder a slight shove so she was lying back on the mattress. "Too much thinking can ruin really good sex, Amelia. How about we just let our bodies do the work?"

He was right, of course. The logical side of her brain was trying to pop in and interrupt what her body wanted.

There was nothing going on with the two of them other than a one-night stand. Nothing wrong with that. She needed it, she wanted it and she was going to let herself have it.

Then he pulled his shirt over his head, revealing his gorgeous tattoos and his rather outstanding chest.

Logic fled the room and desire took over. She rolled over onto her side. "Please continue with the unveiling. And I'm going to warn you now that I'm going to map every one of those tattoos."

"With your tongue, I hope."

She watched as he dropped his pants, and saw the tattoos continued into his boxer briefs. Her sex quivered.

"Visually and tactically. Most definitely."

He dropped his briefs and his cock sprang out. She couldn't resist a smile of pure feminine appreciation. He was built rock hard, all muscle that spoke of what he did out on the football field.

"Your turn," he said.

She started to pull off her shirt, but he came over and grasped the hem, drawing her shirt over her head.

She had to admit it was a little daunting to have a man watch her undress. But Flynn seemed to be appreciative of the unveiling, so she tossed her shirt on the bed, then wriggled out of her jeans—with his help.

"I'll never understand women and their tight jeans," he said as he tugged them down her legs.

"You appreciate our asses cupped in them, though, don't you?"

He lifted his gaze to hers. "That I do. And your ass is very nice."

He rolled her over onto her stomach and smoothed his hands over her butt. When she felt his lips there, she giggled.

"I've always wanted to have a man kiss my ass."

He gave her butt a light smack. "I could do a lot of fun things with your ass, Amelia."

Oh, the images that swirled in her head. She swung around to face him. "Could you?"

"Yeah." He placed his hands on the mattress, pressing them flat on either side of her shoulders. "But we'll table that thought for another time."

Before she could absorb that he thought they'd have more than just this one night, he leaned in and kissed her. She felt the heat emanating from his body and arched up, needing to feel his skin against hers. She still wore her bra and panties, but when he skimmed his body on top of hers, all that delicious heat sizzled between them.

Plus, his cock, nestled between her thighs, hard and surging against her sex, made her quiver with a desperate need to feel him inside of her. It had been such a long dry spell for her and she was unashamedly anxious to have him buried balls deep.

Flynn, on the other hand, must be having lots of sex with many women, because he took his sweet-ass time rubbing his lips against hers, flicking his tongue against the tip of hers and generally driving her bat-shit crazy. All in a good way, of course. She had no complaints about the kissing. He was very good at it. It was just that she desperately craved an orgasm and he kept rubbing his cock against her clit, which made her incessantly needy. She was certain that once she had an orgasm—or two—she'd settle down.

She palmed his shoulders and he lifted.

"Am I too heavy for you?"

"Not at all. I like your weight on me. I'd like it even more if your cock was inside of me."

His lips curved in a knowing smile. "You in a hurry?"

"A big damn hurry for an orgasm. I haven't had one in a while. So feel free to cut the foreplay down to like . . . nothing."

"I see." He lifted off of her. "You know, Amelia, I'm a big believer in giving a woman what she wants."

Then he unhooked her bra and she pulled it off, tossing it to the floor. He reached for her panties and ever so slowly slid them off her hips and down her legs. She wasn't sure if Flynn was giving her what she wanted or tormenting her further. Because he didn't immediately grab a condom. Instead, he parted her legs and then . . .

Nothing.

"What are you waiting for?"

"I'm just . . . looking at you. You're very beautiful, Amelia."

"Thank you. Now fuck me."

He laughed. "And they say guys only think about fucking. How about we slow down the train a little? We have all night."

"I don't want the damn slow train, Flynn. I want the bullet speed train to orgasm-land."

"Are you sure?" He crawled between her legs and shouldered her thighs apart. "Because I can give you a mind-blowing slow ride."

She lifted up on her elbows, arching her brow. His breath was hot on her sex as he smiled up at her.

"You're a teasing bastard, Flynn."

"Yeah. But I'm the bastard who's going to make you come over and over tonight."

Before she could come up with another retort, he put his tongue on her sex.

Her head dropped back and all she could do was close her eyes and feel how hot his lips were as he surrounded her clit, and how wet his tongue was as he bathed her sex with slow, easy strokes.

She'd wanted a quick climax. What she got instead was nirvana—a delicious ride on the ecstasy train. She felt his movements in every nerve ending, wading out from her sex and encompassing her entire body like a warm bath of electric currents. And when he slid his finger in and began to pump slowly in and out of her along with the timing of his mouth, she wanted that sensual train to take a long, unhurried trek to the far reaches of the universe and back.

Her nipples puckered. She reached up to grasp them and rub her fingers over them, only heightening every delicious sensation.

Her orgasm wasn't a quick release, it was a leisurely tumble that left her poised on the edge, unable to catch her breath as she felt it near. And when he hummed against her sex and sucked on her clit, she and the train jumped the tracks. Her entire body shook with her climax—over and over and over again, an endless fall of ecstasy. It felt like a lifetime before the tremors subsided. When they did, Flynn kissed his way up her body, lingering long enough at her breasts to lick and suck her nipples, revving that locomotive's speed up all over again. By the time he took her mouth, she wound her leg around his hip and arched against him. He groaned against her lips and she knew he was right there with her.

This time, slowing the train down would not be an option.

Apparently he felt the same way, because he rolled over and grabbed a condom out of his nightstand drawer, tore into the wrapper and slid the condom on, then parted her legs.

"You ready for me?"

She swept her fingers across his brow. "I've been ready for you."

The curve of his lips when he smiled at her had a devastating effect on her.

"You have no idea how much I like hearing that."

He inched inside of her and her entire body shuddered as he entered her fully.

She'd forgotten how damn good it felt to have a cock buried inside of her. And Flynn's was exceptional.

When he began to move inside of her, she realized he didn't simply excel at having extraordinary anatomy. He knew what to do with it. He moved with his entire body, rubbing his chest over hers, then leaned in to kiss her.

It was a full-body experience, and she immersed herself in every sensation. When he rubbed his pelvis against her clit, she moaned.

Flynn lifted his lips from hers. "I like that sound, Amelia. It makes my balls quiver."

She met his gaze, drowning in the blue depths of his eyes. "You make my everything quiver."

His lips curved. "Yeah, I can feel your body vibrate, squeezing my cock."

He surged against her, and a tremor of pure bliss quaked within her. He rolled to his side, taking her with him, lifting her leg and draping it over his hip so he could slide deeper into her.

Oh, yes. This was so good.

When he cupped her breast and brushed his fingers over her nipple, she thought she might die from the pleasure of it.

"You're sensitive here."

"Yes. Touch me more."

He was good at taking direction, too, because he moved his fingers all over her, giving her just what she needed to elicit arcs of pleasure.

"I like the way you touch me," she said. "I like your mouth, too."

He kissed her, then pulled back. "So I heard when I made you come."

She shuddered, her pussy tightening around him. "Keep talking like that and I'll come again."

"That's the idea."

He surged against her, rubbing his body against her clit. She moaned, gripped his arms and held on as he took her right to the edge.

She didn't have words for him because she was too busy breathing him in, feeling him, being so aware of this moment she couldn't do anything but feel. And when he took her nipple in his mouth and sucked, she gasped.

"Yeah. I like to hear those sounds you make," he murmured, then licked her nipple before sucking it between his teeth as he continued to thrust into her.

She grasped his upper arms, raking her nails over his skin as he pumped into her with slow, easy thrusts. She felt full and ready to burst but she wanted to hold back, needing to suspend this moment for a while longer.

But her body had other ideas and as she began to whimper, control was no longer hers. Flynn began to drive into her with earnest, deep strokes. She lost it then, coming powerfully with a loud cry. She felt that sweet free fall of bliss as she clenched around his cock with deep, forceful contractions, each one more intensely pleasurable than the last. Flynn took her mouth in a hard, penetrating kiss that left her dizzy until, finally, he groaned against her lips and shuddered against her.

It took a few minutes of heavy breathing on both their parts, but finally, she settled and Flynn rolled over onto his back, then off the bed. He disappeared into the adjoining bathroom for a few seconds, then came back and drew her against his chest.

She waited for that weird, awkward after-sex moment. It wasn't like she was used to having sex with other guys. The last man she'd had sex with was her husband, and they hadn't done it for at least a year before their divorce. She was out of practice. What did couples do after first-time sex? Talk? Fall asleep? Flynn couldn't just leave since they were at his house. But he could get up and get dressed so he could take her home if he wanted to get rid of her.

Though he didn't seem to be in any hurry to do that. He held her against his chest and drew circles on the skin of her back.

"You okay?" he finally asked.

"I'm fine. Uh . . . you?"

"Yeah. Though you seem tense."

She tilted her head back to look up at him. "I do?"

"Yes. And it kind of pisses me off."

Uh-oh. "I'm not tense. And why are you pissed off?"

"Because I just worked hard to relax you. Obviously I didn't do a good enough job."

She laughed. "Oh. First, you did a phenomenal job. I came twice. Second, I might have been a little tense. I'm sort of out of practice with the post-coital thing."

"Really."

"Yes. My ex and I hadn't done it in a really long time before the divorce. And you, lucky guy, are my first since then."

He smiled down at her and didn't seem at all nervous or upset about what she'd just revealed to him.

He smoothed his hand over her back. "Now I do feel lucky. Thanks for choosing me."

She didn't know how to answer him. A "you're welcome" seemed weird.

"So why were you tense?"

She rolled over onto her back. "I don't know. I guess I don't know how things are done now."

He laughed, then shifted to lean over her. "First, I highly doubt it's been so long for you that some unnamed rules of sex have changed. Second, there aren't any rules. We'll do whatever feels right for you and for me, okay?"

That did make her feel better. "Okay."

"Now tell me. What feels right for you about now?"

"I'm a little thirsty."

"Me, too. You want some wine, iced tea or ice water?"

"Water sounds great."

"Good. I'll be right back."

He hopped off the bed, giving her a wonderful view of his amazing ass as he made his way out the door and down the hall. She propped herself up against the headboard using the pillows. When he came back, he handed her a glass of water.

"Thanks."

"I see you managed to hog all the pillows while I was gone."

"Hey, you left. You snooze, you lose."

He took several long swallows of water, giving her ample opportunity to ogle his incredible shoulders and abs while he did. Then he set the glass on the bedside table and climbed onto the bed, situating himself right beside her.

When she gave him a look, he said, "You have all the pillows, remember?"

"Yes, I do."

"Besides, you want my hot body keeping you warm, don't you?"

She wasn't going to complain about that. "Absolutely."

After taking another sip of water, she set her glass on the table, then shifted to face him. "What I'd really like is to explore your tattoos. They're intriguing."

"Sure. Touch me all you want to."

She let her fingers map a trail over his shoulders and down his arms, as if she were reading a treasure map. There were scrolling patterns and sharp points, but no words.

"What do they mean?"

"Nothing, really. I just like the ink. At some point I might think about putting some literature on here. Maybe something that inspires me."

"They're beautiful."

"Thanks."

She sat back and looked at him. "So nothing like 'Mom' or some ex-girlfriend's name on here?"

He laughed. "No. I'm not a momma's boy, and so far no woman has inspired me enough to ink her name on my body."

"So far."

"Yeah. Maybe when I get married I'll do something permanent like that."

"You do realize that fifty percent of marriages end up in divorce."

He frowned. "Mine won't."

"So sure of that, are you?"

"Yes."

She leaned back and he shifted, moving down the bed so he could pick up her foot to massage it. He really did have great hands. She thought about what he'd said about marriage.

"While I admire your confidence, I can assure you that everyone goes into marriage thinking it's forever. It doesn't always work out that way."

He lifted his focus from her foot onto her face. "While I can appreciate you're coming from a point of cynicism since you've gone through a divorce, I only intend to get married one time. And I intend for it to be forever."

"I'm sure the guy who had 'I Love Patty for All Time' tattooed on his body and then had to have a giant Chevy truck tattooed over it thought his tattoo would last forever, too."

He arched a brow. "You know this guy?"

She laughed. "No. I made it up. I'm just using it as a random example."

He picked up her other foot, and she couldn't resist a moan when he dug his thumb into her sore arch.

"I think your ex made you lose faith in love."

"Maybe. I'd think all those women who prefer camera time over their interest in you would make you lose faith."

He shrugged. "They just weren't the right one."

"And you still think the right one is out there for you."

He wasn't focusing on her foot. He was looking at her. "Yes, I do."

His gaze was warm. Intense. And she had to admit, she felt relaxed with him, all that tension and after-sex weirdness completely gone.

"Why?"

"Why what?"

"Why do you believe in love, Flynn?"

"Because I've seen it in action with my parents. They've had difficult times and through it all, their love for each other has never once wavered. I've seen it with my brothers, who've all found amazing, smart, beautiful women who love them unconditionally. And believe me, my brothers aren't easy guys to love. If they can find it, so can I."

This was a new side to him. She'd seen the business side of him and the sports side of him. In both, he was driven. She'd seen him be funny and fun. But she'd never seen this serious side. This was a man ready to fall in love.

Too bad she wasn't the woman for him. Because she was never going to give her heart over to a man again. She'd had it crushed once by someone she trusted, and it had hurt horribly.

Flynn was a nice guy, and she liked him. She was sure there was a woman out there who deserved him. It was really too bad it couldn't be her.

Unfortunately, tonight was just that. Just this one night. Because a man like Flynn could be habit forming. She'd fallen down that rabbit hole once before, and she'd never allow that to happen again.

She gently extricated her foot from his grip. "It's probably a good idea for you to take me home."

He gave her a quizzical look. "You don't want to stay tonight?"

She wanted to. And that was the problem. She shook her head and slid off the bed to stand.

"I have a lot of things to do tomorrow. Early."

He got up and came over to where she stood, sliding his arms around her. "I get up pretty early."

His body was warm and she was tempted to turn around and curl into him, let him coax her back into his big bed.

But he was dangerous to her mind and her body, and most especially her heart. So she stepped away, turned around and smiled at him. "I had fun tonight. But no. I need to get home."

Fortunately, he read her signals and nodded. "Sure. I'll throw on some clothes and drive you home."

She got dressed and grabbed her things. They got into his SUV and he drove her the short distance to her house. When he got out and walked her to her door, for a split second she thought about inviting him in. But that would defeat the purpose of putting an end to their night together.

She pulled her keys out of her purse, unlocked the door then turned to him. "Tonight was amazing."

He pulled her against him. "I thought so, too. I'll see you soon."

Before she could walk inside, he tugged her close and kissed her. She fell into the kiss, making her wish they were still naked and in his bed.

One time with Flynn was definitely not enough. Her body curved into his and wanted more. So much more. She finally had to break the kiss with her heart and pulse pounding and everything within her trembling with desire.

"Good night, Flynn."

He smiled in that devastating way she could only describe as lethally sexy. "Night, Amelia."

She waited while he walked down the steps and got into his SUV. Since he didn't drive away, she assumed he was waiting for her to get safely inside. Because he was a gentleman, of course. So she went inside and shut and locked the door.

Then exhaled, because she was still pent up and turned on from his kiss and all that body contact on her doorstep.

She tossed her bag on the sofa, shrugged out of her sweater, then went into the kitchen and poured herself a tall glass of wine. She picked up her phone and looked at the time.

It was one in the morning, too late to call Laura so she could talk to her best friend about tonight, which left her alone to dissect her own thoughts.

She took the wine into the bedroom and laid it on the nightstand. She stripped and climbed into bed.

She wasn't remotely tired, so she grabbed the remote and turned the TV on, surfing until she found a movie to watch. She sipped her wine, feeling a hundred times stupid for asking Flynn to take her home.

She actually had nothing to do early tomorrow, she'd just gotten scared listening to him talk about finding his forever woman. She knew that wasn't her, but it didn't mean they couldn't have some fun together in the interim.

So now she was alone in her bed watching an old romance movie on TV where the characters were getting a lot more action than she was right now instead of getting some real-life action with the hottest man she'd ever been with.

She lifted the wineglass and stared at the contents. "Dumbass move, Amelia."

TEN

FLYNN HAD A WHIRLWIND WEEK OF PRACTICES AND meetings. Then he'd had to leave town for a Thursday-night road game against Dallas, so he'd barely had time to breathe.

At least they'd won their game, and winning on the road was always tough. But he hadn't had a chance to talk to Amelia after their time together, and he'd wanted to do that in person. He wasn't much of a texting guy—not with women he was sleeping with. He'd called her to tell her he was going to be out of town all week, and he wanted to see her this weekend. She said she and her friend Laura had planned a girl's weekend to the wine country.

He remembered her mentioning that when the restaurant had first opened, that she'd need time off for this event. He told her he'd talk to her next week.

But right now he felt unsettled, as if that great night they'd had together was unfinished. He wanted to see Amelia. But his sister was flying in this week, and that would put a crimp in his plans.

After practice and the team meeting on Tuesday, Flynn stopped at the restaurant early to take care of some business with Ken, then headed home and cleaned the house. He had a woman who cleaned for him once a week, but he still picked up the kitchen, ran the vacuum, made sure there were extra towels in the guest-house and stocked the mini fridge for his sister. After, he took a shower and checked his phone. Mia's flight had touched down about thirty minutes ago. She'd texted him and told him she was on her way to get her rental car and she should be at his house within the hour.

Since it was before rush hour, she shouldn't have too much trouble with traffic.

He'd texted his mom to tell her Mia was on the way. She texted back and asked that Mia call her when she got to the house.

His sister might be an adult now, but she was still Mom's baby and Flynn knew it.

He was glad he had a home game this weekend since Mia was in town. Even better, it was the game against St. Louis, which meant she'd get to watch the game where he'd beat up on Grant. He grinned as he thought about it. He'd get to spend extra time with her, and she could come to the restaurant and to the game.

He was in the kitchen fixing some snacks when he heard a car pull into the driveway. He washed and dried his hands and headed outside. Mia was pulling her luggage out of the trunk of the rental car. She looked up at him and grinned.

"Hey," she said.

"Hey yourself." He went over to her and folded her into his arms.

She wrapped her arms around him. "It's really good to be here." She stepped back. "You look good. Been working out?"

He laughed. "Nah, just beating up on guys on Sundays."

"It seems to be working for you."

"You look good, too. And you cut your hair."

She swept her chin-length brown hair behind her ears. "It was getting in my way a lot so it's more functional this way."

He grabbed her luggage and they headed into the house. "You're still gorgeous."

"Thanks."

His sister was beautiful, even more so now that she had cut her long hair. She had the kind of face that made people stop and look twice. It was heart shaped, and she had the sharpest blue eyes in the entire Cassidy family. The fact that she was also the smartest Cassidy didn't hurt, either.

"This place is amazing, Flynn," Mia said as she stepped inside. "I love everything about it. It's got the fifties flair of a Craftsman with all the modern touches. And this kitchen—wow."

He let her wander into the kitchen while he headed toward the back door, where he set her suitcase.

"Thanks. I really like it. You want a tour?"

"You know I do."

He took her around the upstairs, where the bedrooms were, then out back, along the walkway leading to the guesthouse.

"I love this," she said as he set her luggage just inside the door. "It's perfect for guests. You give them plenty of privacy with a bedroom, bath and living area, a wet bar and mini fridge for snacking, and yet it's still close enough to the main house. And still far enough away not to infringe on your action."

He laughed. "There's no action going on in the main house. Not at the moment anyway."

She gave him a wry smile. "Too bad for you."

"Why don't you get unpacked? I was fixing lunch for us when you drove up. I should have that finished when you're done."

"Okay."

He started to turn to leave, then stopped. "Oh, and call Mom and let her know you're here. I told her you would."

"I'll do that right now."

He left and went into the kitchen. The water had already been on to heat when he heard Mia drive up, so he kicked it into high gear. When it started boiling he put in the penne pasta, then made a salad and dressing.

Mia came in.

"Something smells good. What can I do to help?"

He handed her a knife and motioned to the cutting board. "Slice bread."

"I can do that." She washed and dried her hands at the sink, then began to slice the bread. "It's weird seeing you in the kitchen."

He pulled his focus from the salad and put it onto Mia. "Weird how?"

She shrugged. "I don't know. I guess I'm just not used to seeing you so . . . in charge here."

"I like to cook. I've helped Mom cook tons of times."

"Maybe I just wasn't paying attention. How's the restaurant going?"

"Good so far. We'll eat there tonight."

"I can't wait. I'm planning to be extremely critical."

He forced back a smile. "You do that."

He drained the pasta and poured the sun-dried tomato pesto sauce over it, adding basil and fresh Parmesan.

"My stomach is growling loud and insistent over here," Mia said, laying the bread into a basket. "And that looks amazing."

"Of course it's amazing. I cooked it."

"I'll decide if it tastes as good as it smells."

"Prepare to be wowed."

She rolled her eyes and they headed into the dining room.

Flynn had already set the table, so all he had to do was pour iced tea for them and bring in the salad.

He waited while Mia dug into the salad. "Balsamic vinaigrette?" she asked.

"Yeah."

"Really good and not from a bottle. I can tell because that bottled stuff is crap."

"Picky, aren't you?"

"Absolutely." She scooped up some of the pasta next, and made a "mmm" sound. "This is really good, Flynn."

He grinned. "Thanks."

They ate and chatted about his football season and her year at school.

"Are you thinking of entering the PhD program as soon as you finish your master's?"

She took a sip of iced tea, then set the glass down. "I don't know. It's a long commitment and to be honest, I'm kind of burned out on school. I'd like to work for a while."

She paused, pushing her food around on the plate. Flynn knew his sister, and he knew that meant she had something on her mind she wanted to talk about, so he waited.

"Actually, what I'd really like is to start my own business."

His brows shot up. "Seriously?"

She nodded.

"What kind of business?"

"I've been floating around an idea that's gaining steam, at least in my head."

"And what's your idea?"

She paused again, this time taking a few more bites of food. He wanted to ask her, but he knew he had to be patient while she worked out in her head how she wanted to say whatever it was she wanted to say to him.

"A sports management company."

He laughed. "You hate sports."

She frowned. "I do not. How could I hate sports? My entire life has been deeply immersed in it."

"Yeah, and you complained about it constantly."

"Okay, maybe I did say I hated all jocks and everything having to do with sports or the mention of sports or anything connected to sports. But that was then and this is now. And now sports is a mega-billion-dollar industry and if there's one thing I know a lot about, it's sports and athletes."

He could tell this was something she was not only serious about, but passionate about, so he reined in his initial objections. If there was one thing he knew about Mia, it was that she would never jump into something without thoroughly vetting it. "Okay. Tell me your thought process."

"If there's one thing an athlete needs during the course of his career, it's cohesion. He—or she—is bombarded with contracts and lawyers and social media and marketing. I intend to offer a one-stop shop, if you will. One place where they can be offered not only training before they're even drafted, but also how to manage every aspect of their career, from legal to financial to public relations to social. And I intend to do it better than anyone else by hiring the best people out there, from agents to lawyers to the best PR people in the sports management game."

Flynn blinked. "Wow. You really have thought about this."

"Not only have I thought about it, I've been talking to a lot of people who are interested in coming on board. I honestly believe I can do this, Flynn. I might not have the years of experience, but I've got the family name, which I never thought I'd use, but if it works to get me in the door, then I'll use my knowledge after that to get athletes on board."

He leaned back in his chair and took several large swallows of iced tea. When had his baby sister grown up and become a power player in the world of sports? It was the absolute last thing he'd ever expected.

Mia leaned her forearms on the table. "You're very quiet and it's making me nervous."

"I'm just . . . Wow, Mia. This is huge. Have you talked to Mom and Dad about this yet?"

"I haven't talked to anyone in the family about this. You're the first."

He felt honored that Mia had chosen him to discuss the possibility of a future business with. "This is a big damn deal, Mia. You realize that, right?"

"Of course I do, Flynn. This isn't me with a notebook drawing hearts and circles and a maybe someday I'll be a mogul kind of thing. I'm damn serious about this, I've done the financial research and I believe I have the skills to make a success of this venture."

If anyone could do this, it was his sister. "I believe you do, too. Now tell me who you have lined up as players in your company."

She listed two agents, two attorneys, and a handful of highly successful people in the PR world. And he recognized every name. They were all power players in the industry.

"No shit. All of these people would join your company."

"Yes."

"And how did you convince them?"

"By giving them a list of the prospective clients I have who have agreed to come on board. Not to mention who they could bring. Together, we could have one hell of a dynamite company in the first year alone. I'm hardly a dumbass, Flynn. I've written one-year, five-year and ten-year business plans."

Of course she had. For someone who wasn't even twenty-five years old yet, his sister had the potential to be an ass kicker.

"Where would you set up shop?"

"Here in San Francisco. That's one of the main reasons I'm here. I do have a meeting set up at Stanford, but I also have other meetings as well. And after this I'll be flying down to L.A. to meet with some key players in my potential business venture."

He was stunned. She'd done her homework. This wasn't a pipe dream for her, a someday kind of thing. This was . . . right now. "Jesus, Mia. I don't even know what to say."

She smiled. "Say you support me."

"Hell, I'll do more than that. Do you need investors?"

She laughed. "Not yet, but I appreciate it. I have investments from the money Grandpa left me. I intend to use that and I'll get business loans. I want to do this all on my own."

"You know Mom and Dad won't want you to go into debt."

"And I don't want this to be a company that Mom and Dad bought for me. I'll do it my way."

Argumentative and stubborn, as always. "I think it's a great idea, Mia. Now you have to tell Mom and Dad."

"We'll see how everything goes this trip. It's not a one hundred percent done deal yet, but I can't tell you how good it makes me feel that you believe in me."

"Honey, you could shovel shit for a living or decide your next goal is to win the Nobel Peace Prize and I'd be in your corner. I love you."

Tears welled in Mia's eyes. She pushed her chair back, came around and hugged him. "I love you, too, Flynn."

Having taken all this in was not only a surprise, but the details of it had been more than a little overwhelming. All this time he'd been thinking his baby sister was going to stay in school. He'd always thought maybe she'd go into teaching.

This was anything but teaching.

He knew plans changed, but . . . wow. "Now I need a beer."

She laughed. "Me, too."

After lunch they cleaned up the kitchen, then headed to Toro-
nado on Haight Street, one of Flynn's favorite beer bars. Mia had
a Valencia Gold and Flynn had a Blind Pig.

"So why haven't you talked about this with Mom and Dad yet?"
he asked as they sipped their beers.

She shrugged, staring at her mug. "I want to be sure first. Mom
will be supportive and let me make my own decisions. But you
know how Dad is. He's pushy. He'll want to know everything, and
get all up in my business, and then he'll take out the checkbook.
That's the last thing I want. I have to do this—succeed or fail—on
my own."

He understood that need to make a success out of yourself on
your own merits. He'd been walking in his father's footsteps his
entire life, but he'd like to think he'd forged his own way, had made
a name for himself on his talents alone. Otherwise he wouldn't
have been playing as long as he had. The Cassidy name could only
take a football player so far. After that, you had to make it or break
it on talent, sweat and hard work.

And as he looked across the table at his sister, he realized the
fire that had burned in his belly all those years ago when he'd first
started out in his career burned just as hot in her. She knew exactly
what she wanted and she was going after it.

He reached out and grabbed her hand. "You can do this. All on
your own. I know you can."

"Thanks." She inhaled deeply, then blew out a breath. "Now
that it's out in the open, at least with one member of the family, it's
starting to feel real. I have a lot to do."

He laughed. "Yeah, you do. But before you go charging full
steam ahead with this new venture, tell Mom and Dad."

"Well, I have a lot to do before I talk to them. I want to be sure
everyone is on board and I have something to present to our parents that's real and tangible."

They finished their beers and went back to his house, then sat and talked for hours about her business plan. He had to admit he was impressed. She had it all laid out, had a vision, had her chosen personnel and her financing in place. She knew exactly what she wanted and was confident in her approach. With every passing minute he knew for a fact she could make this business a success.

But she'd have to work damn hard at it. He didn't doubt she would. Just like he didn't doubt she'd succeed. And he'd continue to worry about her because that was his job.

"You know, I get that you're all into being your own woman and self-reliant and all that shit, but if you ever need me, I'm right here. And I'm serious about being an investor. If you need me at all, I won't get in your way. I'll just fork over money and wait for you to double my investment."

"I know that. And thanks. The money part I might definitely consider."

He caught and held her gaze. "I mean it, Mia. I'm not just blowing smoke. If you need me for anything."

"And I meant it when I said I know, Flynn. You've always been there when I needed you. I don't doubt you will be in the future."

He caught her genuine smile. Damn this kid who wasn't a kid anymore. She made him feel like an old man.

Was this how Dad felt, watching them all grow up and get lives of their own? Mia's maturity caused an ache in the pit of his stomach and made him realize how quickly time passed. It wasn't that long ago that she was chasing him in the dirt on the ranch, her ponytail flying and her tennis shoes kicking up dust. He could still remember her high-pitched squeals when she laughed.

Now she was a grown woman.

Jesus. Time to stop thinking about that.

He finally picked up his phone. "We should head over to the restaurant. I don't know about you, but I'm hungry."

"No surprise there. You're always hungry."

"True."

They got into his SUV and drove to the restaurant. Mia was busy on her phone texting with someone, so he stayed quiet, figuring she was either chatting with friends or conducting business. He parked on the street, leaving space in the small restaurant parking lot for patrons.

They got out and walked toward the restaurant.

"This place is awesome, Flynn," Mia said as they headed to the door. "I love the feel of the neighborhood. It's right on the corner, with shops all around. And you're within walking distance for a lot of folks."

"Yeah, we've already got people who live nearby who we consider regulars."

"That's amazing."

He held the door for her and they walked in. Mia took in a deep breath.

"I can tell by the smell I'm going to love everything in here."

He grinned. "I thought you were going to be super critical."

She shot him a look. "This *is* me being critical. And shut up."

He laughed and waved at Ken, who came over and shook his hand.

"Hey, Ken. This is my sister, Mia. Mia, this is Ken, my restaurant manager."

Ken shook Mia's hand. "Nice to meet you, Mia. Flynn's told me all about you."

"All the awesome things, no doubt."

Ken smiled. "Of course. Are you two having dinner with us tonight?"

"Yeah. Is Amelia here?"

Ken nodded. "She is. And she said she wants to talk to you, but as you can see we're pretty busy right now."

"Okay. I won't bother her while she's slammed."

Ken got them a table, then Candace, one of the waitresses, came by. Flynn introduced her to Mia, then Candace took their drink order and left menus for them.

Mia looked around. "The ambiance is fantastic. It's not fussy, but it's not lowbrow, either. It's very homey feeling." She met his gaze. "That's what it feels like, Flynn. It's like being at home. Kind of a rustic yet modern feel to it."

He smiled at her. "Good. That's what I was going for."

"And who is Amelia?"

"She's the head chef."

"Oh. Okay."

They ordered their food and several people stopped at their table to chat. The one thing that Flynn liked about Ninety-Two was how friendly everyone was. And he made a point to make himself accessible to his patrons. So he signed a few autographs, took some pictures and chatted with a few fans. After they left the table, he focused his attention back on Mia, who was grinning at him.

"What?"

She shrugged. "I just never think of you as some big-time sports star. You're just my dumb brother."

"No, I'm your smart brother. And the best-looking one of the bunch."

She rolled her eyes, then picked up her glass of wine. "If that's how you can face yourself in the mirror every night."

He laughed. "Smartass."

"So you're playing Grant's team this weekend?"

"Yeah."

"You know they're playing exceptionally well this season."

He arched a brow. "Which means what, exactly?"

"Don't get your panties in a twist, Flynn. It means that I'll get to see a good game. I wouldn't want to watch a game where you steamroll the other team."

"I'd like that."

"I'm sure you would. But I'll be more entertained if you have to work for it."

"You're mean, Mia."

She waved her hand in dismissal. "Yeah, yeah."

The salads arrived and they dug into those, jabbing verbally at each other through the course. There was nothing he enjoyed more than having one of his siblings visit. It made him miss the family dynamic, when he and his brothers and sister would sit at the dining room table and toss barbs at each other through dinner. His parents would mostly laugh as long as they weren't truly mean to each other. And since all the Cassidys had a healthy sense of humor, no one's feelings were ever hurt.

Mia had had to toughen up at an early age since she'd grown up with four older brothers, but she had the best sense of humor out of all of them, and had learned to hurl insults at them from an early age. It was sink or swim in the Cassidy family, and Mia had been born a champion swimmer.

The main course arrived. It didn't surprise Flynn at all that after their discussion last week Amelia had already incorporated the caramelized bluefin tuna into the menu, so as soon as he'd seen it he'd ordered it. Mia was having crab ravioli.

He dug into the tuna, which was tender and delicious.

"Oh, my God, Flynn," Mia said after taking a sip of her wine. "This ravioli is incredible."

"I'm glad you like it."

"Now let me have a bite of your fish."

He sliced off a piece and laid it on her plate. She took a taste, her eyes widening. "Do you eat here every night? I would eat here every night."

He laughed. "No, not every night. But I do come here a lot."

"I can understand why. This is amazing."

He knew she was being nice, but his sister was nothing if not brutally honest. If she didn't like the food she'd tell him. He felt good hearing her praise and he knew Amelia would, too.

He glanced toward the kitchen, wishing he could see Amelia, but the restaurant was super busy right now and the last thing she needed—or wanted, he knew—was him sticking his nose in her kitchen. He could wait.

But he really wanted to talk to her.

Besides, he had Mia to keep him company for now.

They finished their meal and opted for dessert, even though Mia protested she was already too full to eat anything else. She had sorbet and he had cheesecake. By the time they finished dessert it was a lot less crowded in there.

"Excuse me for a minute. I need to dash into the kitchen to talk to Amelia."

"Sure. Oh, and have her come out here," Mia said. "I want to praise her cooking."

"I'll see if she has a few minutes to spare."

He headed over to the kitchen. Everyone was busy, so he stepped inside to see Amelia reviewing orders. He moved up behind her.

"Hey."

She spun to face him. And there was no smile on her face. "I need to talk to you."

Uh-oh. Something was up. "Okay. Sure."

"Stefanie, take over. I'll be right back."

"Okay, Amelia."

Amelia stepped out of the kitchen and Flynn followed. He expected her to talk to him there in the hall, but he was surprised when she made a right turn out the side door.

Ah, okay. Maybe she wanted a kiss. Now, that, he was on board for.

She pulled him down the sidewalk, midway between the door

and the back patio. He leaned in close but she put her hand to his chest.

"What the hell gives you the right to fire one of my cooks?"

He blinked. This was not romantic, and definitely not a kiss. "Huh?"

"You fired Jeff. My prep cook. The one I told you about the other night. The next day, you went and fired him."

"Oh. Right. I figured I'd deal with that so you didn't have to."

"And I told you I'd deal with it. So what did you do? You dealt with it without discussing it with me first."

"Amelia—"

She cut him off before he could say anything else. "Before you hired me I made it very clear that the kitchen staff would be mine to hire, supervise and fire. You and Ken both agreed."

He scratched the side of his head. "Well, yeah, but—"

"Do not *but* me, Flynn Cassidy. You undermined my authority in my kitchen by firing one of my staff. You let your male asshole ego take control and decided you knew what was best. I realize this is your restaurant, but we agreed this was my kitchen. And I'm pissed as hell about what you did."

He opened his mouth to object, but then realized he'd fucked up. "You're right. I'm sorry. I did agree to give you full control in the kitchen. If it means anything to you, my heart was in the right place. I know you have your hands full and I knew Jeff was a problem. I'm a problem solver and I thought I could fix this for you, which I now see was wrong. I apologize for stepping on your toes. And for being an asshole."

She was standing across from him like a fierce blond warrior, her arms folded across her chest as if she was ready to do battle with him. But then her shoulders relaxed—a little.

"Okay. I appreciate the apology. But don't ever do that again.

Just because we had sex doesn't mean you get to make all the decisions for me."

Flynn heard someone clearing their throat behind him. He turned around to find Mia standing by the door.

"Sorry. Went looking for you and someone said they thought you and Amelia were outside. So, you two are dating, huh? Or are you just having sex?"

Well, shit.

Flynn turned back to Amelia, giving her a pained smile. "Amelia, I'd like to introduce you to my sister, Mia."

ELEVEN

AMELIA GAPED AT THE GORGEOUS DARK-HAIRED YOUNG woman who was looking at her with a smile on her face.

She was still pissed off at Flynn, so her emotions were running a little hot. And now she was confused as well. She dragged her attention back to Flynn.

"Wait. What? This is your sister?"

"Yeah. I meant to tell you I was bringing her by but I didn't have the chance."

"Obviously. And now I need to get back to the kitchen. Oh, and hi, Mia. It's very nice to meet you. I'm so sorry you had to witness me yelling at your brother."

"Oh, it's not a problem. I very much enjoyed it. Dinner was awesome, by the way."

Her anger somewhat subsiding, she smiled at Mia. "Thank you."

Amelia headed toward the door, with Mia following.

"You should come by the house when you get off work," Mia

said. "I'd love to spend some time getting to know you, seeing as how you're having sex with my brother."

"Mia, knock it off," Flynn said.

Amelia laughed, though she was cringing inwardly. "Sorry you had to hear that part, too."

"I'm not. This is a new side to my brother and I'm intrigued. I'll be in town for a week and I'd love to see you. Will you be around?"

She paused just inside the door. "I suppose I will, providing your brother doesn't fire me for calling him an asshole."

"Not firing you."

"Good. Now I have to go. See you later, Mia."

M   ⁀gled her fingers. "Later, Amelia."

Amelia headed back to the kitchen, mortified about her behavior. Not toward Flynn, of course. He'd had it coming. But to do it in front of his sister?

Yikes. That had been unfortunate. But she couldn't take it back so she'd have to figure out how to deal with it.

Later.

She washed her hands and got back to work. Fortunately, the rest of the night was as busy as the beginning had been, and for that she was grateful. Diving full speed into work was the best way to not dwell on problems. They'd already hired another prep cook to replace Jeff, and the new one was working out great, so tonight's dinner service had flowed smoothly.

Not that she had helped much, because after her altercation with Flynn, she'd felt . . . scattered. She hadn't seen him since he'd dropped her off at her house after she'd spent the night with him a week ago. He'd called her and texted her, but he'd had to leave town because of a road game, and they hadn't really . . . connected. And she'd been so angry with him after he fired Jeff, which had left her feeling out of sorts in so many ways. She'd wanted to see him in person and talk to him about that.

She'd ended up watching his game on TV on Thursday night. He'd looked really good. No surprise there. But now that she'd seen him naked, there was an underlying heat to the way she viewed him and she found that kind of disconcerting.

"Amelia."

She snapped her attention to Tony, one of the cooks. "Sorry. Yes?"

"We're all cleared out here. Is there anything else you need us to do?"

She looked around, doing a mental check off. "No. It looks great. Thanks for another good night, everyone."

She really had to get her head back in the game and off of Flynn. This job was her priority, and he was way too distracting.

She drove home and immediately kicked off her shoes once inside the front door. She changed into yoga pants and a long-sleeved Henley, headed right into the kitchen, grabbed a bottle of pinot grigio and poured herself a full glass.

She dug her phone out of her purse and checked her messages. There was one from Laura asking her to call. It was after eleven, so she decided to wait until tomorrow. Maybe they could have lunch since Amelia had the day off tomorrow.

The next message was from Flynn.

Text me when you get home.

She arched a brow. That was rather commanding of him, wasn't it? Not a request or a "Hey, if you're not busy, could you text me?" kind of thing.

Whatever.

She decided to ignore him, instead grabbing her e-reader and wineglass. She settled in to read a book from one of her favorite authors, letting the tension of the day melt away.

She was four chapters in when her phone rang. She picked it up.

Flynn.

With a sigh, she pushed the button.

"Hi, Flynn."

"Did you get my text message earlier?"

She decided not to blast him. At least not right away. "I did."

"You're home, right?"

"I am."

"What are you doing?"

"Reading a book and having a glass of wine."

"Okay. So you decided not to answer my text message?"

She took in a deep breath before answering. "Yes, that's exactly what I decided."

He waited a few seconds before he responded. "You're still mad at me."

"I wasn't, but I didn't appreciate the commanding tone of your message."

"The . . . Huh?"

Was it just her, or was he that obtuse? "You said for me to text you, as if I was at your beck and call."

"So you *are* still mad at me. I said I was sorry about firing Jeff. I meant it."

She set her glass of wine on the side table and rubbed her temple where a headache was forming. "I know you did. I think I need to just go to bed. It's been a day."

"I'm sorry if you had a bad day. I probably didn't help that."

"It's not all on you. I didn't get in the mussels I ordered so I had to do a quick substitution on the menu, and the fried eggplant didn't turn out like I wanted it to. It was just one of those days."

"The bluefin tuna was excellent."

"You had that?"

"I did. I'm really glad you added it to the menu. It was spectacular. Mia loved it as well, though she had the crab ravioli and raved about it."

That, at least, made her smile. "I'm so glad to hear that."

"She wants to see you. Which was why I wanted to talk to you. I know tomorrow is your day off and you have a million things you probably need to do, but if you aren't too busy would you have some time to spend with us?"

"I was going to have lunch with my friend Laura."

"I have practice tomorrow anyway until about four, and Mia has meetings. How about dinner? I'll cook, or we can go out to eat."

She owed him that for being such a bitch about the text message. She might be tired, but Flynn didn't deserve to be the recipient of her mood. "Either sounds good."

"Great. I'll text you and I promise it'll be loaded with all kinds of *Would you like to*s and question marks. No commands of any kind."

She laughed. "Okay, Flynn. I'll see you tomorrow."

"Get some rest, Amelia. Good night."

"Good night."

She put her phone down and found herself staring at it for a few seconds, then shook it off.

She hadn't intended to have anything to do with Flynn after the night they spent together, firm in her resolve to keep their relationship strictly professional. But since his sister had requested they spend time together, it would be rude of her to say no.

So this was a special occasion. Or at least that's what she told herself.

After that, though, no personal time for the two of them. And she'd make that very clear to Flynn when she saw him tomorrow.

TWELVE

IT WAS AN EVENT WHEN AMELIA AND LAURA HAD A DAY off at the same time. They were set to meet at noon at Laura's place. Laura had texted her that the door was unlocked and she was running late, so Amelia let herself in.

"I'm here," Amelia hollered as she closed the door.

"I'm upstairs getting dressed. I'll be down in a sec."

Laura's house was a train wreck and she made no excuses about it. She often picked up double shifts at the hospital, and her husband, Jon, wasn't any better at housekeeping than Laura. Shaking her head and smiling, Amelia shifted the pile of books on the sofa along with the blanket and cleared out a space to sit down.

She checked her e-mail while she waited.

"Sorry," Laura said about ten minutes later as she dashed down the stairs, her shoes dangling from one hand. "I'm so sorry. I overslept."

"As often as you work, honey, sleeping is a good thing."

Laura picked up a laptop that was on a chair and set it on top of a pile of papers on the table next to the chair, then sat to slide on her shoes. "Well, I sure as hell don't get enough of it, so thanks for being so understanding. Sorry the place is such a wreck. Decluttering is on my to-do list for later this afternoon."

"Unless we decide to go shopping."

Laura cocked her head to the side. "Do not tempt me with shopping. I'm on a strict no-shopping budget until next month. Or possibly the month after that. Jon told me if he spies another pair of new shoes in our closet he's filing divorce papers."

Amelia grinned. "Right. Like he'd ever do that. The man adores you."

"'Tis true. But I did agree not to buy any more shoes until after the first of the year."

"So just purses, then, right?"

Laura slid her a lopsided grin. "You are such an enabler, Amelia."

"That's why you made me your best friend in college. Because I was the one who said, 'Go ahead and have another Jell-O shot.'"

"And because you held my hair when I paid the consequences for said extra Jell-O shots."

Amelia laughed. "True. And on that revolting note, let's go get some lunch. I'm starving."

"Me, too."

They ended up deciding on Thai food. A restaurant they both loved was nearby, and they were seated at a window table. It was always nice to have a day off on a busy workday. There was something about enjoying the hustle of everyone else having to work while you didn't.

Amelia sipped her tea. "How's work?"

"Intense as hell. How about you?"

"The same."

"How's the hot boss?"

She hovered over her straw for a few seconds before taking a sip, then answered. "Fine, I guess."

Laura cocked her head to the side. "That was interesting."

"What?"

"That pause before you answered."

"It was hardly a pause, and I was taking a drink."

"Uh-huh. Tell me what's going on with sexy football player boss."

She shifted in her seat. "Nothing's going on. Okay, maybe something. But not really anything because I work for him."

Laura cocked a brow. "Do tell."

"Let's not tell. In fact, let's forget I even said anything."

Laura changed chairs so she now sat right next to Amelia. "What the hell, Amelia? Did you two have sex?"

"What? Of course not. What made you think that?"

"You are so lying to me. You had sex with him."

Dammit. The greatest thing about having a best friend was they knew everything about you. The worst thing about having a best friend was them being able to read the subtlest change in your body language. Amelia had never been able to hide a thing from Laura. Not in college when she'd had that ridiculous crush on her humanities professor, and not now.

"Fine. We had sex. But just once and it's not happening again."

"Why? Was he bad at it?"

She laid her chin in her hand. "God, no. It was amazing."

"Did he take the tongue train down to your southern lands? Because any man who doesn't do that isn't worth a second ride."

She choked out a laugh at the train metaphor, one she used all too often herself. "Why, yes. As a matter of fact, he did. And it was a mind-blowing trip."

"Excellent. So why wouldn't you want another ride?"

"Obvious reasons. He's my boss and there's a conflict of interest there."

Laura waved her hand in dismissal. "Only if you make it one."

"Come on. He's my boss. I work for him. You know how complicated that could be. I like my new job and I don't want to lose it."

"Have you talked to him about your concerns?"

"Not exactly."

"Then you should. Before you put an end to something that hasn't even started yet."

She shook her head. "Not to mention I'm freshly divorced and not looking for a relationship."

"First, you're not so freshly divorced, and second, who says you have to marry the guy? Just hook up with him. He's hot and sexy and obviously great in bed. So what are you waiting for?"

She had no idea. "I don't know, Laura. I'm just . . . hesitant."

"Quit hesitating. Frank was a dick and you hung in there for about two years longer than you should have. You were miserable and heartbroken by the time you got out of that marriage. And ever since then you've been focusing on changing cities, changing careers and getting settled. Don't you think you're due for some fun?"

When she put it that way, Amelia realized Laura was right. She'd taken her life—herself—all too seriously these past couple of years. It was time to let go and enjoy herself. And what better way to do that than with someone like Flynn? He was a fun guy.

She could be fun, too. She lifted her gaze to Laura. "I can be fun."

Laura grinned. "I know you can. I think you just forgot how. So it's damn time you remember. Tell me what you have set up with him next, and I don't want to hear 'nothing.'"

"Actually, I'm having dinner with Flynn and his sister tonight."

Laura's brows rose. "Meeting the family already, huh?"

"It's not like that. His little sister is in town for a visit. I met her at the restaurant yesterday. She wants to spend some time with me."

"Because . . ."

"No reason."

Laura slanted a look her way.

"Okay fine. She overheard Flynn and me arguing outside last night."

"About?"

"Work stuff. And I might have mentioned us sleeping together during that conversation and Mia overheard that part."

"Oops."

Amelia nodded. "Yeah. So she knows there's something going on between us. But mainly I think it's because she liked my cooking."

Laura gave her a knowing smile. "If she's like most nosy sisters, she probably wants more details about you and Flynn. She wants to check you out, make sure you're legit and you aren't out to hurt her brother."

"You seriously think that?"

"Of course I do. You remember what it was like when things got serious between Jon and me. His sister Rebecca interrogated the hell out of me for four hours over dinner one night."

"That's different. You and Jon *were* getting serious. Flynn and I are—"

Laura stared at her. "You and Flynn are what?"

"That's just it. We're nothing. We had sex. Once. We work together. It's a fling."

"A fling that could either get messy complicated, or could get serious."

She sighed. "It's not going to get serious."

Laura wagged a finger at her. "You can't predict the future, Amelia. You might believe right now that you're headed down Flingstown Road with Flynn, but you could end up making a sharp turn onto Love Lane."

Amelia shook her head. "Not gonna happen. I've been to Love Lane and that road was filled with hazardous potholes. I don't intend to travel down that particular road ever again."

"Many people have tried to detour and failed, my friend. I'll lay money you can't help yourself and you end up down that road again."

"Nope."

"We'll see."

"Yes, we will." Amelia picked up her drink, and fortunately, lunch arrived so that particular conversation ended, much to her relief.

After lunch, she and Laura ended up going shopping—but not for shoes. She pondered some lingerie, prodded by Laura who insisted that if she was going to have a hot sex affair, then she needed new underwear.

"You probably haven't bought new, sexy underwear in years. What are you living in? Some cotton stuff, right?"

She lifted her chin. "My cotton stuff is serviceable and comfortable for work. Besides, my lack of scandalous lingerie didn't keep Flynn out of my pants the other night."

"Touché, my friend. But still, we're stopping in the lingerie department and buying you something fun and sexy. To make you feel good about yourself and not for Flynn."

When Laura put it that way, how could she resist?

She had to admit, fingering the silks and laces and deep lavender colors—her favorites—did make her feel good. And admittedly it had been a while since she'd shopped for anything this pretty. She certainly hadn't been interested in wearing anything that would turn on her ex, and after they'd split, underwear from the discount stores had suited her just fine.

Now she had a bag filled with hot lingerie she couldn't wait to try out. And maybe—just maybe—she'd think about whether she wanted Flynn to see any of it.

Okay, she was already thinking about stripping down and climbing on top of him wearing the dark lavender bra and panties. Her body tingled just pondering the thought of straddling him, his cock hard as she slid across it wearing next to nothing—

"Are you all right?"

They were riding the escalator and her attention snapped back from her oh-so-inappropriate fantasy to her friend. "I'm fine. Why?"

"Your cheeks are flushed." Laura put her hand on the back of Amelia's neck, sliding it forward to feel her forehead. "You don't feel feverish."

Amelia laughed. "It's just hot in here and I have on too many clothes."

Way too many clothes for that fantasy she'd just conjured up.

They hit nearly every department, chatting the entire time as they tried on clothes, browsed makeup and perfume and looked at shoes, much to Laura's whimpering. In the end, Laura decided on a few pairs of socks, which made Amelia laugh.

"Jon will be so proud you only bought socks," she said as she dropped Laura off at home.

Laura opened her door. "He likely won't believe that's all I got and I fully expect him to inspect the closet. And possibly the trunk of my car."

"If he needs confirmation, tell him to text me. I promise to vouch for your ability to resist that gorgeous pair of sparkly silver heels."

Laura whimpered again. "Don't remind me."

They hugged. Laura grabbed her bag and said, "Call me tomorrow and let me know how it goes over dinner tonight. Unless of course, you're in an after-sex stupor. Then just text me and let me know you lived through the night."

"Funny. I'll call you tomorrow."

When she got home, she went inside, checked her mail and her e-mail, then grabbed something to drink. She had a couple of hours to kill before she was due over at Flynn's house, so she picked up around the house, did that morning's dishes and folded some laundry. After that she headed upstairs to change clothes. What she was wearing was okay, but for some reason she decided to change into some of her new lingerie. And, of course, she chose the dark lavender bra and panties.

She stared at herself in the mirror, turning from one side to the other. She didn't have a curvy body and in fact was kind of stick straight. Her friend Laura got all the lush curves and she'd always been kind of jealous. But admittedly, she looked okay in the new underwear. The bra pushed up what little breasts she had, and the double straps on the panties sat nicely on her hips. Her stomach was flat—mostly—and she felt prettier than she had in a long time.

She had long legs, which Laura had always said were Amelia's best assets. So tonight she decided to wear a dress instead of her usual pants. Especially since she was going to officially meet Flynn's sister. And maybe because she felt extra special in this underwear.

She washed up, redid her makeup, brushed out her hair and decided on a black silk and cashmere dress with long sleeves. It was cool out so she went with her black heeled boots. She finished off the look with a long silver pendant and her silver earrings.

She hoped she wasn't too overdressed, which meant she had to ponder her choice of outfit for fifteen minutes, deciding whether or not she should change into jeans. She finally texted Laura.

I'm wearing a dress. Is that too much?

Laura replied almost immediately. *No. It's easier for Flynn to take off of you later. Are you wearing your new underwear?*

Amelia rolled her eyes. *First, we aren't having sex tonight. His sister is visiting. And yes, I'm wearing new underwear.*

Laura replied: *If you aren't planning sex, why the new lingerie—hmmm?*

Sometimes her friend was a pain in the ass.

Shut up, Laura.

Laura replied with: *LOL. The dress is a good choice. Go have fun tonight and quit second-guessing yourself.*

Laura was right, of course. She grabbed her purse and her keys and headed out the door. She was going to enjoy a night out, some dinner, and that was all that was going to happen.

THIRTEEN

AFTER A GRUELING DAY AT PRACTICE, FLYNN FELT
tight in his right quadriceps. He knew better than to ignore it, so
he'd had one of the team therapists work him out for about an hour
and a half after practice, which meant he was late running all his
errands afterward.

He'd planned a menu for tonight's dinner, and he wanted to
have a lot of it done before Amelia showed up.

Fortunately, Mia was home by the time he got there, so he
enlisted her help.

"You're sure going all fancy for dinner," Mia said.

"Not really. I just want it to be something other than burgers
on the grill."

She nudged him as they stood side by side at the island. "Or
because you want to impress your girlfriend, the chef."

"She's not my girlfriend, Mia."

Mia lifted her gaze to his. "But she could be?"

He waited for a few seconds before responding. "I don't know. I haven't had much luck in that department lately."

"This one's different from the women you typically date, though, right?"

"Yeah. She's different."

"Good. I want you to be happy, Flynn. No one deserves that more than you."

Dammit. He liked it when they teased each other much more than when she got all serious and emotional. He nudged her back. "Thanks, kid."

And then she nudged him hard. "Not a kid anymore."

He groaned. "Quit reminding me. And hey, how did your meeting go today?"

"It went well. Everything seems to be on track so far."

"I'm glad to hear that."

"Me, too. I have another meeting tomorrow. I'll know more after that, but I'm pretty sure it's going to go well."

He liked this confident side of his sister, this motivation to build something. "I'm sure it will, too. Do you need anything from me?"

She turned to face him. "Actually, I do."

That surprised him. "Okay, sure."

"You can pass me the tomatoes."

He rolled his eyes. "Smartass."

Within an hour they had the lasagna in the oven and the salad had been made. Flynn opened a bottle of wine to let it breathe. Mia had gone to the guesthouse to change clothes and make some calls.

The doorbell rang, so Flynn went to answer it.

Amelia looked beautiful. She'd worn her hair down and the wind blew a strand across her cheek.

"Come on in," he said.

"Thanks."

She stepped inside and he inhaled a deep breath as she brushed past him. Her scent was always so unique—something sweet like vanilla, but with an exotic undertone. He didn't know if it was perfume or something she cooked with, but whatever it was, he really liked it.

"A dress tonight, huh?"

She turned around. "Too much?"

He stepped toward her. "No. Definitely not too much. You look beautiful."

As if she was self-conscious about it, she crossed her arms. "It is too much. I knew I should have worn jeans."

He wound his arms around her and tugged her against him. "I haven't had a chance to be alone with you in over a week, Amelia. And you come in dressed like that? No, it's not too much. You look damn perfect."

He was going to kiss her but then the back door opened and Amelia took a very large step back and turned around to face his sister.

"Hello, Mia," Amelia said.

"Hey, Amelia. I'm so glad you came tonight. Flynn's been going all out on dinner to impress you."

Flynn frowned as they made their way toward the kitchen. "I have not. I'm just fixing dinner."

"Oh, right." Mia grabbed a glass and began to pour wine. "Like you make smoked oysters, crab salad and lobster lasagna every night."

Amelia lifted a brow. "That sounds very good."

He shrugged. "I thought it might be."

And maybe he wanted to impress her. You didn't just toss burgers on the grill when you had a chef over to dinner. For Mia, he'd totally do that. For Amelia, absolutely not.

Mia poured wine for everyone.

"Let's go sit in the living room. We have time before dinner."

"Is there anything I can do to help?" Amelia asked.

"No," Flynn said as they made their way to the living room. "Tonight's your night off and you're not cooking."

Amelia took a seat on the sofa and Flynn noticed Mia grabbed a spot on the chair, so he sat next to Amelia.

"You do know I like to cook," Amelia said. "I cook on my days off, too. It's not a burden and I'm happy to pitch in and help."

"Good," Mia said. "Because I highly dislike cooking, so you can feel free to be Flynn's assistant. He's been barking orders at me for the past couple of hours."

"Mia," Flynn warned.

Mia laughed. "What? It's the truth. You're very cranky in your kitchen."

Amelia smiled over the rim of her wineglass, then took a sip. "Most chefs are very particular about their cooking."

"I'm no chef," Flynn said. "But I am particular about how I want things done in the kitchen."

"That's not a bad thing, Flynn. And I'm looking forward to dinner tonight."

"How long have you been a chef, Amelia?" Mia asked.

"About eight years. I started as a prep cook at one of Seattle's finest restaurants right out of college, then worked my way to sous chef at the same restaurant. After I got married and moved to Portland, I got a position as head chef at a restaurant up there and remained there until Flynn hired me to run the kitchen at Ninety-Two. But I've been cooking my entire life. I've always had a passion for it."

Mia nodded. "There's nothing like being devoted to something you love."

"So true. And what do you do, Mia?"

"Right now I'm about to graduate with my MBA. I was planning to get a PhD, but at this point I'd like to take a break from school, so I'm looking at starting a business."

Amelia's eyes widened. "Wow. Good for you. What kind of business?"

Mia looked over to Flynn, who nodded. "I'm laying some groundwork to start a sports management company."

"That sounds incredible, Mia. I'd love to hear more about it."

Flynn sat back and listened as Mia told Amelia about her plans for starting up her company. The more he listened to his sister lay out her ideas, the more impressed he was with her forethought and organizational skills.

"It's definitely a risky venture," Flynn said.

Mia nodded. "I agree, but anything worth having is worth the risk, right?"

"Agreed. But you need to be sure before you move forward that you're ready to take this on."

Mia smiled. "Spoken like a true big brother."

"Hey, I'm just looking out for you. I want you to succeed. I believe in you, you know that."

"I know you do."

"Tell me about the risks, Mia," Amelia said.

While the two of them talked, he got up and finished prepping the appetizer. They had already set the table before Amelia had arrived, so when he pulled the oysters out of the smoker, he took the sliced lemon and cocktail sauce he'd made earlier out of the fridge and set everything in the dining room.

Mia and Amelia came in and Mia poured more wine for them.

"These smell amazing, Flynn," Amelia said.

"Thanks. I hope you like them."

"I'm not sure where you found the time to learn how to cook,"

Mia said. "But, I'm glad Amelia is here tonight because otherwise I'm sure I'd be getting burgers on the grill."

Flynn shot a grin over at Mia. "You probably would."

"Hey," Amelia said. "I like burgers on the grill. You didn't have to do anything fancy on my account."

"I'll keep that in mind for next time." Flynn gave Amelia a knowing smile. She gave him an enigmatic, polite one in return.

After the oysters, he finished prepping the crab salad.

"This is just as good as the appetizer," Amelia said after she finished the salad. Maybe I could hire you as my assistant at Ninety-Two."

"Funny. And maybe you can try out as a linebacker."

"You know, I never said I wanted to play football."

"Are you insinuating that I'm 'playing' at being a cook?"

Amelia calmly took a sip of wine before replying. "I didn't insinuate a thing. You're very sensitive for a tough guy."

"Now you're insulting my manhood?"

"I didn't realize we were bringing your penis into the discussion. And at the dinner table, in front of your sister. Really, Flynn, how could you?"

Mia laughed. "You two are hilarious. And I really like you, Amelia. Not many people can go toe-to-toe with my oldest brother. You're doing a fantastic job. If my other brothers were here I think they'd stand and applaud."

Flynn glared at his sister. "Shut up, Mia."

Mia just snickered and got up to clear the table. When she left, he turned his attention on Amelia.

"And here I expected you to be all quiet and shy in front of my sister."

"You did? Why would you think that?"

"I have no idea."

Mia came back in. "Oh, please don't change your personality on my behalf, Amelia. I like you just the way you are."

"I like you, too, Mia."

He felt ganged up on. Maybe this was how Mia felt being surrounded by all guys growing up. Deciding it was best to ignore both of them, he let it slide and went to pull the lasagna out of the oven.

Amelia had made her way into the kitchen.

"That smells amazing, Flynn. I can't wait to taste it."

He liked that she could tease him and throw insults one minute, and be complimentary and sweet the next. One didn't survive in the Cassidy family if you held on to anger or insults for long.

"Thanks. I hope it tastes good."

She laid her hand on his shoulder. "I have no doubt it will."

"Oh, come on, you two," Mia said. "I like it better when you're flinging insults at each other."

"Give it five minutes," Flynn said, looking at Amelia. "I'm sure they're coming."

Amelia gave him a warm smile, squeezed his shoulder, then headed back into the dining room.

The dinner conversation was decidedly less controversial. Both Amelia and Mia raved over the lobster lasagna, and Flynn couldn't help but agree. It had turned out great.

"There's a hint of something spicy in here, Flynn. What is it?" Amelia asked. "Did you add jalapeños or something?"

"Red pepper flakes and a touch of cayenne pepper. Just enough to give it a hint of heat."

"It's excellent. Lasagna can often get bogged down in the sweetness of the tomatoes and cheese. I really love the idea of adding a little spice to it. We should put this on the menu."

Coming from a chef, that was one hell of a compliment. "You can feel free to experiment with your own recipe and, yeah, we can add it to the menu."

"Good. I'll work it in around the pasta selections."

After they finished dinner, they sat back and drank more wine.

"I'm sorry to have to tell you I didn't make dessert. I'm not a dessert-making kind of guy."

"I can whip something up," Amelia said. "Provided you're in the mood for dessert."

"I don't know about Flynn," Mia said, "but I'm always in the mood for dessert."

"That's not necessary, Amelia. I told you, it's your night off."

She leaned over and patted his hand. "And I told you that I love to cook. Let's take a stroll into the kitchen and see what you have available."

He sighed. "Fine."

He watched while she examined the contents of his refrigerator and pantry. "You have strawberries. I could make us some short-cakes and we'll have it with strawberries and whipped cream."

"Just like that." Mia had taken up a spot at the island.

Amelia let out a short laugh. "Some baking would be in order, but yes."

Flynn shrugged. "If that's what you want to do."

"Absolutely. Let's get these dishes out of the way and I'll take care of dessert."

Flynn shoved the sleeves of his Henley up to his elbows. "I'll do the dishes."

Mia slid off the bar stool. "No, you're both cooking. I'll handle dishes."

In the end, Amelia and Flynn helped put food away while Mia did dishes. With the three of them it took no time at all to clear the kitchen. Flynn and Mia finished up while Amelia started on the shortcake. Since Flynn didn't have individual pans for making smaller cakes, she ended up going with one large cake. He cleaned and sliced the strawberries while she prepped the cake and put it into the oven.

"You didn't have to do this, you know," he said.

Amelia smiled. "How many times are you going to say that so that I have to reply that I love to cook? If a day goes by where I'm not cooking I don't feel like it's a complete day. So get over it, Flynn."

"Yeah, Flynn," Mia said. "Get over it. Amelia loves to cook, so get out of her way."

He supposed he was going to have to get used to the idea that cooking wasn't burdensome to her. He'd wanted to give her a night where she could put her feet up and relax, but maybe this *was* her way to relax.

As she leaned against the counter and sipped on her glass of wine, Amelia said, "Let me put it this way. If you and your brothers— or a bunch of your teammates or friends—were together and someone suggested you go outside and play a game of football, would you balk and say, 'No, I don't want to because that's too much like work for me'?"

He frowned. "Hell, no. I love playing football."

She nodded. "Exactly. That's how I feel about cooking."

He began to see her point. "Okay, I get it. Rock on with your shortcake, Amelia."

She laughed. "I intend to."

The smell of the cake baking filled the kitchen with a delicious sweetness. Baking wasn't something he got into, but maybe he'd have to expand his horizons, because he sure as hell loved desserts. And when Amelia pulled the perfect cake out of the oven, it was all he could do to wait until it cooled. While it did, Amelia made whipped cream.

"Can you come live with me and be my personal chef and my new best friend?" Mia asked.

Amelia grinned. "Sure. When you make that new business a go and you're rich and successful, give me a call."

"Hey," Flynn said, shooting a frown at his sister. "No stealing my talent."

"Is that what she is?" Mia asked. "Your talent? Or is she more than that? Because we haven't yet discussed what I overheard the other night about the two of you having sex."

"And we're not ever going to discuss that, Mia, because it's none of your business."

Flynn had shot a warning glance over to Mia. She might have had a few glasses of wine, but his sister knew when he meant what he said.

"Okay, fine. Let's talk about how soon we can eat the shortcake instead."

"Actually, right now," Amelia said. "Flynn, can you get the strawberries out of the refrigerator?"

"Sure."

He was glad he wasn't going to have to press the point any further with his sister. Instead, they all sat down and ate what had to be the lightest shortcake he'd ever eaten, topped by the best damn whipped cream he'd ever had.

Was there anything Amelia couldn't do?

"This is so damn good," Mia said. "I'm totally serious about declaring my undying love for you, Amelia."

Amelia laughed. "I'm glad you like it."

"I don't just like it, I love it. And wait until my mother meets you. She's a total foodie." Mia looked over at Flynn. "Which reminds me, Thanksgiving is coming up. What do you typically do for Thanksgiving, Amelia?"

Amelia gave a deer-in-the-headlights look to Flynn. He had nothing to offer, so she said, "I . . . don't know."

"Where's your family?" Flynn asked.

"My father died ten years ago. My mom remarried and she and her husband typically go to his parents' house for the holidays."

"So you go there to visit?" Mia asked.

Amelia shook her head. "My mother and I . . . well, let's just say we don't see eye to eye on a lot of things, so we haven't shared many holidays together in the past several years."

Mia gave her a sympathetic look. "That just sucks. You should come to the Cassidy ranch for Thanksgiving. It's a huge free-for-all with my brothers and their fiancées and my parents and uncles and aunts. It's insane but friendly. And my mom would love you. Wouldn't she, Flynn?"

Amelia gave Flynn a helpless look, but he didn't like the thought of Amelia being alone for Thanksgiving. "Yeah, she would. Come to the ranch."

"I . . . couldn't. It would be such an imposition. Plus, there's work."

Mia let out a scoffing sound. "Please. It's not like the boss won't give you the time off. Right, Flynn?"

The more Flynn thought about it, the more the idea held appeal. "Absolutely. You should definitely come spend time with us for the holiday, Amelia. The restaurant is closed for Thanksgiving, and you can take a couple extra days off."

Amelia looked from Flynn to Mia and shrugged. "I . . . guess so?"

Mia got up from her chair and hugged Amelia. "That's great. You'll enjoy it on the ranch and my whole family is going to love you."

They finished dessert, then cleaned up the kitchen. After hanging up the dish towel, Mia yawned. "I'm tired and I have an early meeting tomorrow. So if you don't mind, I'm heading to my little house in the backyard to go to bed."

"Sure, Mia," Flynn said. "I'll see you tomorrow morning."

Mia hugged Flynn, then Amelia. "It was so great spending time with you. I hope I get to see you again before I leave town. Oh, wait, you're coming to the game on Sunday, aren't you?"

Amelia blinked. "I hadn't planned on it."

"Oh, you definitely have to. St. Louis is coming to town and my other brother Grant is the quarterback for that team. It'll be a family thing. Brother against brother. You can't miss it."

Amelia lips quirked. "Brother against brother, huh?"

"Yes. We'll get a pass for the skybox and we can drink and eat food and root for . . . I dunno, whomever."

Flynn frowned. "Whomever my ass. You'll be rooting for me."

Mia laughed. "I take no sides when it comes to my brothers and you know that. Anyway, Flynn will give you the details. Say you'll come?"

Amelia looked at Flynn. "Is she always this pushy with her invitations?"

"Always. You might as well say yes now or she'll be at the restaurant hounding you until Sunday."

Amelia shook her head. "Then, yes. I wouldn't want to miss two brothers beating up on each other."

Mia laughed. "Awesome. Grant's playing quarterback so it'll mostly be him dodging Flynn, who'll be trying to get past the offensive line so he can grind Grant into the ground. Fun stuff."

"Sounds like so much fun," Amelia said with a tilt to her lips. "I'll see you on Sunday."

"Great. Night." Mia started to turn away, but she stopped. "Oh, and by the way, I have plenty to drink, and snacks in my little house in the backyard, just in case you two decide to get busy tonight. You don't have to worry about me popping in on you."

"Good night, Mia," Flynn said, giving his sister a very direct look.

She laughed and waved as she walked out the door.

Which left Flynn alone with Amelia. Amelia was sitting on one of the kitchen bar stools. She looked up at him, a shocked expression on her face.

"Your sister. She's kind of a force of nature, isn't she?"

"Understatement."

And then Amelia went quiet, staring down at her lap. He could tell she had something on her mind. When she lifted her gaze, she said his name.

"Flynn?"

"Yeah?"

"About Thanksgiving. I mean, it was nice of Mia to invite me, but I totally understand if you don't want me there."

Ah. He walked over to her and pulled her off the stool. "I want you there."

"But—"

"No *buts*. I want you there."

"Are you sure?"

"Yes. I'd love for you to come with me to Texas. My mother would love you. She likes food."

"Well, that's nice and all, but isn't that like a family thing?"

"Not with the Cassidys. I mean, yeah, the family comes. But friends do, too. And whoever else shows up. Thanksgiving is a free-for-all with us. Whoever shows up is always welcome."

"You're sure."

He rubbed his hands up and down her arms. "Yes. So don't make a big deal about this, okay? Besides, I want you there. You'll come hang out with my family at Thanksgiving. Nothing more than that."

She nodded and smiled. "Okay. That makes me feel better."

"Good. Now that we got that out of the way, my sister's gone to bed for the night. We're alone and she won't come through those doors again until morning."

He waited, gauging her interest in his statement. She didn't budge, and when he leaned in and brushed his lips across hers, he tasted the sweetness of whipped cream mingled with the tartness of wine.

She snaked her hand up his arm, then pulled back. "So now you've got me alone, Flynn Cassidy. What do you intend to do with me?"

His breathing quickened and he pressed his forehead against hers. "Do you want a written list, or would you just like me to show you?"

"Writing takes too much time. Show me."

FOURTEEN

AMELIA HAD PLANNED TO JUST MAKE THIS NIGHT about dinner and conversation. But then she'd had wine. Great food. Excellent conversation. And a really good time.

She'd also learned a lot about Flynn in the process. Like how much he adored his little sister. How protective he was of her, but also how much he respected her. And that made her warm to him even more than she already had. Which had melted any residual resistance she might have had. Not that she'd had much to start with once he'd opened the front door to her earlier tonight. He'd had on worn jeans that hugged his muscular thighs, and a partially unbuttoned black Henley with the sleeves rolled up.

In theory, saying she was done with him was one thing. When confronted with all that hotness, it was another.

Now he held his hand out for her and pulled her toward him. She slid willingly into his arms and he tugged her against him.

"I missed you last week," he said. "And while I love having my sister here for a visit, I wanted to be alone with you tonight."

She inched closer, loving the feel of his hard body pressed against hers. "We're alone now."

"Yeah, we are. So how about we take this to the bedroom, where I can close and lock the door and make sure we're not disturbed?"

"That sounds like a really good idea."

He took her by the hand and they walked toward the bedroom. They made it as far as the landing to the stairs before Flynn pushed her against the wall.

Her lips curved as he looked at her.

"What?"

"I had a conversation with my friend Laura recently, where I told her I'd never had hot, dirty, up-against-the-wall sex."

His brows shot up. "Is that right? Let's fix that right now."

His mouth came down hard on hers. She felt every bit of his passion as his tongue slid between her lips and swept along hers. She whimpered against his mouth, needing him as much as he needed her. She lifted her leg and wound it around his hip, his answering groan her reward. When he rubbed his hard cock against her, she thought she might slide to the floor, grateful she had the wall and his body for support.

He pulled his mouth from hers, his eyes dark and filled with desire as he looked down at her. "I'm not sure we'll make it to the bedroom."

Her sex quivered. "You keep grinding against me like that and I'll come before we make it up two steps."

"You said you'd never had it up against the wall. Isn't that what you want, Amelia?"

Just thinking about it made her body respond with a flash of heat. "Yes."

He laid another blistering-hot kiss on her, the kind that made every nerve ending explode within her. He trailed his lips over her jaw, her neck, his hands roaming her body as he did. He cupped her breasts, teasing her nipples through the material of her dress and her bra. Even with her clothes on he elicited a reaction. Her nipples ached for his touch, for his mouth, her body quivering under his touch.

He dropped to his knees and raised her dress over her hips, then looked up at her with a wickedly sexy smile.

"Don't you look all hot and sexy in purple."

She smiled down at him, so happy he'd noticed her new underwear. "Thank you."

He held the material of her dress in his hands, then shoved it at her. "Hold this."

He reached for the strings at her hips and pulled her underwear down her thighs, letting it drop to her ankles. She stepped out of it.

"Spread your legs for me, Amelia."

Her legs shook as she widened her stance and he moved in between her thighs. His soft hair tickled her thighs as he drew in, then flicked his tongue out and teased her sex by drawing circles around it.

"Flynn." His name fell from her lips in a soft, needy whisper.

"Yeah, I know." When he laid his mouth fully on her, she rested her head against the wall, overcome by the sensations of heat and wetness from his mouth and tongue. He was taking her to nirvana one torturous lick at a time, and she wasn't sure she'd be able to stay upright. But it felt so damn good, and in no time at all she was crying out with an orgasm that hit her like a lightning strike. Sharp, delicious pulses soared through her, and Flynn grasped her hips and held on while she bucked against him with her climax.

He took her down slow and easy while she gasped for breath. When he stood, he held her panties up with one finger.

"Yeah, purple is damn sexy on you. Does the bra match?"

She smiled. "Yes."

He tucked her panties into his jeans pocket. "We'll get to that later. Now you get hot, dirty sex up against the wall."

Her breath caught as he disappeared for a few seconds and came back with a condom in his hand. He tore the wrapper off, unzipped his jeans and shoved them down his hips. He pulled her leg around him and stepped into her, fitting his cock against her sex.

He cupped her face. "You ready, Amelia?"

"Yes." Her answer fell from her lips in a breathless whisper, her heart racing as she waited for him to enter her.

And when he did, he shoved into her, her butt cheeks bouncing against the wall.

It was glorious. Wicked and hot and everything she could imagine.

He didn't kiss her, just made eye contact with her as he slowly pumped into her. Her pussy squeezed tight around his cock as he eased in and out of her, teasing her. She felt the stirrings of orgasm, her sex clenching around his shaft.

"I think you like this," he said, leaning in to brush his lips across hers.

"I think you're right. Make me come, Flynn."

He grasped her butt and ground against her clit, burying himself deep. She shuddered, crying out as he quickened the pace and gave her what she needed.

It was a whirlwind of heat, his body moving against hers in a way that made her weak in the knees. She felt the clench of his fingers around her butt cheeks, the sweat of his body as he slid against her, and it was the hottest, most thrilling thing she'd ever experienced. Her pussy clenched around his cock as the first wave of orgasm hit her.

When she came, she grabbed on to his shoulders, needing Flynn to anchor her through the maelstrom of pleasurable sensations that flowed through her. He buried his face in her neck while he shuddered through his own orgasm and she clasped tight to him.

She felt breathless. Exhilarated. Ready to do this all night long. Except now she was hot in this dress and couldn't wait to get it off.

Flynn withdrew and kissed her. "Meet me upstairs. I'll get us some water."

She nodded and made her way up to the bedroom, holding on to the banister as she did. Her legs were still shaking.

But oh, wow, had that been good.

She sat on the bed and took a few deep breaths. Flynn arrived with two glasses and handed one to her. She took several long swallows before setting the glass down on the nightstand.

Flynn looked down at her. "How was up against the wall?"

She smiled at him. "Better than I could have hoped for."

"Good." He pulled her panties out of his pocket. "Now let's get that dress off so I can check out the bra that matches these."

The underwear had been a good call. She didn't think he cared, but she sure felt sexier with them on. Though right now they were off, and Flynn seemed to enjoy twirling the panties around his fingers, which only turned her on more.

He dropped the panties on his dresser and pulled off her boots and socks. Then she stood and turned her back so he could unzip her dress. He kissed her back and shoulders, then slid the dress off of her.

She shivered at the contact of his mouth on her skin. She turned around to face him. He traced his finger over the swell of her breasts, teasing a fingertip along the lacy cup of her bra.

"You need to wear this set more often."

She arched a brow. "So purple is your favorite color, too?"

His lips curved. "On you? Hell yeah."

He bent and licked around her breasts, then reached behind

her to unclasp the bra and pull it away. His lips captured one nipple, sucking it between his teeth. She inhaled sharply as the sensation shot straight to her sex, making it tighten and quiver.

She would have thought after two orgasms, she'd be satiated.

Apparently not. Because Flynn's mouth and hands awakened her body in ways that amazed her.

He laid her on the bed, cupping one breast while he licked and sucked the other nipple. A lot of guys paid lip service—and only momentarily—to her breasts and nipples. Flynn made it an art form, plumping and plucking and licking until she writhed against him, silently begging for more.

And he gave her more, his hand snaking down her body to cup her sex and leisurely taking his time to prime her until she was shaking and ready to go off again.

He'd tormented her, taking her to the brink over and over again, only to pull away to cup her hip or play with her ribs. It was maddening. And he was still dressed.

Two could play at this game. She sat up. "Time for your clothes to make a hasty exit. I need you naked."

"I was going to make you come again first."

"Plenty of time for that. Get undressed."

"Yes, ma'am." He hopped off the bed, rid himself of his shirt and pants, then was about to get back on the bed.

"Wait," she said. She grabbed a pillow and threw it on the floor, then slid off the bed and onto her knees. She grasped his hard cock in her hands and flicked her tongue over the head.

He looked down at her. "Oh, fuck yeah. Suck it, babe."

She loved hearing the hard, gritty sound of his voice as she took his cock between her lips and drew it into her mouth. Drops of salty fluid spilled over her tongue and she welcomed it, especially when accompanied by Flynn's groans. She wanted to pleasure him, to string him up on a rack of taut pleasure as he'd done for her. She snaked her hand up his thighs, feeling the tension in his muscles as she moved her mouth back and forth over the length of his shaft. She swirled her tongue over the head, then engulfed his cock deep into the recesses of her throat.

"Christ, Amelia. That's so fucking good. Take it deep. Take all of it. Make me come."

His words were such a turn-on for her, spurred her on to give him what he needed. She lifted up and cupped his ball sac, giving it gentle squeezes while using her other hand to stroke the base of his shaft while she sucked him.

"Oh, yeah. That's it. I'm going to come."

She wanted nothing more than his pleasure, and his harsh groans as the first spurt of come hit her tongue undid her as much as it did him. Her nipples tingled as he came apart for her. His body shuddered with his release and she held on to him while he spilled into her mouth. She swallowed all he had to give, then licked his shaft as she withdrew.

Flynn was shaking and breathing hard as he lifted her off the pillow and pulled her to a standing position. He slid one hand into her hair and kissed her. She moaned against his lips, her entire body enflamed with need for him.

But she also knew he was going to need a few minutes to recover, so she took a step back. "Drink?"

"Yeah." He downed the contents of his glass of water in a few gulps. "Now I need a refill. I'll be right back."

"Okay."

She grabbed her glass of water and took several swallows, then set it back on the nightstand. She climbed onto the bed, unable to resist sliding her hand between her legs to massage the incessant, throbbing ache that Flynn had built up within her. It felt good to build up that tension again, to feel herself climbing ever closer to orgasm.

"Hey, you started without me."

She looked up to find Flynn standing in the doorway.

She tapped her fingers on her sex. "Maybe. But I won't finish without you."

"Good." He took several long swallows of water from his glass, set it on the table, then climbed on the bed next to her. "Now, where were we?"

"I was needing another orgasm."

"Oh, right." He gently pushed her to lie down, then slid his hand between her legs. "You're wet. Did sucking me turn you on?"

She turned her head to look at him. "Incredibly."

His fingers teased her in ways that made her arch against his hand. "It makes my dick hard when I lick your pussy. You taste amazing, and the way you writhe against my face makes my balls pull up tight. All I can think about then is sliding inside of you."

He tucked a finger inside of her, using his thumb to swirl over her clit. She gasped at the sensations.

"You grip my finger tight, just the same way you clench around my cock when I'm inside of you, Amelia. Can you feel it?"

She was so close. "Yes."

He fucked his finger in and out of her, then used the heel of his hand to rub against her clit. She grabbed hold of his wrist and held his hand right where she wanted it.

"That's it," he said. "You control it. Tell me what you need."

"Right there. Now harder." She lost herself in the movements of his hand, the way he watched her face. She was locked on his eyes, and when he bent to kiss her, she whimpered against his mouth and went over into orgasm, arching up against his hand. It was pure bliss to fall so deliciously into her climax, giving full control over to Flynn, who mastered her body with every movement of his fingers and hand.

He removed his fingers but still pet her body with light touches, keeping her fully connected to him. She also noticed his rock-hard erection pressing against her hip. It didn't take long before those featherlight touches grew bolder, and he'd brought her around to full arousal once again.

In between panting and moaning, she said, "You're really good at this."

He grinned. "At what?"

"Turning me on."

"Yeah, you do the same to me." He leaned over and grabbed a condom, put it on, then rolled over on his back. "Ride me."

She quivered at the thought of climbing on top of him and being able to slide her hands over his body. She straddled him, easing down over his rigid shaft. He held on to her hips and thrust up as she sat down on him, the contact between them electrifying. She could feel him swelling inside of her and she stilled, content to just . . . feel.

"Good?" he asked.

She made a happy moaning sound. "Incredible. You feel so good inside of me."

She began to move, sliding forward, then back, her clit dragging across him, sending shocks of pleasure to her core. "Oh, so good."

"Lean forward. I need to touch your breasts."

She did, and he brushed his thumbs over her nipples, sending shock waves into her pussy. She tightened around him and stilled, feeling the waves of orgasm threatening.

Oh, no. Not yet. She wanted more of this wickedly delicious feeling to continue. She let her hands roam over his chest, digging her nails into his shoulders as she lifted off of his cock, only to make a slow slide down over him again, repeating the movement and watching his eyes darken in reaction.

His breathing deepened, his nostrils flared, and with every

movement of her body against his, she felt more connected to him in ways she'd never thought possible. Yes, it felt good, but when he took her hand and twined his fingers with hers, drawing her lips to his for a kiss, she felt a blast of emotion that nearly blinded her in its intensity.

Forcing herself to keep it physical, she drew back, smiled down at him, then rocked against him.

"What you do to me," he whispered against her mouth, lifting against her to give her exactly what she needed.

She responded with an "Mmmm," lost in sensation, in the quickly spiraling knots of pleasure signaling her orgasm was imminent. And when it hit, she straightened, grinding against him so he was buried deep within her. Flynn groaned and went with her, his hands gripping her hips as he thrust over and over into her, his body shuddering against her.

She was shaking as she fell on top of him. He wrapped his arms around her and held her, the two of them sweat soaked and embracing while they breathed heavily together. She didn't know how long she stayed like that. Long enough that her limbs started to cramp. Only then did she climb off and head into the bathroom. Flynn followed and dragged her into the shower with him for a quick rinse. They dried off and she took a couple of sips of water to quench her thirst, then followed Flynn into bed.

She'd thought about heading home, but she was so tired—she'd had quite a few glasses of wine and more than a few orgasms, and the idea of cuddling up next to Flynn and falling asleep was too damn appealing.

He curled his arm around her and she was asleep in less than a minute.

FIFTEEN

AMELIA WOKE EARLY TO FIND HERSELF ALONE IN BED. She turned on the bedside lamp so she could search out her clothes. She couldn't remember where they'd been flung the night before. Surprisingly, they were all neatly folded on the chair by the bed, her boots sitting next to the chair.

Flynn must have done that. Her heart squeezed at the sweet gesture. She went into the bathroom to wash up and found Flynn's toothpaste on the counter, so she used some of it to finger brush her teeth, then fluffed her hair as best she could, got dressed and went downstairs.

Flynn was in the kitchen and she smelled coffee. She really needed a cup of coffee.

"Hey, you're awake. You want coffee?"

"Desperately."

He poured her a cup of coffee and handed it to her. She went to the refrigerator to add some cream, then took a few sips of the eye-jolting brew.

"Oh, yes. Now I'm going to live."

Flynn laughed. "I know the feeling."

She leaned against the counter, and now that her eyes were fully open she checked him out. He wore sweats and a T-shirt, both only adding to the allure of the man's magnificent body. The shirt stretched tight over his massive chest, his tattoos peeking out from the hems of the sleeves. The sweats were low slung yet cupped his ass perfectly.

Not that she was ogling his ass when he turned around to make another cup of coffee. Okay, so she was.

She'd thought one or two or three times with him in bed would have satisfied her and she'd be over the whole need-for-sex thing.

Apparently not, because her nipples tingled and all she could think about right now was stripping off her clothes and taking him back to bed. Or, even better, doing it right here in the kitchen.

She bet he'd be up for it. If she suggested—

The back door opened and Mia stepped in, greeting them with a bright smile. "Hey, good morning, you two. And here I thought I'd be the first one up."

Flynn gave her a look. "Please. You know I'm always the first one up."

"In your dreams." Mia looked over at Amelia. "Morning, Amelia."

"Good morning, Mia. How did you sleep?"

"Like the dead. How about you? Or did you sleep at all?" Mia gave her a knowing look.

"I plead the fifth on that one."

Mia laughed and headed over to the coffeepot. "And I'm not going to press you for details because you're sleeping with my brother and that's way more information than I ever want to know."

"Good idea," Flynn said, kissing the top of Mia's head. "What's on your to-do list today?"

"Heading to Stanford today."

Flynn nodded. "Going through the motions with that?"

"Not really. I do intend to get my PhD at some point. And if they could put together a program I'd be interested in, I might put off the business project for a while. The only problem with the PhD program is the time commitment. It's a full-time gig and while I'd be teaching, it's that many more years before I could work or launch a business. I'm just not sure I'm willing to wait. But I want to do the research into it, so that's partly why I'm here."

"It's good that you're weighing all your options," Amelia said. "That way you can make an informed decision."

Mia nodded. "I agree."

"How do you think Mom and Dad will react if you don't pursue the PhD right away?" Flynn asked.

Mia shrugged. "I think they'll be disappointed at first, but then excited at the prospect of me starting a business. And then terrified at the prospect of me starting my own business." She ended with a laugh.

Flynn took in a deep breath, then let it out. "You're the baby of the family, Mia. We'll all be terrified for you. But at the same time we all have faith in you. And you know I'm going to throw this out again. I'm here for you."

Mia moved in next to Flynn and put her arm around him. "I'm the baby of the family, but not a baby anymore. Trust me. I know what I'm doing and I'm not going into anything blindly."

Amelia watched the interplay between Flynn and Mia, so struck by Flynn's protectiveness over his little sister, while still letting her know how much he believed in her. It gave her these warm feelings she didn't know what to do with.

"I should go," Amelia said.

Flynn frowned. "I was going to make breakfast for all of us before I had to head to practice."

"I have errands to run and bills to pay and I have to do laundry and grocery shopping, all before I have to go to work tonight."

"Are you sure? It won't take long for me to whip something up."

"Absolutely sure. Spend time with Mia. I'll see you later."

"Okay."

She gathered up her purse.

"I'll see you Sunday at the game, right?" Mia asked.

She'd almost forgotten about that. "Yes. Definitely on Sunday."

"Great." Mia hugged her. "See you then."

Flynn walked her to the door, then, after turning to see where Mia was, walked her outside and shut the front door behind him. He pulled her against him and wrapped his arms around her. "I'm glad you stayed last night."

She inhaled his scent, always so masculine. "Me, too. I slept hard. You exhausted me."

His lips curved. "Good."

He tipped her chin and brushed his lips across hers. "I'll talk to you later. Have a good day, Amelia."

She definitely would now. "You, too, Flynn."

He waited on the porch while she got into her car and backed down the driveway. He was still on the porch watching her when she got to the end of his street and turned the corner.

She didn't know how to feel about Flynn. She wanted to keep this light and easy, but there was nothing light and easy about Flynn Cassidy.

SIXTEEN

FLYNN DIDN'T GET TO SEE HIS BROTHERS ALL THAT often, so it was great when one of them came to San Francisco. Even better when they played against each other in football.

He'd been busy with practices and with Mia this week—plus Amelia, which had been a nice bonus. Now that his brother Grant was in town, he was looking forward to seeing him off the field. Come Sunday, he'd lay Grant flat. Today, they'd have beers together.

They both had practices today, so they made plans to meet up after. Grant wanted to go somewhere where they could kick back, relax and not have to deal with fans. Mia was going to be in Palo Alto today, and Flynn in Santa Clara, which was also near where Grant was having practice, so at least they were all close.

Mia said she was craving pho, so Flynn sent them both directions to Tamarine. Flynn got there first so he went in and got a table in the far corner and ordered an iced tea, then texted Mia and

Grant and let them know where he was sitting. Mia arrived shortly after and found him.

"How was practice?" she asked as she slid into a chair next to him.

"Hard. How was your meeting today?"

"Productive."

"Are you intending to tell Grant about what's going on?"

She shrugged. "I don't know. I don't want to tell too many more family members before I tell Mom and Dad, ya know?"

"I understand. I won't say anything to Grant."

"I appreciate it."

He saw Grant walk in so he waved to him. Since it was near the end of the lunch shift, there were hardly any people in the restaurant. Grant spotted them right away and headed over.

Flynn stood and hugged his brother. "Hey," he said.

"Hey," Grant said, then hugged Mia.

"I'm so glad I'm here at the right time to see both of you," Mia said. "You're not going to hurt each other this weekend, are you?"

Grant looked over at Flynn and cracked a smile. "Of course not."

Flynn grinned. "Wouldn't dream of it."

Mia scanned both of them and then frowned. "You're both lying. You guys suck."

Grant laughed. "Come on, Mia. You know how it goes. We're going to play each other like we play any team. Tough, and to win."

"Exactly," Flynn said. "If I break through Grant's offensive line—and I will—I'm not going to pull up just because he's my brother. I'm going to lay him flat."

"Just as I'd expect from you. Not that it's going to happen, because I have the toughest offensive line in the league, and you aren't going to get anywhere close to me."

"Uh-huh. We'll see, Little Brother."

"Yeah, we'll see your defense huffing and puffing as they run after my receivers all the way into the end zone."

Mia rolled her eyes. "It's going to be like this all through lunch, isn't it?"

Grant's lips lifted. "Most likely."

"I should have grabbed a burger at In-N-Out."

Grant slanted a glance at Flynn. "That does sound good. Should we leave now?"

"It shouldn't be crowded this time of day."

Mia sighed. "You're both assholes."

Flynn laughed. "Don't worry. I'm on board for eating here."

"But we don't promise to behave ourselves," Grant added.

Mia picked up her menu. "I don't know why I agreed to have lunch with you two."

Flynn knew why. She was hungry. Plus, she loved both of them as much as they loved her, and with all of the siblings spread around the country, they didn't see each other much. Flynn was more than happy to have his brother and sister in town this week.

Mia ordered pho, Grant ordered the duck and Flynn decided on the sea bass. For appetizers, they went with shrimp spring rolls and lettuce cups.

He was suddenly starving. Then again, a hard practice always worked up his appetite.

"Will Katrina and the kids be joining you this weekend?" Mia asked.

Grant shook his head. "Katrina's in Singapore this week on a photo shoot, and both Anya and Leo have tests so we didn't want to pull them out of school. Plus, Thanksgiving break will be coming up soon and everyone will get together then."

"Oh, good," Mia said. "I haven't seen Katrina or the kids in a while. I'll be happy to see them at the ranch in a few weeks."

Grant looked over at Flynn. "You'll be there?"

"For at least a couple of days."

Mia took a sip of her water, then smiled. "He's bringing his girlfriend, too."

Grant's brows popped up. "You have a girlfriend? One you've managed to keep for more than a week?"

Flynn glared at Grant. "Screw you. And she's not my girlfriend. Or I don't know. Maybe she is. We're kind of seeing each other."

Grant slid a confused glance over at Mia. "What the hell does that even mean?"

Mia shrugged. "I have no idea. She's the head chef at Ninety-Two. She's smart and gorgeous and a lot of fun. Her name is Amelia. She'll be at the game this Sunday."

"Oh. Great," Grant said. "After my team wins, maybe I'll get a chance to meet her."

"After *my* team wins, I might introduce her to you. Loser."

"Don't make me go sit at another table." Mia shot both of them warning glances.

Flynn laughed. "Now you sound like Mom."

"I could get her on the phone, ya know."

"I think even she'd laugh at you if you tried that," Grant said.

Fortunately for Mia, appetizers arrived and Flynn and Grant both shut up long enough to shove food in their mouths. And when conversation started up again, it was fairly benign. They talked about Mia's trip to Stanford, and it was obvious she had decided not to tell Grant about her potential business venture, which meant he'd have to keep quiet about it. He made a mental note to mention that to Amelia as well, though he doubted she'd bring it up in conversation unless Mia was the one to initiate it.

After lunch, which was amazing, they went outside.

"What are you doing tonight?" Flynn asked Grant.

Grant shrugged. "Nothing. I have to be at practice in the morning pretty early."

"Yeah, here, too. Why don't you come to the house? We can go to the restaurant tonight if you want. Or I can fix dinner."

Grant slanted him a suspicious look. "I don't know about having dinner with you. You might be trying to give me food poisoning and knock me out of the game."

"You're both stupid," Mia said, rolling her eyes. "I'll see you at the house."

Flynn laughed after Mia left. "She's so serious all the time."

Grant grinned. "Too grown up for my liking. Maybe she needs a boyfriend."

Flynn shook his head. "No, she doesn't. In fact, that's the last thing she needs right now. She's got her head on straight and she's focused. She doesn't need some asshole derailing all of that."

Grant shoved him as they made their way to the parking lot. "Now *you* sound like Dad."

"Fuck off."

Grant laughed. "I'll follow you to your place."

SEVENTEEN

AMELIA JOTTED DOWN NOTES AS SHE WORKED THROUGH a particularly complex stir-fry recipe.

Her kitchen was a wreck, but she was happy about the way this braised eggplant with chilis and garlic had turned out. Though she loved meats and cooked with them often, she wanted to include a vegetarian and vegan section in her cookbook.

She took a taste of the finished product.

"Mmm, that's good." She picked up her phone to check the time. Just enough time to put the food away in her freezer and clean up the mess she'd made before she had to get ready for work.

She'd spent the majority of her day cooking, cleaning pots and pans and then cooking again, but today was the day she'd set aside for trying recipes for her cookbook. She'd ended up creating three dishes. Two worked out well. One was a throwaway. All in all, not too bad.

Once she'd done all the dishes, she dashed upstairs and into the shower, dried her hair and tossed it into a high ponytail. She got dressed, put her regular clothes into a bag and drove to the restaurant.

She liked to get there about an hour before they opened so she could get a feel for the menu items on tap for the day, plus check in on her staff, who would prep the night's meals.

Her new prep cook, Eugene, was working out well—and he was always on time, which was a bonus. If his probationary month worked out well, he would be getting a raise.

She went over tonight's menu. They didn't have enough stock of the giant prawns, so she crossed those off the menu and replaced them with a new scallop and pasta dish she'd wanted to introduce.

Once the menu for tonight was finalized, she set her staff to work.

"Can I see you for a minute, Amelia?" Ken asked.

"Of course."

She stepped out of the kitchen and into the main dining room. "What's up?"

He pulled up his phone and handed it to her, a grin on his face. "It's a boy."

She looked at a photo of a red-faced newborn. Her eyes widened. "He's here? I thought your surrogate wasn't due until around Thanksgiving."

"He came a little early. Like early this morning, as a matter of fact. But he's perfectly healthy. He weighs six pounds, ten ounces and is nineteen and a half inches long. And he's gorgeous."

She heard the pride in Ken's voice and she couldn't blame him. His son was beautiful.

"He definitely is. But what are you doing here? Get yourself home and to your new baby."

Ken laughed. "Adam's with him now. I just dashed in to check on things and to ask if you wouldn't mind pulling some double duty tonight. The other manager couldn't make it in tonight, but I'm working with her to cover my other shifts for the next couple of days since George made an early arrival. The temporary manager I hired will be able to start on Sunday."

"Of course I can handle things. I'll make sure the assistant chef handles the kitchen. Let me run home and change into something more managerial." She couldn't hold back the tears that pricked her eyes. "And you named him George—after your dad."

Ken smiled. "Yeah. George Louis after my dad and Adam's."

She squeezed his arm. "That's so sweet. Now, you—go home. I'm so happy for you and Adam."

Ken couldn't keep the grin off his face. "Me, too."

She threw her arms around him and hugged him. "I can't wait to come by and see him."

"We can't wait to show him off. But give us some time to get used to being parents."

"Of course. You just call or text me and let me know when you're ready to have people come by."

Ken's eyes glittered with tears. "I'll do that. Thanks, Amelia."

She squeezed his hands, her own eyes welling with happiness. "You're welcome. Give Adam my best. And give that baby a kiss for me."

"I will."

Ken left. Amelia ran into the kitchen to let Stefanie know she'd have to take over management of the kitchen tonight. Then she drove home and changed out of her work uniform and into a skirt, blouse and heels, fixed her makeup, pulled her ponytail out and flat ironed her hair. Now she looked more presentable. She finished off with some jewelry to complete the look.

By the time she hurried back to the restaurant it was nearly time to open. Fortunately, she'd made it in time. She stepped into the kitchen to check on things and found that Stefanie had it all under control, just as Amelia knew she would. Amelia only hired assistants who could do her job as well as she could. Stefanie was a couple of years younger than Amelia and might not have Amelia's level of experience, but she was a damn good cook and an exceptionally strong manager. Amelia had every confidence in her abilities. Plus, she'd still be right there at the restaurant to oversee things.

She checked on the bar and waitstaff, went to the front reception area to make sure the reservations and greeting area was prepared, and checked on tonight's reservations. By then people had started filing in, so she got out of the way and let the more than competent staff do their jobs.

It was hectic, but manageable. She managed to dash into the kitchen a few times to check on things, but Stefanie was managing fine despite being one person down, which allowed her to deal with the overall managerial duties of the restaurant.

"Amelia, Flynn's on the phone for you."

She nodded and went to grab the phone.

"Hi, Flynn."

"Ken called me. Is everything all right there?"

"Everything's perfect. I have Stefanie taking over head chef duties in the kitchen and I'll be managing tonight."

"Okay, thanks. My brother's at the house with my sister and me. We were going to come in for dinner, but if you think all of us being there will be a hassle for you, we can go somewhere else."

Her lips curved. "Flynn, this is your restaurant. Of course you should come."

"How full up are we tonight?"

"About as busy as we typically are for a Friday night."

He cleared his throat. "Can we get a reservation for eight, then?"

She shook her head. "You come in whenever you want. I'll make sure there's a table for you."

He laughed. "Okay. See you then."

She hung up, smiling as she made her way back to the dining area. It was sweet of him to call, but ridiculous that he'd even consider not coming to his own restaurant. Then again, that was Flynn—always concerned about how things affected her or other people.

He was actually a really nice guy. And she wasn't going to think too much about that because there was work to be done, and that's where her mind should be.

They were at least three hours into the dinner hour when Flynn came in, accompanied by Mia and a striking-looking man who looked remarkably like Flynn. That had to be Grant, because the resemblance was close. Same dark hair, same intense look. They were roughly the same height except Flynn was more muscular.

Flynn came over to her right away. "How's it going?"

"It's all going fine. Stefanie's doing a great job in the kitchen. I've tasted everything and it's perfect. We've had a packed house tonight but service has been smooth."

"Great."

She motioned for one of the hostesses, who brought over the menus. "And we have a nice table set aside for you and your brother and sister."

"Thanks." Flynn turned and motioned to the dark-haired man standing next to him. "Amelia, this is my brother Grant. Grant, this is Amelia Lawrence."

Grant smiled, and the effect was devastating. "Nice to meet you, Amelia."

"You, too, Grant. And hi again, Mia."

"Hi, Amelia," Mia said.

One of the hostesses motioned to her. "I'd love to stay and talk, but I have to run. Carol will take you to your table. I hope you have a wonderful dinner."

She ran off and attended to a mixed-up reservation, but kept her eye on Flynn and the others while they were seated. Hopefully everything would go smoothly for them. In fact, she'd make sure of it.

"So that's Amelia, huh?" Grant asked after they put in their dinner orders.

Flynn watched Amelia handle something one of the waiters asked her. She motioned with her head, then was immediately off in the opposite direction. She looked beautiful in her gray skirt and white blouse. And those heels defined her legs in ways he shouldn't be imagining while in the company of his brother and sister.

"Beautiful, isn't she?" Mia asked. "And she's smart and accomplished and she's funny. I don't know why she likes Flynn."

Flynn managed to hear the last part enough to pull his gaze away from Amelia and center it on his sister. "Hey."

Mia laughed. "I was wondering if you were even listening to me, since you couldn't seem to take your eyes off Amelia."

"She is beautiful," Grant said. "She seems out of your league, though."

"Like Katrina is out of yours?"

Grant smiled. "Yeah, like that."

Dammit. Hard to insult his brother if he wouldn't take the bait. Their drinks arrived and Flynn took a long swallow of iced tea.

"How'd your practice go today?" he asked Grant.

"Perfect. We're prepared to kill you on the field on Sunday."

Flynn knew better than that, but since Mia was there, he decided not to argue the point.

"Did you know that Mom and Dad are looking to buy the two hundred acres of property adjacent to theirs?" Mia asked.

Flynn frowned. "No, I didn't. Which one? The one to the north?"

Mia shook her head. "No. East. The ones the Clearmonts owned. They've decided to retire and move to South Carolina to live near their son and daughter-in-law and grandkids."

"That's some prime grazing pasture. Is Dad looking to get more cattle?" Grant asked.

"I have no idea," Mia said. "Mom mentioned it in passing when I talked to her on the phone last night. Bud Clearmont talked to Dad last month about the whole thing, and Mom and Dad discussed it and I guess they're in negotiations now."

Grant looked at Flynn, who shrugged. "I'm surprised he didn't mention it to any of us."

"He didn't say anything to me, for sure," Grant said. "Then again, maybe they were waiting for the sale to be finalized, just in case it didn't go through. Either way, it's a big addition to the land."

"Yes," Mia said. "And if he's adding more cattle, he'll need more hands. Leave it to Dad to be a big cattle mogul."

Flynn laughed. "Yeah, but he loves it. Now I can't wait to get out there this month and find out what's going on."

If there's one thing his father never did after retiring from playing football all those years ago, it was settle down. He'd made a go of his ranch and both he and Flynn's mother loved working the land. His dad had loved playing football. He loved being a rancher just as much. Now that Dad could spend all his time with Mom, he might love the ranching part even more.

Flynn hoped to do the same someday. He wanted to buy land, definitely, but he wasn't sure about becoming a rancher. He just hoped he'd find something to be as passionate about as his father was.

It was something he thought about after their dinner arrived and the table quieted while they ate.

"You know, we can only play football so long," he said to Grant. "At some point we'll have to live the next stage of our lives."

"Yeah," Grant said. "I think we all ponder what that'll be. I imagine yours will involve food."

Flynn tilted his head. "You think so?"

Grant looked around. "I don't see why not. This place looks pretty good and you seem to have a passion for it."

Grant was right about that, but Flynn wasn't near retiring yet. He honestly never thought past the current season. He invested the lion's share of his income, knowing that someday he wouldn't be playing football. Beyond that? It wasn't time to think about it yet.

"How are we all doing?"

Flynn looked up to see Amelia standing at their table.

"Great," Mia said. "The food is amazing, of course."

"I'm so glad to hear that. I hope you enjoy the rest of your meal."

She turned to walk away, but Flynn grasped her wrist. "Don't leave. Have you eaten yet?"

"No. I'll grab something later."

"How about now? It doesn't seem busy."

"Yeah, stay and eat with us," Grant said.

Amelia hesitated. Flynn was right in that it wasn't busy, but her job didn't include sitting and eating. Still, she was absolutely starving. Normally she never worried about grabbing a meal because she tasted everything in the kitchen when she cooked and she always ended up perfectly full.

She looked around to make sure no one needed her for anything. It seemed they didn't, so she nodded. "All right."

Flynn motioned for their waitress, who dashed over. "What can I get for you?"

He looked to Amelia, who ordered a salad and scallops, along with a glass of water.

"I'll have those right up for you," the waitress said, then left.

"How's your visit to San Francisco going, Grant?" Amelia asked.

"Good so far."

"We were discussing the guys' post-football futures when you came to the table," Mia said.

Amelia looked at Flynn. "Oh? And what's in your future?"

Flynn shrugged. "I'm thinking international spy."

Amelia laughed. "Yeah, because you blend in as such an everyday guy."

Flynn frowned. "Hey. I can be an everyday guy."

Amelia cocked her head to the side and gave his body a once-over. "No, you couldn't."

Grant laughed. "She's right. Those tattoos are a dead giveaway. Plus, your ugly face is too remarkable. People would easily remember you."

"Funny comment coming from you considering the two of us look so much alike."

"Oh, hell no. I'm much prettier."

Amelia looked at Mia. "Are they always like this?"

"Worse. And wait until Tucker and Barrett are along for the ride. You'll need tranquilizers."

Though she'd had some trepidation about the trip, Amelia was looking forward to Thanksgiving now. His parents had been to Ninety-Two's grand opening. But she'd been slammed that night and she'd never even met them. She was looking forward to meeting them at the ranch, even if she did feel a bit odd about spending the holiday with Flynn.

"Actually, we were talking about Flynn becoming a world-famous restaurateur after he retires from football," Mia said.

Amelia looked at Flynn, who frowned at his sister.

"That is not at all what we were discussing. You and Grant decided for me."

Amelia nodded. "I could definitely see that. You've done well here. And you do like to cook."

"He just likes to eat," Mia said with a smirk on her face. "I think the cooking thing sprang up from a sense of self-preservation. Maybe midnight hunger pangs or something. Probably after way too many beers. You found yourself on the sofa, strung out and unable to move because you were loaded, and you were bored and channel surfing. Then you landed on a cooking show and voilà, your second career was born."

Flynn rolled his eyes. "Sure. That's exactly how it happened."

Amelia enjoyed watching him spar with his siblings. He was always so confident, so filled with quips. It was nice to see his brother and sister take him down a peg.

As an only child, she'd never had anyone to do battle with, so for her, this was new.

Her dinner arrived, and she'd noticed that Flynn, Mia and Grant had waited for her food to show up before they finished theirs. It had been unnecessary, but at least she didn't feel like she was eating alone now. They all ate and she got to sit back and enjoy more verbal sparring among the siblings.

Over dinner she learned that Grant was engaged to a fashion model. She'd heard of Katrina Korsova—who hadn't? What she didn't know was that Katrina had single-handedly raised her two younger siblings—now teenagers—from the time she was eighteen years old. What an admirable woman.

"Tucker is engaged as well," Mia said to her. "You'll love meeting Aubry, and Barrett's girlfriend, Harmony. And knowing how things are going, you'll get to hear all about the two weddings that are happening next year since that's all we ever talk about."

Amelia smiled. "I love hearing talk of wedding planning. I can't wait."

After dinner, Grant and Flynn had dessert. Amelia and Mia

declined, and Amelia excused herself to get back to work. Flynn got up and followed her toward the kitchen.

He picked up her hand. "What are you doing after work tonight?"

"Collapsing in a heap of exhaustion, probably."

His lips curved. "That rough, huh?"

"Actually, not at all. The staff here is more than competent. It's been fine. What did you have in mind?"

"I thought maybe I could see you."

She couldn't help but react to the way his thumb brushed over the skin of her hand. Despite people filing past them, she wanted to be immune, but she couldn't. He had an effect on her and she had to come to grips with that.

"Sure. But wouldn't you rather go out with your brother and sister?"

"Grant's heading back down south, and Mia has some paperwork she wants to do. So why don't you invite me to your place?"

She couldn't resist smiling at the way he'd invited himself over. "Flynn, would you like to come to my place after I get off work tonight?"

"I'd love to. Why don't you text me when you leave and I'll meet you there?"

"I'll do that."

He looked around, then picked up her hand and kissed it.

Butterflies. She had butterflies in her stomach. Ridiculous, but they were there anyway. Damn the man.

"See you later, Amelia."

He turned and walked back to the table. Amelia heaved in a sigh and headed into the kitchen.

EIGHTEEN

FLYNN HUNG OUT AT A BAR AND PLAYED SOME POOL with Grant and Mia until he got Amelia's text.

"Gotta go," he said.

Grant frowned. "We're in the middle of a game."

Flynn hung up his cue. "I've got other plans."

"In other words," Mia said, "he's going out with Amelia and she's prettier than you."

"How can that be?" Grant asked. "No one's prettier than me."

Flynn shook his head. "Good night, you two."

He left the bar and stopped by his house to pick up a bottle of wine, then drove to Amelia's house and rang the bell. When she answered the door, she was on the phone, so she motioned for him to come inside. He followed, shutting the door behind him.

She'd already changed into black yoga pants that hugged her ass in the best possible way. She was wearing a white tank top that pressed to her breasts and, damn, she looked hot.

She led him into the kitchen. When she saw the bottle of wine, she reached into a drawer and pulled out the opener, handing it to him, then pointed to an upper cabinet. He figured that's where the glasses were.

He opened the bottle and poured the wine into the glasses.

"Sorry," she said as she laid her phone on the kitchen counter. "My friend Laura just got off work so she wanted to chat."

"I need to meet your friend Laura."

"You'd like her. She'd like you. She's married and lives down the street with her husband."

He handed her a glass. She took a long swallow of wine.

"This is your friend from college?"

"Yes."

"We should do a double date."

Amelia arched a brow. "Is that what we're doing? Dating?"

"Aren't we?"

"I don't know. I thought we were just having sex."

"And I thought we were dating."

"Hmm." She took another swallow of wine and didn't answer, which made him frown.

He went over to her and took the wineglass out of her hand and set it on the counter. He drew her against him. "If I hadn't made it clear before, or if in any way you're confused about what's going on between us, Amelia, I like you. I want to see you, outside the bedroom. On dates. In public. With or without other people."

She wound her arms around his neck. "Does that mean you don't want to see me *in* the bedroom?"

"Oh, I definitely want to see you in the bedroom. Or outside the bedroom. In the living room. In the hallway." He looked around her. "Or how about on the back porch?"

She feigned a gasp. "Mr. Cassidy. Are you suggesting we have sex in a public place?"

"I don't think the thought of it shocks you as much as you'd like me to think."

"And now I'm even more scandalized. Just what kind of girl do you think I am?"

"My kind of girl."

Her lips curved. Damn, he liked when she smiled. And when she teased him. And okay, when she breathed. He liked everything about her.

"Come on, grab your wine and show me your porch."

She picked up her glass and led the way. "Is 'porch' some kind of sexual euphemism?"

He laughed. "Not that I'm aware of, but we can make it one if it turns you on."

She chose a spot on the small couch and he sat next to her. The porch had windows, but it wasn't heated out there. Still, it wasn't all that bad. He picked up her legs and placed them over his, then grabbed the blanket that was lying over the back of the sofa and draped it over her legs.

"I'm not cold," she said.

"Does that mean you're hot?"

She cast him one sexy look. "Isn't that your call?"

He ran his hand over her thigh. "If it is, you know my answer."

She scooted onto his lap, straddling him. "We're not going to drink our wine, are we?"

He smoothed his hand down her back, then let his hand rest over her butt. His cock was getting hard and all he could think about was touching her and kissing her. "No."

He cupped the back of her neck and kissed her. She fit her body against his and leaned into him. He groaned as he breathed her in and felt her melting against him.

He moved his mouth from hers and kissed his way down her

neck, his lips feeling the fast rhythm of her pulse. He licked along that pulse point, and she tilted her head back.

"More of that," she said, her voice a throaty whisper.

He swept his hand along the long column of her neck, then moved down between her breasts as he kissed her collarbone. He tilted her back so she rested on his arm, then lifted her tank top, exposing her stomach. He palmed her warm skin, raising the shirt over her breasts. She wasn't wearing a bra, which suited him just fine. One less piece of clothing in his way. He brushed his fingers over her nipples, watching them harden.

"You are so damn beautiful," he said as he lifted her so he could put his mouth over one of the buds. When he sucked, she moaned, and the sound of her voice shot right to his cock. He rocked against her, letting her know what she did to him.

He slid his hand inside her pants. She was hot, wet, and as he dipped his fingers inside her underwear, she arched against him.

"Yes, touch me."

It would be a lot easier to do that if she didn't have pants on. "How do you feel about being naked out here?"

She shifted, sitting up. "How do you feel about turning off the light in the kitchen?"

"I'll be right back." He got up and went into the kitchen. When he came back, Amelia was standing in the middle of the porch. It was midnight dark out there now, but he could still see her. She pulled off her tank top, then shimmied out of her pants and underwear.

"You next," she said.

He shucked his clothes in a hurry, then grabbed the blanket from the sofa and tossed it on the floor. He knelt on it and spread her legs so he could put his mouth on her.

She gasped and laid her hand on his head while he spread his tongue around her clit. Her tart flavor was the best aphrodisiac, filling his senses with a desire to make her come on his tongue.

She was hot and wet and lifted up against him. He flicked his tongue around her, giving her what she needed to get there. He loved the feel of her muscles tensing, the way she gave herself over to him as he flattened his tongue against her clit.

And when she came, her body trembled and she whimpered in such a damn delicious way it was all he could do not to stand up and drive his cock inside of her just so he could feel the quakes of her orgasm. But this was for her and he wanted her to ride the wave of her climax all the way through.

Finally, he stood and Amelia moved into him, putting her mouth on his and sliding her tongue inside to wrap around his in a deep, passionate kiss that made his balls draw up tight with need. He tugged her close and rocked his cock between her legs, sliding against the wetness there.

She finally pulled back, pressing her hands against his chest. "Sit."

He parked it on the sofa, and Amelia came over and leaned down to him. She reached over on the table next to the sofa and picked up a condom packet.

He arched a brow. "Just happened to have one of those sitting on the porch?"

"I never reveal the whereabouts of my secret condom stash."

He grinned, then took the packet from her, tore it open and slid it on. "How do you want it?"

She grinned back. "Inside me. But how about this way?"

She straddled his thighs and slid down over his cock, leaning back enough so he could watch his cock disappear within her. There was nothing hotter than seeing the two of them connected, to feel himself buried deep inside of her. When she was fully seated on top of him, he grasped her hips and drew her forward so he could take a nipple into his mouth. The bud was soft and he flicked his tongue over it before sucking it.

She hissed and raked her nails across his shoulders. "Oh, yes. Suck it, Flynn. Harder."

The edge in her voice made his balls quiver. He could spill inside of her right now just feeling the way she moved against him and the taste of her soft nipple inside his mouth.

He released her nipple, grasped her hands and held on while she rode him, taking in the view of her body as she undulated against him. She was a beautiful goddess, in control of both of them as she rocked him to oblivion. And when she spasmed around his cock, tilted her head back and lost control with her orgasm, he thrust into her with his climax, spilling inside of her with his own release.

It was a damn good feeling, a euphoria he didn't want to let go of.

Amelia clasped on to him and lay her head on his shoulder, breathing deeply as she recovered. He wrapped his arms around her and let them both settle.

"We could just stay like this all night," she murmured against him.

"We could, but it might get a little cold. And eventually there'd be sunrise."

She lifted her head. "True. Let's go get in my bed."

She lifted off of him. He dashed into her bathroom to get rid of the condom. When he came out, Amelia was propped up on the bed, beautifully naked and holding her glass of wine. She motioned with her head over to the nightstand.

"Yours is over there."

He came toward the bed. "Huh. I thought mine was right there." He motioned to her.

She laughed. "I meant the wine."

He picked up the glass and climbed onto the bed next to her, then took a swallow of wine before setting it down on the night-stand. He turned to her.

"Tell me about your ex."

She shot him a raised brow. "That's your idea of after-sex small talk?"

He shrugged. "We're dating now. We should get to know each other better. And I want to know about your life before you came here."

Amelia took a sip of wine. Then another. Flynn could tell talking about her ex was something she didn't enjoy, that it made her uncomfortable. He hadn't meant to make her uncomfortable, but he was being honest when he told her he wanted to know her better. And her ex was part of her past—obviously a big part of her past. He wanted insight into what made her leave Portland and come here.

When she took yet another sip of wine and still hadn't answered him, he decided maybe he should get the conversation started. "You moved from Seattle to Portland for him."

"Yes. Frank—that's my ex—received a really wonderful job offer. We had been dating for a year when we got engaged. We got married eight months later and a month before the wedding Frank got a job offer in Portland he couldn't refuse. So after the wedding we moved there. Actually, he moved before the wedding since he had to start his new position right away. I joined him after the wedding."

"That's kind of stressful on a new marriage."

"It was fine. I was fine with it. We were in love and it seemed like a new adventure. I found a job at a wonderful restaurant and climbed up the chain of command there. I was happy. We were happy—for a while."

He toyed with a lock of her hair. "So what happened?"

"I don't honestly know what changed. I can't pinpoint when it happened or why. Maybe it was the stress of his job. Frank was in a tech job and it was very challenging for him, so he depended on me a lot. His family was in Seattle, so I was all he had and, honestly, my situation was similar. My dad is gone and my mother and I are estranged, so I liked having Frank in my life, someone to count on. Both of us really loved being just the two of us, you know?"

Flynn nodded.

"But after a while, he began to lean on me a little too much. He'd text me all the time asking what I was doing, who I was with. He'd want to review my calendar with me. He worked long hours, which gave me a lot of free time. I was okay with that because I supported his job. I got to know the people I worked with and when he worked late, I'd go out with those friends.

"He . . . I guess he grew jealous that I developed a life that didn't include him."

Flynn frowned. He didn't like the direction this was going. "Surely he couldn't expect you to spend all your time with him, especially if he worked long hours."

She circled her finger over the rim of her wineglass. "Actually, he did. He wanted me home when I wasn't at work. And he wanted me to account for every minute of my time when I wasn't at work. He wanted me to text him when I left the house to go out with friends. He wanted to know who I was with. After a while, he didn't want me to even see my friends in social situations that didn't include him."

"That's ridiculous."

She nodded. "I thought so, too. It got to the point where I felt like he was smothering me, that he didn't trust me. Actually, he didn't trust me. And there was no reason not to trust me. I loved him.

"But his insecurities got the best of him and he went off the deep end. He told me I had to stop seeing my friends altogether and I told him he was being ridiculous and jealous and petty. That's when everything went haywire for us. And that's when he accused me of having an affair with my boss."

Flynn blinked. "Jesus. You can't be serious."

Amelia dragged in a deep breath and sighed. "Yes. It was, of course, completely unfounded. Craig, my boss, was married to a lovely woman and had two amazing little boys and he was utterly devoted to his family. Craig and I got along very well and I enjoyed working for him. I had a wonderful job at the restaurant. I loved all my friends there. And Frank made my life a living hell. He'd show up at the restaurant and get a table just to watch me. He'd tell me he had to keep an eye on me to make sure I behaved. "

"Christ, Amelia. That borders on stalking. He was stalking his own wife."

She nodded. "I know. I tried to convince him there was nothing going on between Craig and me. I think the stress of his job finally got to him. Or something. I don't know. I suggested we go to counseling but he refused. I even offered to get a job at another restaurant, thinking maybe there was something I'd done that gave him the wrong impression. But he said me working somewhere else would be ideal and would be easier for Craig and me to see each other."

Flynn raked his fingers through his hair. His gut tightened and he wanted to fold Amelia into his arms and remove all the pain she'd gone through. But he couldn't. He'd opened up this can of horror from her past by asking her about it. Now that he had, he needed to let her finish. "So what happened?"

"I finally couldn't take it anymore. His refusal to believe in me, to trust me, to even consider going to couples counseling, was the end of our marriage. I told him if he didn't stop this nonsense that I'd leave him. One night it came to a boil and he screamed at me and told me that's exactly what I wanted all along—freedom so I could be with Craig. I cried so hard, tried to convince him that there was only him in my life, but by then he wasn't seeing reason. I packed up and left the house that night. I filed for divorce, quit my job and decided to move. I thought about moving back to Seattle, but what I really needed was a fresh start."

She lifted her gaze to his and offered up a tremulous smile. "And that's how I ended up in San Francisco."

He saw the tears shimmering in her eyes. As one slid down her cheek, he swiped it away with his thumb.

"I'm sorry, Amelia. I shouldn't have brought it up."

"It's okay. It's in the past now."

He took the wineglass from her hands and set it down on the table, then pulled her against him and wrapped his arm around her.

"The past has a way of not staying in the past. Obviously it still lingers."

She shuddered as she took in a breath. "A little."

Probably more than a little. Flynn would like to shove a fist into that bastard's face for hurting Amelia. "Thanks for telling me about him. I'm so sorry he hurt you."

"Me, too."

He smoothed his hand over her hair. "You realize none of this was your fault, right?"

"I do now. For the longest time I tried to figure out what I'd done wrong, how I could have managed it better, what I could have done to make him trust me. I went to counseling and the therapist helped me realize it wasn't me at all. I did everything right. It was all on Frank."

He was glad she was smart enough to seek help to support her through a terrible experience. "Good. Because your counselor was right. None of this was on you."

He let a few minutes pass while he stroked her hair and her back. He really felt shitty about her marriage. What kind of man was that guy, anyway? The more he thought about it, the angrier he got.

"Amelia."

"Yes?"

"Your ex-husband is a dick. Never cry another tear over that worthless piece of shit again. He didn't deserve you."

She laughed, then straightened and shifted to face him. "Thanks for that. It does make me feel better."

And now he needed to shove that part of her past where it belonged—in the past.

He pushed her onto the mattress. "I've got something that'll make you feel even better."

She raised her arms above her head as he moved next to her. "Oh, really? And what might that be?"

"A bedtime story."

"Do tell."

"Once upon a time there was a tongue, a pair of hands and a really big cock . . ."

She sighed as he bent to lick her breasts. "I do love a good bedtime story."

NINETEEN

AMELIA ENJOYED WATCHING A GOOD FOOTBALL GAME, but admittedly she'd never actually been to a stadium before. This was going to be a first for her.

Since Flynn had to be at the stadium super early that morning, she wouldn't show up until later. She made arrangements to meet up with Mia and take Caltrain and the light rail to the stadium, since she knew traffic would be a nightmare. Flynn had offered to arrange for a private car to drive them there, but Amelia and Mia decided public transportation would be a lot more fun. They'd be able to engage with the other fans that way. And Mia had insisted they wear Sabers gear so they could get into the spirit of the game.

Amelia wasn't about to let either Mia or Flynn know that she didn't own Sabers gear. What kind of fan—or girlfriend—would she be if she admitted she didn't own Sabers gear?

Not that she was Flynn's girlfriend or anything. Or was she?

She had no idea. She wasn't much for labeling. They were dating. That was enough to admit for now.

Before she headed into work on Saturday she stopped into one of the pro gear shops in the city and bought a jersey. And she just happened to find a number Ninety-Two jersey with *Cassidy* on the back. If she was going to gear up, she might as well do it right.

She drove over to Flynn's house several hours before game time. Mia came out wearing a Sabers long-sleeved shirt and a jacket and climbed into the front seat.

Mia grinned at her. "Nice jersey. Is it new?"

She knew she should have dirtied it up some. Then again, the thought of wearing a dirty jersey made her shudder. "It might be. Don't tell Flynn."

Mia laughed. "Your secret is safe with me."

They drove to the train station and parked, bought their tickets and climbed aboard. As she suspected, at each stop the train filled with more and more Sabers fans. By the time they got to their transfer stop, everyone on board was talking about today's game against St. Louis, and their entire car made the transfer over to the light rail system that would take them to the stadium.

They rode with a happy crowd of people to the stadium. She was so glad they'd decided to travel this way. It really amped up her enthusiasm for the game.

Flynn had gotten them passes to the suite where the players' wives and families sat and watched the games. After they showed their passes at security and made their way upstairs to the suite, Amelia could only gape in awe.

"Wow," she whispered to Mia. "Fancy."

"Right?"

The room had plenty of seating in front of floor to ceiling windows with a perfect view of the fifty-yard line.

"Hi." A beautiful dark-skinned, dark-haired woman came over.

"I'm Tiffany LaSalle. My husband, Randy, plays wide receiver for the Sabers. Is this your first time here?"

Mia nodded. "I'm Mia Cassidy. Flynn is my brother. This is Amelia Lawrence, Flynn's girlfriend."

Amelia didn't know what to make of Mia's ease in introducing her as Flynn's girlfriend, but Tiffany gave them both a wide smile.

"It's so great to meet both of you. We've had Flynn's parents here before, and a couple of his brothers. Come on in and I'll introduce you to everyone."

She met so many people she wished they were all wearing name tags, because she was never going to remember everyone. But they were all friendly and welcoming, so her immediate nervousness evaporated.

"I don't know about you, but I need a drink," Mia said after the meet and greet. She hooked her arm in Amelia's and dragged her over to the bar, where they each ordered a glass of wine.

They wandered over to one of the sets of windows. Amelia looked down onto the field. They had a really nice view of the Sabers players.

"They're doing warm-ups right now," Mia said.

"I don't usually get to see a lot of the warm-up portion when I watch it on TV. Maybe a brief view, and then they go back to the sportscasters or commercial."

She was fascinated watching them on the field. Okay, so she was watching Flynn and his teammates stretching, running and shoving each other. He looked fine in his uniform. There was no doubt the man had a stellar ass, and it was shown off to perfection in that uniform. He looked so formidable, so fierce out there.

And when the other team came out and they did the coin toss, Amelia and Mia settled into their chairs. Amelia realized she was tense. She had always watched the games, but more with one eye on the TV while she was cooking, more as a passive observer.

Today, though, her attention was riveted to the field. Whether that was because she was here in person and that made the experience more vivid for her, or whether it was because her feelings for Flynn were growing, she wasn't certain.

Either way, it was kickoff time and she so hoped Flynn and the Sabers had a good game.

IT WASN'T OFTEN THAT FLYNN GOT TO PLAY AGAINST his brother, especially on his home turf. He loved Grant, and he knew his brother loved him, too, but once on the field, they were just competitors. And both of them would do anything to win, no matter what it cost the other.

After the kickoff, the Sabers got the ball first, which meant Flynn would have to cool it on the sidelines while Mick Riley and the Sabers offense went to work.

Mick was efficient as ever, chewing up yardage with good passes. The run game was on point, too, and with six minutes off the clock they were in the red zone on the eighteen-yard line.

Flynn and the rest of the defensive players stayed out of the way but kept their bodies limber by moving around behind the benches. And when Mick threw a sharp touchdown pass to Ernie Truskey, their tight end, the entire Sabers sideline cheered, along with everyone in the stadium.

It had been textbook Riley, and Mick got lots of head slaps on his way back.

After the extra point, Flynn and his defense huddled with the defensive coordinator to work out their strategy for this series while the special teams prepared for the kickoff.

St. Louis would have the ball on the twenty-two-yard line.

It was time for Flynn and the defense to work some magic.

After the huddle, he lined up on the right side, breathing in the smell of fresh turf. Turf smelled like winning to him and he could never get enough of it.

He dug his knuckles into the grass and focused only on the player in front of him. That was his target, the player who stood in the way of him getting to the quarterback.

At the snap he pushed off and went head to head with the offensive lineman, who managed to hold him back long enough for Grant to get off a short pass to the wide receiver on the left side. Grant made a quick turn in time to see Junior take the receiver down after a short five-yard gain.

Good enough.

They huddled, then lined up again. This time it was a run through the middle and Flynn piled onto the runner, who ended up with no gain.

Now it was third down and this was the key to stopping the Traders' drive.

"It's third and five," Flynn said in the huddle. "It could go either pass or run, so be ready for it with man-to-man."

They'd gotten their instructions from the sidelines, so they knew what they had to do.

They broke and lined up in man coverage, expecting anything. When Grant dropped back to pass, Flynn pushed off and broke around the lineman, heading straight for the quarterback. Grant danced around him and threw the pass a fraction of a second before Flynn could get to him.

The pass was incomplete. Fourth down.

Grant shot him a glare. Flynn grinned.

The Traders would have to punt, so it was a damn satisfying series. Anything that kept the Traders from the end zone was a win in his book.

They traded back and forth the next several series, with no one scoring. But Flynn had a goal in this game, and that meant getting

to his brother. So far, that hadn't happened and by the end of the
first half Flynn's team was up by one touchdown. That meant
defense was tough on both sides, which suited Flynn just fine. He
liked a hard-fought defensive game.

He'd like it better if the Sabers put more points on the board in
the second half, something their coach pounded into the offense
when they hit the locker room during halftime.

"We've got a lot to be proud of," Flynn said to the defensive
line while they took a breather at halftime. "We've held them
scoreless. Let's keep that momentum going in the second half."

"You know you want to shove your brother into the ground,"
Hey Man said with a grin.

"Well, yeah. But to be honest, it's important to keep our heads
in the game. I know Grant is their quarterback, but to me he's just
like any other quarterback. If one of us—any of us—get to him for
a sack, that's icing. The most important thing is winning the
game. Let's keep our minds focused on that."

He wasn't going to let himself get distracted about having his
brother on the other side of the ball. He wanted to make sure the
other players stayed the same way.

So when they took to the field at the second half, he knew the
defense was determined to keep it a scoreless game for the Traders.
The crowd was fired up, and so was the defense. He got into position
and pushed off the offensive lineman, heading straight for Grant.

His brother had good feet, though, and Flynn only grabbed a
piece of Grant's jersey before Grant sprinted out of his grasp. But
he had to throw the ball away for an incomplete pass that left them
with a second and ten.

Flynn felt the tension rising as Grant came under center and
handed off to the running back. They smothered the back behind
the line of scrimmage for a loss of yardage, which left the Traders

with a third and long. Grant would have to pass on this down and the defense would come in with a hard pass rush this time.

And this time, Flynn blitzed past the lineman. He had Grant in his sights. So did Junior on the other side. Grant had nowhere to go but down, and Flynn pancaked him.

"Fucker," Grant mumbled.

Flynn grinned, leaped up and held his hand down for his brother, who grudgingly let him haul him to his feet.

They shared the briefest of glances, but Grant eventually grinned back at him.

"I'm going to burn you all for a touchdown later," Grant said, pulling turf out of his helmet.

Flynn laughed. "Doubtful."

As he walked off the field to wild cheers from the stadium, Flynn was elated. But the game was far from over. And true to his word, Grant threw a long pass early in the fourth quarter to his best wide receiver, who outran the Sabers corner for a touchdown.

Fuck.

Okay, so there'd be no shutout today.

The Sabers recovered on their next drive when Mick drove them down the field and LaSalle ran in a touchdown from the six yard line, taking over the lead again.

So much for Grant's earlier touchdown. Flynn knew Grant would be pissed about that.

After that it was all defense, and the Sabers held the Traders, who got close to field goal range by late in the fourth quarter, but couldn't get the ball in the end zone.

The Sabers ended up winning the game, fourteen to seven.

After the game ended, Flynn found Grant on the field. They embraced, with cameras all around them, which meant they couldn't say what they really wanted to say to each other, which was a lot of trash talking. That would come later, on the phone, since Grant would have to catch a plane home right away.

"Good game," Grant said.

"You played tough. Your whole team did."

Grant grinned. "Mom still likes me better."

Flynn laughed. "You'd like to think that, wouldn't you?"

"I'll see you in a couple of weeks at the ranch. Love you."

Flynn wrapped his hand around his brother's neck, and they touched foreheads. "Love you, too."

They walked away and Flynn headed toward the locker room to celebrate with his teammates.

TWENTY

IT HAD BEEN AN EXTREMELY LONG DAY. AND AN EXHIL-arating one. For her first live game, Amelia had an amazing time. It probably helped that the Sabers had won. She and Mia had screamed uncontrollably, along with the entire room. It had been crazy in there, and so much fun. She couldn't remember ever attending a public sporting event, and if they were always like this, she wanted to do it again.

She'd also had so much food and drink she wasn't sure she was going to be able to get out of her most comfortable chair. Mia didn't seem in any hurry to move, either, since she was scrolling through her phone.

"Flynn sent us both a text message," Mia said. "He said we can ride home with him, but he's doing media interviews so we can stay put."

"Oh, good. I wasn't relishing the thought of the train. Or, actually, movement of any kind."

Mia nodded. "I know the feeling. So I guess we'll just sit here until he texts. I was thinking maybe a nap."

Amelia laughed. "I like the sound of that. Think they'll kick us out if we sprawl across several of the seats?"

"Only if we snore. You don't snore, do you?"

Amelia shrugged. "I have no idea. I don't think so. Do you?"

"I don't know since I typically sleep alone, so I get no complaints."

"Then we're good." Amelia leaned back and closed her eyes. Just for a few seconds. That wine had been so good. It was probably wise she'd stopped drinking at the end of the third quarter because she'd been caught up in the game and the excitement and the liquor had been flowing . . .

She felt the buzz of her phone and jerked awake. How long had she been out? She looked next to her to see Mia blinking her eyes open to look at her.

"Was I snoring?"

"If you were, I wasn't awake to hear it." Amelia checked her phone. "Flynn said he is heading up here."

"Oh, good." Mia stood and stretched, then looked around. "Bartender's still here."

Amelia turned. "Yeah, but he's only here because he's cleaning up. No more wine for us."

"Sad."

Amelia laughed. "I'll bet Flynn could use a beer."

"I'll bet he could. We should stop for dinner and drinks. Or . . . just drinks."

Amelia snickered.

The door opened and Flynn walked in. He had showered and was wearing jeans and a long-sleeved button-down shirt. She walked over to him and curled her fingers into his hair, which was still damp.

"You smell good," she said, lifting up on her toes to brush her lips against his.

His brows rose. "So do you."

Amelia couldn't help but get lost in the sea blue depths of his eyes.

Until Mia cleared her throat. "Hey, good game."

Amelia reluctantly stepped away so Flynn could hug his sister.

"Thanks. I don't think Grant is very happy about it."

Mia shrugged. "He'll get over it. Can't win all the games."

"It was a really good game," Amelia said. "And the way you trampled your brother—I had concerns for his health."

Flynn laughed. "He was fine."

Mia grabbed her purse. "You should see the way they all go at it when they're playing touch football on the ranch. It's much worse than that tackle Flynn laid on Grant."

"Hey," Flynn said. "You play with us on the ranch."

"I play on the periphery. In other words, I catch passes and run like hell so none of you can tackle me."

Amelia grinned. "So you're fast."

Mia nodded. "Fast enough to stay away from Flynn and my other brothers."

Amelia did not like the sound of that potential game situation. "In that case, I'll be sure to stay out of the way when I'm there this month."

"Oh, no," Flynn said. "We'll get you in the game."

"Ha." Amelia grabbed her bag and followed Flynn and Mia to the door. "I'm steering clear of you bloodthirsty Cassidys."

"You are not lumping me into that group of heathens. You and I can sit on the sidelines, drink margaritas with my mom and make fun of them."

"Sounds like a plan."

Flynn held the elevator door for them. "I will get you in the game, Amelia."

She leaned against the wall and gave him her best smile. "We'll see about that, Flynn."

When they reached the main floor and got out, Flynn led them through the complex and out one of the back doors to a parking lot. Mia climbed into the backseat of Flynn's SUV.

"We thought we'd stop for drinks somewhere, and food," Mia said.

"But mostly drinks," Amelia added.

Flynn gave both of them a look. "I think you both drank your way through my game today."

Mia shrugged. "Maybe."

They drove back to the city, and that took a while because of all the postgame traffic. But they talked about the game. Flynn asked her if she enjoyed it, and Amelia was honest in telling him she had. Even if she'd been sitting at the top of the stadium in the wind and cold, she'd have had a great time. There was something about being at a game instead of watching it on TV that was exhilarating.

"I don't know if it was the noise of the crowd, with everyone screaming every time the Sabers made a play, or the camaraderie of the group we sat with, but it was like a shared experience. So much fun, a lot of laughing."

"Don't forget the drinking," Mia added from the backseat.

Amelia laughed. "Yes, there was definitely that. And the wine was very good. Whoever makes the bar selections has superior taste."

Flynn's lips curved. "I'll be sure to pass that along to the stadium folks."

"You do that," Mia said. "Because good wine is everything in a football game."

Amelia frowned. "Who said that? Chaucer?"

"I think it was Hemingway."

"I think I should take you two home, fix you a meal with some coffee and put you both to bed."

Amelia wrinkled her nose. "Are you insane? It's still early."

"In case you forget, we played the late game today. It's already dark outside."

Amelia craned her neck to look out the window. "Is not."

Flynn laughed. "You're drunk."

"She totally is," Mia said. "I can attest to that."

"You're drunk, too," Flynn said. "I think we'll order pizza."

"Oooh," Mia said. "I love pizza."

Amelia twisted in her seat so she could face Mia. "Me, too. What kind should we have?"

"Sausage. With mushrooms."

"Now I'm hungry. How could I be hungry? We ate so much food."

Mia shrugged. "I dunno. But I'm hungry."

FLYNN ROLLED HIS EYES FOR THE MILLIONTH TIME AS Amelia and his sister ventured into yet another ridiculous topic, this time which of the "Real Housewives" of Beverly Hills was the biggest bitch. He had no idea who the housewives were or what they were talking about.

All he knew was that he was damn happy when he pulled into the driveway of the house. The two of them had babbled nonstop at each other the entire way home, mostly about nonsensical stuff. For God's sake, they'd spent twenty minutes dissecting nail polish colors.

Then again, that topic had been better than the female things. They'd even discussed their periods and cramps and tampons. In front of him. As if he wasn't even there. And one of the women in the car was his sister.

This was stuff he did *not* need to know about.

"I'm ordering pizza," he said as he whipped out his phone. "Tell me what you want."

"Sausage and mushroom," Mia said.

Amelia nodded. "Sounds good to me."

He ordered a pizza for them and another for himself. He was hungry and figured they could split one and he could have another for himself. While the two of them poured iced tea—thankfully nothing alcoholic—from the fridge, he grabbed a beer.

He definitely deserved a beer. Or maybe five. It had been a hard-fought battle on the field, and then a long drive home.

He laid his phone on the counter and headed into the living room.

"So then he said to me—'Oh, babe, I don't like to eat pussy.' Like I was supposed to be okay with that?"

"What an asshole," Amelia said. "And he thought it was okay for you to give him a blowjob, but he wouldn't return the favor by going down on you? I assume you ended it after that."

"You have never seen a woman kick a guy out of her bed faster."

Flynn blinked listening to the conversation between his girlfriend and his sister, turned around and walked out of the room.

He even considered leaving the house entirely, but pizza was on the way. So he wandered upstairs and answered some e-mails and texts on his phone until he heard the pizza guy pull up in the driveway. He figured it was safe to come downstairs then, so he paid for the pizza and they all sat and ate at the kitchen island.

"Where did you disappear to?" Mia asked.

"Upstairs. Had to answer some e-mails."

"Oh, okay."

He wasn't about to tell them he'd run like hell when they'd gotten into sex talk. He wasn't shy about sex by any means. And he sure as hell would love to talk sex with Amelia. But with his sister around? That was a big N-O. He knew she was of age and no doubt had an active sex life, just like any normal, healthy woman. But to be in the middle of two women discussing oral sex, one of those women being his sister?

He intended to nope the hell out of that one for the rest of his life.

Fortunately, right now they were both stuffing their faces, so neither of them were talking, which suited him just fine.

After they ate, Mia put her plate and glass in the dishwasher. "I need to pack."

Amelia frowned. "You're heading back to Texas tomorrow?"

"Unfortunately, yes. Fortunately, though, I'll see you in just a couple of weeks."

Amelia slid out of her seat and pulled Mia into a hug. "I'll miss you. Text me."

"I will. I want that recipe for the corn chowder."

"I'll e-mail it to you."

"Awesome."

Flynn looked over at Mia. "I'll probably drive Amelia home, so I'll be back later."

Mia nodded. "Not a problem. I intend to pack, then I'm going to put on my pajamas and pass out. So I'll see you in the morning."

"Okay. Good night."

"Good night, Mia," Amelia said.

"Night."

After Mia walked out, Amelia looked at him. "Is that my cue that you'd like me to hurry up and finish my pizza?"

"No. It was me telling my sister that if she happened to wander back over here, I might be gone."

"Good. Because I intend to finish this piece. It's really good."

He ended up eating another slice of pizza, too.

"I'm glad you get along so well with Mia."

She gave him a quizzical look. "I love your sister. Why wouldn't I get along with her?"

"I didn't mean it like I was surprised or anything. It just makes me happy. My girlfriend and my sister get along. You know. It's like a good thing."

She crinkled her nose. "Oh. I see. And now I'm your girlfriend? First we were just dating."

"Are you being cranky or is that some kind of problem?"

"Which part? The girlfriend or the dating?"

He rolled his eyes. "Both, I guess. Which part were you talking about?"

"Neither. I just didn't know I was your girlfriend. Then again, I didn't know we were dating, either, until you told me."

Amelia confused him. "Okay. I'm . . . sorry?"

"You don't sound sorry."

It had been a long day. He was tired. He knew Amelia was probably tired, too, and this was the wrong damn time to have this conversation. But now he was irritated. "So because I called you my girlfriend I've pissed you off."

"No . . . I don't know. Maybe. Maybe I'd just like to be asked once in a while instead of told."

Flynn dragged his fingers through his hair and dragged in a deep breath, then let it out. "Okay, so you don't want to be called my girlfriend. How about the woman I'm fucking?"

She leveled a glare at him. "Now, that was insulting."

He widened his arms. "Then I don't know how to talk about us, Amelia. What do you want from me?"

"I don't want anything from you, Flynn. We're just going out. We're having some fun together. Isn't that enough? Why do we have to put labels on it? Why do you have to attach yourself to me? Or why can't we talk about it before you announce that I'm your girlfriend? You don't own me, you know."

And now it was ownership. He had no idea how this conversation had taken such a wrong turn. He'd had enough and before things got ugly between them he needed to put a stop to it. "Okay, I think I should take you home."

"That sounds like a really good idea." She got up and grabbed her purse and headed toward the door, obviously as ready for some separation as he was.

They went outside and it was clear she didn't want to be anywhere near him, because she shot around to the passenger side of the SUV in a hurry, so he didn't even bother trying to go over there to open the door for her. Instead, he slid into the driver's side.

The short drive to her place was made in tense silence. When he pulled in front of her house, Flynn struggled to say something, anything to break the tension between them. But Amelia unbuckled her seat belt and opened her door, apparently in a hurry to get away from him.

"Thanks for letting me come to the game today. I had a good time."

"You're welcome."

"Good night, Flynn." She shut the door and headed inside her house without even a backward glance.

He thought maybe the short drive would have cooled off her temper. He guessed not.

Fine. This wasn't his fault. Calling Amelia his girlfriend wasn't some kind of crime. He put the car in gear and headed home.

TWENTY-ONE

AMELIA STARED INTO HER CUP OF COFFEE, LOOKING for answers. Or maybe a cure for the raging headache that throbbed incessantly between her temples.

Never again was she going to drink that much wine, because it obviously made her behave like a complete bitch.

She was so glad today was her day off, because if she had to go to work tonight it would be brutal.

She'd come home last night, tossed her purse on the sofa, then opened a bottle and had yet another glass, which had only ended up tasting sour to her. In the end, she'd gone to bed but had been unable to sleep, convinced she'd been in the right. Her subconscious, on the other hand, had other ideas. She'd lain awake for hours, unable to sleep while she'd replayed the conversation between Flynn and her.

So he'd called her his girlfriend. Why had that irritated her so much? She'd spent several hours staring at the dark ceiling of her bedroom last night trying to figure that out.

She'd been leery of relationships ever since her divorce. The last thing she'd wanted was to tumble into yet another relationship with a man who'd want to control her. So maybe Flynn's labeling of her as his girlfriend triggered something that made her uncomfortable, and she hadn't even realized it. Then, subconsciously, she'd lashed out at him for no reason at all. Because if there was one thing she knew, it was that Flynn was nothing like her ex-husband. He was kind and encouraging and not at all controlling.

She heaved a sigh, then took another sip of coffee.

She owed Flynn a huge apology. If he intended to ever speak to her again.

When her phone buzzed, she reached across the table to check it. Surprisingly, it was a text from Flynn.

Are you awake yet?

She smiled and texted back. *Having coffee. What are you doing?*

Just got home from taking Mia to the airport.

At least he was speaking to her. That was a good sign.

If you're not busy, would you like to come by for coffee? She texted back to him, then waited, chewing on her bottom lip.

Be there in 10 mins.

She hadn't realized she was holding her breath on his reply until she received it. She exhaled, then dashed into the downstairs bathroom to examine herself. She'd showered when she first got up to see if that would help jolt her awake, so her hair, though kind of a mess, was at least clean, as was the rest of her. But she definitely looked like she hadn't slept last night. There were dark circles under her eyes and she didn't have time to make herself look presentable.

With a sigh, she turned off the bathroom light and went to brew more coffee. She wondered if Flynn had eaten breakfast this morning. If not, she could—

He knocked at the door so she went to answer it. Her heart

pounded as she took in the sight of him wearing a dark blue pea-coat and black jeans. It was cold out this morning so she shut the door after him in a hurry.

"Hey," he said.

"Hey. I made coffee. Take your coat off and come have some."

"Okay, thanks."

He followed her into the kitchen. She poured a cup of coffee and handed it to him.

"Thanks." He wrapped his hands around the mug.

"It's cloudy and cold outside today," she said, feeling ridiculous for talking about the weather.

"Yeah. Looks like it could rain."

At least he'd jumped all over the weather conversation. But since she'd started their fight, and he'd been nice enough to text her this morning, it was up to her to break the icy wall between them. "Flynn. About last night."

"Yeah, about that. Look, Amelia. I'm really sorry. I assumed our relationship and that's on me."

"No. You didn't do anything wrong. I had too much to drink, and then my mouth opened and everything awful came out. I did a lot of thinking and not sleeping last night and I came to the realization that I thought you were trying to control me. Which, by the way, you weren't. I guess it was ghosts of the ex coming back to haunt me and I was being overly sensitive. Which, by the way, is no excuse. So I'm the one who's sorry. I was out of line. Like . . . really out of line."

He came over to her and swept his hand over her hair. "It's okay. You're entitled. You had a bad experience and it's all right if that affects you every now and then. Now, can you forgive me for not reacting well?"

"Given how shitty I behaved, there's nothing to forgive. I'm surprised you're even speaking to me. Frankly, I'm shocked you didn't fire me."

He frowned. "Amelia. Let's get one thing straight right now. Our relationship is now and always will be separate from the job. One has nothing to do with the other. You could tell me right now to go fuck myself and you'll still have a job tomorrow. You understand?"

She nodded. "Yes."

"Okay."

She appreciated the line of demarcation separating their personal relationship from their work relationship. And he'd given her a really nice out considering her bad behavior from yesterday. She laid her forehead against his chest. "Thank you for understanding about yesterday."

He put his coffee cup down on the kitchen island, then tipped her chin up with his finger. "So we're okay now?"

She smiled at him. "Yes, we're okay now."

He leaned down and pressed his lips to hers. This was what she needed, that affirmation of affection, of warmth between them. She'd felt so awful last night and this morning, not only because of how she'd behaved, but also because she'd missed him. She was grateful to find him so understanding.

And now, as he pulled her against him, she wanted to show him how much she appreciated him as a man. She leaned into him, pressing her body against his hard muscle, drawing in his strength as he deepened the kiss. When he let his hand roam down her back to cup her butt and draw her sex closer to his rigid erection, she moaned against his lips.

He pulled back. "I need to fuck you."

She nodded, every part of her trembling with the same need. "Yes. Right now."

She thought he'd take her hand and lead her to the bedroom. Instead, he swept her sweater off her shoulders and laid it on the bar stool, then pulled her tank top off, filling his hands with her breasts. His mouth was next and she whimpered at the heat and wetness as he sucked her nipple. She held on to his arms as he took her to that place where every part of her quivered with awareness.

When he popped her nipple out of his mouth, he took her lips in a scorching kiss that only heated her desire to flaming levels.

He quickly removed his shirt, then toed off his tennis shoes and shrugged out of his jeans and boxers, leaving him standing in her kitchen oh so erect and incredibly gorgeous.

He kneeled on the floor to pull her sweats down and followed through with her underwear. But instead of standing, he leaned in and swiped his tongue across her sex.

She reached for the counter for support as he buried his tongue inside of her.

"Flynn." His name fell as a needy, desperate whisper from her mouth. And when he moved from her pussy to her clit, using his tongue to tease and torture her until her legs were shaking, she leaned both elbows against the counter and spread her legs, giving him better access.

His reply to that was to hum against her, the sound and sensation flooding her senses until she couldn't stand it any longer. She came with a rush and cry, shoving her sex against his face, demanding her orgasm from him.

And oh, did he ever give it to her. He wrapped his arm around her buttocks and held tight to her as he buried his face against her while she came. Her climax obliterated her senses so hard she thought she might collapse onto the floor. Thankfully she had the counter and Flynn for support.

When he stood, he kissed her, this time a slow, languorous kiss that sent her from simmer to fiery hot all over again.

He turned her around and bent her over the counter, then fished into the pocket of his jeans for a condom.

She looked at him over her shoulder, looked at the condom in his hand and gave him a crooked smile. "Sure thing?"

He leaned over her and nipped at her shoulder. "Babe, you are anything but a sure thing."

She liked the sound of that.

He put the condom on, moved in between her legs and smoothed his hand over her hip.

"You came good."

She made a murmuring sound of approval. "Hell yes I did."

"Do it again." He slid into her with a slow, easy glide that made goose bumps pop onto her skin.

She grasped the counter as he moved within her with slow, measured movements.

"Tell me what feels good for you," he said.

"This feels good. Just like this."

He swept his hand around to fondle her breasts, to tease and pluck her nipples. The sensations took her breath away, making her push back against him.

"Oh, yeah," he said. "Now, that's what I like. Push yourself onto my cock."

She loved hearing him talk. The sound of Flynn's deep voice was an aphrodisiac all on its own. And when he moved inside of her and spoke to her, encouraging her with whispered, naughty words, all she wanted to do was come.

She reached between her legs to rub her clit. As she moved her hand over the bud, her pussy tightened around Flynn's shaft.

"That's it," Flynn said. "Make yourself come. Make me come, too."

He drove into her with precise movements, using his cock, his hands and his mouth to take her right to the edge. She used her own hand to soar right over.

"I'm coming," she said, tilting her head back and rocking against his cock as she shook all over with her orgasm.

Flynn gripped her hips and thrust faster, then groaned as he drove deeply into her again and again as he came.

She was out of breath when she came down from that amazing, quivering high.

Flynn scooped his arm around her and pulled her upright, then withdrew, turned her around and cupped the side of her face with his hand.

"I can barely breathe," she said, grinning.

"Ditto."

He kissed her, this time a soft, gentle kiss that sent those familiar quakes dancing around in her stomach.

He took her hand and they went to the bedroom. After he disposed of the condom, they climbed into bed.

"I don't know about you, but I didn't sleep much last night," she said.

He curled up behind her and kissed the side of her neck. "You don't have anything to do today, do you?"

She yawned. "Nothing super important. Just laundry and paying bills and . . . things."

She wasn't sure she finished the sentence before she was asleep.

AMELIA WOKE WITH A START. SHE LOOKED BEHIND her. The bed was empty. The clock on the wall in her bedroom said it was noon. She'd slept for two hours.

Okay, then. She did feel a lot better after that nap. She stretched, got up and went to the bathroom, then threw on underwear and a tank top and wandered down the hall to look for Flynn.

When she entered the kitchen, she halted mid stride.

Flynn was standing at her stove, cooking . . . something. While naked and wearing one of her aprons.

Now, that was a sight Amelia didn't see every day. Or ever. A gorgeous, tattooed, apron-wearing naked man cooking in her kitchen.

She walked into the kitchen, trying to be as quiet as possible as she moved in behind Flynn. She scooped her arms around him. "Did anyone ever tell you that your ass looks amazing in an apron?"

He looked over his shoulder at her and grinned. "All the time."

She cocked a smile at him. "What are you doing?"

"Cooking."

She rolled her eyes. "Obviously. Looks like eggs Benedict. And asparagus."

"I already did a Caprese salad. That's in the fridge."

Her stomach rumbled. "Now I'm starving."

"I figured you might be hungry. I was about to wake you up."

"Wearing that getup, I hope."

He laughed. "Maybe. Now that I know naked apron-wearing guys are such a turn-on for you, I'm going to have to buy one."

She went to grab the salad and her pitcher of iced tea out of the fridge. "Why buy one, when my pink and black teapot apron looks so good on you?"

He grabbed a plate and started preparing the main course. "You have a point. Fine. I'm keeping this one. It makes my eyes stand out, doesn't it?"

"No, it makes your ass stand out." She poured two glasses of iced tea.

He brought a plate over and placed it in front of her, then grabbed his and set it on the island. "I'll be right back."

While he was gone, she served up the Caprese salad on both of their plates and pulled out silverware. When Flynn came back into the room, he was wearing his jeans.

"Now I'm sad. I was so enjoying the apron show."

He pulled up a seat at the island. "I'm sure you were. But I don't think you want my naked ass on your cloth seats."

She took a napkin and set it on her lap. "I'm happy for you to place your naked ass wherever you want."

He lifted his gaze to hers and shot a hot smile at her. "And how about your naked ass, Amelia?"

She shrugged. "I don't know, Flynn. What would you like to do with my naked ass?"

He lifted his fork. "This conversation is making my dick hard. I'm filing it away for future reference."

"You do that." She knew the feeling. Just discussing sex of any kind with Flynn made her belly—and other parts south—quiver. She was so incredibly sexually attracted to him.

But there was so much more depth to him. Like this meal, for example. She was certainly hungry, but she also took the time to savor each bite of the Canadian bacon, poached egg and biscuit. And the hollandaise sauce was creamy and delicious.

"You didn't use the store-bought biscuits I had in the fridge."

He frowned. "Bite your tongue, woman. That's fine if you want to slather some butter and jelly on them. But for this you need scratch biscuits."

"You are a man after my own heart, Flynn Cassidy."

He gave her a look she didn't quite know how to decipher. Something between a smile and a look of confusion.

Then again, it didn't surprise her since their relationship was often confusing to her. Last night she'd been an utter bitch to him. This morning there'd been hot sex. And now he'd cooked for her. He was smart and focused and talented and ridiculously good-looking, not to mention panty-dropping sexy. He was oh-dear-God fine in the sack, too. The man knew his way around a woman's body.

Was she crazy to be so wary of a relationship with him considering he was maybe the perfect man?

No. No man was perfect. Flynn certainly had flaws. She just hadn't seen them yet.

"You're kind of quiet over there."

She lifted her gaze to his, along with her fork. "Stuffing my face over here. And thank you for fixing food for me. Not only food, but delicious food."

He shrugged. "I know basic stuff, nothing fancy. And you're welcome."

"Don't downgrade your abilities in the kitchen, Flynn. You could have whipped up some scrambled eggs and toast, but you didn't. This is fancy."

"Thanks."

Amelia got an inkling that maybe Flynn enjoyed cooking more than he let on. That maybe he wanted to cook more than he let anyone know. For a guy, especially a guy whose job it wasn't to be a chef or a cook of any kind, dabbling in the culinary arts could—to some people—maybe seem less than masculine.

Which, to her, and to a lot of people, was utterly ridiculous. Times had most definitely changed and everyone loved cooking now, from men to women to children. But coming at it from Flynn's perspective, here was a man who played football in a very highly testosterone-laden environment. He had three brothers. It could possibly be that he didn't want to give the impression that cooking was his passion.

Which was okay, but she knew he loved Ninety-Two. No reason not to love the cooking part of it as well. She could see him becoming more involved behind the scenes there. She wasn't some crazy chef who didn't let anyone into her kitchen. Flynn was the owner. If he wanted to come in and dabble . . .

"So, you love cooking."

He looked up at her. "I like it, yeah. Why?"

She leaned back in the chair, trying to take the easy, no-big-deal approach. "I think you like it more than you let on. Plus, you're a great cook, Flynn."

"Thanks. Like I said, I dabble and I can whip up some things, but it's not like it's my career. That's your career."

"Very true. I was wondering, though, if you wouldn't want to learn . . . more."

He frowned. "More what?"

"More about cooking. Especially as it relates to Ninety-Two. I realize you like to eat and you're very involved in Ninety-Two's menu, but wouldn't it be fun when you're in town and not at practice if you, let's say, stepped into the kitchen at Ninety-Two and did some dabbling now and then?"

He cocked a brow. "Trying to put me to work, Amelia?"

She laughed. "Not at all. I just think you have a lot to offer your guests."

"Like what? Burned caramelized tuna?"

She gave him the side eye. "Please. As if that would ever happen. As if I would allow it to happen in my kitchen."

He shrugged. "I don't know. Maybe. I'd have to think about it."

"Sure. Okay." She didn't want to push him, so she went back to finishing her meal. But then the best idea ever occurred to her.

"Oh. Flynn. I have such a great idea."

He smiled at her. "Is it sex related? Do you get to wear the apron naked now?"

She laughed. "No, it's not sex related. It goes back to you cooking at Ninety-Two."

"Okay."

"What if you developed a signature dish that we could put on the menu? We could call it the Cassidy, and indicate that you developed the dish."

He gave her a dubious look. "Oh, sure. No pressure there, Amelia."

"Oh, come on. You have great ideas. I'm sure you'd come up with something amazing. And it would be incredible PR for Ninety-Two."

He looked at her, then nodded. "Yeah, it would, wouldn't it? It's not the worst idea ever."

"Wow, thanks so much for that vote of confidence."

He cracked a smile. "I didn't mean that. It's actually a pretty amazing idea. I'm only sorry I didn't think of it first."

She laughed. "Jerk."

After they finished eating, they did dishes and put away the pots and pans.

"I noticed you had some cookbook notes out on the island," Flynn said after they finished drying the last pot and Amelia put it away in the drawer.

She gave him a look. "Yeah, just something I'm doodling on in my off hours."

"I saw the recipes. I wasn't snooping or anything, they were just lying there so I took a peek."

"It's okay. I wasn't trying to hide it."

"Good. Anyway, they look delicious. Are you trying to publish it?"

"Not really. Like I've told you before, cooking relaxes me. So I like to work out some recipes that are in my head, create them and see how they taste. If they're a success, I write them down. I don't know that I'll ever do anything with them. Maybe someday I'll pass the collection on to my kids." She smiled at him.

He smiled back. "Or you could publish it. You're a great chef, Amelia."

She laughed. "There are a lot of good chefs out there, Flynn. And do you know how difficult it is to get a cookbook published? I mean, yes, I could self-publish it and maybe Laura would buy a copy and maybe a few other people I know. No, thanks, I don't need that kind of rejection in my life."

"Hey." He smoothed his hand down her arm. "You're good. Really good. And I don't think you give yourself enough credit. We could always have copies printed and make them for sale at Ninety-Two."

She shook her head. "That's muddying the waters. Ninety-Two is about you. Not me. Let's keep it that way."

"Okay. But if you do decide to publish your cookbook, you have my full support."

She looked at him, and something in that belly region fluttered again. "Thank you, Flynn. It's been a long time since someone supported me."

"You're welcome. Now, what do you have planned for the day?"

"Nothing really. House chores."

He leaned back in the chair. "I could get into watching you vacuum."

"Funny. More like doing laundry and paying bills."

He wrinkled his nose. "No fun there. That doesn't even sound sexy. Unless you want to have sex on top of a pile of dirty laundry."

She laughed. "You would do that, wouldn't you?"

"Hey, I'm game for anything. Or anywhere. As long as it's with you." He leaned over and rubbed his hand over her thigh. And damn if it didn't perk up all her nerve endings.

She could while away the entire day in bed with Flynn if she allowed herself the luxury. Unfortunately, there was a lot more on her to-do list for today than just the two items she'd told him about. So she slid out of her chair and moved away from him. "Sorry. I also have to go to the bank, run to the grocery store and get a manicure and pedicure. Hey, have you ever had a mani-pedi? You could come with me."

He gave her a horrified look. "That is definitely my cue to leave."

"No way. You'd look cute with pink painted toes. They'd match your apron."

"Funny." He grabbed his shirt and drew it on, then put on his socks and tennis shoes. She walked him to the door and handed him his coat.

He pulled her against him. "Thanks for this morning. For the nap. And everything in between."

She kissed him, letting the kiss linger, regretting that she couldn't spend the day in bed with him, especially when his hands wandered over her butt. Yeah, he definitely had her number there. With a sigh, she stepped back. "And thank you for making brunch for me."

"I'll call you later."

"I'd like that. Bye, Flynn."

She watched him leave, and with great regret, went to the kitchen island and grabbed her notebook so she could start making out her list of things to do for the day. Maybe if she finished early enough she and Flynn could have dinner—or something—together later.

She smiled at the thought of what that "something" might be.

Now, that was something to look forward to.

TWENTY-TWO

THE TEAM HAD FINISHED UP PRACTICE EARLY, AND since he had an out-of-town game that weekend, Flynn wanted to stop by and see Amelia. They had spent nearly every day together for the past week, either her staying at his place or him coming by after she got off work to spend the night at hers.

They were getting closer and he liked it. When she wasn't with him he missed her. He was getting used to waking up with her warm body nestled against his and the scent of her hair against his nose.

It was a good thing.

He knocked on her door and she opened it with a smile. Her smile always made something in the region of his gut tighten.

"Hey. Your hair is wet."

"I just got out of the shower. Come on in."

He shed his jacket and hung it on the rack he'd installed for her one night last week after they'd discussed how she didn't have a coat closet or a coat rack. So they'd gone shopping and she'd picked out a simple wooden board with hanging pegs that she said would work fine for coats because it didn't take up a lot of space.

At least now there was a spot for hanging coats in her living room. They'd made fun of each other for being domestic and shopping for house things together like a couple. He wasn't sure if she was making light of it because she thought it was funny, or because it genuinely freaked her out. So he made sure to keep it fun and uneventful so it didn't seem like a big deal.

Baby steps. He knew how much Amelia's ex had screwed with her head and he didn't want to put any pressure on her. He wasn't going anywhere.

"What time do you have to be at work?" he asked as he followed her into the kitchen.

"Four."

He looked at his phone. It was three. Not enough time. There was never enough time.

She turned and looked at him. "What are you doing the rest of the day today?"

"Not much."

"You should come to work with me and cook."

He cocked a brow. "Why? Are you shorthanded?"

She laughed. "No. I meant you should work on your signature dish."

"Oh." He pondered the thought. "I wouldn't be in your way?"

"Of course not. Plus, it's your restaurant. I promise you we'll make room for you and stay out of your way. And you'd have me to assist you."

"Okay, I'll do that."

"Awesome. Now I'm excited."

He came closer and put his arms around her. "And you weren't excited about going to work before? I might have to report this to your boss."

She wound a hand around his neck and pulled his mouth close to hers. "Asshole," she whispered against his lips before kissing him.

There was something about having Amelia's body next to his that fired him up faster and hotter than blitzing an offensive lineman on a short third down. And when she pressed in closer against him, aligning her body with his, he was ready for action, his cock going hard.

He pulled back and searched her face. "Enough time?"

"Not if you keep talking." With a sexy smile, she reached for the button of his jeans, then shoved the denim down his hips. When she reached into his boxers and pulled his cock out, then began stroking his shaft, he groaned.

Obviously she was in need as much as he was, fired up as much as him. One of the things he liked a lot about her was the way her sex drive matched his.

Okay, he liked a lot of things about her that had nothing to do with sex. This was just a bonus.

Fortunately, she was still in her robe, so he untied the sash and pulled it aside so he could put his mouth on her nipples. She whimpered and tangled her fingers in his hair, tugging hard on it when he sucked a nipple into his mouth.

His cock tightened.

"No foreplay," she said. "I need you inside me."

He all but dragged her into the bedroom. She threw off her robe and he fished a condom out of the box in her nightstand drawer. She lay on the bed and spread her legs, sliding her fingers over her sex. He was pretty sure the strangled sound he heard came from him as he stared down at the beautiful woman lying on the bed, her legs spread as she teased her fingers over her pussy.

He grasped his cock in his hand and stroked it, watching her attention shoot toward the movements of his cock.

"I love watching that," she said. "Seeing you jack yourself off is such a turn-on for me."

"Does it make you wet?"

She dipped her finger into her own moisture and used it to coat the bud of her clit. "Oh, yes."

"Show me how you do it. Show me what you do when you're alone."

Her gaze went from curious to wickedly hot in a second. "I will if you will. Come closer."

He complied quickly and with much pleasure as it gave him an even better view of what she was doing with her fingers. And when she dipped one inside her pussy, his balls drew up and he tightened his fist around his cock.

"It's like watching a live version of porn, right in front of me," she said, lifting her feet and planting them on the bed. She arched her hips and the smell of sex filled her bedroom.

"Yeah. Do you have any idea how hot it is watching a woman touch herself?" As he increased the movements of his hand over his shaft, sweat beaded in the small of his back and around his temples. He could so easily come, could already envision jettisoning a stream over her belly. Now, that was a porn fantasy. He wanted to be buried inside of her, to feel her hot walls quivering and squeezing him when he came. But this—watching her as she moaned, her eyes closing as she lost herself in what she was doing—this was worth jacking off to.

Her lids lifted and the lazy, sensual look she gave him nearly undid him.

"Tell me when you're ready," she said, her voice soft and filled with desire.

"I'm ready when you are. Trust me, babe, when you come, so will I."

She reached up to tease her breast with the tip of her finger. "Here? On me?"

"Is that what you want?"

"Yes. I want to watch come spurt from your cock. All over me."

Christ, she was driving him crazy. "Scoot to the edge of the bed."

She adjusted her body accordingly. It was positioned perfectly and his desire soared. "Oh. Yes. I'm ready. And I need to see you come."

Her fingers moved faster in and out of her pussy and she used her thumb to tease the crest of her clit.

"That's it, baby. Make yourself come. Make me come." He was sweating now, and doing whatever it took to hold back. Because he was drawn up so damn tight his legs were shaking.

"I'm coming, Flynn. I'm coming."

She cried out, and it was the sweetest sound and the hottest thing he'd ever seen, watching her thrash around on the mattress with her orgasm. He couldn't hold back as a stream of come spurted forth from his cock and onto her breasts. He jerked uncontrollably as his orgasm jettisoned from him and onto her sweet creamy flesh. And when she slid her fingers into his come and rubbed it over her nipples, he felt light-headed and more turned on than he could remember being in a long damn time.

Out of breath, he leaned down and brushed his lips over hers, then deepened the kiss, wishing they had all damn day to play together.

"Mmm," she finally said. "I wish we had more time."

"My thoughts exactly."

"But now I need to clean up—again."

He grinned down at her. "Sorry about that."

"Don't be sorry. That was amazing."

He moved aside, then held out his hand and helped her up off the bed. They went into the bathroom together and washed up. He left Amelia alone to get ready while he dressed and went to the kitchen to find something cold to drink. He poured both of them a glass of ice water.

"I could definitely use that," she said, accepting the glass of water from him after she came out of the bedroom. "You made me thirsty."

"You make me horny. Like all the damn time, Amelia."

She laughed, wound her hair up in a bun and stuck a couple of hairpins into it. "You ready?"

"For more sex? Hell yeah. Let's do it."

She laughed. "No. To go to work. Though I like your idea better."

He leaned in and pressed his lips to hers, lingering a bit as she met him and kissed him back. His cock twitched and came to life again. "I am the owner, ya know. You could call in sick with no repercussions."

Unfortunately, she pulled back and drank more water. "Ha. That's not my style. Plus, I love my job."

"Fine, then. I'm ready to leave. As soon as my hard-on goes away."

She looked down at him, then smiled. "I'll keep that in mind for after work."

"Yeah, you do that."

He grabbed his coat and let Amelia walk out the door, then shut it behind him. He followed her to Ninety-Two and parked near her, a couple of blocks down the street from the restaurant. He met her at her car, then took her hand.

She looked down where their hands were clasped. "Are you sure that's a good idea?"

"Holding hands? Always a good idea."

"No. Your employees seeing us holding hands."

"You got a problem with holding my hand?"

"I don't have a problem with it, but some of your employees might see favoritism in this. And that could be an issue for me."

He wanted to argue about it, but the logical side of him saw her point, so when they got closer to the restaurant he let go of her hand.

She turned to face him. "Thank you for understanding and for not making a big deal out of it."

"Hey, the last thing you need are disgruntled cooks."

She laughed. "So true."

"You go on inside. I think I'll head to the market and buy the ingredients I'll need to cook tonight."

She wrinkled her brows. "You're just giving me a head start so no one sees us walking in together."

"Would I do that?"

"You would, and I'd kiss you for that except we're too close to the restaurant and someone might see us. So imagine me kissing you."

"If I think about you kissing me right now, my imagination will go a little crazy and then my dick will get hard and then I'll have to go sit in my car."

She laughed. "I'll see you inside."

She walked through the door and he went down the street where there was a great fish market. He already had an idea of what he wanted to make, so he purchased some sea bass and lobster, then headed back to the restaurant. When he entered, he greeted Clifford, the manager on duty, since Ken was still out on leave.

"Hey, boss," Clifford said. "Didn't expect to see you here tonight."

"It was a spur of the moment thing. I'm going to be in the kitchen if someone needs me."

Clifford didn't even blink or ask questions about why the owner was going to the kitchen. Which suited him just fine because explaining it might be awkward. "Sure thing."

Flynn stopped in the kitchen long enough to put his purchases in the refrigerator, then washed his hands and headed back onto the main floor to say hello to some of the regular guests. That took about a half hour. When he was satisfied he'd done his PR job, he returned to the kitchen to see that Amelia had things well under way.

"Mind if I step in?"

Amelia did a fine job of acting as if this was the first time she'd seen him today. She smiled at him. "Oh, hello, Flynn. You're more than welcome to come in. Would you like to see what's on the menu for tonight?"

"Sure." He walked around and greeted everyone, tasted a few things then went back to Amelia.

"I was thinking of trying out a dish. I actually stopped at the market to buy some things. Mind if I cook in here tonight?"

"Not at all. What would you like to fix?"

"Pan-seared sea bass with lobster risotto. And maybe snap peas."

She grinned and nodded. "That sounds amazing. Do you need some help?"

"No, I think I know what I'm doing, but you'll be the first person I yell to for help if I screw it up."

She laughed. "Sure. You can work over on the left side burners near where I cook."

"So you can keep an eye on me and make sure I don't burn your kitchen down?"

She fought a smile. "Something like that."

"Thanks."

Flynn washed up and got started with the risotto. It wasn't long before he got into a rhythm. He'd had the dish in his head for the past week. Now he just had to put it all together.

Amelia was busy, so she didn't stop by to check on him until he had the entire meal plated. Only then did she come over and lean in to inspect it. He could tell she was giving it her critical chef's eye, which was what he expected from her. It had to pass not only the taste test but the visual one as well. A dish had to look appetizing before the guests would want to eat it.

"Visually, it's stunning," she said as she waited for his approval. When he nodded at her, she reached for a fork and slid it into the fish, taking a small bite. He'd made extra so he could taste everything while he was cooking. He knew it was good. The question was—would Amelia think so, too?

He realized as he waited while she sampled the sea bass, the risotto and the snap peas that he was actually nervous. He knew what he was doing on the football field. No question there. Here, he was a novice, so there was a chance he could screw up.

Amelia chewed thoughtfully, but hadn't said anything.

"Stefanie, come over here, please."

Well, hell. Now she was asking for a second opinion. Maybe she hated it but she wanted someone else to back her up.

Her assistant chef came over. "Yes, boss."

"Taste this, please. It's pan-seared sea bass with lobster risotto and snap peas."

She handed the plate to Stefanie, who did the same thing. She slid her fork gingerly into the fish, then tasted the rice and the peas.

Stefanie nodded at Amelia. "It's outstanding. Did you make this?"

"I did not," Amelia said with a smile. "Our owner did."

"No shit. I mean, no kidding. Mr. Cassidy, this is amazing."

Flynn finally expelled the breath he'd been holding. "So, you both like it?"

Amelia laid her hand on his biceps. "Flynn, it's really good. Like, really good."

Amelia turned to Stefanie. "Flynn has wanted to make a signature dish for the restaurant. Something he can put his name on."

"I'd eat it. Like every day," Stefanie said. "The sea bass is moist and flaky, the risotto is filled with flavor. The lobster is tender and the peas are crisp. Perfectly balanced. I think our clients will go crazy for it."

"I agree," Amelia said. "Thank you, Stefanie."

Stefanie nodded and went back to her station. Amelia turned to Flynn and finally grinned. "It really is outstanding. I think we can safely put the Cassidy dish on our menu."

Flynn sighed. "I'm really glad. I'd been pondering this idea for a while, and I thought it tasted good when I sampled everything. But man, it was nerve-racking watching both of you taste it."

She nodded. "It's always hard introducing new dishes. And I don't always succeed with them. But I want you to know that Stefanie is extremely tough. If she doesn't like something, she is brutally honest about it. She takes her job very seriously and she will not let anything leave this kitchen unless it's perfect. So I trust her judgment implicitly."

"Good to know. And thanks for letting me cook here. It really did make a difference. I don't know that I would have worked as hard on it if I'd done this at home."

"Of course you wouldn't have because you wouldn't have had the added pressure of Stefanie and me to judge you."

He laughed. "Well, thanks for that. I think I'll get out of your way now so you can get back to work."

"Yes. Get out of my kitchen, please."

He leaned in close so only she could hear. "I'll see you later."

"Yes, you'll see a lot of me later."

With that vision in his head, he headed out of the restaurant with a giant grin on his face.

So far, it had been a really great night.

TWENTY-THREE

FLYNN WAS ALWAYS AT EASE WITH PEOPLE. ONE OF the reasons he liked having the restaurant was that he was comfortable around strangers. Meeting his restaurant guests and talking to them? No problem. Doing interviews with the media after games? Never an issue, even if the Sabers lost. Nerves never came into play. He was a rock.

Until tonight. Tonight he was meeting Amelia's best friend, Laura, and Laura's husband, Jon. After he'd cooked at the restaurant yesterday, Amelia had told him that Laura was dying to meet him, so they'd planned a very informal dinner at Laura and Jon's house for tonight.

After practice, he ran errands, went home, did laundry and took care of work calls. Then he showered and stared at his closet, trying to figure out what to wear. After five minutes he realized he was still staring into his closet, undecided.

What the fuck? He was a dude. Guys didn't do this. He pulled out a long-sleeved button-down shirt and put it on, then grabbed a pair of jeans and finished getting dressed.

He had no idea why he was nervous. But as he walked down the stairs and buttoned the cuffs of his shirt, he knew the answer.

Because it was Amelia's best friend. Best friends held all the power. If Laura didn't like him, it could affect his relationship with Amelia.

He should buy a nice bottle of wine for them. Maybe some flowers, too. He had plenty of time before he had to pick up Amelia, so he stopped at the flower shop and picked up a nice bouquet, then drove to the liquor store and searched out a bottle of pinot grigio, and on second glance, pulled a good cabernet as well. Hopefully Laura would like both.

He drove to Amelia's house and went up to ring the bell. She came to the door and he inhaled her fragrance. Not perfume, but something citrusy that smelled fresh and made him want to shut and lock the door and bury his face in her neck. He wished they had time for some getting naked and fooling around, but they didn't, so he pulled her against him and kissed her instead, letting her know how much he really wanted her.

When she drew back, she planted her hands on his chest. "You're affectionate tonight."

"I'm insulted by that statement. I'm affectionate with you all the time."

"I stand corrected. Yes, you are. Did I mention how much I like that?"

"No, you haven't. Care to show me?"

She laughed. "I'll show you later. Otherwise, we'll be late. Or no-shows."

She was right and he knew it. If he started touching her or kissing her he'd never stop. "Let's go."

She took a glance at the backseat as she climbed into his SUV. "Aww, you got her flowers. She'll love that."

"I got wine, too," he said as he backed out of the driveway. "Two bottles."

"She'll love that even more."

It didn't take long to drive to Laura's place since she lived just down the street from Amelia. They could have walked, but an uncharacteristic rain was threatening tonight, so he wanted to make sure they had a vehicle just in case. He parked and he grabbed the wine and flowers from the backseat.

"I warned you that Laura isn't a great housekeeper," Amelia said. "And she's really nervous about having you here, so be kind."

"I am always kind, and shouldn't I be the one who's nervous?"

They stood on the sidewalk and Amelia turned to face him. "You're nervous?"

"Well, yeah."

"Why?"

"Because Laura is your best friend. She gets veto power."

Amelia's lips curved. "Veto power."

Flynn nodded. "If she hates me, we're over."

Amelia laughed. "She's not going to hate you."

"She might."

"Just tell her you love clutter and you have as many subscriptions to magazines as she does. Trust me, she'll love you."

"Done. And you should have seen my room when I was growing up. I love clutter."

She gave him a warm smile as they walked up the steps and onto the porch. Amelia rang the bell and they waited.

The door was opened and a nice-looking guy with short dark hair and a goatee answered.

He grinned. "Hey, you must be Flynn. I'm Jon Perry."

Flynn shook his hand. "Nice to meet you, Jon."

"Come on inside. Oh, and hi, Amelia."

Amelia gave Jon a grin. "I was wondering if you were going to notice I was here."

Jon laughed. "Sorry, I'm kind of a fan."

Jon and Amelia hugged after they came inside. "Laura's giving herself a nervous breakdown in the kitchen," Jon said. "Something about meatballs."

Amelia laid her bag down on the chair next to the front door and shrugged out of her sweater. "Uh-oh. I think I'd better go help her."

"Would you mind taking these in to her?" Flynn asked, handing Amelia the wine and the flowers. "I don't know if those will help."

"They will."

"Come on into the living room," Jon said. "She made me clean."

"You really didn't need to do that."

"Oh, I really did. Laura likes her clutter, and normally doesn't care even when we have company over. Apparently, you're something special."

Flynn smiled. "I like my own share of clutter, so I wouldn't have minded."

"If only I'd known that before I shoved the entire contents of our living room into the closet. Just don't open the closets, okay?"

Flynn laughed. "Definitely won't do that."

Amelia came down the hall bearing two glasses of wine, a beautiful brunette following behind her with two more glasses.

"Amelia made me leave the kitchen."

The woman handed a glass of wine off to Jon, then turned to Flynn. "I'm Laura."

"Nice to meet you, Laura. I'm Flynn Cassidy."

She shook Flynn's hand. "Oh, I know who you are, Flynn. I

knew everything about you even before you started to date my best friend."

Jon put his arm around Laura. "She's sort of into football."

"More than sort of. I'm kind of a stats whiz, so if you'd like to know your tackles, assists, sacks or interceptions, I can quote any of those statistics for you for any year you've played."

Flynn arched a brow. "Really."

"Yeah, really," Jon said. "She's really annoying about it."

Laura looked over at her husband. "Really brilliant, you mean."

Jon nodded, then slid a glance at Flynn. "Yes, brilliant. That's what I meant."

Flynn grinned. He could see the connection between these two. It was cute.

"So I've attempted to make spaghetti and meatballs for dinner," Laura said. "I will say up front that I am not a cook, and by not a cook I mean not anything close to the cuisine you're used to from Amelia. I mean I make basic stuff."

"I like basic stuff," Flynn said. "And thank you for inviting me over for dinner."

"She also lies," Amelia said, smiling at her friend. "She's a very good cook."

Laura shrugged. "If you like home-style food. Or the stuff that comes from cans."

Jon rubbed her back. "But you can give us CPR if one of us collapses. Or first aid if we fall down the stairs."

"Amelia told me you're a nurse," Flynn said, "which is so much more important than spaghetti and meatballs. Now I know who to call next time I get an ankle sprain."

Laura let out a snort. "I believe you already have a highly skilled and likely overpaid medical team to take care of those things for you."

"Then they monitor me and I can't play. Wouldn't it be easier for you to ice it and wrap it for me so I can sneak an injury past the team docs?"

Laura laid her hand on her chest and feigned shock. "What? You'd lie to your medical team in order to get game time?"

"In a heartbeat."

Laura turned to her husband. "I'm sorry, Jon, but I'm leaving you for Flynn. You know how I feel about football."

Jon gave a resigned nod. "I knew this would happen. I've already packed."

Amelia laughed. So did Flynn.

They moved into the dining room and they all helped Laura serve up the salad and the spaghetti, along with amazing home-made bread, despite Laura's protests that her meal was nothing but average fare.

"What did you use in the meatballs, Laura?" Amelia asked as they ate.

"Veal, beef and pork. I told you, just basic stuff."

Flynn could have eaten all the meatballs, but he had to be polite and share. "I don't know what you consider average stuff, Laura, but these are damn fine meatballs. I'd serve them at Ninety-Two."

"Really?"

He nodded.

So did Amelia, who said, "I'm thinking of stealing your recipe and serving them at the restaurant."

Laura looked from Flynn to Amelia. "Now you're both trying to make me feel better."

Jon had taken a sip of wine and laid his glass down. "Accept the compliment babe. They're right. This is exceptional."

Laura beamed a smile. "Thank you. All of you. I might actually start cooking."

"Don't tease me, woman," Jon said.

Laura laughed. "Oh, shut up."

After dinner, they had coffee and a buttery cake that Laura said she'd picked up at the bakery.

"I would have liked to make dessert myself, but I pulled a double shift and couldn't manage it."

"The dinner was amazing, Laura," Flynn said as he accepted a piece of the cake. "I appreciate you making dinner. I'm sure finding any spare time to cook is tough with the hours you work. Amelia said they're somewhat erratic."

She shrugged. "We don't have kids yet, and Jon has similar crazy hours, so right now I don't mind doing the erratic times. At some point we'll start a family and I'll have earned the right to work more stable shifts."

"What do you do, Jon?" Flynn asked.

"I'm a software engineer, so I have the luxury of making a lot of my own hours. Which means when she works, I work."

Flynn nodded. "Sounds like an ideal situation for both of you."

"It works for now," Laura said. "I'm starting to feel the burnout of all the hours, so probably within the next year I'll be ready to start popping out some babies."

"Really?" Amelia grinned. "I'm ready for that, too."

Laura grinned. "To pop out babies of your own?"

"Ha. No. To cuddle your babies."

"Oh. But wouldn't it be fun if we had babies together?"

"That would be great, but my timeline isn't the same as yours."

"It could be." Laura shot a pointed look to Flynn.

"Don't look at me. I mean, I like you and all, Laura, but I'm not having any babies in the next year."

Jon snorted out a laugh.

"Oh, you're no fun at all, Flynn Cassidy," Laura said.

He grinned.

"So I guess that means I'm back in the running as baby daddy?" Jon asked Laura.

Laura sighed. "I suppose. And you are supremely hot and tall and exceptionally smart. I suppose your genetics will work for me."

Jon smiled at her. "Nice of you to say."

They spent hours talking about everything from sports to having babies to world events.

It had been a great night. Flynn was surprised how at ease he'd been with Jon and Laura from the minute he'd walked in the door. He hadn't realized how much time had passed until Amelia nudged him and told him Laura had an early morning call, so it was time for them to leave.

He shook Jon's hand, hugged Laura and thanked them both for inviting him to their house for dinner. Then he left them an open invitation to have dinner at Ninety-Two on him whenever they had a free night, because it sounded to him like they both worked damn hard and could use a night out.

"I'd love that," Laura said. "How about tomorrow?"

Jon laughed. "I don't think he meant tomorrow."

"No, seriously. I mean whenever you want. Tomorrow is good. I'll leave your name at the front desk and whenever you want to eat there, you can have a table."

"Thank you," Jon said. "That means a lot. And we will take you up on that."

They said their good-byes and left. Flynn drove Amelia home and walked her to her door.

"You're not coming in?" she asked with a concerned frown.

"Not tonight. I have an early call tomorrow morning."

She laid her palms on his chest. "I'll miss you tonight."

"Me, too. I hope I did okay with your best friend."

She smiled. "I think my best friend is slightly in love with you. Or maybe more than slightly. So I'd say you passed the test, even though there really wasn't a test."

"Good." He drew her against him and kissed her, wishing he

didn't have to get up so early tomorrow morning. Because as his mouth moved over Amelia's, he wanted nothing more than to feel his entire body moving against hers.

But a little restraint was a good thing sometimes. So he took a step back.

"I'll see you soon."

She had a death grip on his jacket. "Yes, you will."

"Good night, Amelia."

She released her hold on him with a sigh. "Good night, Flynn."

He walked away with a smile on his face.

TWENTY-FOUR

WITH FLYNN'S OUT-OF-TOWN GAME AND HER WORK being so busy, Amelia hadn't seen much of him the past week. And now it was time to leave for their Thanksgiving trip, and she was so stressed about it she could barely breathe.

"Did you remember to pack shorts?"

Amelia looked up from her suitcase to stare at Laura. "Honey, it's November."

Laura had come over at seven in the morning to help Amelia pack. Only her best friend would give up sleep in order to see her off for her trip.

"Yeah," Laura said, flipping through her phone. "And I checked the weather in the part of Texas you're flying to. It's supposed to be eighty degrees there."

Amelia frowned. "Wait. What? Eighty? Are you sure?"

"Yup."

"Well, hell." She stared into her suitcase, where she'd packed long pants and sweaters. "That could change, though, right?"

"Doesn't look like it's going to. At least put a pair of capris and a sundress in your suitcase."

"Fine." She pulled out one of the sweaters and her jeans, replacing them with a pair of capris and a sundress, which felt weird for this time of year. But Laura was right. The last thing she wanted to do was sweat all over Flynn's family.

"You'll be much happier if you're cooler. And dressed appropriately."

After thinking, she threw in another pair of capris and a couple of short-sleeved tops, along with her brown flat sandals and higher platform black ones, then closed her suitcase. "What would I do without you, Laura?"

"You'd sweat without me, that's what you'd do."

"You're right about that." She felt better about what she was taking.

"So you're off work for a few days, and you're traveling to Texas to meet Flynn's family. How do you feel about that?"

She sat on the bed and zipped up her suitcase. "You sound like my therapist."

Laura laughed and sat on the other side of Amelia's suitcase. "I do, don't I? Are you ready for that big a step?"

She slanted a curious look at Laura. "Is it a big step? I'm only going because Mia invited me. Flynn said he wanted me to go and it was no big deal, but I still think he kind of had to say, 'Oh, Amelia, sure, you're totally invited.'"

Laura gave her that look, the one that said she was full of shit. "Really? He could have said nothing, which would have meant he thought his sister's suggestion was a bad idea. Instead, he invited you. More than once. He likes you, Amelia. Get on board with that because it's obvious you like him, too."

She did like him. She more than liked him. Which meant her heart was getting involved, and that was scary as hell.

"Yes, of course I like him."

"But . . ."

Once again, this was what happened when your friend knew you all too well. Amelia realized she couldn't escape having this conversation.

"But I'm afraid."

Laura got up, shoved the suitcase to the end of the bed and sat next to Amelia. "What are you afraid of? That you're going to fall in love with Flynn and he's going to break your heart like that asshole you were married to?"

She sighed. "You know, sometimes you cut right to the heart of the matter like a surgeon."

Laura beamed a smile. "You sure know how to throw a compliment. I'm right, aren't I? Are your feelings for Flynn more than fun, dating and sex?"

"Yes, they're more than all of those."

"Are you in love with him?"

Laura had softened her voice when she asked the question.

"Maybe. I don't know. I thought I was in love with Frank. I gave my whole heart to him. I thought I knew everything about him, that we were destined for forever. That turned out to be a nightmare. He wasn't who I thought he was. So what do I really know about love?"

"You're afraid to give a guy your heart again. You're afraid your feelings are going to be crushed. I totally understand. But don't let one jerk keep you from trusting in love. It's out there and it's waiting for you. The right guy is out there. The right guy could be Flynn."

"Maybe. I don't know."

Laura sighed. "You said that already."

She lifted her gaze to her friend, needing Laura to understand, to be there with her. "Because it's true. I don't know what to believe in. I can't trust my own heart or my own feelings. I just need . . . time, I guess."

Laura went quiet for a few seconds, then finally nodded. "You're right, and I'm being pushy. I'm sorry. I just want you to be happy. I want you to feel good again, to fall in love again. This time, with the right guy."

Amelia leaned against Laura and laid her head on her best friend's shoulder. "I know you do and I love you for that. But this time, I'm going into it with my eyes wide open. I'm never going to let a man hurt me again."

Laura put her arm around her shoulders. "It's good to be wary, but don't close yourself off to the possibility that love could be out there for you. Give it a chance. Give Flynn a chance. He's a nice guy and he seems really into you, so don't close the door, okay?"

"I promise I won't."

After Laura left, Amelia finished up the few things she needed to do around the house—washing dishes, taking out the trash—then took a shower and got ready, her eye constantly on the clock. Flynn was picking her up at nine, so she made certain she was ready to go by eight thirty.

Her stomach grumbled and she realized in all the rush she hadn't eaten yet. Too late now. She'd grab a muffin at the airport or something.

To calm her nerves while she waited for Flynn, she sat at her breakfast bar and made notes about three new dishes she planned to create for Ninety-Two's holiday menu. When Flynn knocked on the door, she put her pen and paper aside, grabbed her travel bag and opened the door.

"Hi. I'm ready."

His lips curved. "A little anxious about the trip?"

"Maybe a little."

"Don't be. It's going to be fine. We're going to have fun. And good morning." He stepped in, grasped her arms and pulled her against him for a kiss. She leaned into him and let the warmth of him surround her for a few seconds. But then she realized they were on a timetable, so she pressed her hands against his chest and took a step back.

"Okay, enough of that."

"You're no fun," he said.

"I'm tons of fun and you know it. Grab my suitcase."

He shot a frown at her. "You're very bossy when you're stressed."

"I am not stressed. Can we go now?"

She was totally stressed and she didn't know why. Okay, she knew why. There was a lot of pressure on this visit, and it was all pressure she was putting on herself. She really needed to relax. Maybe she'd have a muffin before the flight and a glass of wine on the plane.

Though the combination made her wrinkle her nose.

They got to the airport with plenty of time to check in and make their way to the gate. She also grabbed a muffin and an orange juice.

She was surprised to discover they were flying first class. She'd argued with him a couple of weeks ago when he'd told her he was paying for her ticket, but he'd won that argument. If she'd known then it was a first class ticket, she would have argued more.

"First class is frivolous," she said as they waited to board.

"You won't think that when we get on the plane."

"Whatever. I'm fine with coach, you know."

He gave her a look that told her he was just about out of patience with her. "Want me to switch out your ticket?"

"No. I want to sit with you."

"Then we're sitting in first class. I'm a big guy. I like bigger seats. And I can afford first class seats for both of us, so quit complaining about it."

She rolled her eyes and decided to let him have this one. Plus, the seats and extra legroom were awesome, so complaining did seem bitchy.

The plane took off. Not long after that the flight attendant asked her what she wanted to drink. She looked at her watch and saw it was ten thirty. Too early for wine, she supposed, so she ordered a sparkling water. They also took orders for lunch, and she had her choice of grilled chicken salad or pasta. She chose the grilled chicken salad.

She settled in to read a book on her e-reader, while Flynn took out his netbook, shoved in his earbuds and started watching a movie. It wasn't long before she was peering over his shoulder at the movie he was watching. He finally noticed and took out his earbuds.

"You want to watch with me?"

"That might be hard to do."

"Not really." He handed her one of his earbuds. She laughed and shoved it in her ear, nestled close to him and watched the movie over his shoulder until their lunch arrived.

Lunch was amazing, and included wine—and dessert—which made her very happy. Then they showed an in-flight movie, so she put in the earbuds they provided. The flight went by so fast that before she knew it they were landing in Austin. Which made her wish she hadn't turned down that refill on the wine, because now she was nervous again. But she kept her nervousness to herself and followed along as Flynn picked up the rental car and they climbed in.

"It's about an hour to the ranch from here," he said after he pulled out of the lot. "Do you need to stop for anything? Do you want a drink?"

An entire bottle of wine would be good. But she doubted that arriving blitzed to meet Flynn's parents would go over well. "No, thanks. I'm fine."

She could already imagine the greeting she was going to receive. What would his parents think of her?

She knew what they'd think. That she was head chef at Flynn's restaurant, sleeping with Flynn in order to get ahead. God, why had she agreed to this? In the back of her head she'd known it was a bad idea from the start.

"You look a little pale, Amelia," Flynn said after about twenty minutes on the road. "Are you sure you're feeling all right?"

She turned and offered up her best smile. "Oh, I'm fine. Totally fine. Very excited to meet your family."

That hadn't sounded at all sincere.

Ten minutes later, Flynn said, "You know, they're not ogres."

She frowned. "Who?"

"My parents. They're really nice people. Warm and welcoming. I think you're mentally working yourself up over nothing. This isn't a big deal."

"Maybe not to you. But I can't help but think they're going to assume I have some ulterior motive in dating you."

Even though he was wearing sunglasses, she saw his brow go up. "What kind of ulterior motive?"

"Like the evil chef screws the hot football player and owner of the restaurant where she works in order to get a leg up in the business."

Flynn stared at her for a few seconds, then snorted out a laugh.

"It's not funny."

"Hell yeah it's funny. How exactly would sleeping with me help your career?"

She crossed her arms, miffed that he wasn't taking her seriously. "I . . . don't know exactly. But I'm sure I could take advantage of you in some way. If nothing else, it would give me better job security at Ninety-Two."

"Your cooking stands on its own. You don't need to sleep with me to keep your job. As for helping you in the industry, I know very few chefs and have almost no contacts in the restaurant industry. How much help could I give you?"

When he put it like that, it did sound stupid. "I don't know. I just don't want your parents to think I'm using you."

"Trust me, Amelia, my parents won't think that. I'm pretty sure they know me well enough to realize that if I'm bringing a woman home for Thanksgiving, it's because I trust said woman. A woman who has no nefarious intentions where I'm concerned."

"Ooh, nefarious. I like that word. It makes me sound like a femme fatale."

He rolled his eyes. "I'm sorry, babe, but you're more of a sweet muffin than a femme fatale."

She frowned at him. "I am not."

"Being a sweet muffin is a bad thing?"

"Well, no. But I'd like to think I'm at least a little mysterious."

"Okay, you're totally mysterious. You probably have a stiletto dagger tucked into your garter."

Now she laughed. "I don't think the airline would allow me to carry a stiletto through security. But the garter sounds fun."

He slid his hand down her thigh. "Yeah, it does. And if it'll make you wear one, I'll totally buy you a sexy dagger."

"Done deal. But let's wait until we get back home so airport security doesn't confiscate it."

"You got it." He gave her thigh a gentle squeeze, and she suddenly wished they weren't in the car so she could touch him freely. But she needed his concentration on driving, not on her, so she stared out the window.

As they pulled off the highway and drove into more rural territory, she was so intrigued with everything she saw. Having lived all of her life in urban areas, seeing such wide-open spaces intrigued her. Miles of fenced-in green grass, and the occasional acreages housing horses and cows were amazing.

She turned to him. "You grew up here?"

He nodded. "Mostly. After my dad retired from football they bought the ranch. Before that, we lived in Wisconsin."

"What was that like?"

He smiled. "Cold winters, but really nice. I had good friends. I learned to ice skate there."

"And yet you didn't become a hockey player."

He laughed. "No. We played a lot of football. And once we moved down here to Texas, football was king."

"But one of your brothers plays baseball."

"Yeah, what can I say? We couldn't beat that love of baseball out of Tucker."

She stared at him. "You're joking, right?"

At a stop sign, he turned to her. "Of course I'm joking. Sort of."

She rolled her eyes. She never knew when he was kidding. Having grown up without siblings put her at a disadvantage regarding how siblings behaved toward one another. For all she knew, they beat up on each other every day. Then again, she'd seen him with his brother Grant, and his sister, Mia. Though there was a lot of teasing, there was also genuine affection between them all.

She was looking forward to observing the family dynamic. And when Flynn reached the gates of the ranch, her eyes widened. The dark iron double Cs affixed above the huge metal gate looked imposing. Flynn rolled down the window, punched in a code and the gates opened.

They drove down a dirt road for quite a ways until Amelia spotted the house, a beautiful two-story home with bright shutters next to all those windows, plus an amazing wraparound porch. Dogs came running as soon as Flynn pulled in front. Like . . . a lot of dogs.

Amelia inhaled and let it out.

Flynn turned to her and smiled. "Ready for this?"

She managed a smile. "Sure."

She got out at the same time he did. Dogs surrounded them as they came around to the front of the vehicle.

"Dogs, meet Amelia. Amelia, meet the dogs."

There were at least five of them, but surprisingly they were all well behaved. She kneeled down and loved on all of them until a short whistle sent them all scurrying away. Amelia stood and saw a man who looked an awful lot like an older version of Flynn standing on the porch. He hugged Flynn, then came over to her with a smil   's face.

"Scoundrels love the attention. They'll let you pet them all day. I'm Easton Cassidy, Flynn's dad."

Amelia held out her hand. "I'm Amelia Lawrence. It's very nice to meet you, Mr. Cassidy."

"Call me Easton. Welcome to the Double C ranch. Come on in out of the hot sun. Flynn, grab the bags."

Flynn cracked a smile. "Sure, Dad."

Amelia looked back at Flynn, who made a motion with his hands for her to follow his dad, so she headed up the steps and walked inside when Easton held the door for her.

Easton was right. It was hot outside, so it felt supremely cooler indoors. And the house was lovely, with its mix of rustic and modern décor.

"Lydia is in town getting groceries with Aubry and Harmony," Easton said.

"Aubry is my brother Tucker's fiancée and Harmony is Barrett's girlfriend," Flynn said after he set their luggage inside the front door.

Amelia nodded. "Got it." For the past couple of weeks, she had received the full rundown from Flynn on all of the Cassidy family members. She already knew Mia, but she'd wanted to have a general idea of who everyone else was before the family gathering. Flynn was the oldest brother. Grant, who she'd already met, was next, and Grant was engaged to supermodel Katrina Korsova. Katrina had custody of her teen siblings, Anya and Leo. The twins, Tucker and Barrett, were the youngest Cassidy brothers. Tucker was engaged to Aubry Ross, a doctor, and Barrett's girlfriend was Harmony Evans, an interior designer. Of course, Mia was the youngest Cassidy sibling. And Flynn's parents were Easton and Lydia. Now she just needed to meet them all. She was both excited and terrified.

"Thought we heard you pull up."

They walked into the kitchen at the same time an absolutely stunning man came through the back door.

Flynn put his arm around Amelia's waist. "Amelia, this is my brother Tucker. This is Amelia Lawrence."

Another guy came through the back door. He looked eerily similar to Tucker, though he was broader and more muscular.

"And that one is Barrett."

She knew they were the twins, so the similarity between them made sense.

"Hi, it's nice to meet both of you," Amelia said, recalling that Flynn had told her Tucker wore dark glasses that did absolutely nothing to distract from his stunning good looks.

"Great to meet you, Amelia," Tucker said with a smile as he stepped forward to shake her hand.

"Good to meet you, Amelia," Barrett said. "Sorry to hear you're dating our brother. We'll try to talk you out of that over the next few days."

"Nice try," Flynn said. "Won't happen. She's overcome with adoration for me."

Amelia coughed. "Well, I wouldn't exactly say that."

Tucker grinned. "I like her already."

"Where's Grant?" Flynn asked.

"He's out in one of the pastures with Elijah fixing fencing," his dad said.

Amelia knew Elijah was one of Easton's brothers, so Flynn's uncle.

Flynn's lips curved. "Didn't take long for you to put him to work."

"Put us to work," Tucker said. "We've already replaced tires and changed oil in Dad's old junker of a tractor."

"Not a junker," Easton said. "That baby will trudge on another twenty years."

Amelia noticed the look that passed between Flynn and his brother.

"Sure it will, Dad," Flynn said.

And the guys were off, talking farm equipment, giving Amelia time to take a mental step back and watch Flynn engage with his father and his brothers. It was quite the sight, especially when Grant walked in. Amelia waved at Grant, who came over to hug her.

"Hey, good to see you again, Amelia," Grant said.

"Likewise, Grant."

That was all she got before Grant entered the argument.

It was awesome. She pulled up a seat at the oversized kitchen island and watched the interplay between father and sons, each one convinced they were right. If it weren't rude, she'd love to get this on video.

"It's been like this my entire life."

Amelia turned to see a grinning Mia walk in, followed by a very attractive older woman who had to be Mia's mother, Lydia.

"Are they arguing again?" Lydia asked as she set down a bag of groceries. "Hey, all of you, knock that off. There's food in the car. Go bring it in."

And just like that, the disagreement stopped and all the men walked outside. Lydia had to be a miracle worker.

Mia grinned. "It's so nice to see you again." She came over to hug her.

"You, too."

"This is my mom, Lydia. Mom, this is Amelia Lawrence."

Amelia held out her hand. "It's very nice to meet you, Lydia."

Lydia folded her into a hug instead. "I'm very happy to meet you, too, Amelia. Mia has told me a lot about you."

"And judging by what I just witnessed, I'm already a big fan of yours."

Lydia frowned, then her eyes widened and she offered up a wry smile. "Oh, that?" She waved her hand. "They're all like little boys."

"And they know she means business when she tells them to do something. Even Dad knows not to mess with her."

Amelia's mouth ticked up. She could well imagine this petite woman running this household with iron fists. She'd have to with four boys.

Two more women entered the kitchen carrying grocery bags. After depositing them on the counter, they both turned to Amelia. The gorgeous blonde leaned forward to shake Amelia's hand. "I'm Aubry Ross, Tucker's fiancée."

"Hi, Aubry. Great to meet you."

The other woman, a beautiful dark-haired woman with a stunning smile, stepped forward and hugged her. "I'm Harmony Evans, Barrett's girlfriend."

Wow. The Cassidy men sure had gotten lucky in landing such amazingly beautiful women. Starting with Lydia, who was so beautiful with her soft brown hair and amazing blue eyes.

"It's so great to meet you, Harmony. Honestly, it's nice to meet all of you. Flynn has told me so much about everyone in the Cassidy family that I feel like I know all of you already."

"This family can be imposing," Harmony said with a smile. "You just have to dive right in because they're the nicest people I've ever met."

"How was your flight, Amelia?" Lydia asked as Mia began emptying grocery bags and putting things away.

"It was great, thank you. And thank you for letting me spend Thanksgiving in your home."

"One of the things I love the most is when the family is home for the holidays. And extra family is always welcome."

"Thank you for that."

The men all came in bearing the rest of the groceries, so she moved out of the way while everything was put away in a matter of minutes.

Aubry had pulled lemonade out of the refrigerator and filled glasses.

"Lemonade?" she asked her.

"I'd love some."

Within the next few minutes, the front door opened and she also met the striking Katrina, Grant's fiancée, along with her younger siblings, Anya and Leo. Then Easton's three brothers appeared, along with their wives, and she was overwhelmed by people. Flynn must have sensed her trepidation though. While she sat in the dining room getting to know everyone, he sat next to her rubbing her back. She was glad he wasn't shy about being familiar with her in front of his family.

"How's the restaurant going, Flynn?" his mother asked.

"Great, actually. Amelia takes good care of the customers."

She warmed at the compliment. "Did Flynn mention that he prepared a signature dish for the restaurant?"

Lydia looked over at him. "He did not. Tell us about it."

Flynn explained the dish he'd created, and Amelia was happy that the focus was off of her and on Flynn, as it should be.

"So now you're the chef in the family, huh?" Easton asked. "And all this time I thought it was your mom."

"Oh, it's still Mom," Flynn said. "Always will be. I would never have learned to cook if it hadn't been for her."

"Mom will always be the best," Grant said.

"I don't think we'll talk about my cooking when we have a professional chef in our midst," Lydia said, smiling over at Amelia.

"Home cooking for your family always trumps restaurant food," Amelia said.

"I'm glad you think that. Now I won't feel so pressured to come up with five-star meals the entire time you're here."

Amelia laughed. "Even I don't make five-star meals, Lydia. Please, don't feel any pressure just because cooking is my job. I'm really looking forward to spending time with your family. And, of course, I'd be delighted to help with the cooking."

"I'd be delighted to let you help with the cooking."

"That's our mom," Mia said. "Always willing to corral bodies to help slice and dice in the kitchen."

Amelia laughed. "I'm always in the kitchen. Even though I work at a restaurant, when I'm home, I'm usually trying out new recipes. So trust me when I tell you I'll be happy to hang out in the kitchen with you."

Lydia looked over at Flynn. "I like her."

Flynn's lips ticked up. "Knew you would."

It wasn't long before Lydia got up and moved into the kitchen. Mia followed, as did Aubry, Harmony, Katrina and Anya, so Amelia naturally went with them. Lydia started pulling things from the refrigerator, and without knowing what they were going to fix, Amelia dived in to assist.

Then it was a melee of cooking and conversation. Amelia felt right at home talking with the women as she diced onions and tomatoes while conversing about Aubry's medical residency, Harmony's interior design firm and Katrina's modeling career. It was equal parts bizarre and utterly fascinating, but she enjoyed every moment of fixing dinner with this unique family. Eventually some of the guys made their way into the kitchen, including Flynn, who created a rub for the ribs and carried those out back to be grilled.

"How did you decide to become a chef, Amelia?" Lydia asked her.

She spent some time explaining her love of food and her background to Lydia and the rest of the women.

"My plan is to go to culinary school and become a chef," Anya said. "First I have to get my undergraduate degree, because Katrina and Grant won't allow me to do it any other way."

"You've got that right," Katrina said.

Amelia laughed and nodded. "It's the smart road to take, Anya. And I'll be happy to recommend some wonderful cooking schools for you if you'd like."

"I would definitely like that."

She'd found a kindred spirit in the young Anya, who was in her first year of college. Obviously Grant and Katrina were looking out for Katrina's siblings in the best way.

She ended up working side by side with Anya. Together, they made salsa and guacamole, along with hummus and baked beans to go with the ribs. Lydia also made potato and green salads. There was a Caprese salad, and Mia had prepped corn on the cob for the guys to roast on the grill. Amelia had found time to whip up a dessert, too.

By the time dinner was ready, her stomach was gnawing with hunger. Katrina had baked bread and Amelia was ready to tear into the food. Aubry had made margaritas, and Harmony had squeezed lemons for another round of lemonade and sliced limes to go with the margaritas. Lydia had opened some wine, the guys had beers, and the spread at the dining room table was to die for.

Amelia had a margarita in hand and had already had a few sips. It was delicious.

"Let's eat, everyone," Lydia said after Easton had placed a huge plate of ribs in the center of the table.

Dinner was loud, with several conversations going on at once. Flynn placed his hand at the small of her back.

"Everything going okay?" he asked, his voice low so only she could hear.

She smiled up at him. "It's perfect. You have an amazing family."

He grinned. "Thanks. I think so, too."

The food was wonderful. Amelia tried a little bit of everything, and it was all delicious. By the time they'd finished, she was full.

"Amelia made dessert," Lydia said.

Flynn looked over at her and raised a brow.

"Nothing fancy. Just a raspberry ricotta cake and an apple pie."

"While we were outside cooking you made two desserts?" he asked.

"I told you they weren't fancy."

"I don't care if they're fancy or not," Easton said. "They both sound good. Let's have at them."

"Then I guess you boys better clear off dinner so we can have dessert," Lydia said.

The guys cleared the table, and Amelia went into the kitchen to bring out desserts, while Anya and Leo brought out plates and utensils.

"I made coffee, too," Lydia said, "for anyone who wants some."

They all sat and cut into the desserts and doled them out. Amelia was too full to eat, but she did help herself to another margarita and waited for the verdict.

"Damn, woman," Easton said after he tasted the apple pie. "This is fine."

"I'll say," his brother Elijah said. "I love raspberries, and this cake is really good."

They all loved the desserts, which made her happy.

"This raspberry cake is delicious, Amelia," Lydia said. "You'll have to share your recipe with me."

She couldn't hold back her smile. "I will definitely do that."

"I'm putting you on pie-making duty tomorrow, Amelia," Lydia said. "How are you with pecan pie?"

Amelia laughed. "I can definitely handle pies. And pecan is my specialty. Or it will be by tomorrow."

Lydia smiled and nodded. "Just what I needed to hear."

"Oh, let's do a cherry pie, too, Amelia," Anya said. "I love cherry pies."

"Me, too, Anya," Amelia said.

"Don't forget pumpkin or it won't be Thanksgiving." Flynn shot Amelia a hopeful smile.

"Pumpkin pie is his weakness," Barrett said. "He'll eat an entire pumpkin pie by himself."

"Yes, I will, so don't even think about stealing a slice."

"I don't intend to now that Anya suggested cherry pie."

Amelia loved the conversations about food, and made mental notes about some of Flynn's favorites.

After everyone finished dessert, she was surprised when all the guys got up to clean up the kitchen, leaving the women to savor their coffee and drinks in the dining room.

"You have them well trained, Lydia," Amelia said.

She shrugged and sipped her coffee. "For a while I did all the cooking. Then I decided if I was going to cook for these hordes of men, they were going to do the cleanup. To be honest, I got no complaints. And after a while the boys wanted to learn how to cook, so for some meals we all cooked together and shared in the cleanup. But I still did most of the cooking."

"Flynn is a very good cook," Amelia said.

Lydia's lips lifted. "I'm so happy to hear that."

"Tucker holds his own in the kitchen as well," Aubry said.

"Barrett is no slouch, either," Harmony said.

"Grant cooks as well," Katrina said. "When Anya and I let him in there."

Lydia laughed. "Yes, I imagine that's a battle with the two of you being such good cooks."

"Anya is much better at it than I am, and honestly, she's more gracious about letting Grant cook with her."

Anya smiled. "Grant's not bad as an assistant. At least he doesn't scorch the rice."

"We miss your cooking now that you're away at college," Katrina said.

Anya grinned. "Oh, but my roommates love me."

"That's the best part about being a great cook," Amelia said. "You are very popular in college."

Anya nodded. "I found that out very quickly, especially among the microwave-and-Top-Ramen crowd."

Amelia laughed. "Yes, I remember those days very well. Just don't give any recipes away."

"Hey, I'm not stupid. I've already scored concert tickets and history study notes in exchange for my awesome culinary skills."

"That's my smart sister," Katrina said with a nod.

After a while Lydia broke up the party, saying she was tired and was going to bed. It turned out Amelia and Flynn would be staying at the guest cottage down the road—ostensibly to give them some privacy since they were a new couple.

It was sweet and as Flynn brought their luggage into the cottage, Amelia was in awe of what Lydia considered a "cottage." This was a house, and a fairly sizable one at that.

"Shouldn't Grant and Katrina and the kids be staying here?" Amelia asked. "It's huge."

"It's not as big as the other house on the property," he said as she followed him down the hall and into the main bedroom. "Grant and Katrina are staying in that house."

She blinked. "There's another house?"

He flipped on the light and turned to her with a smile. "There's a few. My parents have a lot of land."

"Wow." She had no concept of owning so much land that you could build several houses on it. "That's kind of amazing."

"Yeah. This house is on the smaller side. Just two bedrooms."

She laughed. "Right. Just two bedrooms. And about . . . what? Fifteen hundred square feet, I'm guessing?"

"Sixteen hundred. With a fold-out couch in the living room for extra guests. You're pretty good."

"Thanks. This bedroom is lovely. And a king-sized bed, too."

"Yeah, always plenty of room for one of us big guys to roll around in."

She moved over to him and put her arms around him. "Or one of you big guys with a plus one."

He turned to face her and framed her face, brushing his lips across hers. "Definitely that. You want something to drink? Mom has no doubt stocked the fridge."

"I think I'm so full I might explode if I eat or drink anything else. So I'm good for now."

"You probably need a walk."

"That sounds amazing. I'd love to."

He took her hand and they headed out the front door. It was so remote out here, no lights, nothing like living in the city. She looked up and saw what she thought were a million stars overhead in the clear night sky, so she tugged on Flynn's hand to stop him.

"Look at all those stars."

"Oh. Right. I forget you're used to living in the city. It's pretty amazing, isn't it?"

"It's unbelievable. You had this every night?"

"Every clear night, yeah. My brothers and Mia and I would lie out in the dirt and spot the constellations. Then we'd argue over which one of us was right."

She tore her gaze away from the stunning sky to look at him. "Which one of you was usually right?"

"Mia. But don't tell her I said that."

She laughed. "Oh, so it's a secret, huh? What's it worth to you for me to keep it?"

He grabbed her around the waist, then hauled her against him. "You'd sell my secrets?"

"Maybe. Depends on what you're willing to sacrifice to buy my silence."

He rubbed against her, and she felt him getting hard. "I've got something that might interest you."

She pressed her hands against his chest. "I'm intrigued. Go on."

He looked around, then took her hand and walked her farther down the road. The road curved away from the house, and it was suddenly very dark. All she could see was Flynn and the night sky. Since there wasn't much of a moon, she could only make out the shapes of trees. She inhaled and caught the smell of hay, and heard cattle in the near distance. But otherwise, she had no idea what was out there.

Until Flynn pushed her up against a wood fence post and pressed against her. Before she could say anything his mouth was on hers, hard and passionate. She lost herself in the kiss, in the wild, hungry taste of his lips moving over hers.

His hands roamed her body, sliding along her rib cage and up and over her breasts. For a brief moment she wondered about the possibility of someone wandering by and seeing them, but that moment was lost when his fingers brushed across her nipple. A shock of brutal pleasure made her gasp as a rush of sensation shot through her. She knew Flynn wouldn't put her in an embarrassing position with his family, so instead she focused on the hazy pleasure.

He moved his hand along her stomach—and lower—his fingers dipping into the waistband of her pants. Ripples of sensation curled along her nerve endings and she moaned against his mouth.

"Flynn."

He pulled back and looked at her, his fingers teasing her sex. "I like the way you say my name when you're all hot and bothered. I want to hear you moan my name when I make you come."

Part of her wanted to object. They were out here in the middle of— Well, she actually had no idea where they were.

"No one's here, right?"

He swept his fingers over her clit and she bit back that moan he was talking about.

"Babe, no one's going to come. Except you. You're all hot and wet under my fingers. Just relax and let me touch you."

He kissed her again while his expert fingers did a magical dance across her sex. She gasped as he slid a finger into her.

"Feel that?" he murmured against her mouth. "Your pussy, gripping my finger. You are so tight, so hot. I wish I was inside you right now."

She was coming undone, overcome by the heat and pleasure of Flynn's hands and fingers as he pumped in and out of her while he rubbed her clit with his thumb. She was drowning right here in the great outdoors with nothing but Flynn as her lifeline.

And when she came, it was his name that spilled from her lips as she quivered and reached for him.

"That's it, babe. Let me have it all."

She was sailing on a crazy sea of incredible sensation. She lost herself in the moment, arching her pussy against his hand, letting him take over as he coaxed her over the wave of her orgasm.

When he lifted his hand from her pants, she laid her head on his shoulder so she could catch her breath.

"Now, that was good," he said.

"It was definitely good for me." She lifted her head and pressed her lips to his. "Thank you."

He deepened the kiss, wrapping an arm around her to tug her close. His erection bumped her hip and she realized how in need he must be. And kissing him ratcheted up her desire for him all over again. But now she wanted to be naked so she could touch him and feel him inside of her.

She pulled back and smoothed her hands down his chest, over his stomach, and teased her fingers over his hard-on. "How about we take a stroll back to the house?"

"Great idea. Only let's sprint, not stroll."

She smiled and took his hand, and they walked briskly back to the house. When they got inside, Flynn closed and locked the door, shut off the porch light, then turned to face her.

"Just to make sure none of my family comes by to visit."

Her eyes widened. "You told me no one would come by."

"No one was going to. I was pretty sure."

She rolled her eyes. "Flynn."

He smoothed his hands down her arms. "Hey, you came, and no one saw us. Don't worry."

"Well, I wasn't worried then, but now I am. No more outdoor sex."

"Oh, but I haven't even shown you my secret place."

She laughed and shook her head. "I'm not falling for that. I don't think you even have a secret place."

He had started walking her backward, down the hallway toward the bedroom.

"I have a lot of secret places on this property. Trust me, no one would ever find us."

"Uh-huh. I think you just want to get me naked on the grass somewhere."

"We could do it outside right now, under the stars. Ever had sex under the stars, Amelia?"

They had made it through the doorway and Flynn moved in closer, placing his hands on her hips to guide her toward the bed. When the back of her knees hit the mattress, he pushed her onto the bed and climbed on after her, pulling her on top of him.

"No, I've never had sex under the stars. Or outside."

His eyes gleamed hot with desire. "You're missing out."

"Am I? Or will I end up with mosquito bites on my ass?"

He lifted her top over her head, discarding it, then unhooked her bra, sliding the straps down her arms.

"Oh, come on. Where's your sense of adventure? Besides, it's November. All the mosquitos are gone for the season."

"First, I don't believe you about the mosquitos. Second, I have a great sense of adventure. I'm just a little uncertain about the mosquito bites on my ass."

He cupped her butt and squeezed. "I promise to take very tender care of your very fine ass."

She rocked against him and he groaned. "Promise?"

"Yes. Now get naked and slide that sweet pussy over me."

She shivered at the harsh, needy tone of his voice. She slid off of him only long enough to remove the rest of her clothes. Flynn did the same and when she climbed back on him, he was naked, with a condom in his hand.

"And where did that come from?"

"My cock or the condom?"

She laughed and took the condom packet from him, waving it back and forth. "This."

"My pocket. I grabbed it out of the luggage earlier."

"Aren't you just so smart?" She tore the wrapper off and slid the condom over his cock, watching the way his eyes darkened as she grasped the base of his shaft when she applied the condom.

"I like your hands on me, Amelia. Now slide your hot pussy all over me and make us both come."

She climbed over to straddle his thighs and inched down onto his cock, teasing both of them by taking her time. The heat and length of him felt like sweet, hot steel thickening within her. She dug her nails into his chest and he hissed.

"Yeah, baby, it's that good for me, too." He arched up, filling her with his delicious cock, causing goose bumps to spring up all over her skin. She scraped her nails along his chest, teasing his nipples with her fingertips.

Then she rocked back and forth against him, giving herself the friction she needed. He grasped her hips and dragged her forward, sending shots of pure pleasure through her. When she bent down to kiss him, he tangled his fingers in her hair, winding the strands around his hand to tug on it as he intensified the kiss.

It was all too much. She came with a strangled moan. In answer, he groaned against her lips, dug his fingers into her hips and drove into her, taking her climax to new heights as he thrust hard and fast into her as he came.

She lay there for a while, her body splayed over his in what felt like a drunken stupor. Flynn drew lazy circles over her back and buttocks and she was certain if they stayed like this all night long she'd be perfectly content.

But eventually she climbed off of him and they made their way to the bathroom. She stared at the sink and looked at him.

"We haven't even unpacked yet. I need to brush my teeth."

His lips curved into a sexy smile. "We were busy doing other things and I guess we forgot that part. I'll go bring the luggage in."

She turned around and rested her hip against the sink. "Okay."

She felt blissfully relaxed. Considering how pent up and anxious she'd been this morning, she realized she'd had nothing to worry about.

This was going to be a great trip.

TWENTY-FIVE

ONE OF FLYNN'S FAVORITE PARTS ABOUT BEING HOME was hanging out with his dad, his uncles and his brothers. At some point there would be a football game, typically started out in one of the fields, and always involving over-the-top boasting, a lot of bullshitting and occasionally a bet about who would win.

Flynn knew he was the best and had often proved it. Okay, his dad had been the best and no one ever disputed that. Dad wasn't as young as he used to be, but he could still throw a damn football like he was a twenty-five-year-old, with his rocket arm and pinpoint accuracy. And not one of them would dare try to tackle him or you'd find yourself being assigned some heinous chore, like mucking out the horse barn. Definitely not worth it.

Amelia had wanted to get up early this morning, saying she had made plans with all the women to start cooking, which had suited Flynn just fine since he always enjoyed working out early in the day. He drank a large glass of orange juice, then left Amelia the keys to the SUV, gave her a kiss and set out on his run.

He never minded running at the gym or the team facility, but there was nothing like being home and having the freedom to roam the dirt roads of the Cassidy ranch. Dawn was just creeping up, the sun a hazy bright spot through the early morning fog that had blanketed the ranch overnight. The chill in the air felt good, especially when he quickened his pace. He didn't mind the fog. He knew this land and every curve of the road. He'd run it with his brothers and his sister for years, so he knew when to make a turn. He could do this with his eyes closed.

It felt damn good to be home. No city sounds, no horns honking, no one huffing and puffing next to him on the treadmill. Just Flynn and his own thoughts. His thoughts right now were on home, family and burning off all the calories he was going to eat later today.

He grinned and dug in harder, watching the fog scatter across a green meadow. Yeah, this was his goal. Someday he'd own land like this. When he was retired and he didn't play anymore, he'd raise his kids somewhere they could roam for miles and not be afraid of running into the street.

He'd loved his childhood, and he wanted the same thing for his kids.

His imaginary kids right now.

He made a left turn and took the back road toward the main house, slowing his pace when he got about a half mile out. The last quarter mile he did at a walk to get his heart rate back to normal. Barrett was sitting outside with a cup of coffee when he walked up the porch steps.

"Missed you on my run this morning."

Barrett lifted a brow. "You must have gotten up later than I did. I did mine about four thirty."

"Bullshit. You were sleeping at four thirty."

Barrett took a sip of his coffee. "Guess you'll never know, will you?"

Flynn laughed and went inside. Everyone was gathered in the kitchen, which was typical. He didn't know how his mother handled cooking with a room full of people, but it never seemed to bother her. Then again, she usually put people to work if they were in there, so maybe that was all part of her plan.

Clever woman.

Amelia was busy at the stove flipping bacon. She lifted her head when he came over. He brushed his lips across hers and she smiled.

"You're all sweaty. How was your run?"

"Great. I could use a drink."

"There's a pitcher of lemon ice water over on the dining room table," his mother said, patting him on the back. Then she rubbed her fingers together. "You *are* sweaty. Go into our bathroom and wash up. And change your drenched T-shirt before you sit down to breakfast."

"Yes, ma'am."

Feeling good, he took the stairs two at a time, to reach the second floor where his parents' bedroom was located. He washed up in their bathroom, then went into their closet, where he grabbed one of his dad's old Green Bay T-shirts to throw on. He knew his dad wouldn't mind.

When he came downstairs, his dad grinned. "Good choice."

"I knew you'd think so." He poured himself a glass of water and drained it in a few swallows. He refilled the glass and headed into the dining room, sipping it this time.

"Good run today?"

He turned to find Katrina's teenage brother, Leo. "Yeah."

Leo had filled out a lot since Flynn had first met him. He was a junior in high school now, and a star on his football team. He'd gained about half a foot in height and about fifty pounds of muscle. With his dark brown hair and blue eyes, the kid was a true lady-killer. And from what Grant had told him, a damn good football player, too.

"How's football this season?"

Leo smiled. "Good. Really good. We made state."

"That's great news. You getting a lot of playing time?"

"Every game."

Flynn saw the pride in Leo's eyes when he said that. He was really happy for the kid.

They talked stats for a while. Flynn was impressed with Leo's abilities as a wide receiver, especially since Leo hadn't played football until his freshman year of high school. But with Grant's guidance, Flynn had no doubt the kid would do well.

"Okay, everyone," his mom said, "get your plates and start filling them up. Breakfast is ready."

"I don't know about you," Flynn said to Leo, "but I'm starving, so you'd better beat me to the line or I'm taking all the bacon."

Leo cracked a smile. "You're older and slower than me. Not a chance."

Flynn laughed. When Leo had first met the family, he'd been sort of shy. It was great to see him so bold and confident now. He was quickly becoming a Cassidy family member.

Despite his boasts to Leo, Flynn met up with Amelia and waited for their elders to serve themselves first. Then they got in line behind Grant and his family.

Breakfast was a full meal, as was typical on a ranch. They had eggs, bacon, sausages, fried potatoes, fruit salad, oatmeal, toast and biscuits and gravy, along with coffee, milk and three types of juice, all freshly squeezed. It was more like a buffet than a breakfast.

"I'm going to be fueled for the rest of the day by the time I finish breakfast," Amelia said.

Flynn smiled. "Mom's used to cooking for my dad and uncles

and several ranch hands, who often don't stop for lunch. Breakfast is always a big deal. Plus, everyone will be busy cooking Thanksgiving dinner today. So lunch will be light."

Amelia nodded. "Lydia already has the turkey in the oven. It's great that she has the double oven, so after breakfast I'll start on the pies. Once the turkey's done, we can work on some of the sides."

He leaned over and brushed his lips against her ear. "I can hardly wait to taste what you've cooked."

"What *we've* cooked. It's going to be a joint effort today."

They settled in at the table and Flynn dug into his meal. He was always really hungry after a run, so he ate—a lot.

Then again, so did his brothers. Their plates were piled as high as his, so he didn't feel too bad about those four pieces of bacon. And two sausages. And all those eggs.

"How did you feed all these guys when they were growing up, Lydia?" Amelia asked, her eyes wide as she surveyed Flynn's and his brothers' plates.

His mom laughed. "It was a challenge. We were very lucky that we could afford four growing, hungry boys. And Mia was no slouch in the eating department, either."

Mia shrugged. "I'm nothing if not competitive. Of course that meant I also had to get out and run with these beasts to burn it all off."

"If Lydia hadn't had a job as a lawyer and I hadn't played professional football, we probably would have had to start selling off kids just to pay the mortgage," Easton said, then winked at Amelia.

She laughed. "I'm making a mental note to have no more than two children."

"Easton and I thought we'd only have two kids," Lydia said. "Then after Flynn and Grant, the twins came. They were a surprise."

"And what an awesome surprise we were," Tucker said with a grin.

"Hell yeah we were."

Tucker and Barrett high-fived.

Mia rolled her eyes.

"Oh, right," Flynn said. "I was fine by myself. Then I had Grant to contend with. I figured, okay, I can handle him. Then Mom comes home from the hospital with two babies—both boys. God, it was awful."

Amelia laughed. "You poor thing."

He looked at her. "You don't even know how horrible it was. Like a nightmare."

"Uh-huh. I'm sure it was."

"And you wanted a girl," his dad said to his mom, "so we tried one more time."

"And I was convinced Mom was going to have yet another boy," Flynn said.

"I think by that point we were all certain it was going to be a boy," Grant said, then he looked over at Mia. "And then you showed up and ruined everything."

Mia laughed. "No, I finally gave Mom and Dad what they really wanted after those first four wasted efforts." She beamed a smile.

Amelia laughed. "Quite the handful, this family."

"Oh, Amelia, you have no idea." Lydia shot a wry smile over at Amelia. "But every one of these kids has been worth it. We've had such an amazing, happy life."

To hear his mother say that meant everything to Flynn. He loved his parents, and he knew the sacrifices they had made—especially his mom—to raise five children. Sure, his dad had made a good living as a quarterback, and his mother had done exceptionally well as an attorney. But when they decided to buy the ranch, his mother had given up her career, choosing to dedicate her time to raising all of them.

"Mom, I don't know that I ever told you how much I appreciate you sacrificing your career to raise us," Flynn said.

His mother cocked her head to the side. "It was never a sacrifice, Flynn. It was a choice. I didn't give up a thing."

"Well, thank you. Because we all benefitted from it."

She got up and came around the table, put her arms around Flynn and kissed his cheek. "Thank you. That means a lot."

"Oh sure, say the nice thing," Tucker said. "Now we're all going to have to hug her."

"Yeah, and the next thing you know there'll be a group hug," Barrett said.

Mia grimaced. "Not the Cassidy family group hug. I hate those."

His mother laughed. "All of you finish your breakfasts. We can group hug later."

"Thank God for that," Mia said. "Because I'm shorter than all of you and I always get stuck in the middle of those group hugs. It's like being squashed by bears."

The more time she spent with the Cassidys, the more Amelia wished she had grown up with siblings. Of course, her mother had barely known what to do with her, let alone more than one child. Career had been everything to her mother. She'd had little interest in raising a daughter. If Amelia hadn't had her father around, she wouldn't have had much parenting at all. Or any love.

Her father's death had left a giant hole on the parenting front. Being here was filling a well Amelia hadn't realized had felt so empty for the past ten years since her father had died. And she intended to let that well fill with love and laughter for as long as she was here.

She was also filling the well of her stomach, and she was afraid her clothes weren't going to fit by the time she left. It was a good thing they were only here for a couple of days. If she ate like this all the time, she'd have to get up in the mornings and start running with Flynn, and she wasn't a runner.

Once breakfast was finished, they all took their plates into the kitchen and the guys did cleanup. She couldn't quite get used to seeing that, but she had to admit she enjoyed watching Flynn, his brothers, his dad and his uncles do dishes and clean the kitchen. She made a mental note to train her sons—if she had any—early on how to clean a kitchen and do dishes. It was such an admirable trait.

"It is fun to watch them, isn't it?" Aubry asked as she came up beside Amelia.

"It's something you don't see every day. Something I don't see every day, anyway."

"Oh, come on," Mia said as she came up to lean against the counter on Amelia's other side. "You're a head chef. Surely you employ male staff who do dishes."

"That's different. In my personal world, this is unique. I've dated men—hell, I married one—who never once stepped foot in a kitchen, either to cook or to do the cleanup."

Mia slanted a look of surprise at her. "Really?"

"Yes. I guess some men are still married to traditional gender roles."

"I guess so."

"Those men aren't in this kitchen, obviously," Harmony said. "And I for one am so grateful for that. Barrett is more than willing to wash dishes, do laundry and cook a meal."

Aubry nodded. "My schedule is always so whacked out that it's not like I'm home at five o'clock every night. And I don't have to worry about him starving, because Tucker knows how to fix a meal for himself. And often I'll come home after working a hellishly long shift at the hospital and he'll have fixed something and left it in the fridge for me to warm up."

"Aww, that's so sweet," Amelia said.

"It really is."

"It makes me appreciate Flynn so much more because he does spend a lot of time not only in his kitchen, but also never has a problem mixing it up in mine, including the cleanup part."

Aubry smiled. "That's great."

"If you all are going to continue to wax poetic about my brothers, I'm going to lose my breakfast," Mia said. "Knock it off."

Amelia laughed. "Sorry."

"They are kind of atypical," Harmony said.

"More like ass-holical," Mia said. "But that's my perspective because I grew up with them. I've seen them crack jokes about buttholes and B.O. and seen them shove things up their noses that you do not want to know about."

Amelia looked over at Aubry and Harmony. "That does make Flynn seem a lot less attractive to me."

Harmony grimaced. "I'm going to have to break up with Barrett and go home."

Aubry nodded. "Agreed. I'm calling off the wedding right now."

Tucker's gaze shot up from where he was standing at the sink. "Wait. What did you just say?"

Aubry laughed. "He has very good hearing." She looked over at Tucker. "Just joking around, babe."

"You'd better be. We are getting married and you don't get to change your mind." Tucker scanned their group. "And quit talking to Mia."

"He knows I know all his secrets." Mia nodded and shot Tucker a knowing smile. "They all know that. I should start asking for money."

"You really should," Amelia said. "You could amass a small fortune."

"It could be an amazing side business. Or source my future endeavors. I could call it Mia's Extortion Fund."

Aubry grinned. "I love this idea—and this wickedly smart entrepreneurial side of you, Mia."

"Thank you, Aubry."

Amelia nodded. "If you're really smart you could double down by not only taking their money, but then selling their secrets to their girlfriends, fiancées, wives. Double the money."

Mia turned to her. "That's diabolical. And brilliant. I like this side of you, Amelia."

Amelia shrugged, but had to fight back a laugh. "Thank you. And if you need a partner, just let me know."

"I will."

All joking aside, Amelia was very impressed with how thorough—and how quickly—the guys cleaned up the kitchen. Within twenty minutes they were out of the way so the women could all get in there and start cooking dinner.

Flynn stuck around to help, so they ended up having plenty of hands. Amelia, along with Anya, made several pies while the rest of the group concentrated on fixing side dishes. Before long it was steamy hot in the kitchen and Lydia turned on the air conditioner. Katrina had made sangria, so they were all sipping the cool drink and talking while they did their respective cooking tasks.

Amelia had slid the pies into the oven, so she took her glass of sangria and stepped outside on the front porch for a minute before diving into the next task.

Lydia came out soon after and sat beside Amelia on the porch swing.

"You work so quickly," Lydia said. "It takes me hours just to make one pie, and you've done six."

"I'm used to working fast because of the restaurant. And it's all about having the ingredients laid out and the tasks in order in my head. Plus, it's my job, so that makes it easier for me."

"I imagine that's true. Stuff that seems difficult for someone else is probably cake for you."

"Well, I couldn't walk into a courtroom and argue a case because that's not my area of expertise. Whereas you probably watch all those courtroom dramas on television and roll your eyes at the lack of accuracy."

Lydia laughed. "You have no idea. It's so frustrating."

"I'm sure it is."

"How do you feel about the cooking shows on TV? Do they drive you crazy?"

"Some of them do if they're all about dramatic effect with no substance. But a few are actually pretty good. If they can show the viewer the passion behind the cooking, and give them real world information on how to create something, then I'm all for it. I enjoy quite a few shows."

"So do I. Which ones do you like?"

They talked about which were their favorites. It turned out they shared a number in common, from cooking shows to a couple of the reality competition shows.

"I know you told us all yesterday how you started your career in cooking. But I'm interested in your earlier life. Did you learn to cook from either of your parents, Amelia?" Lydia asked.

"Oh, no. In high school, actually. I took a basic cooking skills class and fell in love. The instructor encouraged me to take an advanced class, which I did, and from there I was hooked. In college I got my bachelor's degree in management, found a job at a restaurant and worked there while I went to school. After graduating, I attended culinary school."

"It's great that you knew what you wanted and went after it."

She nodded. "Yes, much to my mother's disappointment."

Lydia frowned. "She was disappointed? Why?"

"She thought it was a frivolous career with no earning potential. She was a financial analyst, so money was everything to her."

"Oh. Well, that's disappointing. For you."

Amelia shrugged. "My mother was always about career. A lot less about home and family. I was kind of an afterthought to her."

Lydia reached out and laid her hand on Amelia's arm. "I'm sorry."

Amelia looked over at Lydia, horrified that she'd spilled so much personal information. "I'm . . . sorry I brought it up. I never do. I don't know why I said anything. I honestly wasn't looking for sympathy."

"No, you said it because you wanted to talk to someone about it. Am I right?"

"Maybe. I think it's also because I'm so fascinated by your family dynamic. You have such a warm and loving family. The siblings all get along, your husband's brothers live nearby. It's such a tight-knit group."

"And you didn't have that."

"Not really. My father loved and adored me. He gave me everything I could ever want in a parent, so I never felt I was missing anything. He passed away ten years ago."

"I'm sorry, Amelia."

"Thank you. My mother remarried about a year after my father died, and she relocated to Arizona where her new husband's family lives."

"Do you see her often?"

Amelia shook her head. "Hardly at all. We weren't close anyway, and the geographical distance only separated us further."

"That has to hurt."

"It did at first. I felt like she'd abandoned me after my dad died. But in actuality, I find I don't really miss her all that much. I suppose it's because she gave me so little affection as a child. I do miss my dad though. A lot."

"I'm sure you do. You don't have any brothers or sisters?"

"No. Just me."

Lydia gave her a sweet smile and squeezed her hand. "Well, you know, family comes in many forms, not all of it blood."

She returned the smile, feeling the genuine warmth and affection that she'd felt from the moment she'd met Lydia. "Now, that I do know. I stayed close with my best friend from college, and she lives in San Francisco. So we've grown even closer since I moved there. She and her husband own a house just down the street from me. It's been wonderful having a best friend nearby."

"That's good. It's important to have a friend you can share all of your secrets with."

Amelia laughed. "Laura definitely knows all of my secrets. And all of my sins. She was there for me, on the phone and in person with many visits when I went through my divorce."

"Oh. I'm sorry about that, too."

"Trust me, I'm much happier now than when I was married. I made a huge mistake and married the wrong guy."

"That happens. But it sounds to me like you're heading in the right direction now. You have close friends and a wonderful career as a chef."

"I am. I'm very happy. I have to say how much I admire you, Lydia, for giving up your career to put your family first."

Lydia smiled at her. "I never felt as if I was giving anything up. Easton and I saw this property and we fell in love with it. We wanted to give the kids a rural lifestyle, away from the city. He was several years away from retiring from football, and we could have waited for that, but I felt it was the right time to buy the ranch before the kids got too old. And I didn't want to miss their childhoods while I was working. I knew staying at home with them was the right decision for me. I couldn't imagine other people raising our children while both of us stayed in Wisconsin and continued with our careers.

"It was an easy decision to make. Easton was concerned, of course, because he knew I loved my job, but honestly? My kids always came first. And I loved having that time with them before they were all grown and gone. We were lucky my staying at home was an option financially."

Amelia blinked back the sting of tears. Her mother would have never made that choice. Asking her to give up her career—even give up a day of it—would have been like asking her to give up a vital organ. "I don't think you really have an idea how much it meant to your children to have you there with them."

Lydia looked out over the property, a warm smile on her face. "Oh, I know. It benefitted all of us, trust me."

And that was what it was like to feel the love of a mother. Even though Lydia wasn't her mother, she could feel the thousand-watt strength of that love pouring out of her.

It made her very happy to know Lydia. To know Flynn, and know that he came from someone as wonderful as this woman.

After sitting outside a few more minutes, they went back in and started on another cooking task.

Lydia was very easy to talk to. Maybe that's why Amelia had blurted out some secrets from her past. She hoped Lydia didn't feel too burdened by them, or think less of her for telling them.

But surprisingly, Amelia felt lightened by sharing a little bit of her past with Flynn's mother. She wasn't sure why, but she felt closer to Lydia for having shared parts of her past. And maybe that was a good thing.

TWENTY-SIX

IF FLYNN ATE ONE MORE THING TODAY HE WAS GOING to explode. Or have to go on a run again tonight. He was so full. There'd been so much food on the table he hadn't been sure he was going to be able to fit it all on his plate.

Oh, who was he kidding? Of course he'd gotten it all on his plate. Just not in the first round.

He'd made the sausage, apple and cranberry dressing. It had turned out damn good. Even Amelia had approved, and so had his mother, who had told him he had to come home every Thanksgiving from now on to fix it. Amelia had made him promise he'd fix it for her again.

Nothing like high praise from your mom *and* your girlfriend to make a guy feel good.

But after they all cleaned up and put away the leftovers, he had to figure out how to find room for all those pies Amelia had made.

Because she'd made six of them. Two pumpkin, one cherry, two pecan and an apple. He wanted a slice of each.

Not gonna happen. He had a game Sunday, which meant in just three short days he was going to have to hustle his body off the mark, not sludge across the line like an overstuffed turkey.

So maybe one piece of pie.

Okay, two, at most.

"Did I tell you that Anya made cherry cheesecake, too?" Amelia said as she came up beside him while he was staring at all the pies on the counter.

He groaned. "You are all trying to kill me. Did I mention I need   fast on Sunday?"

"Why? You never were before."

Flynn frowned as his brother walked past. "Fuck you, Tucker."

Tucker just laughed as he left the room.

"I'm going to bury him on family game day tomorrow."

"I'll be sure to have my phone out for that. Aubry might need it for evidence."

"Please don't kill my fiancé before we get married," Aubry said as she moved by. She stopped and swiveled to face them. "That sounded really bad. Please do not kill my fiancé ever. There, that sounded much better."

Aubry walked away.

Flynn could tell Amelia had been accepted by his family, which meant a lot to him. And after they sampled her wide selection of pies, they told her they were in love with her. They were sitting around the enormous dining room table drinking coffee, everyone groaning about how full they were.

"You have to stay here now," Easton said to her, "so you can make pie for me every day."

She smiled. "I'm so glad you liked it."

"We'd like you even if you couldn't cook, by the way," Easton said. "Just wanted to clarify that."

She laughed. "I'm glad to hear it."

"If you ate three slices of pie every day, you'd be too fat to work the ranch," Lydia said. "So I'm afraid Amelia will have to go home."

Katrina rubbed her stomach. "I'm really glad I don't have a photo shoot until after the holidays. I'm going to have to keep a strict gym regimen or I'm going to be in trouble."

"Is it hard work staying in shape?" Amelia asked Katrina.

"Not too bad for me yet. I'm fortunate to have a fast metabolism, so most of the workouts I do with my trainer are for muscle-toning purposes. Eventually my metabolism will slow down and diet will become a factor. Especially with the way my sister cooks."

"Oh, sure," Anya said. "Blame me. In advance."

"Just did."

"You're perfect. And when you put on weight, you'll still be perfect," Grant said.

Katrina lifted her gaze to Grant and smiled. "Thank you. And I might be perfect in your eyes, but I'll be retired as a model. The cameras are rather unforgiving."

"Eh, screw them," Grant said. "You can do infomercials."

She laughed. "Right. Like that's high on my list."

Flynn's phone rang. He picked it up, surprised to see Spencer Ryan on the other end. Since Spencer handled all his PR, it had to be important or he would never call him on a holiday. He left the table and punched the button.

"Hey, Spence. Happy Thanksgiving."

"Same to you, Flynn. I'm really sorry to call you on a holiday, but I got an offer that I think you might find interesting. If this is a bad time, I can wait."

"No, go ahead."

He listened, then told Spencer he'd get back to him first thing in the morning. He went back to the table and poured himself another cup of coffee from the carafe.

"Is everything all right?" Amelia asked.

"It was my PR person. Spencer said one of the cooking networks called. They want Ninety-Two to participate in some kind of battle of the sports restaurants. It would be televised, with a signature dish from each restaurant cooked and featured on a TV special they want to tape."

"Wow," Anya said. "That sounds amazing."

"It would be great exposure for Ninety-Two," Mia said. "You're not going to turn it down, are you?"

"I told Spencer I'd think about it and get back to him tomorrow."

"What does it entail?" Amelia asked. "How much media will be at the restaurant? You do have your clients to think about and you don't want them to be inconvenienced."

"Yeah, I thought about that. Spencer said it's one day and they're out."

Amelia nodded. "That's not bad. And Mia's right about the exposure. If they're going to feature you and the restaurant, you can't go wrong."

"It is basically free publicity, right?" his mother asked.

"Yeah, I think so."

"I say go for it," his dad said. "If your PR guy says it's a good deal, then he wouldn't steer you wrong."

"No, he wouldn't. Spencer said this is a good network deal. There's no money in it, of course, just free publicity for the restaurant."

"You don't need the money," Tucker said. "But the opportunity to drive more business to Ninety-Two would be great."

"I agree with Tucker," Barrett said. "I can't see how this is a bad deal any way you look at it, Flynn."

"Yeah. I'll think about it tonight, but I'm leaning toward saying yes. They'll have to film when I'm in town, so I can oversee it."

"Of course they would," Amelia said. "Since you'd be one of the features anyway. And hopefully Ken will be back in charge by then as well so he could be there."

"Yes. I'd like that."

"How exciting," Anya said. "I'd get to see your restaurant on TV."

"You are welcome to come out and see the restaurant in person any time you want. I'm sorry you weren't available for the grand opening."

Anya grimaced. "Yeah. School. Ugh. I hated missing it."

"You need to have Grant and Katrina bring you out."

"I do, don't I? Part of my culinary education."

Katrina rolled her eyes. "You think anything and everything is part of your culinary education."

"I know, isn't it great? That's because no matter where you go, there's food. Isn't that right, Amelia?"

Amelia nodded. "She's got you there, I'm afraid."

"Yeah, she's already hitting us up for Paris," Grant said. "Since she's of legal drinking age there, she wants to sample the food and the wine."

"You're a wise young woman, Anya."

"Quit encouraging her, Amelia," Grant said.

Amelia laughed. "Sorry."

"Though I do have a shoot there in the spring," Katrina said. "And maybe if it's during Anya's spring break . . ."

Anya's eyes widened. "Really?"

"Really."

"Hey, that means I get to go, too," Leo said.

Grant nodded. "We'll all go."

"Well, now I want to go to Paris," Amelia said. "I haven't been in years."

She looked over at Flynn.

"Don't look at me. I'm just over here digesting."

She laughed. "Okay, fine. We'll talk about Paris some other time. But I'm making a mental note."

He swept his hand over her hair. "You do that."

The thought of spending some time alone with Amelia in Paris had definite appeal. Flynn had never been there, but he knew she'd enjoy it.

And he'd enjoy anything she loved.

His heart was in deep with this woman, something that was becoming more and more clear to him every minute he spent with her. He'd been trying to take things slowly with her, given her reluctance to even enter a relationship. But maybe it was time to step it up a bit and see how she reacted.

Because he was definitely ready for the next step in their relationship.

TWENTY-SEVEN

FLYNN DID HIS RUN EARLY THE NEXT MORNING BEFORE Amelia was even awake. They'd both stayed up long into the night with the family playing poker, a Thanksgiving night tradition.

Tucker had won all the chips, the bastard. Flynn was certain he'd cheated.

He'd run toward the main house and was about to take the turn to head back to the guesthouse when he saw his mother step out onto the porch with her cup of coffee, so he stopped and walked toward her.

"Sweaty again, I see," his mom said.

He huffed out a few breaths and nodded, then walked back and forth in front of the porch so he wouldn't stiffen up.

"Want some juice or a tall glass of water, or are you going to head back to the guesthouse?"

"I'll take some water, please."

She set her coffee on the table. "I'll be right back."

He stretched, did a slow jog back and forth down the walkway for a few seconds until his mom showed up with his water then headed up the steps and took the glass from her.

"Thanks." He took several deep swallows of water, then set it down on the table and took a seat next to his mom.

"I didn't mean to interrupt your run."

"You didn't. And I'll finish it on the way back."

"Okay." Mom sipped her coffee, quiet as always.

"We had fun last night. And all day yesterday."

"Did you? That's good. I like Amelia, Flynn."

He'd wondered how his mom felt about Amelia. They seemed to get along well, but he'd wanted more details, her specific thoughts about him and Amelia together. It was one of the reasons he'd stopped this morning to talk to her. He hadn't had a chance to get her alone yesterday with the whole family around. He valued his mom's opinion and he wanted to get her take on Amelia.

"Do you?"

"Yes, I do. But you know, my opinion—anyone's opinion, shouldn't matter to you. How do you feel about her?"

He dragged in a deep breath, then let it out. "I'm crazy about her. I think I've been crazy about her since the moment I met her."

That made her smile. "I can see why. She's smart, talented, funny, and she clearly feels the same about you."

"Does she? I'm not sure. She holds her emotions deep inside. She had a rough go of it during her marriage. The guy treated her badly."

Mom frowned. "She told me she was divorced, but she didn't get into details. He didn't abuse her, did he?"

Flynn shook his head. "No, not physically, anyway. But he didn't trust her, accused her of things she didn't do. So she put all of her love and trust in this guy, gave her heart to him, and he stomped all over it."

"And now she's reluctant to give her heart again. That's understandable."

"Yeah. I've given her space and I haven't told her how I feel."

She looked over at him. "And how do you feel?"

"I'm in love with her, Mom." Saying the words out loud were a shock to him. But as soon as he said them, he knew they were true. It felt right.

She laid her hand on his arm. "That's so good to hear. And also terrifying. Because if she doesn't reciprocate your feelings, she could break *your* heart."

"I think she feels the same way I do. But I want to approach her cautiously."

His mother's lips curved. "Like a scared cat?"

He smiled, too. "Something like that. I'm not in any hurry. It took me a long time to find her. She's worth waiting for."

"I hope you're right. I don't want either of you to be hurt. I especially don't want you to be hurt. You're my firstborn. You've always looked out for your siblings, making sure they were the ones who took the right road in life. But there was never anyone to look out for you."

He took her hand. "You're wrong about that. There was you— and Dad. I never felt like I was alone."

Her eyes brimmed with tears. "I hoped you always felt like you could come to us—to me, with anything. That you could talk to me about anything that concerned you."

He held up his glass of water. "Why do you think I'm sitting here with you now?"

She laughed. "I love you, Flynn."

"I love you, too, Mom."

They sat there together for a few more minutes, then his dad showed up with a cup of coffee. He talked to his dad for a few minutes about his parents' plans to buy up the adjacent land, which sounded like a really good deal.

Then he got up, kissed his mom on the cheek and started his run back to the guesthouse.

By the time he got there, Amelia was awake and drinking a cup of coffee at the kitchen table. He grabbed another glass of water, downed it in a few swallows then went over and brushed his lips across hers.

She smiled up at him. "You were up early this morning."

"Yeah. I wanted to get my run in before you got up."

"The bed was cold and lonely without you in it."

Exactly what he needed to hear.

"I guess we could go warm it up again."

"Do you have time before the family football game this morning?"

He cocked a brow. "Did you seriously just ask me to decide between sex with you and football with my family?"

"I guess I did."

"There is no decision. Let's get naked."

She smiled a wicked smile at him, set her coffee cup down, stood up, pulled off her tank top and shimmied out of her pants.

And now she was naked. In the kitchen.

His cock roared to life, hard and throbbing. He jerked his T-shirt over his head, toed off his tennis shoes and pulled off his socks, then shrugged out of his sweats and dragged his boxer briefs off.

All the while, he watched as his girlfriend sipped coffee naked.

"I don't know that I've ever seen anyone get out of their clothes so fast," she said.

"I was incentivized by a hot, naked woman in the kitchen."

She put down her coffee mug, came over to him and wrapped her hand around his cock, stroking it with a firm grip. "I had a hot sexy dream last night about you and me in the kitchen."

His brows shot up. "You did?" His cock tightened. "You know you're going to have to tell me about it. Preferably while I'm inside of you."

"Yes. I woke up wet and ready for you. Sadly, you were gone."

"Now I'm really sorry I went for that early run."

"Oh, that's okay. I just rubbed my pussy and thought about you."

"Christ." He swept his hand around the nape of her neck and put his mouth over hers in a hard, demanding, passionate kiss that made her moan. She flicked her tongue against his, then sucked it, which made him groan against her lips.

She pulled away. "I'm ready for you, Flynn. Hot and wet and ready for you to fuck me on the kitchen counter." She reached over and pulled out a condom packet from a nearby drawer.

"You are ready."

"I told you—I had this dream."

While he put on the condom, she inched up onto the counter. "You gave it to me hard here. Really hard."

He scooped his hand under her butt and she wrapped her legs around his hips while he entered her, driving into her with one fierce thrust. She gasped and raked her nails down across his shoulder.

"Like this?" He powered in, then out, then drove in harder.

She lifted her gaze to his, her eyes all hot passion. "Yes, exactly like that."

It was fast and furious, both of them panting as he shoved his cock in and out of her, making sure to grind against her clit with his body.

Amelia dug her nails into his arms and lifted against him, her pussy tightening around him with each thrust of his cock.

"Oh, yes, yes, just like this," she said, tilting her head back to look at him. "That's going to make me come. Fuck me faster."

He did, and she exploded around him with waves of contractions that unraveled him. He climaxed with her, taking her mouth as he spurted inside of her with a furious rush of violent pulses that made him feel light-headed.

For a while, there was only the sound of both of them breathing heavily. Amelia ran her fingers down his arms.

"I need a shower," she said.

"Me, too. But I think I'll hold off until after the football game."

He hoisted her off the counter and set her on her feet. She grabbed on to him, lifted up on her toes and kissed him.

When she pulled back, she smiled. "You made my dream come true, Flynn."

His heart did a strange leap against his chest. "Glad to hear that."

"I'm off to shower. I'll be right back."

"Okay."

He watched her walk away, enjoying the view of her very fine ass as she disappeared down the hall.

She'd taken his breath away. And his heart, too.

Damn.

TWENTY-EIGHT

IT WAS OBVIOUS THAT THE CASSIDYS TOOK THEIR football very seriously.

Amelia expected a lackadaisical football game, kind of half-assing it, maybe more like touch or flag football.

Oh, no. This was no-holds-barred, might-as-well-be-a-real-game kind of football with tackling in the dirt and everything.

Neighbors had showed up as well, so it was clearly some kind of annual event. Some young guys, some not so young and some in between, so they'd fielded two entire teams.

After they'd had breakfast, Lydia had already started to prepare lunch. There were leftovers from yesterday, along with a ham and some steaks Lydia said they were going to throw on the grill. Lydia was also making potato salad. They'd all pitched in and some of the neighbors brought food, too.

Amelia had met a lot of people and she'd never remember all their names, but now she sat outside in a chair next to Mia, who explained to her that the Cassidy Thanksgiving football game had started out small, but had quickly become an annual event.

"At first it was just the family. Then a few of the guys' friends wandered over. Then some neighbors. Before long, we had fielded enough players that we had teams."

"Obviously it's a serious thing."

"You have no idea."

"You even have team shirts. Green and white. This is like . . . an actual game."

Mia laughed. "All thanks to my dad. I think he misses playing, so this is his chance to get back in the game. He quarterbacks for the green team, of course, and Grant for the white team. Then they do schoolyard picks for the rest."

Amelia looked over the teams as they all put their shirts on. Flynn and Barrett were on Grant's team. Tucker was on Easton's team. Two of Easton's brothers, Elijah and Eddie, were on his team. His other brother, Eldon, was on Grant's team.

"They don't really pick by favorites, do they?" Amelia asked.

"Nah. They just switch it up every year. For example, last year Flynn and Barrett were on Dad's team and Tucker was on Grant's. So this year they swapped. Same with all the family friends and neighbors. Dad and Grant know exactly who was on whose team last year and they just swap. And whoever got picked first last year? They get chosen last this year. That way no one gets their feelings hurt."

"I see. And it keeps things fair that way."

"Right. It's just for fun. Until they start playing. Then it's no-holds-barred, at least to a certain extent. Flynn, Barrett and Grant have games this weekend and everyone knows that. No one wants them to get hurt."

Amelia looked over at Flynn, who had hiked up his sweats and was currently getting ready for his dad's team to have the ball.

"I don't know. Flynn looks like he's tougher than a lot of these guys here. And Barrett looks huge and mean, too."

"Oh, they are. And they know it. Which is why they all gang up on these guys."

Amelia laughed. "Should I be concerned for Flynn's safety?"

"No. Like I said, they'll go after him, but no one wants him to get hurt. They root for him every weekend."

Before she knew it, Easton had hiked the ball. She held her breath as Flynn rushed off the line. He was covered by a swarm of tall, farmhand-type boys who were about ten years younger than he was, and taken to the ground. She was certain Flynn was at the bottom of that pile.

People were cheering, Amelia had no idea where the ball was or who had it because she was concentrating on that Flynn pile. And when they all got up, there was Flynn, laughing, taking the hand that was extended to him by one of the boys.

"Your ass is mine next time, Bennett."

One of the kids, tall and muscular, shot Flynn a smirk. "Good luck trying, Cassidy."

Then it all started over again. This time Flynn got the best of the kid, shoving him out of the way and getting so close to his father that Amelia thought for sure Flynn was going to pile drive Easton right into the ground. But Flynn only grabbed his father around his middle, then the play was blown dead.

Easton patted Flynn on the head. "Do it just like that this weekend, kid."

Flynn grinned. "You know I will."

Amelia must have held her breath for the entire hour the game was played, until Lydia said it was time for lunch.

Then everyone filed into the house, hands and faces were washed and plates were loaded with food. The guys, of course, piled their plates high, no doubt having worked up appetites with all that game play.

Flynn threw an arm around her shoulders. "So, what did you think?"

"I think you're all crazy. But it was so much fun to watch."

"Watch? Oh, no. Second half we bring the women in."

She laughed. "I don't think so."

"He's not kidding," Aubry said. "They're much gentler when we play."

Amelia looked from Aubry to Flynn, who nodded. "We really are. And if someone gets hurt, we have a doctor on board."

"This is true," Aubry said, taking a bite of potato salad. "Providing you don't lay the doctor flat."

"Would we do that?" Tucker asked.

"Given half a chance, yes." Aubry cast a shifty look toward Tucker.

Amelia made sure to stock up on protein over lunch. She was certain she was going to need it.

"I'm not sure what position I'm going to be any good at," she said as she and Flynn sat outside at one of the picnic tables and ate.

He leaned over and whispered to her, "You're excellent at every position you've played with me."

She laughed, then nudged her shoulder against his. "I meant football."

"Oh, did you? My bad."

After lunch they realigned the teams with women included. Lydia begged off claiming a bad knee, but otherwise, all the other women were on board.

Amelia found herself playing wide receiver, hoping she could actually catch the ball if it was thrown at her. She was also on the same team as Tucker and Easton, which meant she was playing against Flynn. She was determined to ignore his presence, because the last thing she wanted was Flynn tackling her.

Unless it was in the bedroom.

She lined up in her position. She was told this was a running play, so she wouldn't get the ball. All she had to do was block Mia, who was playing for the other team.

Mia was smaller than her. She was certain she could do that.

At the snap, she ran and pushed into Mia, who might be shorter than her, but she was tough. They went toe-to-toe, shoving against each other in one hell of a battle. When the play ended, both of them were winded.

"Okay, you're strong," Amelia said.

Mia grinned. "I have to be with these guys around. Plus, lifting weights and yoga pay off."

"I'm making a mental note of that."

She held her own for the next several plays, until Easton told her in the huddle that she was getting the ball, so she should go long and wait for it.

She really hoped she didn't embarrass the Cassidy family by totally missing it. Or even worse, tripping and falling.

She pushed off at the snap and brushed past one of the neighborhood women whose name she didn't recall. At least she had that part down. She ran as fast as she could, turned and, holy crap, there was the ball. It landed in her hands and she outran the guy chasing her and ended up at the end zone.

Suddenly there were cheers, and she caught sight of Easton and Tucker, both of them with their arms up in the air.

She's scored a touchdown. Holy shit.

Even Flynn came over and hoisted her in his arms.

"You did it, babe," he said. "You scored."

She felt exhilarated. No wonder athletes loved playing. This felt really damn good.

She grinned, then pulled herself out of the game so someone else could play. She took a seat next to Lydia, who handed her a glass of lemonade. She savored several long swallows.

"You played well."

Amelia laughed. "I am not an athlete. But it was fun. And I scored. That's one for the memory books."

"As long as you had a good time."

"I did. I also have a new appreciation for what your husband did and what your sons do. That is some hard work. I'm sure every part of me is going to be sore tomorrow."

"They do work hard. Easton used to have a standing appointment with my massage therapist every Monday. He used to scoff at me for getting massages, until I convinced him to go. He still goes to the one I use in Austin a couple of times a month. Ranching isn't any easier than football."

"No, I imagine it isn't."

"You should consider it. You probably spend a lot of time on your feet."

"I do. And I should. Right now a massage sounds like a small slice of heaven."

After the game ended, the party broke up and everyone started leaving. Grant and his crew had to head out, because he needed to be at his team facility early the next morning.

"I'm going to come visit you someday and we're going to have a cooking frenzy," Anya said before she and Amelia hugged each other.

"I really hope you do."

She said her good-byes to Grant and Katrina and Leo as well.

Flynn had an away game this weekend, so he had to report early to his team tomorrow as well, and Amelia had to work, so they packed up and said their good-byes.

She hugged Mia. "Stay in touch."

"I will. Hopefully I'll be out in the Bay Area again soon and I'll see you."

"I hope so."

She loved this family. She had fallen hard for all of Flynn's siblings and their girlfriends and fiancées. Saying good-bye was rough, but she had been so happy to meet all of them.

She said good-bye to Easton, then hugged Lydia. "It was such a pleasure to meet you and spend time with you."

"Same here," Lydia said "I hope we get to see you again."

"I'd like that very much."

"That would be amazing. Do come visit."

She was actually sad to leave the ranch. After having had so much trepidation about coming here, these people felt like family to her now.

She really hoped she'd get a chance to come back here someday.

Like maybe at Christmas. She was crossing her fingers that things with Flynn and her were progressing well, and that maybe, just maybe, this was the relationship that would heal the wounds of the past and propel her toward a happy future.

She had fallen crazy in love with Flynn, and now she was crazy in love with his family.

She hoped like hell she wasn't setting herself up for an awful heartbreak.

TWENTY-NINE

IT HAD BEEN AN INSANE COUPLE OF WEEKS. FLYNN had had an out-of-town game, and the time he'd had in town had been busy.

Amelia and he had finally had a chance to go see Ken and Adam's baby. They'd gone over one night and had brought dinner that Amelia had cooked. Adam had offered to cook, but Amelia had insisted that it was her gift to them.

She'd made penne pasta along with freshly baked rolls, anti-pasto and a salad. Flynn had brought the wine.

George was absolutely gorgeous and he looked a lot like Adam with his dark good looks and thick, dark hair. They'd had a great time catching up and Ken was fortunately going to be back at work in time for the media event. Adam's leave was longer, which Ken said made him feel better about leaving George.

Amelia had spent as much time as possible holding George, and watching her rock the baby in her arms sent weird pangs of need shooting through Flynn. He'd thought a lot the past year about settling down and having kids, but his main goal had been to find the right woman. The whole kids thing had been something that he'd thought was far off in the distance.

Now, though, he could imagine Amelia holding their child. That "someday" was becoming more and more real to him. It was time to have a conversation with Amelia about his feelings for her.

But it would have to wait until after this whole media event at Ninety-Two.

He'd been in constant contact with Spencer and with the producers of the *Battle of the Restaurant Jocks* show, as he'd been informed it was named. Sounded hokey as hell to him, but he wasn't in television, so what did he know?

They were arriving at the restaurant today, and he was grateful he'd been able to arrange it for a week he was going to be in town.

This was Ken's first week back, and Flynn had never been happier to see someone when he arrived at the restaurant on Monday.

"I am so glad to see you. I'm going to tell you right now that you were greatly missed. Not only by me, but by Amelia and the entire staff."

Ken grinned. "I do like being missed. There's nothing worse than no one noticing you're gone."

"Trust me, everyone noticed you were gone. And I'm damn glad you're back, especially today. Though I'm sorry you're being thrust into the middle of this whole TV show thing."

"It's fine. I'm happy to stay busy. Then I won't hide in my office and cry every time Adam texts me a picture of George."

Flynn put his arm around Ken and gave his shoulder a squeeze. "You know you can dash home for lunch or dinner to spend time with your baby. Or Adam can bring him by."

"I'm going to be fine. It'll just take some time getting used to. And thank you for that."

There was a knock at the door. Flynn sighed. "That's probably the film crew," Flynn said. "I'll go let them in."

Ken gave him an understanding nod. "Let's get this party started."

AMELIA HAD SUPERVISED THE FOOD PURCHASES FOR today at the market, wanting to make sure everything was perfect before she headed over to Ninety-Two. She'd spent the past few days reviewing all of the dishes on the menu, trying to select the best. Since Flynn had been out of town the past few weeks, and then busy with practices for this week's game, he'd left it to her to select the dish they'd prepare.

There was some pressure. But she knew what she wanted to do and she made sure to select the freshest ingredients.

By the time she arrived at the restaurant, she noticed the network's two vans were parked out front, along with a couple of other SUVs.

She was not looking forward to this. She just hoped it brought a lot of great publicity to the restaurant.

Entering the side door, she was stopped by a very tall, imposing looking security guard.

"I'm sorry," he said. "No visitors today."

She rolled her eyes. "I'm the head chef here."

The guy pulled up his netbook. "Name."

"Amelia Lawrence."

He scrolled down the list. "Okay, you're clear."

Taking a deep breath, she repeated her internal mantra—she would not be irritated by the intrusion of people into her place of work.

There were cameras and lights and tripods and something that looked like a giant silver foil alien thing. Jeez, what a mess. Amelia wondered how they were going to get actual customers into the restaurant tonight.

She saw Flynn talking to some guy and went over to him. He looked up at her and smiled.

"Hey, Amelia. This is Paul Birch, the producer of the show they're doing. Paul, this is Amelia Lawrence, head chef of Ninety-Two."

Paul smiled and shook her hand. "Pleasure to meet you, Amelia."

"Same here, Paul. We're all very excited that you're featuring Ninety-Two in your show."

"Thanks. We've heard a lot of great things about the restaurant—and the food here. I'm looking forward to seeing what you cook up for us tonight."

"I know you're going to love it."

Paul grinned at Flynn. "She's confident. I like that."

"She's good at what she does," Flynn said.

Paul's phone buzzed. He looked at it. "I need to take this, so if you'll excuse me for a minute."

Paul stepped outside and Flynn turned to her.

"Exciting day, right?"

"Yes. Very exciting."

"I really want to kiss you right now."

Her lips curved. "Probably not a good idea in front of the camera crew. They might be filming, and I don't think you want that kind of exposure."

"I don't know. I wouldn't mind."

She laughed. "Time for me to get to work. I've got a big day ahead of me, and my team needs to make sure it all looks perfect."

"Okay. I'll see you soon."

She walked away, her stomach already a jumbled knot of nerves. She hoped this went over well for Flynn and that she didn't do anything to screw things up.

On her way into the kitchen she met Blaine Hurst, the director, who told her what time they were going to start the shoot.

"We'll interview Flynn about the restaurant, then move into the kitchen to film you and your crew preparing the meal."

She had been informed in advance that's how it was going to work. She wasn't thrilled that she was going to be on camera, but since it was all part of the deal, and all for Flynn and Ninety-Two, she accepted it.

She nodded. "I'll need to do my prep in advance. That way when you're set to film, my team will have everything ready to go."

"Great," Blaine said. "Thanks for being so cooperative, and so coolheaded about it all."

She smiled at him. "We do have our customers coming in tonight as well, so we're prepping to feed them, too. This is just a little addition to our typical evening."

Blaine smiled. "I like you, Amelia."

She laughed. "I'm glad to hear that. Let's hope it stays that way, Blaine."

She hurried off to meet with her staff and battle plan for tonight's event.

THIRTY

IT WAS CHAOS, BUT AT LEAST IT WAS ORGANIZED chaos. The restaurant was quickly filling with customers. Flynn had closed the restaurant tonight to the public and invited some of the regulars who came in all the time, making it a VIP event. Since there was filming involved, everyone would have to sign a release and he wanted to make sure his regulars were okay with that, so he'd put that on the invitations.

He wanted the evening to be fun. God, he hoped it was going to be fun. Plus, tonight's meals were on the house.

Once the restaurant was full, the cameras were turned on him and he did his spiel about why he'd wanted to open Ninety-Two. He hoped he hadn't sounded like an asshole when he talked about his love for cooking and how involved he was with the restaurant. The cooking show host—Ray—was a big name who had several shows and restaurants of his own. He asked Flynn why he hadn't put his name on the restaurant, and Flynn explained that he wanted the draw to be about the food and not his name. Hopefully he hadn't insulted the host by saying that, but it was the truth.

After the interview, Ray moved into the kitchen and it was time for Amelia and her crew to shine. Flynn stayed back while Amelia showed off her and her team's skills in preparing the sea bass, lobster risotto and snap peas. He'd argued with her about fixing the Cassidy, the signature dish he'd created, but she'd told him customers loved it, she thought it was an elegant dish and she felt it would present well for television.

In the end, he'd capitulated because she was the chef and she could decide what would be served.

HE WATCHED HER PREPARE THE DISH, THOUGH HE WAS watching Amelia play to the cameras more than anything.

"We call this dish the 'Cassidy' in honor of Flynn Cassidy, the owner of Ninety-Two. It's a pan-seared sea bass, accompanied by a lobster risotto and crisp snap peas."

As Amelia moved around the kitchen, Flynn noticed she was relaxed and natural with the camera in her face. She showed no sign of nervousness and reacted to the camera—and to Ray—as if she was cooking for one of her friends. Amelia and Ray chatted amiably about cooking, about her background in cooking, the ingredients and Amelia's cooking process. Flynn couldn't be more proud of her. They only had to do a couple of takes until the director called for a final cut.

It had been perfect. He was so proud of her. Everyone stepped out so Amelia and her staff could continue cooking the rest of the meals for the customers.

"She's good," Paul said as he moved up beside Flynn.

Flynn smiled and nodded. "Yes, she is. She's an excellent chef."

"She's more than that. She's a natural in front of the cameras."

Flynn couldn't be more relieved hearing the producer's praise. "She'll be happy to hear that. She was nervous about tonight."

"She shouldn't be. Blaine said she did great."

"Good."

Dinner turned out perfectly, and the crew ate as well. He knew Amelia would make sure everyone had a meal, so that didn't surprise him.

He hadn't had a chance to talk to her yet because she was busy and he'd made sure to stop by all the tables to see how his customers enjoyed the meal. They all seemed to have a great time and didn't mind at all being filmed, which was a relief for Flynn.

All in all, the night had gone perfectly.

He finally spotted Amelia talking to Paul and Blaine and Ray right outside the kitchen. Flynn turned toward them, but then he overheard a bit of their conversation.

"You're a natural in the kitchen and in front of the camera," Paul said. "You're attractive, you have an ease about you and you weren't nervous."

Amelia smiled. "I'm so glad to hear that it all went well. Thank you."

"Have you ever considered hosting your own cooking show?" Paul asked.

Flynn stalled and moved around the corner so Amelia couldn't see him.

"Oh. No. That's not my area of expertise."

Ray chimed in with, "Trust me, Amelia. As someone who has done this for years, you'd be a shoo-in for a network show of your own. You and I hit it off right away, and as someone who's hosted cooking show competitions, I can tell you most people fumble and are nervous. You weren't nervous at all."

"We could get you a gig easily," Paul said. "You have a natural ability and your talents are amazing. What do you think?"

Flynn held his breath, waiting for Amelia to say no.

"I'm so flattered you think so highly of me. Could we step inside the office here?" Amelia asked. "I'd like some privacy to talk to you."

They all went into Ken's office and shut the door.

Flynn's stomach tightened. What the hell had just happened? He'd waited for Amelia to turn them down. Instead, she asked for privacy to talk to them?

That could only mean one thing. They'd offered the bait of her own TV cooking show, and she was going to say yes.

Of course she'd say yes. Her own television show? What chef would turn that down? No one would. She wouldn't. And she wasn't going to, which was why she'd asked to speak to them in private. One, so none of the staff could overhear her, and most important, so he wouldn't see her talking to the producer, host and director of the show.

Goddammit.

He felt sick to his stomach. Betrayed. He'd been so blind and stupid to think that she felt the same about him as he felt about her.

He was in love with her, while all these months she'd been biding her time, waiting for the perfect opening. And now she'd found it and she'd pounced on an opportunity.

Sonofabitch. He felt like the biggest sucker ever.

AMELIA TOOK A DEEP BREATH AS SHE FACED PAUL, Blaine and Ray. The last thing she wanted to do was insult any of them. Flynn's reputation was on the line and she had to make sure this all went well for him. They'd just offered her the opportunity of a lifetime, so she had to make sure to be gracious about this.

"I am so flattered by your offer. But honestly, I'm very happy here at Ninety-Two."

Blaine gave her a look of disbelief. "You realize what we're offering you here."

She nodded. "I do, and I'm extremely grateful. But I love it here. I've established a home and a career that I'm very happy with."

"Happy enough to give up the opportunity to have your own television show?" Ray asked. "Because that kind of opportunity might not come around again."

She nodded. "I realize that. And I'm not discounting this tremendous opportunity you're offering me. I'm so flattered. But I'm going to have to decline with my thanks. I'm honored you think so highly of my cooking and my skills. I'm happy where I am though."

Blaine nodded. "We think you have talent, Amelia. If you change your mind in the next twenty-four hours, you call me." He took out his card and handed it to her.

"Thank you so much."

She hoped she'd been kind and professional and she hoped her refusal wouldn't shed Ninety-Two in a bad light.

After they exited the office, the crew packed up and left. She tucked Blaine's card in her pocket and went back to finish up in the kitchen.

She had been honest with them when she had told him she was flattered. She had gone into this with the expectation that tonight would be all about Flynn, and certainly not all about her. She had showcased his signature dish and had made sure to mention—on camera—that Flynn had been the one to create the dish she'd made tonight. She wasn't sure where they had gotten the idea that she should be on TV. What a ridiculous notion.

Either way, she'd been honest when she'd told them she was happy right where she was. Here at Ninety-Two. In San Francisco. With Flynn.

Speaking of Flynn, she really wanted to find him to tell him about Blaine's offer. He'd probably laugh. Her on television? She couldn't even imagine it.

She found Ken, who was closing out for the night.

"Hey, Ken."

Ken turned to her and grinned. "Great night, right?"

She smiled back at him. "It did turn out well. Have you seen Flynn?"

"Oh, he left. Said he had something he needed to do."

She frowned. "He left?"

"Yeah, about twenty minutes ago. But he was really happy about tonight. He said it went well."

"I see. Okay. Great. Thanks, Ken."

She went back into the kitchen and finished cleanup with her crew, then grabbed her keys and went to her car. When she slid in, she rubbed her stomach.

Flynn wouldn't have left unless something was wrong. Now she was worried about him, and there was no way she'd go home without checking on him. She pulled out her phone and texted him.

Where are you?

She waited, hoping she'd get a response right away. She got nothing, which only made the panic rising up within her worse. She drove off and headed the few miles to his house. His SUV was parked in the driveway so she got out and went to the front door and rang the bell.

He answered within a minute.

"I texted you."

His expression was flat, emotionless. "Yeah, I got that."

He got that? She walked in and he closed the door behind her. She turned to face him. "Why didn't you answer me? I was so worried about you. It's not like you to leave the restaurant without seeing me."

He shrugged. "Seemed to me you were plenty busy."

"Busy? I have no idea what you're talking about."

"With Paul and Blaine, planning your new future."

"With . . . what?" She laid her purse and keys on the nearby table and walked over to him. "Flynn, I have no idea what you're talking about."

"I overheard you, Amelia. I heard you and Blaine talking about the TV show."

"Oh, you did? Wasn't that ridiculous? Can you imagine me doing a TV cooking show?"

"Yeah, I can imagine you. You were amazing today. Natural and perfect on camera."

She had no idea why he seemed so pissed about it. "You're angry with me. Why?"

"Because this is what you wanted all along. And now the perfect opportunity has fallen in your lap and I didn't see it coming."

"Didn't see what coming? I really wish you'd be more clear, because I'm confused."

"Oh, you didn't see it coming? That's hilarious considering the way you set me up." The anger coming from his face scared her.

She took a step back. "I never set you up, Flynn, and honestly, I don't know what you're talking about."

"You planned this from the beginning. Be nice to Flynn, let Flynn think you're vulnerable. Tell him this bullshit story about how broken you are from your past. Then, when he's totally open with you, when he's ready to give you everything, that's when you strike. I've never seen anyone manipulate someone so perfectly, Amelia. Did you know about the network showing up or was it just the right opportunity at the right time? How far were you planning to take this? All the way, or were you just planning to string me along, playing the 'let's take this slow' card until the right score came along for you?"

Realization struck, and every word he said to her was like a knife stabbing at her heart. "You think I planned this? That I used you? That my past was a lie?"

"I don't know. Was it?"

"Of course it wasn't. I've never been anything but honest with you. And the network thing? I don't know what you thought you heard—"

"I heard and I saw. I heard them offer you a TV show, and then saw you take them into Ken's office for some privacy. How convenient to strike up a deal with them where I couldn't see you."

Wow. He thought she manipulated him, that she used him to advance her career.

She felt sick to her stomach. It was like the past had come back to slap her across the face all over again.

He didn't trust her.

"No, I took them into Ken's office because I needed a moment to gather my thoughts. I wanted to make sure I was being polite and professional because your restaurant—your reputation—was on the line. So I wanted to make sure I said all the right things when I turned them down."

He laughed. "Sure you did. An opportunity like that comes once in a lifetime, Amelia. And I'm supposed to believe someone with your talent is going to turn them down."

"Yes, you are supposed to believe it, because it's true. And I did turn them down. Because I thought you knew me. I thought you believed in me. In us. In what we have together. Which is one of the main reasons I did turn them down."

He didn't say anything and she knew she wasn't reaching him. Because he didn't trust her. It was Frank all over again.

What was it with her and men? Did she have a distrustful face? Did she give off some lying aura?

No. This wasn't about her. This was not her fault. This was about Flynn.

"You know what? Fine. Believe what you want." She went and grabbed her purse and car keys. "You know who was the wrong person to trust in someone again? Me. Because I gave my heart to you and you just crushed it under your giant, stupid feet. So maybe I will take that job after all, because I can't work for someone—I can't love someone—who has so little faith in what we have."

"See, I knew it. You are taking the job."

She was so frustrated right now she wanted to pick up the nearest lamp and throw it at him.

"Go fuck yourself, Flynn."

She walked out the door, her entire body shaking with rage and hurt and the need to scream into the night. She held it together while she drove home, opened her door and tossed her purse and keys on the sofa. She went into the kitchen, grabbed a glass and a bottle of wine. She poured a glass, went out onto her porch and pulled her phone out of her pocket.

She texted Laura.

Flynn and I broke up. I need you. Stat.

Then she started drinking, forcing back the tears that pricked her eyes.

Because she damn well would not cry over that asshole.

THIRTY-ONE

IN GAME SITUATIONS, FOCUS WAS EVERYTHING.

For this game, Flynn's focus was shit.

"You've missed easy tackles out there," his coach had told him at halftime. His coach had never lectured him about missing tackles. Flynn was always the leader in tackles on his team.

He needed to pull his head out of his ass or they were going to lose this damn game. They had to win today. They *could* win today and Flynn knew it. There was no way he was going to be the cause of losing this game.

"Something on your mind?" Mick asked him while they made their way out of the tunnel for the second half.

"Yeah. Woman trouble."

Mick grimaced. "That's the worst. We'll go out after we win this game and you can tell me all about it. In the meantime, get your head in the right place."

Flynn nodded. "You got it."

The second half went much better. Flynn put one hundred percent of his focus on obliterating the offensive line. He ended up with two sacks and six tackles.

They won by ten points, because the Sabers offense had fired up hot in the second half. And fortunately, the defense had managed to pull it together. *He'd* managed to pull it together.

Flynn was just relieved he hadn't fucked it all up.

A group of them decided to go out for steaks. Tara had flown in for the game, but she had Sam with her and he was tired since it was a night game, so she was taking Sam back to the house. Mick was going to head out for steak with them.

They waited in the bar while their table was prepared. Mick and Flynn sat next to each other. Flynn grabbed a beer and Mick got a soda.

"You pulled it out in the second half," Mick said.

"Yeah, defense got it together. Offense kicked some ass."

Mick took a long swallow of soda and grinned. "Next week will be even better."

"It will."

"Wanna talk about your woman trouble?"

Flynn said. "It's Amelia. We broke up."

Mick frowned. "Sorry to hear that, man. Tara and I really liked her."

"So did I. But she wasn't who I thought she was."

"Yeah? And how's that?"

"She used me for the prime promotion opportunity—a network show."

Mick looked surprised. "Really? That doesn't seem like Amelia."

"I didn't think it was possible, either. But I overheard her talking to the network people about it."

Mick turned around in his chair to face him. "Are you sure that's what you heard?"

Flynn shrugged. "She told me she was trying to let them down in a professional manner, but I heard her tell them she wanted to talk somewhere private. They went into the restaurant manager's office."

"Okay. And?"

"And, nothing. She used me."

"You verified this with those network people who filmed your show?"

"Well . . . no."

Mick rolled his eyes. "Look, Flynn. The last thing I want to do is to get in between you and your woman. But trust me, the one thing I do know is misunderstanding, and it almost cost me my relationship with Tara. Before you lose her, verify it."

Flynn took a long swallow of his beer. "Fine. I'll do that."

Flynn had a lot to think about, and he did that the long night after the game. The next morning, he got up and made a phone call to Paul Birch, the producer of the show. He started out by thanking him for including his restaurant, figuring that accusing him of trying to steal his head chef wouldn't go over well, and he did have Ninety-Two to think about.

"We were glad to do it, Flynn. The footage came out great, by the way. Did Amelia tell you we offered her a TV spot?"

He was glad he didn't have to bring it up. "She mentioned it."

"She was extremely professional when she turned us down. I've never seen anyone more uninterested in being in the spotlight than Amelia." Paul laughed. "You would have thought we were making her an offer for jail time."

"Really." He felt a stab to his gut.

"Yeah. But she was sweet about it. Hey, I gotta run. We'll send you a link to your spot on the show when it's available."

"Okay. Thanks, Paul."

He dropped his phone on the sofa and dragged his fingers through his hair.

"Shit." He'd fucked up. Not only had he fucked up, he'd done it badly, and he'd ruined his relationship with Amelia.

Everything she'd said to him had been right. He hadn't trusted her, hadn't believed her when she'd told him the truth.

The things he'd accused her of, the things he'd said to her . . .

He was a total asshole, a complete douche.

But why had she turned the job down? It was a great opportunity for her. A once-in-a-lifetime opportunity.

He had to talk to her. The problem was, she hadn't been to work in a week, and he wasn't even sure she was still in town.

He grabbed his keys and drove to her house, figuring since he'd been such a dick, she wouldn't answer her phone if he called. He knocked at her door.

No answer. He rang the bell. Still no answer.

Fuck. He got out his phone and scrolled through his contacts, landing on Laura's number. He was so glad he'd gotten it the night they'd had dinner at her place. He punched the button.

Laura answered. "You are an asshole, Flynn."

"You're right. And I deserve every terrible thing you want to say to me. But I need to find Amelia."

"Why? So you can break her heart even more?"

"No. So I can make things right between us."

Silence. Like, a really long silence.

"Please, Laura."

He heard her sigh. "She's here at my house. But if you make her cry again I will hurt you."

"I believe you. And thanks."

Now he had to gather his shit together and figure out what the hell he was going to say to Amelia. Because even he didn't know how he was going to fix this just yet.

He only knew he was about to head into the most important conversation of his life.

THIRTY-TWO

AMELIA WAS FIXING CHICKEN MARSALA IN LAURA'S kitchen when the doorbell rang.

"I'll get it," Laura said.

Jon was at a meeting downtown and was going to be late coming home tonight, so Amelia wanted to fix something he could easily heat up. She knew this was one of Jon's favorite dishes and he'd been so great about letting her hang out here the past few days. She just couldn't be alone in her house—alone with all her thoughts and her tears. Crying wasn't doing her any good and she was tired of having headaches from crying so much.

Laura had finally convinced her to come stay with them. At least with Laura there was conversation and laughter and she had people to cook for. Cooking was therapy to her, and being alone and cooking for herself wasn't working. Here with Laura she had someone to talk to about the mess that her life had turned into. She didn't know what she would have done without Laura over the past week.

Now she didn't have a job and she didn't know what she was going to do about that, because there was no way she was going back to Ninety-Two. Not after all the awful things Flynn had accused her of.

"Amelia."

She stilled at the sound of Flynn's voice, certain she'd imagined it. He'd been in her head a lot the past several days.

She turned to see Laura standing next to him.

"Don't be mad," Laura said. "I thought the two of you should talk."

All the hurt came rushing back, all the things he'd accused her of.

She shook her head. "I don't want to talk to him."

She turned the stove off and walked away, needing to get away from Flynn before he said something else to crush her heart.

She walked out onto the back porch and zipped up her hoodie, wrapping her arms around herself and fighting back the tears that sprang forward just seeing him again.

The back door opened and she knew it was him. Laura was a peacemaker and she would want her to have closure, if nothing else.

Screw closure. Closure was a stupid concept someone who'd never had their heart ripped out of their chest had come up with. She didn't need closure. She was pissed, and righteous anger felt a whole lot better than closure.

"Go away, Flynn."

"I have to talk to you."

She blinked away the tears and turned to him. "About what? About how you accused me of using you to become a famous chef?"

He looked pained. Good. She hoped he developed an ulcer over it.

"Yes. I was wrong."

"No shit." She went and sat on one of the cushioned love seats out there. It was cool outside, so she grabbed a blanket and laid it over her legs.

Flynn grabbed one of the folding chairs and placed it across from her, then straddled it so he faced her. "I freaked out when I overheard you talking to Paul and Blaine. When they offered you the job, I expected you to turn them down."

"I *did* turn them down."

"No, you asked them into Ken's office for privacy."

"Yes, so I could turn them down while still being professional and polite. I was doing that for you. For the restaurant."

"At the time I didn't know that. All I saw was you looking excited and smiling at them and . . . it doesn't matter what I thought. I was totally off base and I should have known you better."

She nodded. "Exactly. You should know me. You should have trusted me. God, Flynn, the things you said to me really hurt. All those women I watched you with before we got together. I knew what they were about. They were about using you to advance themselves. And you thought I'd do the same thing to you? It's like you never knew me at all."

He looked down at his feet, then back up at her. "I know. I guess I got burned one too many times and trust has been a big issue for me."

"So you lumped me in with them the first chance you got?"

"I did, and I'm sorry." He reached for her but she shook her head and stood up.

"No. I've been through this before with a man who had no faith in me. I can't do it again. I won't do it again. You need to leave."

"Amelia."

She had turned away, refusing to look at him. Because if she did, she might weaken and fall into his arms, begging him to hold her. To love her. Because God, despite everything, she still loved him.

"Go away, Flynn. Leave me alone."

"I'm not giving up on you. On us. I need you. I love you, Amelia."

She couldn't hold back the tears and they fell down her cheeks like a river.

This was the first time he'd told her he loved her. Now, when her heart was torn in two.

She swiped at the tears, needing so badly to feel the touch of his hand, to feel the strength of his arms around her. But she couldn't trust him anymore. And without trust, they wouldn't work.

"Please just leave." She could barely get the words out.

"I'll find a way to make this right."

She heard him walk away and after the porch door closed, she fell onto the lounge, choking out a sob. She shoved her fist against her mouth, hating that she was crying—again. But this sense of loss went deep, so deep that even her bones ached from it.

When the porch door opened again, it was Laura who came and sat down in the love seat with her, put her arms around her and held her while she cried.

THIRTY-THREE

THE FIRST NOTE ARRIVED THE DAY AFTER FLYNN HAD showed up at Laura's house. Amelia had decided it was time to go home and face her life, though Laura had told her she was welcome to stay with her and Jon as long as she needed to.

But she was stronger than her emotions, and she needed to move on. She needed to find a new job and learn to live in her silent, empty house with her sadness.

The envelope had Flynn's handwriting on it and she'd picked it up with her mail.

She hesitated, then opened it.

I love the way you smile. It always hits me right in my heart, because it's so genuine.

I miss your smile, Amelia. I love you.

F

That's all the note said. She ran her fingers over his handwriting. It was a little messy, which made her lips tick up.

No. He would not make her smile. He would not win her back. She tossed the note in the trash.

An hour later she went and pulled the note out of the trash and left it on her kitchen counter.

That evening, she received a delivery.

It was a box. Inside the box was a sizzling steak, baked potato and a salad. And another note from Flynn.

You're probably cooking every day but not eating, and you should eat. I made this because I know you like steak. I made the salad dressing. Hope you like it.

  I love you, Amelia.

                                                                    F

Damn him.

She wanted to toss the meal. But no good meal should be ignored, so she ate the steak while she stared at the note. The salad dressing was a creamy balsamic vinaigrette that was pretty damn good.

The next morning when she got up there was another box at her front door, along with another note.

Inside the box was a gorgeous handmade lap quilt. She ran her hands over the intricate design, then opened the note.

Thought this might keep you warm while you're sitting on your porch.

  I love you.

                                                                    F

With a shuddering sigh, she carried the quilt out to the porch and draped it over her lap while she had her morning coffee.

With her mail that day came another note.

I'm really bad at poetry but I'm going to give this a try:
I'm imperfect, but you are the most beautiful woman I've ever met
We were good together, and yet
I blew it. Please give me another chance
And I know we can make this last.
I love you, Amelia.

F

As poetry went, that was awful. But her heart was melting. He was trying. He was thinking about her every day.

Damn him.

OVER THE NEXT TWO DAYS THERE WERE AT LEAST TWO notes a day. He fed her, gave her wine, a cookbook she'd been coveting that hadn't even been released yet, and wrote another note with even worse poetry than the first one.

Laura had come over and Amelia told her about the notes.

"He loves you. He fucked up badly. He's obviously trying to make amends. What are you going to do?"

She sighed. "I don't know. You know how I feel about trust."

"Yes, I do. But he's not Frank."

"No. He's not."

"I guess that leaves you with two choices. You forgive him and you find your way back to each other, or you walk away forever."

She blinked back tears at the thought of never having Flynn in her life again. "I don't know what to do, Laura."

"Okay, think about this. When you called it quits with Frank, how did it make you feel?"

"Sad. In a remote kind of way. But also relieved."

"And how do you feel now—about the possibility of ending things with Flynn?"

She turned tear-filled eyes to Laura. "It's tearing me apart. I love him so much."

Laura ran her hand up and down Amelia's arm. "I think you have your answer."

Amelia nodded. "I think I do."

Laura picked up one of Flynn's notes and read it. "Honey, no one who is that big of an asshole would go to this much trouble to win you back. Trust me, average guys just don't do this. Also, this is the worst poetry I've ever read."

Amelia laughed. "I know. God, I love him so much."

"So forgive him and let's get your happily ever after started."

"Yes, let's do that."

THIRTY-FOUR

WHEN FLYNN RECEIVED THE TEXT FROM AMELIA ASKing him if he'd like to come over to her place for dinner, it was all he could do not to leave practice right then and rush over.

But they had a big game this weekend, and his focus had to stay on his team and the upcoming game against Seattle. They were in first place in their division, and determined to stay there. It was too close to the end of the season to screw things up now.

He was ready for this game, and he thought the defense practiced tough today. He felt like they were all prepared to do battle on Sunday.

It had been a long grueling day, but once the team meetings were over with, he headed home, then went upstairs and got ready to go to Amelia's house.

He sat on the bed after his shower, pondering what he was going to say to Amelia tonight. He had hoped the notes he had sent her this week communicated the depths of his feelings. But he needed to write her one more note, so after he got dressed he went downstairs, took a note card out of the box and wrote out the note. He put it in the envelope and tucked it in the pocket of his button-down shirt, then headed over to Amelia's house.

His heart was pounding as he rang her doorbell. When she opened the door, he wasn't sure what kind of reaction to expect, but seeing her tremulous smile was the best thing he had seen in the past week.

"Come on in."

"Thanks."

"I'm making pork tenderloin for dinner," she said as she headed into the kitchen. "I need to check on it."

"Sure." He watched her walk away. She was wearing a flowing dark brown cotton dress with long sleeves and all kinds of ripples at the bottom of the skirt. She was barefoot, her hair loose around her shoulders in waves. She looked like a gorgeous hippie and all he wanted to do was put his arms around her and hold her for like . . . an hour or two.

When she closed the oven door, she lifted her gaze to his. "Glass of wine?"

"Yes, please."

She poured from the bottle that was open on the counter and handed him the glass. He took a sip.

"Good."

"Yes."

"Thanks for inviting me to dinner."

"Thank you for all the notes, and all the gifts. They were personal and from the heart, and that meant a lot to me."

Which reminded him of the one in his pocket. "Oh, there's one more."

He took it out and handed it to her. She looked at it, then up at him.

"Should I open it now?"

"Whenever you want to."

She opened the envelope and pulled out the card and read the note aloud.

"'I do trust you. And I was so very wrong not to. Please forgive me. I love you, Amelia, and I want a future with you. I'll do whatever it takes to make that happen.'"

As she read it, he saw her eyes fill with tears. She laid the note down.

"Oh, Flynn." She walked into his arms.

Having the contact of Amelia's warm body pressed against his was the best damn thing ever. It would always be the best thing ever.

He kissed the top of her head. "I'm so sorry for being such a jerk. It'll never happen again."

She tilted her head back. "Don't make promises you can't keep."

He smiled. "Okay. I'll try not to be such a big jerk again."

"That works."

He brushed his lips across hers. "Forgive me?"

"Yes."

He smoothed his hand over her face, unable to believe this amazing woman had forgiven him. "I love you."

"I love you, too."

He wasn't sure he'd ever felt his emotions swell this deeply, but hearing Amelia tell him she loved him was overwhelming.

"I really don't deserve you."

She grinned. "No, you don't. But you have me. Now and for always."

"We have each other. And we're a work in progress. At least I am."

"I am, too. We'll work on our issues together."

He took in a deep breath and kissed her again, this time a deeper kiss. This time a kiss that was filled with love and passion. She pressed against him and his cock got hard. He ran his hands down her back, cupping her butt to draw her against his erection.

She pulled her lips from his. "Make love to me, Flynn. Now."

They moved into the bedroom and clothes were shed fast. He cupped her breasts and sucked at her nipples until she gasped. When she stroked his cock with her soft, smooth hands, it was his turn to suck in a breath. He reached for a condom and put it on in record time, then they rolled on their sides to face each other as he slid into her, teasing her nipples as he thrust deeply in and out of her hot, tight pussy.

She ran her palm over his jaw. "I've missed this, missed you being inside of me."

He felt her tighten around him. "I haven't slept. I don't sleep when you're not with me."

She whimpered as he drove deeper into her. "I love you, Flynn."

He teased her lips with his. "I love you, too, Amelia."

Then there were no more words as they were both caught up in the passion. And when she came, she cried out and dug her nails into his arms. He groaned hard with his climax and emptied into her with a shudder.

After, he tucked her head against his shoulder and held her, feeling like the luckiest damn man in the world.

"You'll come to the ranch for Christmas, won't you?" he asked as he stroked her back.

"Oh, God, yes. I love your family, Flynn. I wouldn't miss it."

"Good. And you'll come back to work at Ninety-Two, won't you?"

She paused for a few seconds before answering. "If you want me to. I'm sure Stefanie is doing a great job."

"She is, but she'd really like you back. She said she needs a couple more years of training before she's ready to be a head chef."

Amelia leaned back to look at him. "She's very good."

"Yeah, she is. You're better. And speaking of you being the best chef ever, you really don't want your own television show?"

She stabbed at his chest with her fingernail. "No. Not now. Not ever. TV is not my thing, Flynn."

"Ow. Okay. Got it. No TV. Not now. Not ever."

"In fact, the next time a film crew comes, I'm taking the day off."

He nodded, willing to give her anything as long as she was happy. "Got it. You're in charge."

"I am?" She pushed him onto his back and rolled over on top of him. "Good to know."

"What about dinner?"

"It's on slow simmer."

He grasped her hips and lifted against her. "Oh, good. Then let's move things in here to a full boil."

She smiled down at him. "See what a good match we are, Mr. Cassidy?"

"Damn near perfect, Ms. Lawrence."

ONE

BRADY CONNERS WAS DOING ONE OF THE THINGS HE enjoyed the most—smoothing out dents in a quarter panel of a Chevy. As soon as he finished, he'd paint, and this baby would be good as new.

It wasn't his dream job. He was working toward that. But with every day he spent as a mechanic at Richards Auto Service, thanks to the shop's owner, Carter Richards, he was pocketing money. And that got him closer to his dream—opening up his own custom motorcycle paint shop.

Somewhere. Maybe here in Hope. Maybe somewhere else. Probably somewhere else, because the town of Hope held memories.

Not good ones.

A long time ago—a time that seemed like an eternity now—he'd had plans with his brother, Kurt, to start up a business together.

That dream went up in smoke the day Brady got the call that his brother was dead.

He paused, stood, and stretched out the kinks in his back, wiping the sweat that dripped into his eyes. Needing a break, he pulled off his breathing mask and swiped his fingers through his hair. He took a step away and grabbed the water bottle he always kept stored nearby. He took a long drink from the straw, swallowing several times until his thirst was quenched, then stepped outside.

It was late spring, and rain was threatening. He dragged in a deep breath, enjoying the smell of fresh air.

He really wanted a cigarette, but he'd quit a little over a year ago. Not that the urge had gone away. Probably never would. But he was stronger than his own needs. Or at least that's what he told himself every time a powerful craving hit.

Instead, he pulled out one of the flavored toothpicks he always kept in his jeans pocket and slid that between his teeth.

Not nearly as satisfying, but it would do. It would have to.

He leaned against the wall outside the shop and watched the town in motion. It was lunchtime, so it was busy.

Luke McCormack, one of Hope's cops, drove by in his patrol car and waved. Brady waved back. Luke was a friend of Carter's, and while Brady wasn't as social as a lot of the guys he'd met, he knew enough to be friendly. Especially to cops.

Samantha Reasor left her shop, loading up her flower van with a bunch of colorful bouquets. She spotted him, giving him a bright smile and a wave before she headed off.

Everyone in this town was friendly. He mostly kept to himself, did his work, and then went home to the small apartment above the shop at night to watch TV or play video games. Some nights he did side work painting bikes. He had one goal in mind, and that was to save enough money to open his business. He saw his parents now and again, since they lived in Hope, but the strain of Kurt's death had taken a toll on them.

Nothing was the same anymore. With them. With him, either, he supposed.

Sometimes life just sucked. And you dealt with that.

His stomach grumbled. He needed something to eat. He pushed off the wall and headed up the street, intending to hit the sandwich joint on the corner. He'd grab something and bring it back to the shop.

He stopped suddenly when Megan Lee, the hot brunette who owned the bakery, dashed out with a couple of pink boxes in her hand. She collided with him, and the boxes went flying. She caught one, he caught one, and then he steadied her by sliding his arm around her.

She looked up at him, her brown eyes wide with surprise.

"Oh my gosh. Thank you, Brady. I almost dropped these."

"You okay, Megan?"

"Yes. But let me check these." She opened the boxes. There were cakes inside. They looked pretty, with pink icing on one and blue on the other and little baby figurines in strollers sitting on top of the cakes. There were flowers and other doodads as well. He didn't know all that much about cake decorations. He just liked the way they tasted.

"They're for Sabelle Frasier. She just had twins." She looked up at him with a grin. "A boy and a girl. Her mom ordered these for her hospital homecoming. I spent all morning baking and decorating them."

He didn't need to know that, but the one thing he did know was that people in this town were social and liked to talk. "They look good."

She swiped her hair out of her eyes. "Of course they're good."

He took the boxes from her. "Where's your car?"

"Parked just down the street."

"How about you let me carry these? Just in case you want to run into anyone else on your way."

Her lips curved. "I think you ran into me."

He disagreed, but whatever. He figured he'd do his good deed for the day, then get his sandwich.

He followed her down the street.

"I haven't seen much of you lately," she said.

He shrugged. "Been busy."

"I've been meaning to come by the shop and visit, but things have been crazy hectic at the bakery, too." She studied him. "How about I bring pastries by in the morning? And I've never brought you coffee before. How about some coffee? How do you take it? Black, or with cream and sugar? Or maybe you like lattes or espresso? What do you drink in the mornings?"

He had no idea what she was talking about. "Uh, just regular coffee. Black."

"Okay. I make a really great cup of coffee. I'm surprised you haven't come into the bakery, since it's so close to the auto shop. Most everyone who works around here pops in." She pressed the unlock button on her key fob, then opened the back door and took the boxes from him.

Man, she really could talk. He'd noticed that the couple of times they'd been together in social situations. Not that it was a bad thing, but for someone like him who lived mostly isolated, all that conversation was like a bombardment.

But he liked it. The one thing he missed the most since his self-imposed isolation was conversation. And Megan had it in droves. He just wasn't all that good at reciprocating.

After she slid the boxes in, she turned to him. "What's your favorite pastry? You know, I've dropped cupcakes off at the auto shop. Have you eaten any of those?"

He was at a loss for words. He always was around her. A few of his friends had fixed the two of them up before. Once at Logan and Des's dinner party, then again at Carter and Molly's wedding.

They'd danced. Had some conversation. Mostly one-sided, since Megan had done all the talking.

He wasn't interested.

Okay, that wasn't exactly the truth. What heterosexual male wouldn't be interested in Megan? She was gorgeous, with her silky, light brown hair and her warm chocolate eyes that always seemed to study him. She also had a fantastic body with perfect curves.

But he was here to work. That was it. He didn't have time for a relationship.

He didn't want a relationship, no matter how attractive the woman was. And Megan was really damned attractive.

"Brady?" she asked, pulling his attention back on her. "Cupcakes?"

"What about them?"

She cocked her head to the side. "Oh, come on, Brady. Everyone has a favorite pastry. Cream puffs? Donuts? Scones? Cakes? Bars? Strudel?"

He zeroed in on the last thing she said. "Apple strudel. I used to have that from the old bakery when I was a kid."

She offered up a satisfied smile. "I make a killer apple strudel. I'll bring you one— along with coffee—in the morning."

He frowned. "You don't have to do that."

She laid her hand on his arm and offered up the kind of smile that made him focus on her mouth. She had a really pretty mouth, and right now it was glossed a kissable shade of peach.

He didn't want to notice her mouth, but he did.

"I don't mind. I love to bake. But now I have to go. Thanks again for saving the cakes. I'll see you tomorrow, Brady."

She climbed into her car and pulled away, leaving him standing there, confused as hell.

He didn't want her to bring him coffee. Or apple strudel. Or anything.

He didn't want to notice Megan or talk to Megan or think

about Megan, but the problem was, he'd been doing a lot of that lately. For the past six months or so he'd thought about the dance he'd shared with her. The laughs they'd enjoyed together and her animated personality. She had a sexy smile—not the kind a woman had to force, but the kind that came naturally. She also had a great laugh and she could carry a conversation with ease. And that irritated him because he hadn't thought about a woman in a long time.

Ever since his brother had died, he hadn't wanted to think about anything or anyone. All he'd wanted to do was work, then head upstairs to his one-room apartment above the auto shop, eat his meals, and watch TV. And on the weekends he'd do custom bike painting. Keep his mind and his body busy so he wouldn't have to think—or feel.

Women—and relationships—would make him feel, and that wasn't acceptable. He'd noticed that right away about Megan, noticed that he liked her and maybe—

No. Wasn't going to happen—ever. He needed to get her out of his head.

He only had time for work and making money. He had a dream he was saving for.

And now he barely had time for lunch, because he had a Chevy to get back to.

TWO

MEGAN GRABBED HER PURSE AND THE CUPCAKES
she'd made for tonight's book club meeting. She was already late
because she'd had so much baking to finish for tomorrow, and
she'd lost track of time. Then she'd had to shower to clean off the
bakery scent—a flour, sugar, and butter combo.

Though the girls probably wouldn't mind that.

She drove over to Loretta Simmons's bookstore, noting that
the street was filled with her friends' cars and she was the last to
arrive. Typically, she was early. Her pulse raced as she got out of
her car and pushed through the door.

She loved this bookstore, which took up the entire first floor of
the renovated old mercantile in downtown Hope. Loretta had
returned to town after her divorce last year and had leased the
first-floor space in the historic building Reid McCormack had
gutted and rebuilt.

Now it was the Open Mind bookstore, and lately it had become her favorite hangout. It not only had tons of books, but also coffee and tea, plus wireless and an electronics bar for people who had e-readers or laptops and wanted a quiet place to work or study. It was perfect for voracious readers, and with the local college nearby, it was also a great place for the students to come by at night to read or study.

Megan wandered to the back and found her friends set up at their regular spot.

"Hey, sorry I'm late," she said.

Her best friend, Samantha, looked up from the book in her lap, her long blond ponytail twirling back and forth as she lifted her head. "You made it."

"Yes, finally." She laid the boxes on the round table in the center. One of the things she loved was all the comfortable seating areas, spaces where groups could come together to meet. This one had several cushioned chairs, a sofa, and a table.

"We're so glad you're here," Loretta said. "And not just because of the cupcakes."

"Well, sort of because of the cupcakes," Chelsea said. "But I brought wine, so we'd have survived if you hadn't made it."

Megan laughed. "I'm sure you would have. But I never miss book club."

She unpacked the cupcakes from the box and arranged them on a plate.

"What have we got tonight?" Molly asked.

"Dark chocolate cupcakes with vanilla buttercream frosting."

Chelsea poured the wine. "Which goes perfectly with zinfandel."

Emma, who was eight and a half months pregnant, laid her hand on her lower back. "I miss wine."

"Your doc said you could have a glass, didn't he?"

"Yes, but I think I'll opt for tea."

Megan looked around. "Where's Des?"

"Opting out tonight," Emma said. "She said she'll see us all at the baby shower this weekend at the ranch, providing she doesn't have the baby before then."

Megan went over and grabbed one of the glasses of wine Chelsea had poured. "Who do you think will go first, Emma?"

Emma delicately lowered herself into one of the chairs. "I'm hoping me."

Molly laughed. "I'm hoping it's you as well. I have tomorrow on the office pool."

Emma arched a brow. "There's an office pool on my due date?"

"Honey, the entire town has pools for your and Des's delivery dates," Sam said. "With both of you due at the same time, how could we not?"

"Well, I have a couple of weeks left, so I don't know what you were thinking, Molly."

Molly shrugged. "That first babies sometimes come early. Though I have you two weeks late on another pool."

Emma rubbed her belly. "My poor baby being gambled on." She paused for a few seconds, then said, "Is it too late to get in on the action?"

Megan laughed. "I don't know, Emma. I think you might have insider information."

"Oh, please. I wish I knew when this little one was coming out. And hopefully it's soon."

While everyone played guessing games about Emma's due date, Megan wandered over to Sam, who was making herself a cup of coffee. "How's the new house coming along?"

"It's hit-and-miss. We got the foundation poured before winter set in, and they're working on plumbing, electrical, and getting the walls and the roof up. But you know they're dancing around the weather, and early spring has been rainy, so we're hoping that calms down somewhat so we can make some headway. In the meantime, we're living at my house. The yard is big enough for Not My Dog, who's perfectly happy as long as he's with Reid and me."

Megan smiled. "And of course he goes to work with Reid every day anyway."

"This is true."

"How's Grammy Claire?"

Sam's smile faltered. "About the same. She has her good days and bad days. Some days she recognizes me, some days she looks at me like she doesn't know who I am."

Megan squeezed her arm. "I'm sorry."

Sam nodded. "We're prepared for it. Physically she's still doing well enough to stay at her home, thanks to Faith, Grammy Claire's best friend, living there with her. I don't know what we'd do without her help. And the nursing staff who come in for regular visits have been lifesavers."

"It also helps that you and Reid are just across the street."

"Yes. We stop by every day and check on her."

"And maybe someday the two of you will have a honeymoon."

"Oh, we don't need that. It was enough that Grammy Claire was able to be at our wedding, and that she had full cognitive function at the time."

Megan saw the tears welling up in her friend's eyes, and knew how much it was hurting her to slowly lose her grandmother to Alzheimer's. "But you two are still newlyweds, so anytime you need my help with anything, all you have to do is ask."

Sam hugged her. "Thank you. I know I can count on you. But speaking of all things love, I haven't seen you dating anyone lately. What's up with that?"

"Oh, well, you know how it is. The bakery keeps me busy."

Sam slid her a look. "And that excuse is getting old. How did things go with that date you had last week?"

"The one with the guy from the newspaper?"

"Yes, that one."

Megan gave her a blank stare. "He was . . . nice."

Sam wrinkled her nose. "Nice? That's it?"

"Yes. That's it."

Sam sighed. "So, in other words, no spark."

"What are we talking about sparking?" Chelsea asked. "Not that I'm eavesdropping, but . . . okay, I'm eavesdropping."

"We're talking about Megan's date the other night."

"Ohh, you had a date?" Chelsea asked, pulling up a spot next to Sam. "Spill the details."

If there was one thing their hot redheaded friend loved, it was gossip. And Megan knew Chelsea had opinions, especially on men and dating. "Unfortunately, nothing to spill. Nice guy. Good job. Great manners over dinner. He was polite, made decent conversation and all, but I felt . . . nothing."

Chelsea's hopeful look disappeared. "Oh. That's unfortunate. As someone who dated more than her share of men in the past—"

"Like the entire male population of Hope," Sam said.

Chelsea shot Sam a look. "Hey. Not the entire population. Maybe half."

Megan laughed.

"Anyway," Chelsea said, "I can attest to the fact that sometimes the chemistry just isn't there, despite how good a man looks on paper."

Megan folded her arms. "Says the woman who landed the hottest bartender in Hope."

Chelsea graced them all with a well-satisfied grin. "I did, didn't I?"

"And she's smug about it, too," Sam said.

"I am, aren't I?"

Megan shook her head. "No cupcakes for you."

"Megan," Chelsea said, looking shocked. "You wouldn't do that."

"A few more bad dates and I might just consider it."

"But you wouldn't deny Sam, who just married the hottest architect in town."

Sam gave Megan an apologetic look and took a sip of her wine.

"Hmm, you have a point, Chelsea. Maybe I'll just keep all the cupcakes for myself."

"Or maybe you should consider dating more," Sam said.

"Okay, there's that. But even Chelsea can attest to the fact that the pickings are slim."

Loretta came over and sat on the edge of the sofa. "What are we picking?"

Sam leaned her head back. "Dates for Megan."

"And I mentioned the prime pickings among men are slim," Megan said.

Loretta nodded her head. "I can see how it would be hard to date in a small town."

"You have a point there," Chelsea said. "However, I think my problem was that I was extremely picky. Now that I've had an opportunity to take a step back and reflect, I can assure you that there are several good-looking and eligible men in Hope."

Megan wasn't buying it. "Name three."

"Jeff Armstrong, Brady Conners, and Deacon Fox."

Leave it to Chelsea to rattle off three names without even hesitating. Jeff was a very attractive doctor, Brady worked at Carter Richards's auto shop, and Deacon owned a construction company. Deacon had also been Loretta's high school boyfriend. She tilted her gaze to Loretta, who seemed to show no emotion when Deacon's name was mentioned. Though she wondered how Loretta felt about Deacon now after all these years.

Sam laughed, then laid her hand on Megan's shoulder. "She's got you there."

"I tried dating Brady," Megan said. "That didn't work out."

Chelsea frowned. "You and Brady dated? When?"

"Okay, so we didn't actually date. We had a couple of fix-ups where we were sort of pushed together."

"Which is not at all like dating," Sam said.

"No, it's not, but he never asked me out."

"I haven't seen Brady go out with anyone since . . ." Molly let the sentence trail off.

"Since his brother died," Chelsea said. "Yes, I know. All that hot studliness going to waste. You should go after him, Megan. Are you interested?"

"She's definitely interested," Sam said.

Megan shot Sam a mind-your-own-business look.

"Oh, I see. So it's a lust thing," Chelsea said. "Well, who wouldn't lust after that man? If I wasn't already taken by a hot guy of my own, I'd be all over Brady Conners. Tall, well-muscled, rides a motorcycle, and that man just exudes sex."

Megan looked over at Chelsea, who shrugged.

"What? Just stating the facts. Come on, Megan, surely you agree."

She couldn't deny it. "I do agree. But I don't know. It seems like a waste of my time to chase after a man who isn't interested."

"I've seen him around town," Loretta said. "Chelsea does have a point. He is fine-looking."

"Maybe you're not dangling the right carrot," Chelsea said.

"I don't think many of Hope's citizens would appreciate me showing up at Carter's shop naked."

Sam snickered. Chelsea laughed. Loretta smiled over the rim of her wineglass. Molly and Emma smiled.

"Not exactly what I meant, Megan," Chelsea said. "You have to make yourself irresistible to him."

"I actually ran into him earlier today. Or, rather, he ran into me and my two boxes of cakes. I talked to him about baked goods."

"That would have gotten Reid's attention," Sam said. "Then again, he's a sucker for a good cinnamon roll."

"All men love sweet things," Emma said. "If you know what I mean."

Megan knew what she meant.

"So bring him some baked goods. And while you're at it, flash him some cleavage."

She looked down at her T-shirt and jeans. "Sexy is not my persona, Chelsea. That's more up your alley."

Chelsea grinned. "Ooh, well thank you. But you don't have to change your appearance, Megan. We love you just the way you are. Which, by the way, is absolutely beautiful."

Considering Chelsea was stunning, with her gorgeous red hair and stylish clothes and beautiful smile, Megan took that as a compliment. "Thank you."

"But how does he react around you?" Chelsea asked.

"Like he's interested. And annoyed about it."

"Hmm," Loretta said.

"That's a very good sign," Sam said.

"I agree," Molly said. "Men aren't like women. They keep their emotions close."

"And you know, Loretta," Chelsea said, "there are plenty of eligible men out there for you as well."

Loretta looked none too happy that the conversation had steered over to her.

"Oh. Um, I'm not interested."

"In men?" Chelsea asked.

Loretta laughed. "I like men very much. But after the divorce, I'm concentrating my efforts on the new business here, and on Hazel. I think that's enough for now."

Megan's gaze drifted to where Loretta's nine-year-old daughter, Hazel, was reading on the floor in the corner of the bookstore, completely oblivious to their conversations. She was such a cute kid, with her jeans and her T-shirt and her ponytailed hair pulled through the back of her baseball cap.

"She's so adorable, Loretta," Megan said.

Loretta sighed, then smiled. "Thank you. I think so, too. Should we start?" She held up the book club selection, Shannon Stacey's newest book. Megan was so excited about this one, since Ms. Stacey was one of her favorite authors. She loved everything she wrote.

Megan poured another glass of wine, and Chelsea pulled her aside.

"Seriously, Megan. You have nothing to lose with Brady, and everything to gain. The man sounds interested. So give him a little shove in the right direction."

She shrugged. "I'll try, but I don't know. He doesn't seem to want to be shoved."

Chelsea laughed. "They never do. Then again, men can often surprise us."

If Brady even once asked her out, Megan would be more surprised than anyone. But she had promised to bring him coffee and something from the bakery tomorrow, so she'd start there and see if anything came from it. The man was hot and sexy and worth pursuing, so why not?

She'd give it one shot—and one shot only—and then see what came of it.

Jaci Burton is the *USA Today* and *New York Times* bestselling author of the Play-by-Play series, including *Rules of Contact, Unexpected Rush, All Wound Up, Quarterback Draw, Straddling the Line, Melting the Ice* and *One Sweet Ride*, and the Hope series, including *Don't Let Go, Make Me Stay, Love After All, Hope Burns, Hope Ignites* and *Hope Flames*. Visit Jaci online at jaciburton.com, facebook.com/AuthorJaciBurton and twitter.com/jaciburton.